Book 5

The
MYSTERY
of the
VANISHED
PRINCE

Also by Enid Blyton

could tell Fatty as soon as he comes then, and he might get us all on to it.'

Bets was thrilled. She went to get the paper. She brought it out to Pip and they both studied it carefully. But there didn't seem to be anything happening at all.

'It's nothing but pictures of frightful women and their clothes, and horses racing, and what hot weather it is, and –'

'Cricket scores, and . . .' went on Bets, in a voice as disgusted as Pip's.

'Oh well – cricket scores are *interesting*,' said Pip, at once. 'Look here – see this bowling analysis here?'

Bets wasn't in the least interested in cricket. She turned the page.

'Just like a girl,' said Pip, in an even more disgusted voice. 'The only thing of real importance in the paper is the cricket – and you don't even look at it!'

'Here's something – look, it's something about Peterswood, our village,' said Bets, reading a small paragraph down in a corner. 'And it mentions Marlow too – that's quite near.'

'What is it?' asked Pip, interested. He read the paragraph and snorted. 'Huh – that's not a mystery, or even anything interesting.'

Bets read it out. 'The weather has been very kind to the school camps on the hills between Peterswood and Marlow. This week two or three interesting visitors have joined the camps. One is little Prince Bongawah of Tetarua State who amused everyone by bringing a state umbrella with him. Needless to say he only used it once!'

'Well, if you think that even Fatty can make any mystery or even be *interested* in a silly thing like that, you'd better think again,' said Pip. 'Who cares about Prince Bongabangabing, or whatever his name is?'

'Bongawah,' said Bets. 'Where's Tetarua State, Pip?'

Pip didn't know and didn't care. He rolled over on his front. 'I'm going to sleep,' he said. 'I'm too hot for words. We've had five weeks of hot sun and I'm tired of it. The worst of our weather is that it never stops when it makes up its mind to do something.'

'I don't care about the weather or anything,'

said Bets, happily. 'It can do what it likes now that Fatty and the others are coming back!'

Larry and Daisy came back first. They arrived home the next morning, helped their mother to unpack, and then went straight round to Pip and Bets.

'Larry! Daisy!' shouted Bets joyfully, as they came into the garden. 'I didn't think you'd be back so early. Gosh, how brown you are!'

'Well, you're not so bad either,' said Daisy, giving little Bets a hug. 'It's been ages since we saw each other! Such a waste of hols when we can't go mystery-hunting together!'

'Hello Bets, hello Pip,' said Larry. 'Any news? I must say you're a bad correspondent. I sent you four postcards and you never wrote once!'

'*You* sent them! I like *that*!' said Daisy, indignantly. 'I wrote every single one of them! You never even addressed them.'

'Well, I *bought* them,' said Larry. 'Hey – any news of old Fatty? Is he back yet?'

'Coming today,' said Bets joyfully. 'I keep listening for his bicycle bell, or old Buster's bark. Won't it be lovely for all five of us – and Buster, of course – to be together again!'

Everyone agreed. Bets looked round at the little group, glad to have Larry and Daisy there – but nothing was ever the same without Fatty. Fatty, with his sly humour and enormous cheek and brilliant brains. Bet's heart swelled with joy to think he would soon be there too.

'There's the telephone,' said Pip, as a loud, shrilling ring rang out from the house. 'Hope it's not for me. I feel I simply cannot get up. I think I'm stuck to the grass.'

Mrs Hilton, Pip's mother, appeared at a window. 'That was Frederick on the telephone,' she called. 'He's back home, and will be round to see you very soon. He says, will you please watch out for him, as he's so brown you may not know him. He probably won't know any of *you* either, you're so tanned!'

Everyone sat up straight at this news. 'Oh, I *wish* I'd answered the phone,' said Bets. 'Fatty has such a nice *grinny* voice on the phone.'

Everyone knew what she meant. 'Yes – sort of chortly,' said Larry. 'Gosh, I wish I was always as sure of myself as Fatty is. He never turns a hair.'

'And he *always* knows what to do, whatever happens,' said Bets. 'I say – do you think he'll come in disguise, just for a joke?'

'Yes, of course he will,' said Larry. 'I bet he's got a whole lot of new tricks and disguises and things – and he'll want to practise them on us at once. I know Fatty!'

'Then we'd better look out for someone peculiar,' said Daisy, excited. 'We simply *can't* let him take us in the very first minute he comes back!'

Fatty was, of course, simply marvellous at disguising himself. He could make his plump cheeks even bigger by inserting cheek pads between his gums and his cheek inside his mouth. He had a wonderful array of false teeth that could be fitted neatly over his own. He had shaggy eyebrows to stick over his own modest ones, and any amount of excellent wigs.

In fact, most of his considerable pocket money went on such things, and he was a never-ending source of joy and amusement to the others when he donned one of his many disguises to deceive them or someone else.

'Now we'll watch out,' said Pip. 'Everyone who

comes in at the gate is suspect – man, woman, or child! It *might* be old Fatty!'

They hadn't long to wait. Footsteps could be heard dragging up the drive, and then a large, feathered hat appeared bobbing above the hedge that ran along the pathway to the kitchen entrance. A very brown, plump face looked over the hedge at them, with long gold earrings dangling from the ears, and ringlets of black curls bobbing beneath the dreadful hat.

The children stared. The face smiled and spoke. 'Buy some nice white 'eather? Bring you luck!'

Round the hedge came a large gypsy woman, in a long black skirt, a dirty pink blouse, and a red shawl. Her feathered hat nodded and bounced on her black curls.

'Fatty!' screamed Bets at once, and ran over at top speed. 'Oh, you're Fatty, you are, you are! I recognised your voice – you didn't disguise it enough!'

2. FATTY ARRIVES

The other three children did not call out or run over. This woman seemed much too tall to be Fatty – though he *was* tall now. The gypsy woman drew back a little as Bets came running over, shouting joyfully.

"Ere! 'Oo are you a-calling Fatty?' she said, in a husky voice. 'What you talking about?'

Bets stopped suddenly. She stared at the woman, who stared back insolently, with half-closed eyes. Then the gypsy thrust a bunch of bedraggled heather at Bets, almost into her face. 'Lucky white 'eather,' she whined. 'Buy some, little Missy. I tell you, I ain't sold a spray since yesterday.'

Bets backed away. She looked round at the others. They still sat there, grinning now, because of Bets' sudden fright. She went very red and walked back to the other three children.

The woman followed, shaking her heather in

quite a threatening manner. 'If you don't want my 'eather, you let me read your 'and,' she said. 'It's bad luck to cross a gypsy, you know.'

'Rubbish,' said Larry. 'Go away, please.'

'What do she want to call me Fatty for?' said the woman angrily, pointing at poor Bets. 'I don't reckon on insults from the likes of you, see?'

The cook suddenly appeared, carrying a tray of lemonade for the children. She saw the gypsy woman at once.

'Now you clear off,' she called. 'We've had enough strangers lately at the back door.'

'Buy a spray of 'eather,' whined the woman again and thrust her spray into the cook's angry face.

'Bets – run and fetch your father,' said the cook, and Bets ran. So did the gypsy woman! She disappeared at top speed down the drive and the children saw her big, feathered hat bobbing quickly along the top of the hedge again.

They laughed. 'Gosh,' said Pip, 'just like old Bets to make an idiotic mistake like that. As if anyone could think that awful old creature was Fatty! Though, of course, she did have rather a husky voice for a woman. That's what took Bets in.'

'It nearly took me in too,' said Daisy. 'Hello, here's someone else!'

'Butcher boy,' said Pip, as a boy on a bicycle came whistling up the drive, a joint of meat in his basket on the front.

'It *might* be Fatty,' said Bets, joining them again, looking rather subdued. 'Better have a very good look. He's got a fine butcher boy disguise.'

They all got up and stared hard at the boy who was now standing at the back door. He whistled loudly, and the cook called out to him.

'I'd know it was you anywhere, Tom Lane, with that whistling that goes through my head. Put the meat on the table, will you?'

The four children gazed at the boy's back. He certainly *might* be Fatty with a curly brown wig. Bets craned forward to try and make out if his hair *was* a wig or not. Pip gazed at his feet to see if they were the same size as Fatty's.

The boy swung round, feeling their stares. He screwed up his face at them cheekily. 'Never seen anyone like me before, I suppose?' he said. He turned himself round and round, posing like a model. 'Well, take a good look. Fine specimen of a butcher's boy, I am! Seen enough?'

The others stared helplessly. It *could* be Fatty – it was more or less his figure. The teeth were very rabbitty though. Were they real or part of a disguise?

Pip took a step forward, trying to see. The boy backed away, feeling suddenly half-scared at the earnest gaze of the four children.

'Here! Anything wrong with me?' he said, looking down at himself.

'Is your hair real?' said Bets suddenly, feeling sure it was a wig – and if it was, then the boy must be old Fatty!

The butcher's boy didn't answer. He looked very puzzled, and put up his hand to feel his hair. Then, quite alarmed by the serious faces of the others, he leapt on his bicycle and pedalled fast away down the drive, completely forgetting to whistle.

The four stared after him. 'Well – if it *was* Fatty, it was one up to him,' said Larry, at last. 'I just don't know.'

'Let's have a look at the meat he left on the table,' said Pip. 'Surely even Fatty wouldn't go bicycling about with joints of meat, even if he *was* pretending to be a butcher's boy. Sausages would be much cheaper to get.'

They went into the scullery and examined the meat on the table. The cook came in, astonished to see them bending over the joint.

'Don't tell me you're as hungry as all that,' she said, shooing them away. 'Now don't you start putting your teeth into raw meat, Pip!'

It did look as if Pip was about to bite the meat; he was bending over it carefully to make quite sure it was a real joint, and not one of the many 'properties' that Fatty kept to go with his various disguises. But it was meat all right.

They all went out again, just as they heard a rat-a-tat-tat at the front door. 'That's Fatty!' squealed Bets and rushed round the drive to the front door. A telegram boy stood there with a telegram.

'Fatty!' squealed Bets. Fatty had often used a telegram boy's disguise, and it had been a very useful one. Bets flung her arms round his plump figure.

But, oh dear, when the boy swung round, it certainly was not Fatty. This boy had a small, wizened face, and tiny eyes! Clever as Fatty was at disguises, he could never make himself like this! Bets went scarlet.

'I'm so sorry,' she said, backing away. 'I – I thought you were a friend of mine.'

Her mother was now standing at the open door, astonished. What was Bets doing, flinging her arms round the telegram boy? The boy was just as embarrassed as Bets. He handed in the telegram without a word.

'Behave yourself, Bets,' said Mrs Hilton, sharply. 'I'm surprised at you. Please don't play silly jokes like that.'

Bets crept away in shame. The telegram boy stared after her, amazed. Larry, Pip, and Daisy laughed till they ached.

'It's all very well to laugh,' said Bets, dolefully. 'I shall get into an awful row with Mother now. But honestly, it's exactly like one of Fatty's disguises.'

'Well, of course, if you're going to think every telegram boy is Fatty, just because Fatty's got a telegram boy's uniform, we're in for a funny time,' said Pip. 'Gosh, I wish old Fatty would come. It's ages since he telephoned. The very next person *must* be Fatty!'

It was! He came cycling up the drive, plump as ever, a broad grin on his good-humoured face, and Buster running valiantly beside the pedals!

'Fatty! FATTY!' shrieked everyone, and almost before he could fling his bicycle into the hedge, all four were on him. Buster capered round, mad with excitement, barking without stopping. Fatty was thumped on the shoulder by everyone, and hugged by Bets, and dragged off into the garden.

'Fatty – you've been ages coming!' said Bets. 'We thought you'd be in disguise, and we watched and watched.'

'And Bets made some simply frightful mistakes!' said Pip. 'She's just flung her arms round the telegram boy! He was really startled.'

'He still looked alarmed when I met him cycling out of the gate,' said Fatty, grinning at Bets. 'He kept looking round as if he expected Bets to be after him with a few more hugs.'

'Oh, Fatty, it's great to see you again,' said Bets, happily. 'I don't know *how* I could have thought any of those people here this morning were you – that gypsy woman, the butcher boy, and the telegram boy.'

'We honestly thought you'd be in disguise,' said Larry. 'Gosh, how brown you are. You haven't got any paint on, have you? I've never known you get burnt so brown.'

'No, I'm just myself,' said Fatty modestly. 'No powder, no paint, no false eyelashes. no nothing. I must say you're all pretty brown yourselves.'

'Woof,' said Buster, trying to get on to Bets' knee.

'He says he's sunburnt too,' said Bets, who could always explain what Buster's woofs meant. 'But it doesn't show on him. Darling Buster! We *have* missed you!'

They all settled down to the iced lemonade that was left. Fatty grinned round. Then he made a surprising statement. 'Well, Find-Outers – you're not as smart as I thought you were! You've lost your cunning. You didn't recognise me this morning when I came in disguise!'

They all set down their glasses and stared at him blankly. In disguise? What did he mean?

'What disguise? You're not in disguise,' said Larry. 'What's the joke?'

'No joke,' said Fatty, sipping his lemonade. 'I came here in disguise this morning to test out my faithful troop of detectives, and you didn't recognise your chief. Shame on you! I was a bit afraid of Bets though.'

Pip and Bets ran through the people who had appeared since breakfast that morning. 'Mrs Lacy – no, you weren't her, Fatty. The postman – no, impossible. The man to mend the roof – no, he hadn't a tooth in his head. That old gypsy woman – no, she really was too tall and, anyway, she ran like a hare when she thought I was going to fetch Daddy.'

'The butcher boy – no,' said Larry.

'And we know it wasn't the telegram boy, he had such a wizened face,' said Daisy. 'You're fooling us, Fatty. You haven't been here before this morning. Go on, own up!'

'I'm not fooling,' said Fatty, taking another drink. 'I say, this lemonade is super. I *was* here this morning and I tell you, Bets was the only one I thought was going to see through me.'

They all stared at him disbelievingly. 'Well, who were you then?' said Larry at last.

'The gypsy woman!' said Fatty, with a grin. 'I took you in properly, didn't I?'

'You weren't,' said Daisy, disbelievingly. 'You're pulling our legs. If you'd seen her, you'd know you couldn't be her. Awful creature!'

Fatty put his hand in his pocket and pulled out a pair of long, dangling gilt earrings. He clipped one on each ear. He pulled out a wig of greasy black curls from another pocket and put it on his head. He produced a bedraggled spray of heather and thrust it into Daisy's face.

'Buy a bit of white 'eather!' he said, in a husky voice, and his face suddenly looked exactly like that of the gypsy. The others looked at him silently, really startled. Even without the big feathered hat, the shawl, the basket, and the long black skirt, Fatty was the gypsy woman!

'You're uncanny!' said Daisy, pushing the heather away. 'I feel quite scared of you. One minute you're Fatty, the next you're a gypsy woman. Take that awful wig off!'

Fatty took it off, grinning. 'Believe me now?' he asked. 'Gosh, I nearly twisted my ankle though, when I sprinted down the drive. I honestly thought young Bets here was going to get her father. I wore really high-heeled shoes, and I could hardly run.'

'So that's why you looked so tall,' said Pip. 'Of course, your long skirt hid your feet. Well, you took us in properly. Good old Fatty. Let's drink to his health, Find-Outers!'

They were all solemnly drinking his health in the last of the lemonade when Mrs Hilton appeared. She had heard Fatty's arrival and wanted to welcome him back. Fatty got up politely. He always had excellent manners.

Mrs Hilton put out her hand, and then stared in astonishment at Fatty. 'Well really, Frederick,' she said, 'I cannot approve of your jewellery!'

Bets gave a shriek of delight. 'Fatty! You haven't taken off the earrings!'

Poor Fatty. He dragged them off at once, trying to say something polite and shake hands all at the same time. Bets gazed at him in delight. Good old Fatty – it really was lovely to have him back. Things *always* happened when Fatty was around!

3. DISGUISES

Bets quite expected some adventure or mystery to turn up immediately, now that Fatty was back. She awoke the next morning with a nice, excited feeling, as if something was going to happen.

They were all to meet at Fatty's playroom that morning, which was in a shed at the bottom of his garden. Here he kept many of his disguises and his make-up, and here he also tried out some of his new ideas.

Many a time, the others had arrived at his shed to have the door opened by some frightful old tramp, or grinning errand boy, all teeth and cheeks, or even an old woman in layers and layers of skirts, her cheeks wrinkled, and with one or two teeth missing.

Yes, Fatty could even appear to have a few of his front teeth missing, by carefully blacking out one here and there, so that when he smiled, black gaps appeared, which seemed to be holes where teeth had once been. Bets had been horrified when she had first seen him with, apparently, three front teeth gone!

But this morning, it was Fatty himself who opened the door. The floor was spread with open books. The four children stepped over the madly-barking Buster and looked at them.

'Fingerprints! Questioning of witnesses! Disguises!' said Bets, reading the titles of some of the books. 'Oh, Fatty, is there another mystery on already?'

'No,' said Fatty, shutting the books and putting them neatly into his bookcase at the end of the shed. 'But I seem to have got a bit out of practice since I've been away – I was just testing my brains, you know. Anyone seen old Mr Goon lately?'

Everyone had. They had all bumped into him that morning as they rode round to Fatty's on their bicycles. As usual, the policeman had been ringing his bell so violently that he hadn't heard theirs, and he had ridden right into the middle of them.

'He fell off,' said Daisy. 'I can't imagine why, because none of *us* did. He went an awful bump too, and he was so angry that nobody liked to stop and help him up. He just sat there shouting.'

'Well, he enjoys that,' said Fatty. 'Let's hope he is still sitting there, shouting, then he won't interfere with *us*!'

'Woof,' said Buster, agreeing.

'What are we going to do for the rest of these hols if a mystery doesn't turn up?' asked Pip. 'I mean, we must all have had picnics and outings and things till we're tired of them. And Peterswood is always half-asleep in the summer. Nothing happening at all.'

'We'll have to wind up old Mr Goon then,' said Fatty, and everyone brightened at once. 'Or what about my ringing Inspector Jenks and asking him if he wants a bit of help on anything?'

'Oh, you *couldn't* do that,' said Bets, knowing quite well that Fatty could do anything if he really wanted to. 'Though it would be really nice to see him again.'

Inspector Jenks was their very good friend. He had been pleased with their help in solving many mysteries. But Mr Goon had not been nearly so pleased. The bad-tempered village policeman had wished many a time that the five children and their dog lived hundreds of miles away.

'Well, perhaps I won't bother the Inspector just yet – not till we've smelt out something,' said Fatty. 'But I was thinking we ought to put in a bit of practice at disguises or something like that – we haven't done a thing for weeks and weeks – and suppose something did turn up, we'd make a muddle of it through being out of practice.'

'Oh, *do* let's practise disguises!' said Bets. 'All of us, do you mean?'

'Oh yes,' said Fatty. 'I've got some fantastic new disguises here. I picked them up on my cruise.'

Fatty had been for a long cruise, and had called at many exciting places. He opened a trunk and showed the four children a mass of brilliant-looking clothes.

'I picked these up in Morocco,' he said. 'I went shopping by myself in the native bazaar – my word, things were cheap! I got suits for all of us. I thought they would do for fancy dress, though they will do for foreign disguises too!'

'Oh Fatty – let's try them on!' said Daisy, thrilled. She picked out a bright red skirt of fine

31

silk, patterned in stripes of white.

'There's a white blouse to go with that,' said Fatty, pulling it out. 'Look, it's got red roses embroidered all over it. It will suit you fine, Daisy.'

'What did you get for me, Fatty?' asked Bets, dragging more things out of the trunk. 'You are a most surprising person. You're always doing things nobody else ever thinks of. I'm sure Pip would never bring me home any clothes like this if he went to Morocco.'

'I certainly wouldn't,' said Pip grinning. 'But then, I'm not a millionaire like old Fatty here!'

Fatty certainly seemed to always have plenty of money. He was like a grown-up in that, Bets thought. He seemed to have dozens of rich relations who showered gifts on him. He was always generous with his money though, and ready to share with the rest of them.

Bets had a curious little robe-like dress that reached her ankles. It had to be swathed round and tied with a sash. The others looked at her, and marvelled.

'She looks like a little foreign princess!' said Larry. 'Her face is so sunburnt that she looks like an

Indian – she might *be* an Indian! What a wonderful disguise it would make for her!'

Bets paraded round the shed, enjoying herself. She glanced into the big clear mirror that Fatty kept there, and was startled. She looked like a real little princess! She drew the hood of the dress over her head, and looked round with half-shut eyes. Fatty clapped.

'Very good! An Indian princess! Here Larry – stick this on. And this is for you, Pip.'

The boys pulled on brilliant robes, and Fatty showed them how to wind cloths for bright turbans. All of them seemed to be transformed into a different nationality altogether. Nobody would have thought them English.

Fatty stared at the four parading round his shed. He grinned. His brain set to work to try and evolve a plan to use these bright disguises. A visiting princess? A descent on Mr Goon for some reason? He racked his brains for some bright idea.

'We might be the relations of the little Prince Bongawah of Tetarua State,' said Bets, suddenly. 'I'm sure we look exactly like them!'

'And who's Bongawhatever-it-is when he's

at home?' asked Larry. Bets explained.

'He's a foreign prince who is staying at one of the school camps on the hills between Peterswood and Marlow,' she said. 'We read about him in the paper. He brought a state umbrella with him, but the paper said he only used it once!'

'I bet he did,' said Larry, grinning. 'Got a state umbrella, Fatty?'

'No,' said Fatty, regretfully. He looked at everyone admiringly. 'Honestly, you're wizard! Of course, your suntans make you look first class in those foreign clothes. *Any*one would think you belonged to a different nationality. I only wish you could parade through the village!'

'You dress up too, Fatty, and let's go parading!' said Bets. But Fatty had no time to answer because Buster began to bark loudly, and tore out of the open door at sixty miles an hour.

'Now what's up with *him*?' said Fatty, in surprise. 'I wonder if old Mr Goon's anywhere about?'

Bets peered out of the door and up the garden path. 'It's three boys,' she said. 'Goodness, I know who one is! It's ERN!'

'Ern!' echoed everyone, and ran to the door.

Three boys were coming down the path towards the shed, and Buster was dancing excitedly round Ern's ankles, barking madly.

Fatty shut the door of the shed and faced the others. His eyes sparkled.

'It's Ern Goon!' he said. 'Old Mr Goon's nephew! Let's pretend you're foreign royalty visiting me. If you speak English, speak it badly, see? And if I speak to you in nonsense language, you speak the same. Let's see if we can take old Ern in properly!'

Ern was, as Fatty said, a nephew of Mr Goon the policeman. He had once been to stay with his uncle and had been involved in a mystery. Mr Goon had not been kind to Ern, but the Five Find-Outers had, and Ern thought the world of Fatty. Now here he was, coming to pay a visit with two friends. What a chance to try out the foreign 'disguises'!

Footsteps came right up to the door. Ern's voice could be heard speaking sternly to his two companions. 'Now you behave yourself, see? Both of you. And spit that toffee out, young Sid.'

Whether Sid spat the toffee out or not could not be gathered by the five children in the shed. Bets giggled and Pip gave her a sharp nudge.

There was a knock on the shed door. Fatty opened it and stared solemnly at Ern. Then his face took on a surprised and pleased expression. He smiled broadly and held out his hand.

'Ern! Ern Goon! This *is* a pleasure! Do come in, Ern, and let me introduce you to my foreign visitors!'

4. ERN, SID AND PERGE

Ern was still the same old Ern. He was plump, red-faced, and his eyes bulged slightly, just as his uncle's did, though not quite so much. He grinned shyly at Fatty, and then gazed in awe at the four silent 'foreigners' dressed in such brilliant clothes.

'Pleased to see you, Fatty,' he said, and shook hands for a long time. Then he turned to the two boys behind him. They were not as old as he was, and very alike.

'These here boys are my twin brothers,' he explained. 'This one's Sid – and this one's Perce. Speak up, Sid and Perce. Remember your manners. Come on, say "how do you do" like I told you.'

'How do you do,' said Perce, and bobbed his tousled head, going a brilliant scarlet with his effort at manners.

'Ar,' said Sid, hardly opening his mouth at all. Ern glared at him.

'You still sucking that toffee, Sid? Didn't I tell you to spit it out, see?'

Sid made an agonised face, pointed to his mouth, and shook his head.

''E means, his teeth's stuck fast again,' explained Perce. ''E can't say a word then. Couldn't speak all day yesterday, neither.'

'Dear me,' said Fatty, sympathetically. 'Does he live on toffee then?'

'Ar,' said Sid, with another effort at opening his mouth.

'Does "Ar" mean yes or no?' wondered Fatty. 'But I'm forgetting *my* manners now – Ern, let me introduce you to some very distinguished friends of mine.'

Ern, Sid, and Perce stared unblinkingly at Bets, Pip, Larry, and Daisy, not recognising them in the least as ordinary children. Bets turned her head away, afraid of giggling.

'You have no doubt heard of the little Prince Bongawah of Tetarua State,' went on Fatty. 'This is his sister, Princess Bongawee.' He waved his hand towards the startled Bets.

'Lovaduck!' exclaimed Ern, staring. 'So this is

the Prince's sister, is it? We've seen Prince Bongawah, Fatty – we're camping out in the field next to his. He's a funny little fellow with a cocky little face.' He turned to Sid and Perce.

'You can see they're sister and brother, can't you?' he said, to Bets' indignation. 'Like as two peas!'

'You're right, Ern,' said Perce.

'Ar,' said Sid, working the toffee round a bit to produce his usual remark.

Bets inclined her head majestically and looked at the three awed boys through half-closed lids.

'Popple, dippy, doppy,' she said in a high and mighty voice.

'What's she say?' asked Ern.

'She says, "Your hair is very untidy,"' said Fatty, enjoying himself.

'Coo,' said Ern, and swept his hand over his standing-up hair. 'Well, I didn't know as we were going to see royalty, like, else I'd have done me hair. Who are the others, Fatty?'

'This is Pua-Tua,' said Fatty, waving his hand towards Daisy. 'She is a cousin of the Princess's, and waits on her – a very nice girl indeed.'

Ern bowed, because Daisy did. Perce bowed too,

but Sid didn't. His toffee had got stuck again, and he was concerned with that. His jaws moved unceasingly.

'And the others are Kim-Pippy-Tok, and Kim-Larriana-Tik,' said Fatty, making Bets long to burst into giggles.

Pip moved forward, put his face close to Ern's, and rapidly rubbed noses. Ern started back in surprise.

'It's all right,' said Fatty, soothingly. 'That is their way of greeting a friend.' Sid and Perce backed away, afraid of the same kind of greeting.

'Pleased to meet you,' said Ern, with a gasp. Then he gazed at Fatty in awe. 'You haven't half got some posh friends,' he said. 'What about those other friends of yours – Larry and Daisy and Pip and little Bets?'

'They're not very far away,' said Fatty truthfully. 'Did you say you were camping out somewhere, Ern?'

'Yes,' said Ern. 'We got a chance of a campout, me and Sid and Perce together – got the loan of a tent, see, and Ma said she'd be glad to see the last of us for a bit. So off we skipped, and put up our tent in the field next to one of the school camp fields. We aren't half having a good time.'

'Sright,' said Perce.

'Ar,' said Sid. He suddenly put his hand into his pocket and brought out a round tin. He took off the lid and offered the tin to Fatty. Fatty peered in. It was almost full of dark brown, revolting-looking toffee in great thick pieces.

'Er, no thanks, Sid,' said Fatty. 'I don't want to spoil my dinner. And don't offer it to my visitors, because they will probably have to make speeches this afternoon, and I don't want them to be struck dumb by your toffee.'

'Ar,' said Sid, understandingly, and replaced the lid carefully.

'Where does he get that toffee from?' asked Fatty. 'I've never seen anything like it!'

''E gets it from the 'oopla stall at the Fair near the camp,' explained Perce. ''E's a nib at throwing rings round things, is our Sid. Gets himself a tin of toffee that way each day.'

'Ar,' said Sid, beaming proudly.

'Tickly-pickly-odgery, podgery, pooh,' announced Larry suddenly. Ern, Sid, and Perce stared at him.

'What's 'e say?' asked Perce.

'He says that Sid looks rather like a bit of toffee himself,' said Fatty, at once. 'Chewed-up toffee, he says.'

There was a pause, in which at least five of the children longed to burst into laughter.

'Bit rude that,' said Ern at last. 'Well, I suppose we'd better be off. Been nice to see you, Fatty. Sorry we couldn't see the others too.'

'Have you seen your uncle, Mr Goon?' asked Fatty.

'Coo, no,' said Ern. 'I'd run a mile if I saw him. Don't you remember how he treated me when I stayed with him last year? Sid and Perce don't like him neither. I say, Fatty – any more mysteries going?'

'Not yet,' said Fatty. 'But you never know when one might spring up, do you?'

'Tooky-oola-rickity-wimmy-woo,' said Pip, solemnly. 'We-go-get-icy-cream.'

'Why, he can speak English!' said Ern, in amazement. 'Hear that? I say, why don't we all go and get ice creams? There's a man down by the river we could go to. I don't want to go into the village in case I meet my uncle.'

Fatty grinned. He looked at the other four, who gazed back expectantly. Their 'disguises' had gone down so well with Ern, Sid, and Perce that they were longing to go out in them. Fatty didn't see why they shouldn't! If they took the river road, they wouldn't meet a great many people or attract a crowd, but it would be fun to see the faces of the few they met!

'Iccky, piccky, tominy, wipply-wop, Kim-Pippy-Tok,' he said, politely bowing to Pip, and waving him to the door. 'We'll all go and get ice creams by the river. The Princess must go first, Ern.'

'Course,' said Ern, hurriedly getting out of the way. 'Now *she* would look fine with a state umbrella like her brother had. It'd suit her all right and, what's more, I wouldn't mind carrying it either, she's such a little duck.'

Bets drew her hood over her face to hide her laughter. Fatty looked at Ern as if suddenly struck with a good idea. The others waited expectantly.

'Ah, yes – of course. I'd forgotten that the Princess Bongawee must not go out without her state umbrella,' he said. 'What a good thing you reminded me, Ern.'

43

'Lovaduck! Has she got one too?' asked Ern.

Fatty disappeared and the others waited. Whatever sort of 'state umbrella' was Fatty going to fetch?

He came back, with an enormous, brightly-coloured umbrella over his head. Actually, it was his mother's golf umbrella, but as Sid, Pearce, and Ern had never seen a golf umbrella in their lives, they honestly thought it was a very grand 'state umbrella'.

'Here, Ern – you can do as you said, if you like, and carry it over the Princess's head,' said Fatty, and Ern nearly had a fit.

'Would she let me?' he asked.

'Dimminy-dooly-tibbly-tok,' said Bets, and gave him a sudden smile. He blushed and looked at Fatty.

'What's she say?' he asked.

'She says, she likes you, and she wants you to carry it for her,' said Fatty promptly.

'The way you understand their language beats me!' said Ern, admiringly. 'But then you always were a one, weren't you, Fatty? Well, I'll be proud to hold the umbrella over Her Highness, or whatever she's called. Sid and Perce, get behind.'

The Five Find-Outers were by now quite unable to contain their laughter. Pip was purple in the face with his efforts to stop exploding. Fatty looked at him.

'Tickly-kickly-koo, jinny-peranha-hook!' he said, and then burst into laughter as if he had made a joke. The others immediately took the opportunity of joining in and Larry, Daisy, Pip, and Bets rocked from side to side, roaring with laughter, holding on to one another, much to the astonishment of Ern and his two brothers.

'What's the joke?' asked Ern, suspiciously.

'It's too difficult to translate it for you,' said Fatty. 'Come on now, the Princess in front, with Ern carrying her umbrella – her cousin, Pua-Tua, just behind – and us following.'

The little procession went down the garden path, passing the kitchen door on the way. The maid stood there, shaking a mat, and she stared open-mouthed as they passed. Ern felt terribly important.

It was very disappointing not to meet more people on the way down to the river. They met old Mrs Winstanton, who was so short-sighted that all she saw was the big umbrella, which made her think it must be raining. She hurried home before she got caught in a shower!

They met the grocer's boy, who stared in amazed and mystified silence. Bets giggled. Ern gave the boy a dignified bow which mystified him still further. What was all this going on? He followed them a little way, and then went to deliver his goods and a tale of 'dressed-up visitors under a HUGE umbrella' to a fascinated housekeeper.

They met nobody else at all. They came to the river path and walked solemnly along it.

'There's the ice cream man!' said Ern, thankfully. 'Pore Sid, he won't be able to have one, what with his toffee and all!'

5. MR. GOON GETS A SURPRISE

The ice cream man was lying on the river bank, fast asleep, his tricycle-van pulled back into the shade. Fatty woke him.

He sat up, amazed at the brilliant group around him, topped by the huge umbrella held by Ern, who was now getting a little tired of its weight.

'What's all this?' said the ice cream man. 'Charades or something?'

Ern opened his mouth to introduce the Princess Bongawee, but Fatty frowned at him. He didn't want the joke to go too far – and he had an uneasy feeling that the ice cream man wouldn't be taken in quite as easily as some people. It wouldn't do to spoil the joke for Ern. Ern, Sid, and Perce were in the seventh heaven of delight to think they had gone walking with a princess and her followers.

'Nine ice creams, please,' said Fatty. Ern corrected him.

'Eight, you mean,' he said.

'You've forgotten Buster,' said Fatty.

'Coo, yes,' said Ern, suddenly remembering that Buster also loved ice cream. Buster had been as good as gold, following the procession solemnly, and hadn't even been to say hello to any dogs he met.

The ice cream man handed out the ice creams, making a few more remarks as he did so.

'Pouring with rain, isn't it?' he said to Ern, who was still valiantly holding the umbrella over Bets. 'Just as well not to get wet.'

'Funny, aren't you?' said Ern.

'Not so funny as you look,' said the ice cream man. 'Where'd you get that umbrella? Out of a cracker?'

'Ha, that's where *you* came from, I spose,' said Ern, at once. 'BANG – and out of a cracker you fell!'

'That's enough, Ern,' said Fatty hastily, seeing a storm about to blow up between the ice cream man and Ern. 'Come on, let's take our ice creams a bit further down the path, where it's cooler.'

The ice cream man remarked that he knew where he could get Ern a clown's hat to go with his umbrella, but Ern was not allowed to reply. Fatty hustled him away, and his umbrella caught in the low-swinging branches of a tree. Bets had to stand still while poor Ern struggled to release it, his ears burning at a few more remarks from the witty ice cream man.

They went on at last again, holding the freezing ice cream cartons in their hands. Sid had one too, and everyone was curious to see how he could manage to eat an ice cream with his mouth still full of toffee. His toffee slab seemed unending. So far as anyone knew, he still had the same piece in his mouth.

And then someone came cycling round the corner of the path – someone burly and red-faced, with a dark blue uniform and helmet!

'It's Uncle!' gasped Ern, in a panic.

'Mr Goon!' said Fatty. 'Old Clear-Orf! Well, well, this is going to be funny!'

Buster recognised Mr Goon with delight. He tore up to his bicycle and jumped at his feet. Goon got off at once and kicked out at the excited little Scottie.

'Clear orf!' he said angrily. 'Here, you, call this dog orf, or I'll push him into the river. Proper little pest, he is.'

'Hello, Mr Goon,' said Fatty, politely. 'I haven't seen you for a very long time. Come here, Buster. Heel, boy, heel!'

Buster ran to Fatty reluctantly, and Mr Goon had time to take in the whole group. He gaped. What a lot of foreigners – and Ern with them. *Ern!* He didn't even know Ern was in the district. He advanced on Ern, who almost dropped the huge umbrella he was still holding.

'ERN! What you doing here?' thundered Mr Goon. 'And bless me, if it isn't Sid and Perce too! What's all this about? And what's the umbrella for?'

'Uncle! Don't shout like that,' begged Ern. 'This is a princess here, and that's why I'm holding an umbrella over her. It's a state umbrella. Don't you know one when you see one?'

Mr Goon didn't even know a golf umbrella when he saw one, much less a state one. He stared at Ern disbelievingly. Ern went on in an urgent voice.

'Uncle, you've heard of Prince Bongawah, who's staying in one of the camps, up on the hills over there, haven't you? Well, this is his sister, Princess Bongawee – and that's her cousin – and . . .'

Goon was amazed. He looked at Bets, wrapped

closely and gracefully in her robes, the hood partly drawn across her sunburnt face. Her face seemed faintly familiar to him, but he didn't for one moment think of Bets Hilton. She stood there rather haughtily, a little scared, without saying a single word.

Goon cleared his throat. He looked at Fatty, who said nothing. 'They were visiting Fatty,' explained Ern. 'And, of course, I told them about Prince Bongawah, who's camping in the field next to us, Uncle – and I'd have known this princess was his sister, they're as alike as two peas.'

'But how did *you* come to be mixed up with them?' asked Goon, suspiciously.

'Your nephew, Ern, came to pay a visit to us, that's all, Mr Goon,' said Fatty, delighted that Ern should be telling Mr Goon such a marvellous tale. 'And the Princess Bongawee liked Ern, and requested him to hold her – er – her state umbrella over her. And Ern's good manners are well-known – so here he is.'

Mr Goon had never had any opinion of Ern's manners at all. He considered that Ern had none. He stared first at Ern, then at the haughty little princess, and then at Fatty. Fatty stared back unwinkingly.

'She a real princess?' asked Mr Goon, in a confidential aside to Fatty. Before Fatty could answer, Bets spoke in a high little insolent voice that amused Fatty immensely.

'Ikky-oola-potty-wickle-tok,' she said.

'What's she say?' asked Goon with interest.

'She wants to know if you're a real policeman,' said Fatty, promptly. 'What shall I tell her?'

Mr Goon glared at him. Bets interrupted again. 'Ribbly-rookatee, paddly-pool,' she said.

'What does *that* mean?' asked Mr Goon. Fatty put on an embarrassed look.

'I don't like to tell you, Mr Goon,' he said.

'Why? What's it matter?' said the policeman, curiously.

'Well, it's rather a personal remark,' said Fatty. 'No, I don't really think I can tell you, Mr Goon.'

'Go on – you tell me,' said Goon, getting angry.

'Yes, you tell him,' said Ern, delighted at the idea of the princess saying something rude about his uncle.

'Ar,' put in Sid, unexpectedly. Goon turned on him at once.

'What you interfering for? And what do you mean by standing there with your mouth full in front of royalty? Go and empty your mouth!'

'Ar,' said Sid, in panic.

'It's toffee, Uncle,' said Ern. 'Stick-me-tight toffee. It can't be spat out.'

Bets went off into a peal of laughter. Then she hurriedly spoke a few more words. 'Wonge-bonga-smelly-fiddly-tok.'

'There she goes again,' said poor Goon. 'You tell me what she said then, Frederick.'

'I couldn't possibly,' persisted Fatty, making Goon feel so curious that he could hardly contain himself. His face began to go purple, and his eyes bulged a little. He stared at the little princess, who giggled again.

'I only say, why he got FROG face!' said Bets, in a very foreign voice. Everyone immediately exploded, with the exception of poor Sid who couldn't get his mouth open.

Mr Goon exploded too, but in a different way. He was very angry. He took a step forward and Ern instinctively lowered the umbrella and put its vast circle just in front of Mr Goon's nose.

'Don't you hurt the princess, Uncle,' came Ern's quavering voice from behind the huge umbrella. Then Buster joined in the fun again, and flew at Mr Goon's ankles, snapping very deftly at the bicycle clips that held his trousers tightly round his legs.

Mr Goon roared in anger. 'I'll report that dog! I'll report you too, Ern – trying to stick that umbrella into me!'

'Mr Goon, I hope you won't upset the relations of the British with the Tetaruans,' said Fatty, solemnly. 'We don't want the Prince of Tetarua complaining that you have frightened his sister. After all, Tetarua is a friendly state. If the Prime Minister had an incident like this reported to him by an angry prince, there might be . . .'

Mr Goon didn't stay to listen to any more. He knew when he was defeated. He didn't know anything about the Tetaruans, but he did know that little states were very touchy nowadays, and he was rather horrified to hear what Fatty said. He got on his bicycle and sailed away in purple dignity.

'I'll have something more to say to you, young Ern,' he shouted, as he pedalled past, with Buster at his back wheel, making him wobble almost into the river. 'I'll come up to your camp, you see if I don't!'

He left Ern petrified by his threat, but still valiantly holding the umbrella. Everyone collapsed weakly on the grass, and even Sid managed to open his mouth wide enough to let out a sudden guffaw.

'Our poor ice creams,' said Bets, suddenly relapsing into English, and looking at the ice cream in her carton. It was like custard. Nobody noticed she was speaking English except Fatty, who gave her a little frown.

They licked up their ice creams with difficulty. Sid managed to pour his somehow into his mouth, between his stuck teeth. Fatty grinned round.

'A most creditable performance!' he said. 'Princess, my congratulations!'

'Binga-bonga-banga,' said Bets, graciously.

'What about fresh ice creams?' said Fatty. But Ern, Perce, and Sid couldn't stay. Ern had heard the church clock striking twelve, and as he had been promised a camp dinner by the caravanners next to his tent if he got back at half past twelve, he felt impelled to go.

He bowed most politely to Bets, and handed the

state umbrella to Fatty. 'Pleased to have met you,' said Ern. 'I'll tell your brother about you when next I see him over the hedge. Like as peas in a pod, you are!'

Sid and Perce nodded a good-bye, and then they all went off to get the ferry across the river to the hills on the other side.

'Thank goodness we can talk properly again,' said Larry. 'My word, Fatty – what a morning! I don't know when I've enjoyed myself so much!'

6. DISAPPEARANCE

Two days later, Fatty, Larry, and Pip all had tremendous shocks. Fatty got down to breakfast before his mother and father, and poured himself some coffee. He took the two papers they had each morning to his own place, and prepared to enjoy them in peace.

The headlines flared at him, big and black. 'Disappearance of a Prince from Camp. Vanishes in the night. Prince Bongawah gone.'

And in Larry's house, Larry too was reading the same headlines out to Daisy, having found the papers on the front doorstep and brought them in.

In Pip's house, Pip was, as usual, trying to read his father's newspaper back to front. The back page was never very interesting to Pip, because it was all about horse-racing, golf, and tennis – none of which he took any interest. Cricket scores were usually in too small print for him to see. So he waited patiently for his father to study the cricket scores himself on the back page, when Pip would be able to read the front page.

And there, staring at him, were some very interesting headlines. 'Prince vanishes. Tetarua informed. Boys in camp questioned.'

Pip nudged Bets and nodded his head towards the paper. She read the headlines too. Good gracious! That must be the Prince Bongawah whose sister she had pretended to be. How very extraordinary! Bets thought hard about it. Would it matter her having pretended? No, it couldn't. They had only done it to play a trick on Ern.

Yet another person was most interested in the disappearance of the young prince. That was Mr Goon, of course. He also read it in his morning newspaper, and a few minutes later, his telephone rang and he had the news from headquarters. He thought rapidly.

My word – I've met the prince's sister, he thought. If we get hold of her, we might get some news! I'd better get on to the Inspector straightaway.

He corrected himself. 'I should say the *Chief* Inspector! He's had a promotion again. I've never had any. Got enemies, I have, no doubt of that. Keeping a good man down, that's what they are. Wait till I get them!'

He brooded for a few minutes on enemies that prevented promotion, and then rang up head-quarters again and asked for the Chief Inspector.

'He's busy,' said the voice at the other end. 'What do you want him for, Goon?'

'Something to do with the Prince Bongawah disappearance,' said Goon, pompously. 'Very interesting.'

'Right. Hold on a minute,' said the voice. Then Goon heard the Chief Inspector's voice – sharp, confident, and a little annoyed.

'What is it, Goon? I'm busy.'

'Sir, it's about that Prince Bongawah, or whatever his name is,' said Goon. 'I've met his sister, sir, the little Princess Bongawee. I wondered if anyone had thought of questioning her. She might know something about her brother's disappearance.'

There was a moment's silence. Then the Chief Inspector's voice came again, sounding astonished.

'Sister? What sister? This is the first time I've

heard of her.'

Goon swelled with importance. 'Yes, sir. I met her two days ago, sir, with her cousin, who looks after her. And two of her train, sir, all very posh and high and mighty.'

There was another astonished pause. 'Is that really you speaking, Goon?' said the Chief Inspector's voice at last. 'This really is so astonishing.'

'Course it's me speaking, sir,' said Goon, surprised and hurt. 'Why shouldn't it be? I'm just reporting something to you, as is my duty. Would you care for me to interview the princess, sir?'

'Wait a minute, wait a minute,' said the Chief Inspector. 'I must ask a few questions of somebody here. We've had no reports of any sister or princess or cousin! I must find out why.'

Goon waited, feeling pleased to have caused such a commotion. Ha – let Chief Inspector Jenks ask all the questions he liked, he'd have to let him, Goon, handle this in the end! That was a bit of luck meeting Fatty with those Tetaruans and their umbrella. A thought struck him. How was it that *Fatty* knew them?

Drat that boy! thought poor Goon. Here I've got

a fine bit of investigation in my hand – and I've got to say it's that big boy who introduced me to the princess! Then the Chief Inspector will get on to that toad of a boy, and he'll take the whole matter out of my hands!'

He sat and brooded about this, the telephone receiver stuck to his left ear. Then he brightened. He could say that his nephew, Ern, had introduced him. After all, it *was* Ern who had given him all the details. That was quite true. He needn't bring Fatty into it at all.

The Chief Inspector's voice came down the telephone again, making Goon jump.

'Are you there, Goon? Well, I've made a few enquiries this end, and nobody seems to know anything about a sister who's called Princess Bongawee. But seeing that you appear to have met her, I suppose we must enquire into it. How did you meet her?'

'Well, sir – my nephew Ern was with her, and he told me about her and who she was,' said Goon.

'*Ern* – your nephew *Ern*!' said the Chief Inspector, astounded. He remembered the plump, rather spotty, extremely plain nephew of Mr Goon quite clearly. Hadn't he been mixed up in another mystery? Oh yes – and had come quite well out of it too, in the end. But *Ern*! In the company of a Tetaruan princess! The Chief Inspector wondered again if this telephone call was a hoax. But, no, it couldn't be. He knew that harsh voice of Mr Goon's only too well!

'What was Ern doing with the princess?' asked the Chief Inspector, at last.

'Well – he was holding a – a state umbrella over her,' said Mr Goon, beginning to feel that this tale of his didn't really sound very credible.

There was another pause. The Chief Inspector swallowed once or twice. Was Goon all right? Had he got a touch of the sun? This tale of a princess – and Ern – and a state umbrella sounded nonsense to him. The Chief Inspector simply didn't know what to make of it at all.

'Look here, Goon,' he said, 'this is all very extraordinary, but I suppose there may be something in it if you think it's important enough to telephone me about it. I think I will leave you to contact this – er – princess, and ask her a few questions. Why she's here, when she came, what she's doing, who she's with, and so on. Go and do that now. I'll send a man over to check what you find.'

'Right sir, thank you, sir,' said Goon, pleased that he was going to handle the matter first. He clicked down the receiver, and went to get his helmet. It was a great pity he had to go and see that toad of a boy, Fatty. Frederick Trotteville. Huh! He'd soon show him he'd got to answer his questions though. He'd stand no nonsense from that pest.

He cycled round to Fatty's house. He knocked sharply at the front door. The maid opened it, and he asked for Fatty.

'He's gone out, sir,' said the maid.

'Where's he gone?' demanded Mr Goon.

Mrs Trotteville, Fatty's mother, heard Mr Goon's rather loud voice, and came into the hall.

'Oh, it's you, Mr Goon,' she said politely. 'Did you want Frederick? He's out, I'm afraid. Was there something you wanted to ask him?'

'Well, madam, I did want to ask him a few questions about the Princess Bongawee,' said Mr Goon. 'But perhaps you can tell me. Was she staying here?'

Mrs Trotteville looked amazed. '*What* princess?' she asked. 'I've never even heard of her.'

'She's the sister of that Prince Bongawah that's vanished,' explained Mr Goon.

This didn't convey anything to Mrs Trotteville at all. She hadn't taken any interest in the morning's report of the prince's disappearance. She had merely thought he hadn't liked cold baths or something, and had run away. And anyway, what was it to do with Frederick?

'I'm afraid I can't help you, Mr Goon,' she said. 'Frederick has only been back home for two or three days and, as far as I know, he hasn't been about with any princesses at all. I feel sure he would have introduced them to me if he knew any. Good morning.'

'But – do you mean to say you didn't ask her in to tea or anything?' said Mr Goon desperately.

'Why should I, if I have never even met her?' said Mrs Trotteville, thinking that Mr Goon must be out of his mind. 'Good morning.'

She shut the door and left a perspiring Mr Goon outside. Now he had got to go and find that boy. Where would he be? He might be round at those precious friends of his – the Hilton's – or those other's – Larry and Daisy somebody-or-other.

Mr Goon cycled first to Larry's house. But again he drew a blank. Larry and Daisy were both out.

'Probably round at Frederick Trotteville's,' said their maid. But Mr Goon knew better. Nobody was going to send him trapesing back there again!

He cycled, very red in the face now, down the road, and all the way to Pip's. He cycled up to the front door, and hammered angrily on the knocker.

The five children were out in the garden with Buster. Buster growled at the knocking and Fatty put a restraining hand on him.

Bets went peeping round the hedge to see who it was at the front door. She ran back, looking scared.

'It's Mr Goon. Old Clear-Orf. He looks very red and cross,' she said. 'Oh dear – do you think he's come to ask us about the princess I pretended to be? He's really so very silly, I'm sure he thinks I was real!'

Fatty got up. 'Come along,' he said. 'Out of the gate at the bottom of the garden we go, top speed. If anyone calls us, we're not here. If Goon is hunting for the Princess Bongawee, let him hunt! Do him good. Shut up, Buster – if you bark, you'll give the game away!'

They all fled silently down the garden to the little gate that opened onto the lane at the bottom. Buster ran too, without even half a growl. Something was up, was it? Well, he could play his part too, then!

When Mrs Hilton took Mr Goon out into the garden to find the children, there was no one there. No one in the summer-house either! How peculiar!

'I am *sure* I heard them out here a minute ago,' she said. 'Pip! Bets! Where are you?'

No answer at all. Mrs Hilton called once more and then turned to the purple Mr Goon. 'I expect you will find them either at Frederick Trotteville's, or at Larry's,' she said. 'Perhaps you would like to go there.'

Mr Goon had a vision of himself chasing from one house to another, endlessly in search of an elusive Fatty. He scowled, and sailed away morosely on his bicycle.

'Really,' thought Mrs Hilton, 'that policeman's manners get worse and worse every day!'

7. ERN AND MR GOON

Somebody else was also very excited that morning, besides the Find-Outers and Mr Goon. Ern was most astonished when he heard the news of Prince Bongawah's disappearance. He learnt it in rather a peculiar fashion.

Ever since he had met the Princess Bongawee at Fatty's house, he had kept a lookout for the little prince over the hedge. He was longing to tell him that he had met his sister.

But, somehow, he hadn't caught sight of him. Still, Ern didn't give up, and that very morning he had squirmed right through the hedge, hoping to find the prince himself.

He was most astonished to find two policemen nearby. They pounced on Ern at once. 'What are you doing in this field?' demanded one, his hand on Ern's neck.

'I only just came over to look for someone,' said

67

Ern wriggling. 'Lemme go. You're hurting.'

'You'll get hurt a lot more if you come interfering here now,' said the policeman grimly. 'You might even disappear – like the little prince!'

This was the first Ern had heard of any disappearance. He stared at the two policemen. 'Has he disappeared?' he said, astonished. 'Coo, think of that! When did he go?'

'Sometime in the night,' said the policeman, watching Ern closely. 'Hear anything? You're camping in that tent, I suppose?'

'Yes. I didn't hear nothing at all,' said Ern at once. 'Coo – to think I met his sister, the princess, a few days ago!'

'Oh yes?' said one of the policemen, mockingly. 'And did you have tea with his mother, the Queen, and dinner with his old man?'

'No. But I had an ice cream with his sister,' protested Ern.

'Oh yes?' said both policemen at once. One of them gave him such a violent shake that Ern almost fell over. 'Now you get along,' he said. 'And just remember, it's always best to keep your nose out of trouble. You and your tales!'

Ern squeezed back through the hole in the hedge, hurt to think that his tale had been disbelieved. He was determined to go and tell Fatty about the prince's disappearance. It didn't occur to him that it was already in all the papers.

He set off by himself, without Sid or Perce. Perce was in a bad temper that morning, and Sid as usual had his mouth full of stick-me-tight toffee, so there was no conversation to be got out of him at all. Ern felt that he wanted a little intelligent company. Neither Sid nor Perce could be called really interesting companions.

He decided to borrow a bicycle from one of the nearby caravanners. There was one there, leaning against the caravan. Ern snooped round, looking for the owner.

He found him at last, a boy a bit older than himself. 'Lend me your bike?' called Ern.

'Cost you,' called back the thrifty owner. Ern parted reluctantly with some money and rode off down the field path to the gate, wobbling over the ruts.

Meanwhile, Mr Goon was cycling grumpily back home again. Just as he turned a corner, he caught sight of a plump boy cycling towards him. It was Ern. Ern, however, was not particularly anxious to meet his uncle, so he turned his bike round hurriedly and made off in the opposite direction.

For some reason, Mr Goon took it into his head to think that the boy in the distance was Fatty in one of his errand boy disguises.

He began to pedal furiously. Oho! So that toad of a boy was up to his tricks again, was he? He was disguising himself so as to keep away from Mr Goon and his questions, was he? Well, he, Mr Goon, would soon put an end to that! He would cycle after him till he caught him.

So Mr Goon cycled. The pedals went up and down furiously, he rang his bell furiously as he rounded the corner, and he looked furious too. Anyone looking at Mr Goon at that moment would have thought that he was on very important business indeed.

Ern took a look over his shoulder when he heard the furious ringing of Mr Goon's bell coming round the corner. He was horrified to find his uncle racing after him down the street. Ern began to pedal very quickly indeed.

'Hey you!' came a loud voice from halfway down the street. Ern's heart almost failed him. His uncle sounded so very stern. But what had he, Ern, done now? Was his uncle going to scold him for protecting the princess with the state umbrella?

Ern pedalled away and shot round a corner. So did Mr Goon. Both got hotter and hotter, and Ern became more and more panic-stricken. Mr Goon began to get very angry indeed. He was absolutely certain it was Fatty leading him this dance. Wait till he got him! He'd pull off his wig, and show him he couldn't deceive him!

Ern turned another corner, and found himself cycling up a path into a barn. He couldn't stop. Hens and ducks fled out of his way. Ern ended up on the floor of a dark barn, panting, and almost in tears.

Mr Goon came up the path at top speed too. He also landed in the dark barn, but not on the floor. He came to a stop just by Ern.

'Now, you just take off that wig,' commanded Mr Goon, in an awful voice. 'And let me tell you what I think of boys who lead me a dance like this, just when they know I want evidence regarding the Princess Bongawee!'

Ern stared up at his uncle in amazement. What was he talking about? Did he think Ern was wearing a wig? It was dark in the barn, and at first Mr Goon did not see that it was Ern. Then, as his eyes grew used to the shadows, he saw who it was. His eyes bulged almost out of his head.

'ERN! What are you doing here?' he almost yelled.

'Well, Uncle – you chased me, didn't you?' said Ern, in alarm. 'I was frightened. Didn't you know it was me? You pedalled after me all right.'

Mr Goon collected himself with an effort. He stared down at Ern, who was still on the floor. 'What did you run away from me for?' he asked sternly.

'I told you. You chased me,' said Ern.

'I chased you because you were running away,' said Mr Goon, majestically.

'Well, Uncle – I ran away because you were chasing me,' said poor Ern again.

'You being cheeky?' asked Mr Goon, in an awful voice.

'No, Uncle,' said Ern, thinking it was time he got

up. He was too much at Mr Goon's mercy on the floor. Anything might happen to him with his uncle so furious! Ern didn't know what was the matter at all. All he had done was to try to get away from his uncle.

'Have you seen that big boy today?' asked Mr Goon, watching Ern slowly and cautiously get up.

'No, Uncle,' said Ern.

'You seen that there princess again?' asked his uncle.

'No, Uncle,' said Ern, in alarm. 'I say – you're not after *her*, are you?'

'Do you know where she lives?' said Mr Goon, thinking that perhaps he might get something out of Ern, if he couldn't find the elusive Fatty.

'Why don't you ask Fatty?' said Ern, innocently. 'He knows her very well. I expect she sees him every day. Coo – she might know something about her brother's disappearance. I never thought of that!'

'Now you listen here, Ern,' said Mr Goon, solemnly. 'You remember Chief Inspector Jenks? Well, I've been talking to him on the phone today, see, about this same disappearance. And he's put me in charge of the case. I'm trying to find that princess to question her. But do you think I can find that pest of a boy to ask him about her? He's nowhere to be found! Makes me think *he's* disappearing too – on purpose!'

Ern picked up his bike, listening hard. He thought it very likely indeed that Fatty was avoiding Mr Goon. Ern considered it was a very sensible thing to do. Perhaps Fatty was on to this case too? Perhaps – oh joy – perhaps a mystery had suddenly turned up right under his very nose? Maybe Fatty was avoiding Mr Goon so that he wouldn't have to give away what he knew about the princess.

Ern grinned suddenly, much to his uncle's astonishment. 'What you grinning at all of a sudden?' he asked suspiciously.

Ern didn't answer. His grin faded. 'Now you look here, young Ern,' boomed Mr Goon, 'if I catch you hanging round Peterswood, hobnobbing with that pest of a boy, I'll have you and Sid and Perce cleared out of that camp in double-quick time – do you hear me? You don't know nothing about this case at all, and you aren't going to know anything, either. I know you and your ways – telling tales of this and that and the other! All you can tell that boy this time is that I'm in charge of this, and if he doesn't tell me all he knows about that princess before teatime, so's I can report to the Chief Inspector, he'll get into serious trouble. Very serious trouble.'

Mr Goon was quite out of breath after this long speech. Ern edged out of the barn. The hens peeping round the door scattered at once, clucking. Ern leapt on his bicycle and rode out at top speed.

'You go and tell that boy I want him!' yelled Mr Goon, as a parting shot. 'I'm not going all over the place after him again!'

Ern cycled quickly to Fatty's, relieved to have got away from his uncle without too much trouble. He hoped to goodness he would find Fatty at home. He was lucky! Fatty was in his shed with the others, keeping a watch for Goon.

Ern poured out his tale, and was disappointed to find that the others already knew about the prince's disappearance from the papers. 'What about that princess, Fatty?' said Ern. 'Don't she know nothing about her brother?'

'Ern – she wasn't a real princess,' said Fatty, thinking it was time to own up to their joke. 'That was only young Bets here dressed up in some things I brought from Morocco. And her cousin was Daisy, and the others were Larry and Pip!'

'Kim-*Larri*ana-Tik, at your service,' said Larry, with a bow.

'Kim-*Pip*py-Tok,' said Pip, with another bow. Ern stared, bewildered. He rubbed his hand over his eyes. He stared again.

'Lovaduck!' he said at last. 'No, I can't believe it! Just you dressed up, little Bets! And you looked a real princess too. Coo! No wonder my uncle's wanting to see you, Fatty, and ask about the princess – and no wonder you don't want to see *him*! Took him in properly, we did! Me with the state umbrella and all!'

Bets began to laugh. 'You were fine, Ern,' she said. 'Oh dear – didn't we talk a foreign language beautifully! Onna-matta-tickly-pop!'

'Beats me how you can talk like that,' said Ern, wonderingly. 'But I say – what's the Chief

Inspector going to say about all this? My uncle says he told him all about the princess this morning, and he's been put in charge of the case! He says I'm to tell you to keep off! *He's* met the princess too, he says, and you've got to tell him where she lives so that he can interview her.

Fatty groaned. 'I knew this would happen! Why did I do such a fool thing! It was just because you turned up when you did, Ern. Well – I suppose I'd better ring up the Chief Inspector and tell him everything. All I hope is that he'll laugh.'

'Better go and do it now,' said Pip, nervously. 'We don't want old Mr Goon round complaining about us again. If you get the Chief Inspector on your side, we'll be all right.'

'Right,' said Fatty, getting up. 'I'll go now. So long! If I'm not back in five minutes, you'll know the Chief Inspector has gobbled me up!'

He went off down the garden path to the house. The others looked rather solemnly at one another. What in the world would the Chief Inspector say when he heard there was no princess?

And worse still – whatever would *Mr Goon* say?

He must have told the Chief Inspector all about her.
He wouldn't like it one little bit when he knew it
was all a joke!

8. TWO UNPLEASANT TALKS

The Chief Inspector was not at all pleased with Fatty's tale. At first, he couldn't make head or tail of it, and his voice became quite sharp.

'First Goon telephones a cock-and-bull story of some princess who says she's Prince Bongawah's sister, and now you ring me and say there's no such person, it was only Bets dressed up,' said Chief Inspector Jenks. 'This won't do, Frederick. A joke's a joke, but it seems to me you've gone rather far this time. You've made Goon waste time on a lot of nonsense, when he might have been doing a bit of more useful investigation.'

'I quite see that, sir,' said poor Fatty. 'But actually it was all an accident – we'd no idea when we dressed up and called Bets the Princess Bongawee that Prince Bongawah was going to disappear. It was a most unfortunate coincidence. I mean, we couldn't possibly have guessed that was going to happen.'

'Quite,' said the Chief Inspector. 'You have a very curious knack of turning up in the middle of things, Frederick, haven't you? Accidental or otherwise. You'll certainly make Goon gnash his teeth over this! By the way, how on earth did that nephew of his – Ern, or some such name – come to be mixed up in this idiotic princess affair?'

'He just happened to barge in on us when we were dressing up,' explained Fatty. 'You know he and his twin brothers are camping in the field next to where the little prince was camping, don't you? It's a pity he's such an idiot or he might have noticed something.'

There was a pause. 'Yes,' came the Chief Inspector's voice, at last. 'I'd let Goon question them, but I don't think he'd get much out of Ern, somehow. You'd better see if you can find out something, Frederick – though you don't deserve to come in on this, you know, after your asinine behaviour.'

'No, sir,' said Fatty humbly, his face one huge grin at the thought of 'coming in on this'! That meant a little detective work again. Aha! So these hols were going to have something exciting, after all!

'All right,' said Chief Inspector Jenks. 'Make your peace with Goon if you can, and tell him to telephone me afterwards. He will *not* be pleased with you, Frederick. Neither am I. You'd better try and rub off this black mark quickly!'

Without saying good-bye, the Chief Inspector rang off, and Fatty heard the receiver click back into place. He put back his own, and stood by the wall, thinking hard. He felt thrilled, but rather uncomfortable. Quite by accident, he had got mixed up with the Prince Bongawah, simply because Bets had dressed up as a princess and Ern had seen her! How could he have known the prince was going to disappear, and that old Mr Goon would immediately spread the news about his mythical sister? Just like Goon! Always on to the wrong thing!

It was going to be most unpleasant breaking the news to Mr Goon that the Princess of Bongawah was just a joke. She didn't really exist. It was only Bets, dressed up, who had taken in old Mr Goon!

I play too many jokes, thought Fatty to himself. But it's going to be a pretty poor life for me and the others if I cut out all the tricks and jokes we like. We play them too well, I suppose. Gosh – there's Mr Goon coming in at the front gate! Now for it!'

Fatty went to the front door before Mr Goon could hammer at the knocker. He wasn't particularly anxious for his mother to hear what he had to say to Goon.

Goon stared at Fatty as if he couldn't believe his eyes. 'Here I've been chasing you all day and you come and open the door to me before I've even knocked!' he said. 'Where have you been?'

'That doesn't matter,' said Fatty. 'Come into this room, Mr Goon. I've something to say to you.'

He took the burly policeman into the little study, and Goon sat down in a chair, feeling rather astonished. 'I've got plenty to ask *you*,' he began. 'Been after you all day to get some information.'

'Yes. Well, you're going to have quite a lot of information,' said Fatty. 'And I'm afraid it will be a bit of a shock to you, Mr Goon. There's been an unfortunate misunderstanding.'

'Huh!' said Mr Goon, annoyed at Fatty's way of speaking. 'I don't want to know about unfortunate misunderstandings, whatever they may be – I just want to ask you about this here Princess Bonga – er, Bonga-what's-her-name.'

'Bongawee,' said Fatty, politely. 'I was going to tell you about her. She doesn't exist.'

Goon didn't take this in at all. He stared at Fatty, bewildered. Then he poked a big fat finger into the boy's face.

'Now you look here – you can pretend all you like that she doesn't exist, but I saw her with my own eyes. She's important in this here case, see? You may want to pretend that you don't know her now, nor where she is, but I'm not having any of that. I'm in charge of this, and I'm going to demand answers to my questions. Where's this princess now?'

Fatty hesitated. 'Well, I've already told you she doesn't exist,' he said. 'There's no such princess. It was only Bets dressed up.'

Goon went a dull red, and his eyes bulged a little more. He pursed up his mouth and glared. *Now* what was this boy up to? The princess was Bets dressed up! What nonsense! Hadn't he heard her talk a foreign language with his own ears?

'You're making up a tale for some reason of

your own, Frederick,' he burst out at last. 'I not only saw the princess, but I heard her. She talked all foreign. Nobody can talk foreign if they don't know the language.'

'Oh yes, they can,' said Fatty. 'I can "talk foreign" for half an hour if you want me to. Listen!'

He poured out a string of idiotic, completely unintelligible words that left Mr Goon in a whirl. He blinked. How did this boy do these things?

'There you are,' said Fatty, at last. 'Easy! You try, Mr Goon. All you have to do is to let your tongue go loose, if you know what I mean, and jabber at top speed. It doesn't *mean* anything. It's just complete nonsense. You try.'

Mr Goon didn't even begin to try. Let his tongue go loose? Not in front of Fatty, anyway! He might try it when he was by himself, perhaps. In fact, it might be a good idea. He, too, might be able to 'talk foreign' whenever he pleased. Mr Goon made a mental note to try it out sometime when he was quite by himself.

'See?' said Fatty, to the dumbstruck policeman. 'I only just let my tongue go loose, Mr Goon. Do try. Anyway, that's what Bets and the others did

– we didn't really "talk foreign", as you call it.'

'Do you mean to say that that procession Ern was with was just Bets and your friends dressed up?' said poor Mr Goon, finding his tongue at last. 'What about the state umbrella?'

Fatty had the grace to blush. 'Oh that – well, actually it was a golf umbrella belonging to my mother,' he said. 'I tell you, it was all a joke, Mr Goon. Ern happened to come along when they were all dressed up, and you know what he is – he just fell for everything, and swallowed the whole tale of princess and lady-in-waiting and all! We went out for ice creams – and then we met *you*!'

Mr Goon suddenly saw it all now. He was full of dismay and horror. To think of all he had told the Chief Inspector too! How was he to get out of *that*? He buried his face in his hands and groaned, quite forgetting that Fatty was still there.

Fatty felt extremely uncomfortable. He didn't like Mr Goon at all, but he hadn't meant to get him into this humiliating fix. He spoke again.

'Mr Goon, it was a silly mistake and most unfortunate, of course, that the Prince Bongawah should go and disappear just after we'd pretended

Bets was his sister. I've told the Chief Inspector all about it. He's just as annoyed with me as you are, but he does see that it was pure coincidence – just an unlucky chance. We're all very sorry.'

Mr Goon groaned again. 'That golf umbrella! I told him it was a state umbrella. He'll think I'm potty. Everyone will think I'm potty. Here I am, struggling for promotion, doing my very best, and every time you come along and upset the apple cart. You're a toad of a boy, that's what you are!'

'Mr Goon, I *am* sorry about this,' said Fatty. 'Look here – let's work together this time. I'll try and make up for this silly beginning. We'll solve this mystery together. Come on – be a sport!'

'I wouldn't work with you if the Chief Inspector himself told me to!' said Mr Goon, rising heavily to his feet. 'Once a toad, always a toad! And what would working with you mean? *I'll* tell you! False clues put under my nose! Me running about at night to find people that aren't there! Me arresting the wrong person while you've got the right one up your sleeve! Ho – *that's* what working with you would mean!'

'All right,' said Fatty, getting angry at being

...alled a toad so often. 'Don't work with me then. ...ut if I can put any information your way I will, ...ll the same – just to make up for upsetting your ...pple cart.'

'Gah!' said Goon, stalking out. 'Think I'd listen ...o any information from you! You think again, ...rederick Trotteville. And keep out of this. I'm in ...harge, see, and I'll solve this mystery, or my ...ame's not Theophilus Goon!'

9. A LITTLE 'PORTRY'

Mr Goon went to telephone the Chief Inspector. He felt extremely gloomy and downhearted. Why did he always believe everything Fatty said and did? Why didn't he spot that the state umbrella was no more than a golf umbrella? What was there about that pest of a boy that always made him come to grief?

I'll never believe a word he says again, thought Mr Goon, picking up the telephone receiver. Never in this world! He's a snake in the grass! He's a – a toad-in-the-hole. No – that's a pudding. Talking about me working with him! What sauce! What cheek! What . . .

Letting your tongue go loose too, he went on thinking. What does he mean? Let's try it – abbledy, abbledy, abbledy . . .

'What's that you say?' asked a surprised voice at the other end, and Mr Goon jumped. 'Er – can I peak to Chief Inspector Jenks, please?' he asked.

The conversation between the Inspector and Mr Goon was short, and much more satisfactory to Mr Goon than he had dared to hope. Apparently Inspector Jenks *was* annoyed with Fatty, and although a little sarcastic about people who believed in false princesses and particularly in state umbrellas, he said far less than Mr Goon had feared.

'All right, Goon,' he finished. 'Now, for pity's sake, put your best foot forward, and get something sensible done. It's in your district. Go and interview the boys up in the camp, use your brains, and PRODUCE RESULTS!'

'Yes, sir,' said Goon. 'And about that boy, Frederick Trotteville, sir – he's not to . . .'

But the Chief Inspector had rung off, and Goon stared at the silent receiver crossly. He had meant to put in a few well-chosen remarks about Fatty's shocking deception, and now it was too late.

Fatty told the others the result of his telephone call to the Chief Inspector, and of his interview with Mr Goon. Bets was sorry for Mr Goon. She didn't like him any more than the others did, but

all the same she thought he hadn't had quite a fa[i]r
deal this time – and it was really her fault becaus[e]
she had passed herself off so gleefully as th[e]
Princess Bongawee!

'We really will try to help him this time,' sh[e]
said. 'We'll pass him on anything we find out.'

'He probably won't believe a word,' said Fatty.
'Still, we could pass anything on through Ern. H[e]
might believe Ern.'

Ern was still there. He looked alarmed. 'Here[,]
don't you go telling me things to pass on to m[y]
uncle,' he protested. 'I don't want nothing to d[o]
with him. He don't like me, and I don't like him.'

'Well, Ern, it would only be to help him,' sai[d]
Bets, earnestly. 'I feel rather awful abou[t]
everything really – especially about the bit where [I]
called him "frog face" in broken English!'

Fatty laughed. 'Gosh, I'd forgotten about that[.]
Fancy *you* doing that, young Bets! He'll be callin[g]
you a toad, if you call him a frog!'

'It was awfully rude of me,' said Bets. 'I can't thin[k]
what came over me. Ern, you *will* pass on anythin[g]
we want you to, to your uncle, won't you?'

Ern couldn't resist Bets. He had a tremendou[s]

admiration for her. He rubbed his hand over his untidy hair, and stared helplessly at her.

'All right,' he said. 'I'll do what you say. But mind, I don't promise he'll believe me. And I'm not going too near him either. I'll tell him over a fence or something. You don't know what a temper my uncle's got.'

'Oh yes, we do,' said Fatty, remembering some very nasty spurts of temper that Mr Goon had shown in the past. 'We don't *really* want to help him, Ern, but we do want to make up for messing him about this time, that's all. We'll make amends, if we can't be friends.'

'I say! That last bit sounds like portry,' said Ern.

We'll make amends,
If we can't be friends.

'See? It's portry, isn't it?'

'No, it just happened to rhyme, that's all,' said Fatty. 'By the way, you used to write a lot of poetry, er, portry, I mean. Ern, do you still write it?'

'Not so much,' said Ern, regretfully. 'It don't seem to come, like. I keep on starting pomes, but that's as far as I get. You know, just the first line or two, that's all. But I've got one here that's three lines almost.'

'Oh Ern, read it!' said Daisy, delighted. Ern's poems were always so very dismal and gloomy, and he was so very serious over them.

Ern fumbled in his pocket and brought out a dirty little notebook with a pencil hanging to it by a string. He licked his thumb and began to turn the pages.

'Here we are,' he said, and cleared his throat solemnly. He struck an attitude, and began to recite his 'pome' haltingly.

> A pore old gardener said, "Ah me!
> My days is almost done,
> I've got rheumatics . . ."

Ern stopped and looked at the others in despair. 'I got stuck there,' he said. 'That's what always happens to me. I just get stuck – in the very middle of a good pome too. Took me two hours and twenty-one minutes to get that far. I timed meself. And now I can't finish it.'

'Yes, I can tell it would be a good pome,' said Fatty, solemnly. 'It goes like this, Ern.'

And Fatty also struck an attitude, legs apart, hands behind his back, face turned upwards – and recited glibly, without stopping.

> A pore old gardener said, "Ah me!
> My days is almost done,
> I've got rheumatics in my knee,
> And now it's hard to run.
> I've got a measle in my foot,
> And chilblains on my nose,
> And bless me if I haven't got
> Pneumonia in my toes.
> All my hair has fallen out,
> My teeth have fallen in,
> I'm really getting rather stout,
> Although I'm much too thin.
> My nose is deaf, my ears are dumb,
> My tongue is tied in knots,
> And now my barrow and my spade
> Have all come out in spots.
> My watering can is . . ."

Larry shouted with laughter and Pip thumped Fatty on the back, yelling. Bets collapsed with Daisy on the rug. 'Don't,' said Bets. 'Stop, Fatty! How do you do it!'

Fatty stopped, out of breath. 'Had enough?' he said. 'I was just coming to where the watering can was feeling washed out, and the spade was feeling on edge, and . . .'

'*Don't*, Fatty!' begged Bets again, giggling helplessly. 'Oh dear – HOW do you do it?'

Only Ern was silent, without a smile or a laugh. He sat on the edge of a chair, struck with absolute wonder. He gazed at Fatty, and swallowed hard. He couldn't make it out. How could Fatty stand there and recite all that without thinking about it?

'Struck dumb, all of a sudden?' asked Fatty, amused. 'How do you like the way your "pome" goes on, Ern? It's a pity you didn't finish it, you know. You could have read it out to us then, instead of my saying it to you.'

Ern was even more bewildered. He blinked at Fatty. 'Do you mean to say, if I had finished that pome that's what it would have been like?' he asked, in an awed voice.

'Well, it's your pome, isn't it?' said Fatty cheerfully. 'I mean, I only just went on with it. I think you work too hard at your pomes, Ern. You just want to throw them off, so to speak. Like this.'

> The little Princess Bongawee
> Was very small and sweet,
> A princess from her pretty head
> Down to her tiny feet.
> She had a servant, Ern by name,
> A very stout young fella,
> Who simply loved to shield her with
> A dazzling . . .

'STATE UMBRELLA!' yelled everyone, except Ern. There were more yells and laughs. Ern didn't join in. He simply couldn't understand how Fatty could be so clever. Fatty gave him a thump.

'Ern! Wake up! You look daft, sitting there without a smile on your face. What's up?'

'You're a genius, Fatty, that's what's up,' said Ern. 'The others don't know it, because they don't know how difficult it is to write portry. But I do. And you stand there and – and . . .'

'Spout it out,' said Fatty. 'It's easy, that kind of stuff. I'm not a genius, Ern. Anyone can do that kind of thing, if they think about it.'

'But that's just it,' said Ern. 'You don't even think about it. It's like turning on a tap. Out it comes. Coo, lovaduck! If I could do portry like that, I'd think meself cleverer than the King of England.'

'Then you'd be wrong,' said Fatty. 'Cheer up, Ern. One of these days, your portry will come gushing out and then you'll be miserable because you won't be able to write it down fast enough.'

'I'd get a shock if it did,' said Ern, putting away his dirty little notebook with a sigh. 'I'm proud to know you, Fatty. If the others don't know a genius when they see one, I do. I'm not a very clever fellow, but I know good brains when I come across them. I tell you, you're a genius.'

This was a very remarkable speech indeed from Ern. The others looked at him in surprise. Was there more in Ern than they suspected? Bets slipped her hand through Fatty's arm.

'You're right, Ern,' she said. '*I* think Fatty's a genius too. But not only in poetry. In everything!'

Fatty looked pleased but extremely embarrassed.

He squeezed Bets' hand. He coughed modestly, and then coughed again, trying to think of something to say. But Larry spoke first, amused at Fatty's modest coughs.

> It was a coff,
> That carried him off,
> It was a coffin
> They carried him offin,

he said in a solemn and lugubrious voice. Whereupon the meeting dissolved in squeals of laughter and yells and thumps. Ern was delighted. What a set of WONDERFUL friends he had!

He s...peered his... hand. He coughed modestly and
then coughed again, trying to think of something
to say. But fatty... ...'t believe in many
modest coughs.

It was call.

10. UP AT THE CAMP

That afternoon, Fatty began to 'investigate' in earnest.
He had studied the papers, but had learnt very little
from them. Apparently, the little prince had joined in
a camp singsong the night he had disappeared, and
had then had some cocoa and gone off to his tent
with the three other boys he shared it with.

These three boys could give no help at all. They
had been tired and had fallen asleep immediately
they had got into their sleeping-bags. When they
awoke, it was morning, and the prince's sleeping-
bag was empty.

That was all they could say.

There's not very much to go on, thought Fatty.
I suppose someone has kidnapped the boy. I'll have
to question Ern and Sid and Perce, though I don't
expect any of them know a thing – and I'll have to
snoop round the camp a bit too, and keep my
ears open.

He cycled round to Pip's that afternoon and found Larry and Daisy there. 'Has anyone got a relation of some sort up at the camping ground?' asked Fatty. 'I haven't as many relations as you have. Larry, can't you produce a cousin or something who might be staying at the camp?'

'No,' said Larry. 'What about you, Pip?'

'What schools are up there?' said Pip. 'Where's the paper? I saw a list of them today.'

They scanned the list carefully. 'Ah, there are boys from Lillington-Peterhouse,' said Pip. 'I know a cousin of mine goes there. He might be at the camp.'

'What's his name?' asked Fatty.

'Ronald Hilton,' said Pip. 'He's older than I am.'

'We could go and find the Lillington-Peterhouse lot,' said Fatty, 'and ask for Ronald. If he's there, you can have a powwow and the rest of us will have a snoop round, and keep our ears open.'

'I don't much want to have a powwow with Ronald,' said Pip. 'He'll think it awful cheek. I tell you, he's older than I am.'

'Do you realise this may be a mystery?' said Fatty severely. 'I know it doesn't seem like one at all, and we've begun all wrong, somehow – but it's a *possible* mystery, so it's your duty to do what you can, Pip.'

'Right,' said Pip, meekly. 'I'll powwow then. But if I get a clip on the ear, come and rescue me. I hope if it's a mystery, it livens up a bit. I can't get up much interest in a little foreign prince being kidnapped.'

'Nor can I,' admitted Daisy. 'But you never know. I bet we don't get much out of Ern, Sid, or Perce, Fatty. They wouldn't notice anything if it went on under their noses!'

'Got your bikes, Larry and Daisy?' asked Fatty. 'Come on then, let's go. We won't use the ferry, we'll go round by the bridge and up to the camp that way. It's not very far on bikes.'

They set off, with Buster as usual in Fatty's basket. He sat up there, perky and proud, looking down his nose at any other dog he met.

'If you get any bigger I won't be able to take you in my basket much longer, Buster,' panted Fatty, as he toiled up a hill.

'Woof,' agreed Buster, politely. He turned round and tried to lick Fatty's nose, but Fatty dodged.

They got to the camp at last. It was in a very

large field, sloping down to the river on one side. Clumps of trees stood here and there. Tents were everywhere, and smoke rose from where a meal was cooking. Boys hurried about, yelling and laughing.

The Find-Outers put their bicycles against a hedge. Fatty spoke to a boy coming along.

'Hey! Where's the Lillington-Peterhouse lot?'

The boy jerked his head towards the river. 'Last tents down there.'

The five children strolled down to the tents. Pip looked nervous. He really didn't like accosting a cousin two years older than himself, and very much bigger. He hoped he wouldn't see him.

But in a moment or two, he got a thump on the back and a cheerful-faced boy, three inches taller than Pip, shouted at him.

'Philip! What are *you* doing? Don't say you've come to look me up!'

Pip turned round. He grinned. 'Hello Ronald!' he said. 'Yes, I did come to look you up. Hope you don't mind.'

It was funny to hear Pip being called by his right name, Philip. Pip introduced his cousin to the others. Ronald stared hard at Fatty.

'Hey! Aren't you the chap Philip is always gassing about – the one that works with the police or something?'

Fatty looked modest. 'Well, I do help the police sometimes,' he admitted.

'Are you on a job now?' asked Ronald eagerly. 'Come and tell us about it!'

'No – no, I can't,' said Fatty. 'We've just come up here to see you – and out of interest because of the disappearance of that young prince.'

'Oh, that fellow!' said Ronald, leading them all into a very spacious tent. 'Don't bother about *him*! Jolly good riddance, *I* say! He was the most awful little beast imaginable!'

There was a long wooden table in the tent and on it were spread plates of jam sandwiches, potted meat sandwiches, buns, and slices of fruit cake. Jugs of lemonade stood at intervals down the length of the table.

'You do well for yourselves!' said Larry.

'Help yourselves,' invited Ronald. 'I'm helping with the catering this week – head cook and bottlewasher, you know. It's a bit early for tea, but everything's ready and we might as well get what we want before the hungry hordes rush in.'

They each got plates, and piled them with food. It really was not more than an hour or so since they had finished their lunches, but that made no difference. All of them could eat, hungrily, at any time of the day or night, including Buster, who was now sniffing about under the table, snapping up all kinds of tasty bits and pieces.

Ronald led them out into the field again, complete with plates of food, and took them down to the river. 'Come on, we'll sit and eat in peace here,' he said. 'My word, Trotteville, I'm pleased to meet you. Philip's told me no end of tales about you at one time and another – and I've told them to my pals too.'

Fatty told him a few more, and enjoyed himself very much. Pip got bored. His cousin took no further notice of him, he was so wrapped up in Fatty. Pip finished his tea and got up. He beckoned to Larry.

'Come on, let's go for a wander round,' he said. 'We might pick up something.'

They strolled round the field. Nobody took much notice of them. Larry stopped a boy going by. 'Where's the tent Prince Bongawah slept in?' he asked.

'Over there, if it's any interest to you!' said the boy cheekily, and hurried off.

Pip and Larry walked over to the tent he had pointed out. Outside sat three boys, munching sandwiches. They were all about Pip's age.

'Good tent, yours,' said Larry to the boys. It certainly was a very fine one indeed, much better than any other tent nearby.

'Supplied by his Royal Highness, Prince Bongawah-wah-wah,' said one of the boys.

Pip laughed. 'Why do you call him that?' he asked. 'Didn't you like him?'

'No,' said the boys, all together. A red-haired one waved his sandwich at Larry.

'He was a frightful, cocky little fellow,' he said. 'And a real idiot. He yelled at everything, like a kid of seven!'

'That's why we called him Wah-wah,' said another boy. 'He was always wah-wahing about something.'

'Did he talk English?' asked Larry.

'Well, he was supposed to know hardly a word,' said Red-Hair. 'He just talked rubbish usually – but he could speak our language all right if he wanted to! Though goodness knows where he picked it up! Talk about Cockney!'

'What school did he go to?' asked Larry.

'None. He had a tutor,' said Red-Hair. 'He was a regular little urchin, for all he was a prince! All his clothes were of the very very best, even his pyjamas – but did he wash? Not he! And if you said you'd pop him into the river he'd run a mile, wah-wahing!'

'Lots of boys are like that,' said the third boy, munching away. 'We've got two at our school. One never cleans his teeth and the other howls if he gets a kick at football.'

'Do you think the prince got kidnapped?' asked Pip, feeling rather thrilled with all this first-hand information.

'I don't know and I don't care,' said Red-Hair. 'If he *is* kidnapped, I hope he stays kidnapped, that's all. Have a look at his sleeping-bag. Did you ever see one like it?'

Larry and Pip peeped inside the marvellous tent. Red-Hair pointed to a sleeping-bag at one side. It certainly was most magnificent, padded and quilted and marvelously embroidered.

'Try it,' said Red-Hair. 'I tried it once. It's like being floated away on a magic carpet or something when you get inside – soft as feathers!'

Pip wriggled inside. It certainly was an extraordinarily luxurious bag, and Pip felt that if he closed his eyes he would be wafted away into sleep at once. He wriggled down a little further and felt something hard against his leg. He put his hand down to feel what it was.

It was a button! A very fine button too, blue with a gold edge. Pip sat up and looked at it. Red-Hair glanced at it.

'One of the buttons off his pyjamas,' he said. 'You should have seen them! Blue and gold with those buttons to match.'

'Do you think I might keep it as a souvenir?' said Pip. He really wondered if by any chance it might turn out to be a clue!

'Gosh, what do you want a souvenir for? Are you daft?' said the second boy. 'Keep it if you want to. I don't reckon Wah-wah will want it again! If he loses a button, he'll be provided with a new set of pyjamas!'

'Did he leave his pyjamas behind?' asked Larry, thinking it might be a good idea to look at them.

'No. He went off in them,' said Red-Hair. 'That's what makes everyone think he was kidnapped. He'd have dressed himself if he had run away.'

Larry and Pip wandered out into the open air again. A loud voice suddenly hailed them.

'Larry! Pip! What you doing up here?' And there was Ern's plump face grinning at them from over the nearby hedge. 'Come on over! We've got *our* tent here!'

11. A LITTLE INVESTIGATION

'Hello, Ern!' said Larry, surprised. He had forgotten that Ern had been camping so near the big camp field. The faces of Sid and Perce now appeared, Perce grinning, Sid very solemn as usual.

Larry and Pip said good-bye to Red-Hair and his friends and squeezed through the hedge to Ern. Pip had put the pyjama button safely into his pocket. He didn't know whether it might be useful or not.

Ern proudly showed the two boys his tent. It was a very small and humble affair, compared with the magnificent one they had just left – but Ern, Sid, and Perce were intensely proud of it. They had never been camping before, and were enjoying it immensely.

There were no sleeping bags in the tent, merely old, worn rugs spread over a groundsheet. Three mugs, three broken knives, three spoons, two forks ('Perce lost his when he was bathing,' was Ern's mystifying explanation), three macintosh capes, three enamel plates, and a few other things.

'Fine, isn't it?' said Ern. 'We get water from the tap over in the camp field. They let us use it if we just go straight there and back. But they won't let the caravanners use it. So we get it for them, and in return they sometimes cook us a meal.'

There were a good many caravans scattered about, and also one or two more small tents. The caravan standing next to Ern's tent was empty, and a litter of papers was blowing about.

'The people there have gone,' said Ern. 'There was a woman and two kids – the kids were babies. Twins like Perce and Sid.'

'Ar,' said Sid, who was following them about, chewing. 'Ar.'

'What's he mean, arr-ing like that?' asked Pip, annoyed. 'Can't he ever talk properly?'

'Not while he has toffee in his mouth,' said Ern. 'Ma don't allow him so much when he's at home, of course, so he talks a bit more there. But here, when he can eat toffee all day long, he never says much except "Ar". Do you, young Sid?'

'Ar,' said Sid, trying to swallow the rest of

his toffee quickly, and almost choking.

'He seems to want to say something,' said Pip, interestedly. 'Do you, Sid?'

'Ar,' said Sid frantically, going purple in the face.

'Oh, it's only to tell you about the twin babies, I expect,' said Ern. 'He was cracked on them, was our Sid. He used to go over to that caravan and pore over the pram for hours on end. He's dippy on babies.'

Pip and Larry looked at Sid with surprise. He didn't seem at all the kind of boy to be 'dippy on babies'.

Sid pointed down to the ground, where there were four different sets of pram wheel marks.

'There you are, you see – I said he wanted to tell you about them twins,' said Ern. 'He used to stand by their pram and pick up all the rattles and things they dropped. I bet he's ready to howl now they're gone. He's a funny one, Sid is.'

'Ar,' said Sid, in a strangled voice, and almost choked again.

'You're disgusting,' said Ern. 'You and your toffee. You've et a whole tin since yesterday. I'll tell Ma on you. You go and spit it out.'

Sid wandered away, evidently giving up all hope of proper conversation. Pip heaved a sigh of relief. Sid and his toffee gave him a nightmare feeling.

'Sid was proper upset this morning, when the twins went,' said Perce, entering amicably into the conversation. 'He went over to joggle the pram like he does when their mother wants them to go to sleep – but she yelled at him and chased him away. That made the babies yell too, and there wasn't half a set-to.'

'What did she want to do that to our Sid for?' said Ern, quite annoyed at anyone yelling at his Sid. 'He's been good to those smelly kids, he's wheeled their big pram up and down the field for hours.'

Pip and Larry were getting tired of all this talk about Sid and the babies. Who cared anyway?

'Ern, did you hear anything at all last night when Prince Bongawah was supposed to be kidnapped?' asked Larry. 'Did Sid or Perce?'

'No. We none of us heard anything,' said Ern, firmly. 'We all sleep like tops. Sid don't even wake if there is a thunderstorm bang over his head. The whole camp could have been kidnapped, and we wouldn't have known a thing. Good sleepers, the Goons are.'

Well, that was that. There didn't seem to be anything at all to be got from Ern. How maddening to know someone living just across the hedge from the prince, and to get nothing out of him at all!

'You did *see* the prince though, didn't you?' said Larry.

'Yes. I told you,' said Ern. 'He was a funny little fellow with a cocky little face. He made faces.'

'Made faces?' said Larry, in astonishment. 'What do you mean?'

'Well, whenever Sid or Perce or me peeped through the hedge, he'd see us and make a face,' said Ern. 'He may have been a prince, but he hadn't been brought up proper. Brown as a berry, of course.'

'Browner than us?' asked Pip.

''Bout the same,' said Ern.

'Why did you say that he and Bets were as alike as peas in a pod?' asked Pip, suddenly remembering this extraordinary remark of Ern's.

Ern blushed. 'Oh well, seemed as if brother and sister ought to look alike,' he muttered, and busily kicked a stone along. 'Coo, I wonder what happened to his state umbrella! You should have seen it, Pip. Somebody came to visit him, and one of them put up this enormous umbrella – all blue and gold it was – and carried it over him. He didn't half scowl.'

'Didn't he like it then?' asked Pip.

'Well, everyone laughed and yelled and shouted,' said Ern. 'It looked a bit strange, you know.'

'Hello there!' suddenly came Fatty's voice over the hedge. 'Why did you wander off like that? You left me to do all the talking, Pip.'

'That's why I went,' said Pip. 'You like talking, Fatty, don't you?'

'Can we come through the hedge?' called Daisy's voice. 'Is there a place where we won't tear our clothes?'

Ern gallantly held aside some prickly branches as the girls squeezed through the hedge. Fatty followed. 'Nice cousin of yours, that fellow Ronald,' Fatty said to Pip. 'We had quite a chat.'

'You must have done quite a lot of "questioning of witnesses" then,' said Pip slyly, remembering the books Fatty had been studying a day or two before.

'Did you get any interesting information about this case?'

'Well, no,' said Fatty, who had actually spent the whole time relating some of his own exploits to the open-mouthed Ronald. 'No. I didn't gather much.'

'What about you, Pip?' asked Bets. 'Have you been questioning Ern, Sid and Perce?'

'Yes,' said Pip. 'But Larry and I didn't get much out of them. They slept all night long and didn't hear a thing. They haven't the faintest idea what happened to Prince Bongawah.'

'Ar,' said Sid, joining them suddenly. His jaws chewed frantically. Pip looked at him in disgust.

'Go away,' he said. 'And don't come back till you can say something else. I shall start "arring" myself in a minute. ARRRRRRRR!'

He made such a fierce noise that Sid gave him an alarmed glance and fled.

Pip took out the blue and gold button from his pocket and showed it to the others.

'This is the solitary clue – if it can be called a clue – that we've found,' he said. 'I found it in the sleeping bag belonging to the prince. It came off his blue and gold pyjamas.'

'Well, what use do you think that is?' asked Fatty. 'Is it going to help us to find out who kidnapped the prince, or when or how, or where he's gone? Not much of a clue, Pip.'

'No,' said Pip, pocketing the button again. 'I thought it wasn't. But you always tell us to examine everything and keep everything just in case. So I did. By the way, he didn't dress, he disappeared in his pyjamas.'

That made Fatty stare. 'Are you sure, Pip? Who told you?'

'The boys who slept in his tent,' said Pip.

'Well, that's funny,' said Fatty.

'Why?' asked Daisy. 'There wouldn't be any time, would there, for him to dress? Besides, wouldn't he disturb the other boys if he did?'

'Not if he stole outside in the dark when they were asleep,' said Fatty. 'He could take his clothes with him and dress quickly. Anyone wandering about in pyjamas would be spotted.'

'But Fatty, surely there wouldn't be *time* for anyone to dress if he was being kidnapped,' said Daisy again. 'They'd just grab the prince out of his tent and make off with him, in his pyjamas.'

'Oh no, Daisy,' said Fatty. 'You're not being very clever. Kidnappers would never creep through a crowded field, falling over tent ropes and pegs, finding their way to one special tent, opening the flap, dragging out one special boy in the darkness, who would surely yell the place down. After all, he was called Bongawah-wah-wah because he howled so much.'

'Oh,' said Daisy. 'Yes, that was very silly of me. Of course kidnappers wouldn't do it like that. What do you think they did?'

'I think somebody arranged for him to steal out after lights-out,' said Fatty. 'Perhaps they said they'd take him to that Fair in the next town – it goes on till all hours! Something like that. You can't tell. And if he was going to be kidnapped, the kidnappers would find it easy – there he would be, waiting at the gate for them, already dressed, thinking what a lad he was.'

'I see – and they'd just whisk him away in a car and that would be that,' said Pip.

'Oh, *now* I see why you're surprised he was in pyjamas,' said Daisy. 'If the kidnapping was planned in that way, he certainly wouldn't be in pyjamas!'

'Correct,' said Fatty, with a grin.

'Maybe he couldn't spot his clothes in the darkness,' suggested Ern, helpfully.

'This isn't a mystery, it's a silly sort of puzzle,' said Bets. 'Nobody heard anything, nobody saw anything. Nobody knows anything. I'm beginning to feel it couldn't have happened!'

12. SID FINDS HIS VOICE

'Come on – it's time we went,' said Fatty, getting bored. 'We're absolutely at a dead end here. Wherever Prince Bongawah is, he's probably still in his blue and gold pyjamas. Good luck to him!'

They rode off, waving good-bye to Ern and Perce. Sid was nowhere to be seen, for which everyone was thankful.

'He chews his toffee like a cow chewing the cud,' said Pip. 'Have you noticed how spotty he is? I really do believe he lives on toffee and nothing else.'

'I never want to see him again,' said Bets. 'He makes me feel sick.'

'Well, there's no reason why we ever *should* see him again,' said Fatty. 'So long as Ern comes alone to see us. *I* don't intend to visit dear Sid and Perce.'

But he did see Sid again, and that very evening too! Fatty was trying on one of his newest

isguises down in his shed, when there came a
nock at the door.

Fatty looked through a hole, pierced in the door
or spying, to see who was outside. Gosh – it was
rn – with Sid! How aggravating, just as he was
;oing to practise this disguise.

Fatty turned quickly and looked at himself in
he big mirror. He grinned. He'd try the disguise
)ut on Ern and see if it worked!

Fatty opened the door. Ern stood outside, ready
with a smile. Sid beside him. The smile faded as Ern
saw, not Fatty, but a bent old man with side-
whiskers, a straggly beard, shaggy white eyebrows,
and wispy white hair on a bald pate. He was
dressed in a loose, ill-fitting old coat, with dragged-
down pockets, and corduroy trousers, wrinkled
and worn.

'Oh, er, good evening,' said Ern, startled. 'Is, er,
is Mr Frederick Trotteville in?'

The old man put a trembling hand behind one
ear and said, 'Speak up! Don't mumble. What's that
you say?' His voice was as quavery as his hand.

Ern shouted, 'IS MR FREDERICK IN?'

'Now don't you shout,' said the old man, in a

cross voice. 'I'm not deaf. Who's Mr Frederick?'

Ern stared. Then he remembered that Fatty wa
always called Fatty. Perhaps this old man onl
knew him by that name.

'Fatty,' he said, loudly. 'FATTY.'

'You're a very rude boy,' said the old man, hi
voice quavering higher. 'Calling me names.'

'I'm not,' said Ern, desperately. 'Look here
– where's the boy who lives here?'

'Gone,' said the old fellow, shaking his head
sadly. 'Gone to live in London.'

Ern began to think he must be in a dream. Fatty
gone to London! Why, he'd only seen him an hour
or so ago. He glanced anxiously at the shed. Had he
come to the right place?

'Why has he gone?' he asked at last. 'Did he
leave a message? And what are you doing here?'

'I'm his caretaker,' said the old fellow, and took
out a big red handkerchief. He proceeded to blow
his nose with such a loud trumpeting noise that
Ern fell back, alarmed. Little did he know that
Fatty was hiding his gulps of laughter in that big
red handkerchief!

Sid backed away too. He slid down the path

ıt Ern caught him by the arm.

'Oh no, you don't, Sid! You've come here to say ᴍething important, and say it you're going to, if ᴛ takes us all night to find Fatty. If you go back to ᴀe camp, you'll fill your mouth with toffee again, ᴀd we won't none of us get a word out of you! ᴏu're the only one of us with a real clue, and ᴀtty's going to know it!'

'I *say*! Has he really got a clue?' said the old man, ᴀ Fatty's crisp, clear voice. Ern jumped violently ᴀd looked all round. Where was Fatty?

The old man dug him in the ribs and went off ᴀto a cackle of laughter that changed suddenly ᴀto Fatty's cheerful guffaw. Ern stared at him ᴏen-mouthed. So did Sid.

'Lovaduck! It's *Fatty*!' cried Ern, overjoyed and ᴛounded. 'You took me in properly. Coo, you're an ᴅd man to the life. How do you make yourself bald?'

'Just a wig,' said Fatty, lifting it off his head and ᴏpearing in his own thatch of hair. He grinned. 'I ᴀas practising this disguise when you came. It's a ᴇw wig, and new eyebrows, side-whiskers, and ᴇard to match. Good, aren't they?'

'You're a marvel, Fatty, honest you are,' said

Ern, wonderstruck. 'But your voice – and yo[ur]
laugh! You can't buy *them*! You ought to be [on]
the stage.'

'Can't,' said Fatty. 'I'm going to be a detectiv[e.]
It's a help to be a good actor, of course. Come i[n.]
What's all this about Sid and a clue?'

'Well,' said Ern solemnly, 'it's like this. S[id]
wanted to tell us all something this afternoon an[d]
he couldn't, because of his toffee. Well, he worke[d]
and he worked at his toffee till it all went.'

'Tiring work,' said Fatty, sympathetically. 'An[d]
then, I suppose, he found his voice again. Can h[e]
really say something besides "ar"?'

'Well, not much,' said Ern honestly. 'But he di[d]
tell us something very strange – very strang[e]
indeed, Fatty. So I've brought him down here t[o]
tell *you*. It may be very, very important. Go on, S[id]
– you tell him.'

Sid cleared his throat and opened his mout[h.]
'Ar,' he began. 'Ar – you see, I heard them yellin[g.]
Ar, I did.'

'Who was yelling?' enquired Fatty.

'Ar, well,' said Sid, and cleared his throat agai[n.]
'They were yelling, see.'

'Yes. We know that,' said Fatty. 'Ar.'

That put Sid off. He gazed beseechingly at Ern. Ern looked back forbiddingly.

'See what happens to you when you get toffee mad?' he said. 'You lose your voice and you lose your senses. Let this be a lesson to you, young Sid.'

'Has he really come just to tell me somebody was yelling?' asked Fatty. 'Isn't there anything else?'

'Oh, yes. But praps *I'd* better tell you,' said Ern, and Sid's face cleared at once.

'Ar,' he said.

'And don't you interrupt,' said Ern, threateningly. Sid had no intention of interrupting at all. He shook his head vigorously, not even venturing another 'ar'.

'Well, this is what Sid told us,' said Ern, beginning to enjoy himself. 'It's peculiar, Fatty, honest it is. You'll hardly believe it.'

'Oh, get *on* Ern,' said Fatty. 'This may be important. Begin at the beginning, please.'

'I told you – at least I told Larry and Pip – that our Sid here is mad on babies,' said Ern. 'He's always going about joggling their prams and picking up their toys and saying "Goo" to them.

Well, next to our tent there's a caravan – you saw it. It's empty now. The people went today.'

Fatty nodded. He was listening hard.

'The woman in the caravan had a couple of twin babies,' said Ern. 'And being twins, Sid got more interested in them than usual – him and Perce being twins, you see. So he played with them a lot. Didn't you, Sid?'

'Ar,' said Sid, nodding.

'Well, this morning, Sid heard those babies yelling like anything,' said Ern, warming up to his tale. 'And he went over to joggle the pram. The woman was in the caravan, packing up, and when she saw our Sid there, she flew out at him and smacked him on the head. A fair clip it was! She told him to clear off.'

'Why?' asked Fatty. 'Sid was only doing what he'd been in the habit of doing. Had the woman ever objected before?'

'No,' said Ern. 'She let him wheel them up and sometimes down, too. And a heavy job it was, because it's a big double pram, made to take twins. Well, she smacked his head and Sid went off, upset like.'

'I don't wonder,' said Fatty, wondering when he point of all this long tale was coming. 'What :ame next?'

'The woman dragged the pram round to the)ack of the caravan,' said Ern, 'where she could :eep her eye on it. But those babies still went on yelling, and our Sid here, he couldn't bear it.'

'Ar,' said Sid, feelingly.

'So when the woman took some things and went off down to one of the other caravans, Sid popped over to the pram to see what was the matter with the babies,' said Ern. 'They sounded as if they was sitting on a safety pin or something. Anyway, Sid put his hand down under them and scrabbled about like – *and he felt somebody else down in that big pram*, Fatty!'

Fatty was really startled. He sat up straight. 'Somebody else!' he said, incredulously. 'What do you mean?'

'Well – just that,' said Ern. 'Sid felt somebody else, and he pulled the clothes back just a little bit, and saw the back of a dark head, and a bit of dark cheek. Then one of the babies grabbed at Sid, and rolled over and hid whoever it was in the pram.'

Fatty was astounded. He sat silent for a minute Then he looked at Sid. 'Who did you think it wa in the pram?' he asked.

'The prince,' said Sid, quite forgetting to say 'ar in his excitement. 'He was hiding there. He didn' know I saw him. Ar.'

'*Well*!' said Fatty, taking all this in. 'So *that'* what happened. He simply crept out of his tent in his pyjamas, and hid in the caravan for the nigh – and in the early morning, the woman packed him into the bottom of that big pram, hidden under the babies! How uncomfortable! He must have been all screwed up – and awfully hot.'

'Ar,' said Sid, nodding.

'Then the woman must have got someone to fetch all her goods, and wheeled the pram away herself, with the little prince in it,' said Fatty. 'Nobody would guess. But why did it happen? What has *she* got to do with it? Why did the prince creep away to her? Gosh – it's a mystery all right!'

'I thought you'd be pleased, Fatty,' said Ern, happily. 'Good thing Sid got rid of his toffee, wasn't it? That's what he was trying to tell us this afternoon. Almost choked himself trying to get the news out.'

'It's a pity he didn't tell somebody as soon as he knew this,' said Fatty.

'He did try,' said Ern. 'But I just thought he wanted to go swimming or something when he kept pointing to the caravan. Sid's never very talkative, even in the ordinary way. His tongue never grew properly, Ma says.'

'I'll have to think what to do,' said Fatty. 'Ern, you must go and tell your uncle. I said we'd tell him everything we found out. You'd better go and tell him straight away.'

'Lovaduck! I can't do that!' said poor Ern. 'Why, he'd give me such a scolding that I wouldn't recover for a month of Sundays!'

13. MR GOON HEARS THE NEWS

All the same, Ern had to go. Fatty didn't want to ring up the Chief Inspector quite so soon after his ticking-off – and if Goon knew, he could report the matter himself. So poor Ern was sent off to Goon's with Sid trailing behind. Neither of them felt very happy about it.

Mr Goon was in his kitchen at the back of his house. He was alone – and he was practising. Not disguises, like Fatty. He was trying to 'let his tongue go loose', as Fatty had advised. *Could* he 'talk foreign' by merely letting his tongue go loose?

He stood there, trying to make his tongue work. 'Abbledy, abbledy, abbledy,' he gabbled, and then paused. For some reason, 'abbledy' seemed the only thing he could think of. He tried to remember the string of foreign-sounding words that Fatty had fired off the other afternoon, but he couldn't. Surely it must be easy to say a string of rubbish?

But it wasn't. His tongue merely stopped when it was tired of saying 'abbledy', and his brain could think of nothing else at all.

Mr Goon tried reciting.

'The boy stood on the burning deck, abbledy, gabbledy, abbledy. No, it's no good.'

Meanwhile, Ern and Sid had arrived. Ern didn't like to knock in case his uncle was having a nap, as he so often did. He turned the handle of the front door. It wouldn't open, so he thought it must be locked from the inside.

'Come on round to the back, Sid,' said Ern. 'He might be in the garden.'

They tiptoed round to the back, and came to the kitchen window. It was wide open. A noise came from inside the room. 'He's there,' whispered Ern. 'He's talking. He must have a visitor.'

They listened. 'Abbledy, abbledy, abbledy,' they heard. 'Abbledy, abbledy, ABBLEDY.'

Ern looked at Sid, startled. That was his uncle's voice. What was he gabbling about? Ern cautiously poked his head a bit further forward and peeped in at the corner of the window. Yes – his uncle was there with his back to him, standing on the rug, looking at himself in the mirror and gabbling his curious rubbish on and on.

Ern didn't like it at all. Had his uncle got a stroke of the sun? Was he out of his mind?

'Abbledy, abbledy,' came again and again. And then, suddenly, 'The boy stood on the burning deck.'

That decided Ern. He wasn't going to interfere in anything like this, important clue or not. He stole down by the side of the house, and made his way to the front gate. But alas, Mr Goon had heard footsteps, and was at the front door at once. He was just in time to see Ern and Sid opening the gate.

'What you doing here this time of the evening?' he roared. 'What you doing going out before you've even come in? You been listening outside the window?'

Ern was terrified. He stood trembling at the gate with Sid.

'Uncle, we only came to tell you something,' quavered Ern. 'A clue. Most important.'

'Aha!' said Goon. 'So that's it. Come along in then. Why didn't you say so before?'

He just stopped himself saying, 'abbledy,

abbledy.' He must be careful. He'd gone and got that on his mind now!

Ern and Sid came in, treading like cats on hot bricks. Mr Goon took them into his sitting-room. He sat down in his big armchair, crossed his legs, put his hands together and looked up at the two boys.

'So you've got a clue,' he said. 'What is it?'

Sid couldn't say a word, of course, not even 'ar'. Ern was almost as bad. However, it all came out with a rush at last.

'Uncle, Sid found the clue. You know that Prince Bongawah that was kidnapped? Well, he wasn't. He put himself in a pram with twin babies and he was wheeled away this morning.'

Mr Goon listened to this with the utmost disbelief. Put himself in a pram? With twins! And got himself wheeled away! What nonsense was this?

Mr Goon rose up, big and terrible. 'And why did you come and tell me this ridiculous nonsense?' he began. 'Why don't you go and tell it to that big boy? Let *him* believe you! I won't. Cock-and-bull story! Gah! How DARE you come and tell me such a tale?'

'Fatty told us to,' blurted out poor Ern, almost crying with fright. 'We told him and *he* believed us. He said we were to tell *you*, Uncle, really he did. To help you.'

Mr Goon swelled up till Ern and Sid thought he must be going to burst all the buttons off his already-tight tunic. He towered above them.

'You go and tell that toad of a boy that I'm not such an idiot as he thinks I am,' he bellowed. 'You tell him to take his tales of prams and twin babies to the Chief Inspector. Sending you here to fill me up with nonsense like that! I'm ashamed of you, Ern. For two pins, I'd give you a hiding. How DARE you!'

Ern and Sid fled. They fled down the hall passage, through the front door, and out of the gate without waiting for another word. Sid was crying. Ern was white. Why had Fatty sent him on such an errand? He, Ern, had known quite well that his uncle wouldn't believe him. And he hadn't.

'Come on back to the camp,' panted Ern. 'We'll be safe there. Run, Sid, run!'

Poor Ern didn't even think of going back to Fatty's to tell him what had happened. He and Sid fled for their lives, looking over their shoulders every now and again, fearful that Mr Goon might be after them.

Perce was thankful he hadn't gone with them when he heard their tale. He was just as much scared of his uncle as the others. Ern had often told him and Sid dreadful tales of the time when he had been to stay with Mr Goon – the punishments and shoutings-at that he had had.

'Still, it was worth it,' Ern would end cheerfully. 'I made friends with those five kids – specially with Fatty. He's a wonder, that boy!'

Meantime the 'wonder boy' was having a quiet little think to himself about Sid's surprising piece of news. It was all very, very extraordinary. Could Sid possibly be right? Could it really have been the young prince huddled down in that big double pram? Of course, such a trick *had* been played before, to get people away in secret.

Just have to take out the two seats, put the person in the well of the pram, and stick the babies on top of him, thought Fatty. Yes – it's easy enough. But why, why, why, did the prince creep through the hedge at night and get himself parked in the pram the following day?

It was a puzzle. Fatty thought he had better sleep on it, and then discuss it with the others in the morning. He wondered what Mr Goon had thought of Ern's appearance and news. Was he acting on it? Had he telephoned the Chief Inspector?

Fatty half-expected Mr Goon to telephone him for his opinion on Ern's news. But no, on second thoughts he wouldn't, decided Fatty. He would want to work out things on his own, so that he could say he had done everything himself.

Well, let him, thought Fatty. If he can unravel the puzzle more quickly than I can, good luck to him! I'm in a real muddle. Why – when – where – how – and, particularly, *why*, seem quite unanswerable!

Fatty telephoned Larry.

'Is that you, Larry? Meet in my shed tomorrow morning, half past nine, sharp. Most important and mysterious developments. Ern and Sid have just been down with amazing news.'

'Great!' came Larry's voice, tense with excitement. 'What is it? Tell me a bit, Fatty!'

'Can't say it over the phone,' said Fatty. 'Anyway, it's most important. Half past nine sharp.'

He rang off, leaving Larry in a state of such terrific excitement that he could hardly prevent himself from rushing down to Fatty's at once! Daisy and he spent the whole evening trying to think of what Fatty's mysterious news could be – without any success, of course.

Fatty telephoned Pip next. Mrs Hilton answered the phone. 'Pip's in the bath,' she said. 'Can I take a message?'

Fatty hesitated. Mrs Hilton was not at all encouraging where mysteries were concerned. In fact, she had several times said that Pip and Bets must keep out of them. Perhaps, on the whole, it would be best not to say much. Still, he could ask for Bets.

So Bets came to the telephone, in her dressing-gown, having a feeling that Fatty had some news.

'Hello Fatty,' came her voice. 'Anything up?'

'Yes,' said Fatty, in a solemn voice. 'Extraordinary news has just come through – from Ern and Sid. Can't tell you over the phone. Meet here at half past nine tomorrow morning, sharp.'

'*Fatty*!' squealed Bets, thrilled. 'You *must* tell me

something about it. Quick! Nobody's about, it's quite safe.'

'I can't possibly tell you over the phone,' said Fatty, enjoying all this importance. 'All I can say is that it's very important, and will need a lot of discussion and planning. The real mystery is about to begin, Bets!'

'Ooooh,' said Bets. 'All right – half past nine tomorrow. I'll go straight away and tell Pip.'

'Now don't you go shouting all this through the bathroom door,' said Fatty, in alarm.

'No, I suppose I'd better not,' said Bets. 'I'll wait till he comes out. But I'll jolly well go and hurry him though!'

Pip was so thrilled at this sudden and unexpected telephone call that he, like Larry, almost felt inclined to dress and shoot off to Fatty. But as his mother would certainly be most annoyed to find him dressing again and going out after a hot bath, he reluctantly decided he must wait.

Fatty sat in his bedroom and thought. He thought hard, turning over in his mind all the things he knew about the young prince. He got the encyclopaedia and looked up Tetarua. He found a store catalogue of his mother's which, most fortunately, pictured not only a single pram but a double one as well, with measurements.

Fatty decided it would be the easiest thing in the world to hide someone at the bottom of a double pram. Probably the most uncomfortable thing in the world too, he thought. I wonder what old Goon is making of all this!

Goon wasn't making anything of it at all. He just simply didn't believe a word, so he had nothing to puzzle over. 'Gah!' he said, and dismissed the matter completely!

14. TALKING AND PLANNING

Before half past nine had struck, the Five Find-Outers (and Dog) were all gathered together in Fatty's shed. Buster was very pleased to welcome them. He pranced round in delight, and finally got on to Bets' knee.

'Now Fatty – don't keep us waiting – tell us exactly what's happened,' said Larry, firmly. 'Don't go all mysterious and solemn. Just tell us!'

So Fatty told them. They listened in astonishment.

'Hidden in the *pram*!' said Larry. 'Then the prince must have known that woman very well. She must have been camping nearby for a reason.'

'Do you think she could have been the prince's nurse, and knew perhaps he wasn't happy at camp, and arranged to smuggle him away?' said Bets.

'Bright idea, Bets,' said Fatty, approvingly. 'I thought of that myself. But the twin babies are rather a difficulty there. I don't feel the prince would have a nurse with twin babies somehow.'

'She might have been an *old* nurse of his, and got married, and had twins,' said Bets, using her imagination.

'It's not much good having theories and ideas about all this until we get a few more actual details,' said Fatty. 'I mean, we must find out who the woman is, if the caravan belongs to her, if she came there when the prince arrived, if those babies are really hers, or borrowed so that she could take that big double pram for hiding purposes – oh, there are a whole lot of things to find out!'

'And are we to snoop round and find all these details?' asked Daisy. 'I rather like doing that.'

'There's a great deal to find out,' said Fatty. 'We'll have to get busy. Anyone seen the papers this morning?'

'I just glanced at them,' said Larry, 'but I was really too excited to read anything. Why?'

'Only because there's a bit more about the prince and his country in today,' said Fatty. He spread a newspaper on the floor and pointed to a column.

Everyone read it.

'Well, as you will see,' said Fatty, 'Tetarua isn't a very big country, but it's quite important from the point of view of the British, because there's a fine airfield there we want to use. So we've been quite friendly with them.'

'And they've sent their young prince here to be educated,' said Larry. 'But, according to the paper, there's a row on in Tetarua between the present king and his cousin, who says *he* ought to be king.'

'Yes. And the possibilities are that the cousin has sent someone over here to capture Prince Bongawah, so that, if he doesn't ever appear again, he, the cousin, will be king,' said Fatty. 'There are no brothers or sisters apparently.'

'An old, old plot,' said Larry. 'Do you suppose they will demand a ransom for the prince?'

'No,' said Fatty. 'I think they want to put him out of the way for good.'

There was a silence after this. Nobody liked to think of the young prince being 'put away for good'. Bets shivered.

Daisy rubbed her forehead, puzzled. 'And yet – though that's what the papers say – *we* know differently,' she said. '*We* know he wasn't kidnapped in the way they think, just swept out of his tent and rushed off in a car somewhere. *We* know that, of his own free will, apparently, he crept out of his tent in his pyjamas, went through the hedge to that caravan, and allowed himself to be hidden and wheeled away in that pram! That couldn't be called kidnapping.'

'No. It couldn't,' said Fatty. 'There's something strange about this. I believe Sid, you know. For one thing, he would never, ever have the imagination to make up all that.'

'Did you ring the Chief Inspector?' said Pip. 'What did he say?'

'Well, as a matter-of-fact, I didn't telephone him,' said Fatty. 'I don't feel he's very pleased with me at the moment – with any of us, as a matter-of-fact – so I sent Ern and Sid round to Mr Goon, to tell *him*. He would naturally ring up the Chief Inspector himself, and get his own orders.'

'But wouldn't the Chief Inspector ring *you*, when he got Mr Goon's message?' asked Pip.

'I rather thought he might,' said Fatty, who was feeling a little hurt because there had been no word at all from the Chief Inspector. 'I expect he's still peeved with me. Well, I won't bother him till I've got something first rate to tell him. Let Mr Goon get on with his own ideas about this – we'll get on with ours! At least I've passed on Sid's information to him.'

There was another silence. 'It's rather a peculiar mystery really,' said Bets at last. 'There doesn't actually seem anywhere to *begin*. What do we do first?'

'Well, as *I* see it, we had better follow up the definite clues we have,' said Fatty. 'We must first of all find out about that woman – who she is. Get her address. Interview her. Try and frighten something out of her. If she is hiding the prince, we must find out where. And why.'

'Yes,' said Larry. 'We must do all that. Hadn't we better begin before Mr Goon gets going? He'll probably be working along the same lines as us.'

'Yes. I suppose he will,' said Fatty, getting up. 'This part is pretty obvious to anyone – even to Mr Goon! Well, let's hope we don't bump into him today. He'll be annoyed if we do!'

'Woof,' said Buster joyfully.

'He says he hopes we *do* bump into him,' said

Bets, hugging the little Scottie. 'You love Mr Goon's ankles, don't you Buster? Nicest ankles in the world, aren't they? Biteable and snappable and nippable.'

Everyone laughed. 'You're an idiot, Bets,' said Pip. 'Are we going up to the camp, Fatty? We shall have to find out who lets out those caravans, and see if we can get the name and the address of the woman who was in the one with the twin babies.'

'Yes. That's the first thing to do,' said Fatty. 'Everyone got bikes?'

Everyone had. Buster was put into Fatty's basket, and off they all went, ringing their bells loudly at every corner, just in *case* Mr Goon was coming round in the opposite direction!

Ern, Sid, and Perce were most delighted to see them. Fatty looked at Sid, but when he saw his jaws working rhythmically as usual, he snorted.

'Not much good asking Sid anything,' he said. 'We'll only be able to get "ar" out of him. Sid, if you get many more spots, you'll be clapped into hospital and treated for measles!'

Sid looked alarmed. Ern spoke to him sternly.

'Go and spit it out. You're a disgrace to the Goon family.'

'Ar,' said Sid, looking really pathetic.

'He can't spit it out,' said Perce. 'It's not the kind of toffee for that. Try some, Ern, and see.'

'No thanks,' said Ern. 'Well, count Sid out of this, Fatty. He's hopeless.'

'Yes – but he's quite important,' said Fatty. 'Well, he'll just have to nod or shake his head, that's all, when I ask him questions. Sid, come here. Stop chewing and listen. I'm going to ask you some questions. Nod your head for "yes", and shake it for "no". Understand?'

'Ar,' said Sid, and nodded his head so violently that some of the toffee went down the wrong way and he choked.

Ern thumped him on his back till his eyes almost fell out of his head. At last, Sid was ready again, and listening.

'Sid, do you know the woman's name?' asked Fatty.

'Ar,' said Sid and shook his head.

'Did you ever see her speaking to the prince?' asked Fatty.

'Ar,' said Sid and shook his head again.

'Don't keep saying "ar" like that,' said Fatty, aggravated. 'It's positively maddening. Just shake or nod, that's all. Did you see where the woman went when she wheeled away the pram?'

Sid shook his head dumbly.

'Do you know ANYTHING about her except that she had twins and lived in that caravan?' asked Fatty, despairing of ever getting anything out of Sid at all. Sid's head was well and truly shaken again.

'A man in a lorry came to get the things out of the caravan,' volunteered Perce, unexpectedly.

'What was the name on the lorry?' asked Fatty at once.

'Wasn't none,' said Perce.

'Well, a fat lot of help you and Sid are,' said Fatty in disgust. 'You don't know a thing – not even the name of the woman!'

'Oogleby-oogleby,' said Sid suddenly, looking excited. Everyone looked at him.

'Now what does *that* mean?' wondered Fatty. 'Say it again, Sid – if you can.'

'Ooogleby-oogleby-*oogle*by!' said Sid valiantly, going red in the face.

'He's talking foreign, isn't he?' said Ern, with a

laugh at his own wit. 'Here, Sid – write it down. And mind your spelling!'

Sid took Ern's pencil and wrote painfully on a page of his notebook. Everyone crowded round to see what he had written.

'MARGE and BURT', Sid had printed.

'Marge and Burt,' said Larry. 'Does he mean margarine and butter?'

Everyone looked at Sid. He shook his head at once, and then pretended to hold something in his arms and rock it.

'*Now* what's he doing?' wondered Bets. 'Rock-a-bye baby – Sid, you're dippy!'

'Oh, *I* know, he's pretending to be holding two babies – he must have written the names of the twins!' cried Daisy. Sid nodded, pleased.

'Ar,' he said. 'Oooogly-oogly.'

'Well, I don't know if it's going to help us to know the name of those twin babies,' said Fatty, looking extremely doubtful, 'but I suppose it might. Thanks for your help, Sid – such as it is. Ern, see he doesn't eat any more toffee. Honestly, it's disgraceful.'

'What are we going to do now?' asked Pip.

'We're going to find out who lets these caravans and see if they'll tell us the name and address of the woman who took that one,' said Fatty, waving towards the empty caravan nearby. 'Come on. We'll go now.'

'Can I come too?' asked Ern eagerly. But Fatty said no, he'd no bicycle. He didn't want Ern, Sid, and Perce trailing round them all morning. It would look rather conspicuous to go about in such a large company.

'All right,' said Ern, mournfully. 'Spitty.'

Bets looked at him in delight. 'Oh, *Ern*! I'd forgotten you used to say that, when you meant "It's a pity". Fatty – don't you remember how he used to run all his words together when we knew him before?'

'Yes,' said Fatty, getting on his bike. 'Swunderful! Smarvellous! Smazing!'

15. AN INTERESTING MORNING

And now began a morning of real investigation for the Find-Outers. They rode off down to Marlow, where the agent lived who let the caravans. Fatty had copied down the address from a big notice in the field.

'CARAVANS TO LET,' it said, 'APPLY CARAVANS LTD, TIP HILL, MARLOW.'

They found Tip Hill, which was a little road leading up a hill. Halfway up, in a small field, stood a caravan marked, 'CARAVANS LTD. Apply here for caravans to be let.'

'Here we are,' said Fatty. 'Who would like to do this part?'

'Oh you, Fatty,' said Bets. 'You always do this sort of thing so well. We'll come and listen.'

'No, you won't,' said Fatty. 'I'm not going to have a lot of giggling and nudging going on behind me. If I do this, I do it alone.'

'All right – do it alone,' said Pip.

Fatty went in through the little gate and up to the door of the caravan. He knocked on it.

It opened, and a youth stood there with a cigarette hanging from the side of his mouth.

'Hello!' he said. 'What you want?'

'I'm anxious to find the person who rented one of the caravans next to the school camp field,' said Fatty. 'Could you tell me her name and address, please? I'd be most obliged. She left before I could ask her what I wanted to know.'

'My word – aren't we la-di-da!' said the youth. 'Think I've got time to hunt up names and addresses of your caravan friends, Mister?'

Fatty glanced at the side of the caravan. He saw the name of the owners there in small letters. 'Reg and Bert Williams.' He guessed the youth was just an employee.

'Oh well, if you haven't time, I'll go and ask Mr Reginald Williams,' said Fatty, at a venture. He turned away.

The youth almost fell down the caravan steps. 'Ere, you! Why didn't you tell me you knew Mr Reg?' he called. 'I'll get the address if you wait half a tick.'

Fatty grinned. It was nice to bring that lazy little monkey to heel! 'Very well. But make haste,' said Fatty.

The youth made haste. Fatty thought that Mr Reg, whoever he was, must be a pretty terrifying person if he could shake up a fellow like this merely at the mention of his name! The youth hunted through a large file and produced a list of the caravans up on the hill by the school camp field.

'Now which caravan is it?' he asked. Fatty had noted the name, of course.

'It was called "River View",' he said. 'Quite a small one.'

The youth ran his finger down a list. 'Ah – here we are – Mrs Storm, 24 Harris Road, Maidenbridge. That's not far from here – 'bout two miles.'

'Thanks,' said Fatty, and wrote it down.

'You going to see Mr Reg?' asked the youth, anxiously, as Fatty turned to go.

'No,' said Fatty, much to the youth's relief. He went out to where the others were waiting.

'Got it!' he said, and showed them the name and address. 'Mrs Storm, 24 Harris Road,

Maidenbridge. About two miles from here. Come on – let's get going.'

Feeling rather excited, the five rode off to Maidenbridge. Had Mrs Storm got the prince? Would she tell them anything at all?

They came into Maidenbridge, and asked for Harris Road. It turned out to be a narrow, rather dirty little street, set with houses in a terrace.

They arrived at number 24. It was even dirtier than the rest in the street. Ragged curtains hung at the windows, and the front door badly wanted a lick of paint.

'I'll tackle this too,' said Fatty. 'You ride to the end of the street and wait for me. It looks funny for so many of us to be standing at the front door.'

Obediently, the others rode off. Fatty stood his bicycle at the kerb and knocked. An untidy woman, her hair half down her back, opened it. She said nothing, but just looked at Fatty, waiting.

'Oh – er, excuse me,' said Fatty, 'are you Mrs Storm?'

'No. I'm not,' said the woman. 'You've come to the wrong house. She don't live here.'

This was a bit of a shock.

'Has she left then?' asked Fatty.

'She never did live here, far as I know,' said the woman. 'I've bin here seventeen years, with my husband and my old Ma – I don't know no Mrs Storm. Not even in this street, I don't.'

'How strange,' said Fatty. He looked at the paper with the name and address on. 'Look – it says Mrs Storm, 24 Harris Road, Maidenbridge.'

'Well, that's this house all right – but there's no Mrs Storm,' said the woman. 'There's no other Harris Road but this, either. Why don't you go to the post office? They'll tell you where she lives.'

'Oh thanks, I will,' said Fatty, 'sorry to have troubled you for nothing.' He departed on his bike, puzzled. He joined the others, told them of his failure, and then they all cycled to the post office.

'I want to find someone's address here please,' said Fatty, who was certainly in command that morning. 'I've been given the wrong address, I'm afraid. Could you tell me where a Mrs Storm lives?'

The clerk got out a directory and pushed it across to Fatty. 'There you are,' he said. 'You'll find all the Storms there, hail, thunder, and snow!'

'Ha, ha, joke,' said Fatty politely. He took the

directory and looked for STORM. Ah – there were three Storms in Maidenbridge.

'Lady Louisa Storm,' he read out to the others. 'Old Manor Gate. No, that can't be her. She wouldn't rent a caravan. Here's another – Miss Emily Storm.'

'She wouldn't have twin babies, she's a Miss,' said Bets. 'We want a Mrs.'

'Mrs Rene Storm,' read out Fatty. 'Caldwell House. Well, that seems to be the only one that's likely.'

They left the post office. Fatty turned to Daisy. 'Now *you* can do this bit, Daisy,' he said. 'You must find out if Mrs Rene Storm has twin children.'

'Oh, I *can't*,' said Daisy, in a fright. 'I simply can't walk up and say, "Have you got twin babies?" She would think I was mad.'

'So you would be if you did it like that,' said Fatty. 'Now – you're a Find-Outer, and you haven't had much practice lately. You think of a good way of finding out what we want to know, and go and do it. We'll sit in some ice cream shop and wait for you.'

Poor Daisy! She racked her brains frantically as they all rode along to find Caldwell House. It was a little house set in a pretty garden. Round the corner was a café, and here Fatty and the others sat down to have ice creams and wait for Daisy.

'A nice big double ice cream for you, Daisy, when you come back with your news,' said Fatty. 'In fact, a treble one if this Mrs Storm is the right one. Remember, we only want to know if she has twin babies.'

Daisy rode off. She rode round a block of houses two or three times, trying to think how she could find out what Fatty wanted to know. And then an idea came to her. How simple after all!

She rode to Caldwell House, and put her bicycle by the fence. She walked up to the front door and rang the bell. A little wizened maid opened the door. She looked about ninety, Daisy thought!

'Please excuse me if I've come to the wrong house,' said Daisy, with her nicest smile, 'but I'm looking for a Mrs Storm who has twin babies. Is this the right house?'

'Dear me, no,' said the little maid. 'My Mrs Storm is eighty-three, and she's a great-grandmother. She has never had twins, neither have her children, nor her grandchildren. No wins in the family at all. I'm sorry.'

'So am I,' said Daisy, not quite knowing what else to say. 'Er – well, thank you very much. I'm afraid she's not the Mrs Storm I'm looking for.'

She escaped thankfully and rode quickly to the ice cream shop. The others were pleased to see her come in beaming.

'Is it the right woman?' said Fatty.

'No, I'm afraid not,' said Daisy. 'I'm only beaming because I managed it all right. This Mrs Storm is eighty-three and a great-grandmother – and there aren't any twins in her family at all.'

'Gosh,' said Fatty dolefully. 'Now we're at a dead end then. That wretched caravan woman gave a false name and address. We might have guessed that! We can go hunting the country up and down all we like, but we'll never find a Mrs Storm with twins!'

'Where's my ice cream?' said Daisy.

'Oh, *sorry* Daisy!' said Fatty. 'What am I thinking of! Waitress, a double ice cream please – and another single one all round.'

As they ate their ice creams, they discussed what

to do next. 'Could we possibly look about for twin babies?' asked Bets.

'It's *possible*,' said Fatty, 'but I feel it would take rather a time, looking for all the twin babies there are in this district!'

'How would you set about it, Bets?' asked Pip, eyeing her teasingly. 'Put up a notice – "Wanted twin babies. Apply Bets Hilton".'

'Don't be silly,' said Bets. 'Anyway, have you got a better idea? What *can* we do next? We haven't a single clue now.'

'Only my button,' said Pip, and pulled out his blue and gold button. He put it down on the table. They all looked at it. It really was a beautiful button.

'Beautiful, but completely useless as a clue,' said Fatty. 'Still, keep it if it pleases you, Pip. If you happen to see a pair of blue and gold pyjamas on a washing line with one button missing, you'll be lucky!'

'Well, that's an idea,' said Pip. 'I shall look at all the lines of washing I see. You just never know!' He put the button back into his pocket.

'What about baby shows?' said Daisy, suddenly

'We might see twin babies there, and find out where they live.'

'*Baby* shows!' said Pip, in disgust. 'Well, if anyone's going to snoop round baby shows, it won't be me. You and Bets can do that.'

Bets gave a little exclamation, and pointed dramatically to a notice on the wall of the shop. They all looked, and jumped in surprise.

'BABY SHOW,' said the notice. 'At Tiplington Fair, 4 September. Special prizes for TWINS.'

16. OFF TO TIPLINGTON FAIR

'Funny coincidence,' said Fatty, with a laugh. 'Now, let's see – where's Tiplington? Other side of Peterswood, isn't it?'

'You don't *really* think there's anything in Bets' idea, do you?' said Pip, in surprise.

'Well, there's just a chance, I suppose,' said Fatty. 'Bets has had good ideas before. Will you and Daisy go over, Bets?'

'Yes,' said Bets promptly and Daisy nodded. 'Why can't you boys come too? After all, it's a Fair. It should be quite fun. We could take Ern too – he might recognise the twins if they *did* happen to be there!'

'Right. We will take Ern,' said Fatty. 'But not Sid or Perce.'

'I don't mind Perce so much, but I can't bear Sid,' said Bets. 'He's so *chewy*.'

'I can think of a lot more things I don't like about Sid,' said Larry.

'So can we all. Let's change the subject,' said Fatty, feeling in his pocket for money. 'Now, how many ice creams did we have?'

'Oh, Fatty – don't pay for all of them,' said Daisy. 'Larry and I have got plenty of pocket money today.'

'My treat,' said Fatty. 'I'm your chief, don't forget, and I expect to pay some of the – er – expenses we run up.'

'Thank you, Fatty,' said Bets. 'You're a very, very *nice* chief.'

'The fourth of September is tomorrow,' said Daisy. 'I hope it's fine. Who'll tell Ern?'

'Pip,' said Fatty, promptly. 'He hasn't done much in the way of jobs today – you and Bets and I seem to have done most. Pip's turn to do something.'

'All right,' said Pip. 'But if Sid comes "arring" at me I shall throw him into the river.'

'Do,' said Fatty. 'It will probably make him swallow all his toffee at once and get rid of it!'

They decided to meet the next day at Larry's, and all go over to Tiplington together on their bicycles. Ern was to join them at Larry's too, and Larry would borrow an old bicycle for him.

'Two o'clock,' said Fatty. 'And tell Ern to wash

his face and brush his hair and clean his nails, and put on a clean shirt if he's got one. My orders.'

Ern took these orders in good part. Nothing that Fatty said could ever annoy him. 'He's the cat's whiskers,' he told Pip. 'A genius, he is. Right, I'll be there, all spruced up, like. What are we going over to the Fair for? Anything cooking?'

'Might be,' said Pip. 'Don't be late, Ern.'

'I won't,' said Ern. 'Slong!'

It took Pip a moment or two to realise what 'Slong' meant. Of course – 'So long!' Where did Ern learn to mix up his words like that? 'Slong!' What a word!

Ern set off joyfully to go to Larry's the next day. He had difficulty in stopping Sid and Perce from coming too. 'Well, you can't,' he said. 'Look at your hair – and your faces – and your nails – and your shirts! Disgraceful! You can't go out in company like that.'

'Well, it's the first time you've brushed your hair or cleaned your nails,' grumbled Perce.

Ern walked down to the river and took the little ferry boat across. He then walked to Larry's. On the way, to his horror, he met his uncle. Mr Goon advanced on him, even redder in the face than usual, with the heat.

'Ha! Young Ern again!' he began. 'And where may *you* be off to, I'd like to know! You got any more fairy tales for me about princes in prams with twin babies?'

'No, Uncle. No,' said Ern. 'I'm afraid I can't wait. I mustn't be late.'

'Where you going?' asked Mr Goon, and a heavy hand descended on Ern's shoulder.

'To Larry's,' said Ern. Mr Goon looked him over carefully. 'You're all dressed up – hair brushed and all,' he said. 'What are you up to?'

'Nothing, I tell you, Uncle,' said poor Ern. 'We're all going over to Tiplington Fair, that's all.'

'What – that potty little Fair?' said Mr Goon in astonishment. 'What are you going there for? Has that big boy got something up his sleeve?'

'He might have,' said Ern, wriggling free with a sudden movement. 'He's brainy, he is. He believes the things I tell him, see? Not like you! We're investigating hard, we are! And for all you know, we're on to something!'

He ran down the road, leaving Mr Goon

breathing hard. Now, did Ern mean what he said? Was there something going on at Tiplington that he, Mr Goon, ought to know about? Why was that toad of a boy taking all his lot over there?

Mr Goon went home, brooding over the matter. He suddenly made up his mind. He would go to Tiplington too! He ought to keep an eye on that boy anyway. You never knew when he would smell out something.

Mr Goon wheeled out his bicycle and mounted it with a sigh. He didn't like bicycling in hot weather. He was sure it wasn't good for him. But duty called, and off he went.

He started before the others, who had waited for Ern, and had had an ice cream each in the sweetshop in the village before they set off. Buster was in Fatty's bicycle basket as usual, his tongue hanging out contentedly. He was at his very happiest when he was with all the Find-Outers together.

Ern was happy too. He had forgotten about his uncle. He was proud to be with the Find-Outers, and proud that they wanted him. He beamed all over his plain, plump face.

'Slovely,' he kept saying. 'Streat.'

'What do you mean – Street?' asked Daisy, trying to work it out.

'He means, it's a treat,' said Bets laughing.

'SwatIsaid,' said Ern, puzzled.

'Swatesaid,' chorussed everyone in delight.

They rode off down the lanes to Tiplington. After about a mile, they caught sight of a familiar figure in dark blue, labouring at the pedals of his bicycle.

'It's Mr Goon!' said Pip, in surprise. 'Surely *he's* not going to Tiplington too! Don't say he's visiting the baby show as well! Ern! Did you tell him we were going to the Fair?'

Ern went red. 'Well, yes, I did,' he said. 'Didn't I ought to have? I didn't think it mattered?'

'You certainly ought not to have,' said Fatty, annoyed. 'Now we shall have him shadowing us all the time. Still, he probably won't want to do the important thing – look at the twins in the baby show! You'll have to take Ern into the baby show with you, Bets and Daisy – in case you want him to identify any twins.'

'Coo,' said Ern. 'Let me off the baby show! I'm not Sid. I'd run a mile from a baby show!'

'Well, you won't run a mile from this one,' said Daisy, firmly. 'If there are any likely twins, I shall fetch you in, Ern. So don't dare to disappear.'

'Sawful,' said poor Ern. 'Really, sawful this.'

'Sagonizing,' said Fatty. 'Sunendurable.'

'You talking foreign again?' asked Ern, with interest.

'Not more than you are,' said Fatty. 'Now – altogether – pass Mr Goon and ring your bells hard. Bark, Buster, bark. And everyone yell, "Good afternoon, how are you!"'

And so, to Mr Goon's alarm, annoyance and discomfort, six children rode noisily past him with bells ringing, Buster barking madly, and everyone shouting loudly.

'GOOD AFTERNOON, HOW ARE YOU!'

Mr Goon nearly went into the ditch. He scowled after the backs of the six speeding cyclists. He was almost exhausted already. Still, Tiplington wasn't really very far away now. He pedalled on manfully. If there was anything at Tiplington that he'd got to know about, he must certainly be there. There was no knowing what that pest of a boy was up to.

The Fair was certainly not much of a show. It was in a small field. In one big tent was a flower show, a fruit show, a jam show, and a baby show. There were the usual sideshows – a small roundabout, swings, and a hoopla stall. A fortune-teller sat in a very small tent, reading people's hands for them, telling them of great good fortune to come, voyages across the sea, and all the usual fairy tales.

Apparently the Fair was to last three days, but the local flower, fruit and baby shows only this one afternoon. 'Lucky we saw the notice yesterday,' said Bets, as they paid the entrance fee at the gate. Buster was let in for nothing, but Fatty put him on a lead.

'When does the baby show begin?' wondered Daisy. 'Look – there's a notice on that tent. And here are some babies arriving too. Goodness, they look hot, poor things!'

Prams of all types were wheeled in. The four boys wandered off, but Daisy and Bets stood watching the babies being wheeled into the tent.

Daisy clutched Bets' arm suddenly. 'Look, a double pram – and another. Twins!' she said. 'Where's Ern? We shall never know if the babies are the ones that were up in the caravan.'

Ern had completely disappeared. He had been having a lovely time on the roundabout, riding on an elephant, when he had caught sight of his uncle wheeling his bicycle in at the gate, red in the face, dripping with perspiration, and panting loudly. Ern didn't like the look of him.

So, when the roundabout stopped, he slipped quietly off the elephant and made his way to the tent of the fortune-teller. He hid behind it, watching Mr Goon's movements. Ern was not going to have any more to do with his uncle than he could help.

Daisy and Bets disappeared into the big tent, for the baby show was about to begin. How annoying of Ern to vanish! Still, perhaps he would come along soon.

'Four sets of twins!' said Bets. 'Oh, aren't these babies fat? I don't think I like them quite so fat. And they look so hot and miserable. I'm sure this tent is too hot for them.'

'Come and look at the twins,' said Daisy. 'I say, we don't really *need* Ern, you know, because we know the twins' names – Marge and Bert!'

'Oh *yes*,' said Bets, remembering. 'We can just

ask the mothers their names. That's easy.'

The first twins, one big and one small, and quite unalike, were called Ron and Mike, their proud mother informed the two girls.

'No good,' whispered Bets. 'They're boys. We want a girl and a boy.'

The next two were both girls – Edie and Glad, so their mother said. The next pair were again boys, exactly alike, down to the same spot on their chins. Alf and Reg.

'Here's a girl *and* a boy,' said Bets. 'What are their names?'

'The girl's Margery, and the boy's Robert,' said the mother proudly. 'Big for their age, aren't they?'

Bets and Daisy thought they were far too big, far too fat, and far too hot. But their names were right – or almost right!

'Margery and Robert!' said Bets to Daisy in a low voice. 'Marge and Bert. Where's Ern? We'll have to ask him to come and look at them.'

They made their way out of the tent in great excitement and, at last, ran into Ern behind the fortune-teller's tent, where he was still hiding. They pulled him over to the tent.

'You simply *must* tell us if we've found the right babies!' said Bets, and got a sudden punch in the back from Daisy! She gave a squeal. 'Why did you . . .' she began.

And then she saw why! Mr Goon was standing just at the entrance to the tent. He was most interested in what Bets had just said to Ern! Oho! So they *had* got Ern over for something special, thought Mr Goon.

Ern went into the tent, followed by Mr Goon. 'Oh blow,' said Bets. 'Ern, it's the babies at the far end of the row. Just walk quietly by them and tell us if they're the ones we're looking for. Nod your head if it is. Shake it, if not. And look out for Mr Goon!'

Ern walked down the row of babies. Bets and Daisy watched anxiously. Would he shake or nod his head? But, most annoyingly, Ern did neither!

17. THE BABY SHOW

Mr Goon also walked down the row of babies. The little things were terrified of his big, blue-clad figure and his brilliant red face. They began to cry. 'Yow!' they wailed. 'Wow-yow-wow!' Mr Goon scowled at them. He didn't like babies. Also, he was worried. He was remembering Ern's extraordinary tale of the prince being smuggled away in a pram with twin babies. And, lo and behold – here was a row of twin babies! Did Fatty really believe that tale then? *Could* there be something in it?

Mr Goon decided to take quite a lot of notice of the twins. He stood gazing at them. He prodded one or two. He watched Ern walk by them all, looking carefully. He watched him go out of the back flap of the tent, and then he followed him.

The mothers were thankful to see him go. 'What's he want to come in here for, frightening our babies?' said one mother. 'He's set them all off crying with his scowls and his prods!'

Ern had found Bets and Daisy.

'Ern, *why* didn't you either nod or shake your head?' asked Bets crossly. 'You said you would. We *must* know if they are the twins or not. Are they?'

'I don't know,' said Ern, helplessly. 'All those babies in there look alike to me. I couldn't tell t'other from which. Oh, Bets – I'm sorry. They're as like as peas.'

'How *annoying*,' said Daisy. 'Especially as those two are called Margery and Robert.'

'Of course, Bert might be short for Albert or Hubert, as well as Robert,' said Bets. 'We don't know that Bert, the twin Sid knew, was short for *Robert*.'

'*I* know!' said Daisy, suddenly. 'Let's look for the pram that Margery and Robert came in. Ern could surely recognise *that* if it was the one.'

'Oh yes,' said Ern, confidently. 'It was – let me see – was it dark blue, or dark green?'

The two girls stared at him, exasperated. 'You're perfectly hopeless!' said Daisy. 'What good are you to us, I'd like to know! You never notice a thing!'

Ern looked very woebegone indeed. Mr Goon emerged from the tent at that moment and, to the girls' great annoyance, Ern at once made off at top speed! Now they would lose him all over again!

'Ern! Come back and look at the prams!' shouted Bets. Mr Goon pricked up his ears again. Prams! Prams! There *was* something up this afternoon. Those kids *were* investigating something, drat them!

Bets and Daisy gave up on Ern. They wandered over to where the prams were neatly set out in a row, empty of their babies. There were two enormous double prams, one fairly big one, altered to take two children, and any amount of ordinary single prams.

'Perhaps we'd better wait about here for Ern,' said Bets, bored. 'He'll come back sooner or later, I suppose. I wonder what the three boys are doing. Oh, do look at Mr Goon. He's interested in prams too!'

Mr Goon was now examining the prams. Could he find anything in them that would help him? He didn't think so. He considered each pram carefully, much to the amazement of a mother coming out to get something for her baby.

'Thinking of buying a pram?' she asked him.

Mr Goon didn't deign to reply. He wandered off

in search of Ern.

Soon the mothers began to bring out their babies to their prams. They had all been judged, and 'Margery and Robert' had a big rosette each, with 'First Prize, Twins' on it.

'Oh!' said Bets, starting forward. 'Did they get first prize! How lovely! Let me carry one for you. I like babies.'

'Well, perhaps you'd just bring me my pram,' panted the mother, loaded down with her two heavy children. 'It's over there.'

'Which one?' asked Bets.

'That one,' said the mother, nodding at a rather shabby small pram. It was a single pram! Bets had been sure she would have had a double one – what a disappointment. Margery and Robert *couldn't* be the twins they were looking for, after all! Ern and Sid had been quite certain that the pram belonging to the twins in the caravan was a double one.

She brought the little single pram over. 'There now, Madge,' said the mother, settling the little girl at one end, and then putting the boy at the other. 'Now now, Robbie – don't you start yelling.

Haven't you got first prize? Laugh then, laugh!'

Daisy looked at Bets. Madge and Robbie – not Marge and Bert! That settled it. They were not the twins and this was not the mother. All this way over to the Fair for nothing!

'Come along, Bets – let's have a bit of fun now,' said Daisy. 'We've done our investigation – and like all our investigations so far, it's just come to nothing. I don't believe we'll ever find anything out in this mystery!'

They went off to the swingboats. Then they had a try at the hoopla and Bets got a ring round a little red vase, much to her delight.

Then up came Fatty. 'Bets! Daisy! Any good? Were they the twins? What did Ern say?'

'Oh Fatty, such a disappointment! There were twins there whose names were Margery and Robert and we felt sure they were the ones!' said Daisy. 'But they weren't. They were called Madge and Robbie! Ern wasn't a bit of good. He had a look at all the twins, but he said they were as like as peas, and he wouldn't know if they were the caravan twins or not!'

'And, anyway, they have a single pram not a

double one,' said Bets. 'We've come all this way for nothing.'

'Oh no, you haven't,' said Fatty, pulling her over to the roundabout. 'Come on, choose your animal and I'll pay the roundabout boy twice as much as usual to go on twice as long. You can have the longest ride you've ever had in your life!'

Bets chose a lion and the roundabout boy set the roundabout going at top speed, so that Bets and the others yelled in glee! He let them have such a long ride that everyone stared in surprise.

'That was fun,' said Bets, getting off her lion and feeling rather wobbly about the legs. 'Goodness, I still feel as if I'm going round and round.'

Fatty suddenly saw Mr Goon in the distance. He grinned. He went over to the roundabout boy, and had a long talk with him. The boy laughed and nodded. Fatty slid some money into his hand and walked away.

'What have you been up to, Fatty?' said Daisy. 'You've got a wicked look on your face.'

'I've just been arranging for Mr Goon to have a nice long ride,' said Fatty. 'Giving him a real treat, I am! Just you watch!'

Mr Goon had given up searching for the elusive Ern. In any case, he would never find him because Ern was lying hidden under a caravan belonging to one of the Fair people at the end of the field. So now Mr Goon was wandering over to where he saw Fatty, Bets, and Daisy. They were joined by Larry and Pip, who had been unlucky at hoopla, and had no money left.

'Watch,' said Fatty under his breath. They all watched, though not quite certain what they were supposed to watch. The roundabout boy and another one got up on the roundabout as Mr Goon drew near. They began to shout at one another.

Everyone turned to see what was happening. 'You give it to me, I say!' yelled one boy. 'Or I'll box your ears!'

'Shan't!' shouted the other boy, and lunged out at the first boy. Down he went on the platform of the roundabout, and rolled about, yelling loudly.

'Don't worry, Bets. It's all pretence,' said Fatty, grinning. 'Now watch what happens!'

Mr Goon heard all the rumpus, of course. He pulled down his tunic, put his helmet quite straight, and walked ponderously over to the roundabout.

'Hey, you boys! What's the matter there! Behave yourselves!'

'Help, help! He's on top of me!' yelled one of the boys. 'Help! Fetch the police!'

Mr Goon mounted the platform of the roundabout, watched by scores of people, looking very impressive indeed. 'Now what's all this?' he began, and then he suddenly clutched at a nearby tiger.

The roundabout boy had slid off the platform and had started the roundabout! Round it went and round, the music sounding very loud indeed in Mr Goon's startled ears. He nearly fell over. He clasped his arms round the neck of the tiger and yelled ferociously.

'Stop this thing! Stop it, I say!'

But nobody heard him through the din of the strident music! The roundabout went faster and faster, it simply WHIZZED round, till Mr Goon's figure could no longer be clearly seen. Fatty began to laugh. The others rolled about, squealing with joy. Everyone yelled. Mr Goon was not popular in Tiplington!

The roundabout slowed down at last. Mr Goon

still clutched the neck of the tiger. He dared not let go. Poor Mr Goon – the world still went round for him, and the tiger seemed his only friend!

18. PIP'S DISCOVERY

'I have a sort of feeling we'd better go,' said Fatty. 'Where's Ern? Oh, there he is. Good thing he saw a bit of the fun!'

Ern came over to them, grinning. 'I say, look at Uncle on the roundabout. He's still got hold of the tiger. Was it an accident, Fatty?'

'Not quite,' said Fatty, with a rich chuckle. 'Do come on, everyone. Mr Goon won't be fit to follow us on his bike for quite a while. He'll probably want to go round in circles for ages.'

He winked at the roundabout boy, who winked back. Mr Goon straightened up, unwrapped one arm cautiously from the tiger, and took a step away from it. But the world immediately seemed to swim round him again, and he embraced the tiger more lovingly than ever.

'If I look any more, I shall die of laughing,' said Larry. 'I've already got a frightful stitch in my side.

I have never laughed so much in my life. Dear old Mr Goon – I feel quite fond of him for making me laugh so much. How he will ever get off that roundabout, I don't know!'

Fatty had to shove everyone along. They all so badly wanted to see Mr Goon get off the roundabout and walk unsteadily over the field. The roundabout boy was now shouting at him. 'Sorry, sir! Quite an accident. Won't charge you a penny, sir! Free ride for the police force!'

Mr Goon decided not to deal with that roundabout boy just yet. His words seemed to swim round in his head. He didn't want to argue with anyone just then. He held the tiger still more tightly, and shut his eyes to see if the world would steady itself again.

The Find-Outers and Ern found their bicycles and mounted them. 'Come down this path,' said Ern. 'It's a shorter way to the road. I saw it when I was hiding under the caravan.'

So they took Ern's path that led across the field, past the caravans, and out into a lane that went straight to the road.

And it was when they were cycling slowly past

the caravans that Pip suddenly saw something that made him almost wobble off his bicycle!

Clothes lines stretched here and there, hung with the washing belonging to the Fair people. Pip glanced at it idly as he went by. He saw a blouse there, a blue blouse made of rather common material – but it wasn't the blouse that gave him such a surprise – it was the buttons on it!

'Gosh!' said Pip. 'Surely they're the same as the button I've got in my pocket – the button that came off Prince Bongawah's pyjamas!'

He took the button out of his pocket and went over to the clothes line. He compared it with the buttons on the blouse. They were exactly the same – blue and gold, very fine indeed.

Pip glanced at the nearby caravan. It was bright green with yellow wheels. He would remember that all right. He rode fast after Fatty, almost upsetting the others on the narrow path as he passed them.

'Stop it, Pip!' cried Bets angrily, as he almost brushed her pedal. 'What's the hurry?'

Pip caught Fatty up at last. 'Fatty! Quick. Stop a minute, I've got something important to say!'

Fatty stopped in surprise. He got off his bicycle and waited by the little gate that led into the lane. 'Wheel your bike out under those trees, so that we can't be seen talking,' panted Pip.

Everyone was soon standing under the trees, surprised and puzzled. 'What is it, Pip?' said Fatty. 'What's up all of a sudden?'

'You know this button that came off Prince Bongawah's pyjamas?' said Pip, producing it. 'Well, Fatty, when we passed those clothes lines I saw a blouse hanging on one – and it had buttons *exactly* like these all down the front! And you must admit they're very fine and very unusual buttons!'

'Gosh!' said Fatty, startled by this remarkable statement of Pips'.

He took a quick look at the button and then walked back the way he had come, wheeling his bicycle. 'I must check up,' he said in a low voice as he went. 'Wait for me. I'll pretend to be looking for something I've dropped in the grass.'

He went along with bent head until he came to the clothes line. He spotted the blouse at once. He went right up to it, still pretending to look for something on the ground – and then took a good

181

look at the blouse which was now almost touching his nose.

He came back quickly. 'Pip's right,' he said, his voice sounding excited. 'This is very important. We thought we'd wasted the afternoon, coming after twin babies – and so we had from that point of view – but we're on to something much better!'

'What?' asked Bets, thrilled.

'Well, obviously those buttons are off the prince's pyjamas,' said Fatty. 'And quite obviously, also, the pyjamas have been destroyed in case they might be recognised. But whoever destroyed them couldn't bear to part with the lovely buttons – and put them on that blouse, thinking they would never be noticed!'

'They wouldn't have been if Pip hadn't found that button, and noticed the washing!' said Bets. 'Oh Pip, you *are* clever!'

'Let's think,' said Fatty. 'Let's think quickly. What does it mean? It means that the prince is probably somewhere here – hiding – or being hidden. Probably in that caravan near the washing line. We'll have to try and find out.'

'We can't very well stop now,' said Pip.

'Mummy said Bets and I were to be back by six – and we won't be if we don't hurry.'

'*I'll* stop behind,' said Fatty, making up his mind quickly. 'No, I won't. I'll go back, change into some disguise, and come back here. I'll get into talk with the Fair people and see if I can pick something up. Yes, that's the best thing to do. One of us must certainly make enquiries quickly.'

'Let me stop too,' said Ern.

'Certainly not,' said Fatty. 'You go back with the others, Ern. Go on. Do as you're told. I'm chief here. Let's ride back quickly because it will take me a little time to put on a disguise.'

'What will you be, Fatty?' asked Bets, excited, as they all cycled quickly down the lane, Ern looking a little sulky.

'A pedlar,' said Fatty. 'Selling something. I can easily get into talk with the Fair people then. They'll think I'm one of them. I simply must find out if there has been a new boy added to their company just lately!'

'Good gracious! From being quite unsolvable, this mystery has jumped almost to an end!' said Bets.

'Don't you believe it,' said Fatty grimly. 'There's

more in this than meets the eye. It's not as straightforward as it looks. There's something funny about it!'

This all sounded extremely exciting. The six of them rode along in silence, each thinking the same tumultuous thoughts. What would Fatty find out? Would he discover the prince that evening? What was the 'something funny' he meant?

They got home in good time. Fatty went straight down to his shed. He knew exactly what disguise he would wear. It was one he had worn before, and he felt it was just right.

It was an ordinary schoolboy who went into the little shed – but an ordinary schoolboy didn't come out! No, a pedlar crept out, a dirty-looking creature with long earrings in his ears, a cloth cap pulled down over his face, a brilliant red scarf round his neck, and protruding teeth. Fatty was in disguise!

Dirty flannel trousers clothed his legs and old gym shoes were on his feet. He wore a red belt and a dirty yellow jersey. On his back was a pack. It held bottles of all kinds marked 'Cold Cures', 'Cures for Warts', 'Lotion for Chilblains', and all kinds of weird concoctions that Fatty had invented himself for his pedlar's pack!

He grinned as he crept up the path. His protruding teeth showed, ugly and white. He had fixed a fine false set over his own, made of plastic. Fatty was going investigating – and nobody in the world would have guessed he was anything but a dirty little travelling tinker or pedlar!

He cycled off, back to Tiplington. That was clever of Pip to spot those buttons. Very clever. It put the mystery back on the map, so to speak. Fatty thought rapidly over his plan.

I'll go to the Fair field. I'll sit down and get into talk with the roundabout boy or someone. I'll find out who lives in that green and yellow caravan, and pretend I know the people there – and perhaps get the roundabout boy to take me over and introduce me. Then I'll see who's in the caravan and have as good a snoop round as I can. Well, I hope the plan will work!

He was soon back at the Fair. There were more people now because it was evening. The roundabout was swinging round bravely. The swingboats were flying high. There was a babble of talk and laughter everywhere.

Now then, thought Fatty, carefully hiding his bicycle in the middle of a thick bush. Now then! Once more into the breach, dear friend – and see what's what!

He sauntered in to the field. No one asked him for entrance money because he looked exactly like one of the Fair folk themselves. Fatty looked round. The roundabout boy was there at his place. Should he have a word with him? No, he was too busy. What about the hoopla boy? No, he was busy too. Fatty strolled along, keeping his eyes open.

He came to the swingboats. The man looking after them was standing holding his arm as if in pain. Fatty walked up. 'What's up, mate? Hurt yourself?'

'One of these swingboats came back and knocked my elbow,' said the man. 'Look after them for me for a few minutes, will you, while I go and get something for it?'

'Right,' said Fatty, and looked after the swingboats faithfully till the man came back, his arm neatly bandaged.

'Thanks,' he said. 'You with us, or have you just come along?'

'Just come along,' said Fatty. 'Heard that maybe someone I knew was here. Thought I'd give them a call-in.'

'Name of what?' said the man.

'I can't remember the name for the moment,' said Fatty, taking off his cap and scratching his head hard. He screwed up his face. 'Let me see now – Barlow, Harlow, no, that wasn't it.'

'What line were they in?' said the man.

'Ah wait – something's coming back to me!' said Fatty. 'They had a green caravan with yellow wheels. Anyone here in a caravan like that, mate?'

'Oh yes, the Tallerys,' said the man, taking some money for a ride in his swings. 'Those who you mean? They've got that green and yellow caravan over there!'

'That's right – the Tallerys!' exclaimed Fatty. 'How did I come to forget the name! Are they all still there, mate?'

'Well, there's old Mum, and there's Mrs Tallery, and there's a nephew, Rollo,' said the man. 'That's all. Old Man Tallery's not there. He's on a job.'

'Ah,' said Fatty, as if he knew quite well what the job was. 'Well, I feel uncomfortable at going along to them if Old Man Tallery's not there. The others might not remember me.'

'I'll take you along, chum,' said the obliging swingboat man. 'Say, what's your name?'

'Smith,' said Fatty quickly, remembering that many gypsies were called Smith. 'Just Jack Smith.'

'You wait till this lot's finished their swings and I'll take you over,' said the man. 'Maybe they aren't there though. I did see Old Mum and Mrs Tallery going off this afternoon.'

'Well, I'd be glad if you'd take me across,' said Fatty. 'You can tell them I knew Old Man Tallery!'

19. ROLLO TALKS A LOT

The swingboat man took Fatty across to the yellow and green caravan. An old woman was outside, sitting in a sagging wicker chair that creaked under her great weight.

She was calling loudly to someone, 'Rollo! Drat the boy, where is he? I'll give him such a hiding when I get hold of him!'

'Hello, Old Mum,' said the swingboat man, coming up. 'That scamp of a Rollo gone again? I'll give him a clip on the ear if I see him, and send him over to you. He's the laziest young 'un I ever did see in my life.'

'He is that,' grumbled Old Mum. 'His aunt's gone down to the town, and he was told to clean the windows of the caravan. They're that dirty I can't see to knit inside!'

She peered at Fatty. 'Who's this? I don't know him. Do you want Old Man Tallery? He's not

189

here. Won't be back for a few days.'

'Oh, I'm sorry,' said Fatty. 'I wanted to see him.'

'Friend of his,' the swingboat man explained to Old Mum. 'Name of Jack Smith.' He turned to Fatty. 'You sit and talk to the old lady a bit. She'll love that! What have you got in your pack? Anything to interest her? I'm going back to my swings.'

Fatty opened his pack and displayed his bottles and tins. Old Mum took one look at them and laughed a wheezy laugh.

'Ho ho! That's your line, is it? Coloured water and coloured powders! My dad was in the same line and very paying it was too. Shut your pack up, lad, I've no use for them things. I'm too old and too spry to be caught by such tricks!'

'I wasn't going to sell you any, Old Mum, or try to,' said Fatty, in a voice very like Ern's. 'When did you say Mrs Tallery would be back?'

'Oh, I never know how long she'll be,' said Old Mum crossly. 'Here, there, and everywhere she is. Here today, gone tomorrow – leaves me alone for days on end, she do. Off she went a few days ago, never said where – and back she comes without a word.'

Fatty pricked up his ears. Could Mrs Tallery be he woman in the caravan – the woman with he babies?

'Let me see now,' said Fatty, 'how many children has she got?'

'She and Old Man Tallery never did have children,' said Old Mum. 'Nary a one. That's why they took on Rollo, though gracious knows why they wanted to pick on him, the little pest. But his Ma's got eleven kids besides him, so she was glad to get rid of him.'

'Oh, of course,' said Fatty, quite as if he knew all about it! He was about to ask a few more questions when the swingboat man came up again, leading a boy by the ear.

'Here's Rollo, Old Mum,' he said. 'Shall I set him to work cleaning the windows, or shall I put him across my knee and give him a hiding first?'

'No!' yelled Rollo, squirming about. 'I'll do the windows, you big beast!'

The swingboat man shook him, laughed, and went off again. Fatty looked at the angry boy. He wasn't very big, about Pip's size, and the scowl on his face made him very ugly and unpleasant. Old

191

Mum began to scold him soundly, the words pouring out of her mouth in an endless stream. The boy made a rude face at her.

He then went to get a pail of water and a cloth presumably to clean the very dirty windows. Old Mum heaved herself up to go into the caravan.

'I'm chilly,' she said. 'Just keep an eye on that boy, will you? Give me a call if he stops his work!'

Fatty helped the old woman into the caravan. She seemed surprised at his help. 'Well, 'tisn't often my son, Old Man Tallery, has friends like you!' she said. 'First time I've known one of them help me up the steps!'

She disappeared into the smelly, dirty caravan. The boy sulkily sloshed water over the windows, and made them so wet and smeary that Fatty thought they were worse than ever!

He sat and waited till the boy had finished. Rollo emptied the water, threw the cloth under the caravan, and made a face at Fatty.

'Here,' said Fatty, taking some money out of his pocket. 'I'm hungry. Go and buy something with this, bring it back, and we'll share it. Skip along!'

'Right,' said the boy, looking less sulky. He took the money and went. Soon he was back with two meat pies, gingerbeer, and four enormous jam tarts. He sat down by Fatty.

'You a friend of Old Mum's?' he said. 'Misery guts she is. I like my aunt better. No nonsense about *her*.'

'You've got plenty of brothers and sisters, haven't you?' said Fatty, eating the pie. He didn't like it at all. It was dry and musty.

'Yes. Eleven,' said Rollo. 'The youngest are twins. Always yelling they are.'

'*Twins*?' said Fatty at once. 'How old are they?'

'Don't know,' said Rollo. 'Just babies. They came to stay with my aunt when my mum was ill.'

'What, here?' said Fatty, munching away. 'I shouldn't have thought there was room for all of you in the caravan.'

'They was only here for a day,' said Rollo. 'Then my aunt got a caravan up on the school camp field and had them there.'

Fatty went on munching solidly, but his eyes suddenly gleamed in his dirty face. Aha! He was on the track now all right! So the aunt was the woman in the caravan – and Rollo's twin brother and sister were the twins in the pram!

'Let me see – Marge and Bert are the twins, aren't they?' said Fatty. Rollo nodded.

'That's right. You know the family all right, don't you! There's Alf, George, Reenie, Pam, Doris, Millie, Reg, Bob, Doreen – and Marge and Bert.'

'And you're the one they chucked out, are you?' said Fatty, gazing at the jam tarts and wondering if he dared to tackle one.

'Ere! Oo said I was chucked out!' said Rollo indignantly. 'What do you suppose Old Man Tallery picked *me* out of the lot for? *I'll* tell you. Because I can act, and because I've got brains, and because I'm jolly useful to him!'

'I bet you're nothing but a nuisance to him, a dirty little rascal like you!' said Fatty, trying to rouse Rollo into telling him a lot more things. Rollo rose to the bait at once. He scowled.

'I'm going to tell you something, Mister,' he said to Fatty. 'I can act anything, I can. I can be a boy leading a blind fellow – that's one way Old Man Tallery and me get money – and I can be a nice kid going shopping with my aunt, and slipping things up my sleeve when Aunt's talking to the shop girl – and I can even be a *prince*!'

Fatty jumped. A prince! Now what did he mean by that? Fatty turned and stared at the gypsy boy, who looked back impudently at him.

'Ah, that made you stare!' said Rollo, triumphantly. 'I bet you don't believe it, Mister.'

'No, I don't,' said Fatty, hoping to lead the boy on and on. His mind was in a whirl. A prince? What did it all mean?

'I thought you wouldn't believe me!' said Rollo. 'Well, I've said too much. I'd better not say any more.'

'That's because you've got nothing to say,' said Fatty promptly. 'You're making up a lot of tales and you know it. Prince, my foot! Dirty little rascal like you a prince! What do you take me for?'

The boy glared at him. Then he looked all round as if afraid that someone might overhear. 'Look here,' he said, 'do you remember the fuss in the papers about that prince being kidnapped. Prince Bonga-Bonga or something. Well, I was him!'

'Go and tell that fairy tale to the twins!' said Fatty scornfully, but inwardly very excited. 'There's a *real* Prince Bongawah, who belongs to a real kingdom called Tetarua – I've seen photographs of him.'

'Well, I tell you, I was him!' persisted the boy, angry that Fatty wouldn't believe him.

'Really? Well maybe you'll tell me how you were kidnapped then, and how you got away, and were taken here,' said Fatty sarcastically.

'Easy,' said the boy. 'I wasn't kidnapped. I just had to stay a few days at the camp, see, and pretend to be the prince and just talk gibberish – and then on a certain night, I had to creep through the hedge, find my aunt's caravan, and hide there. You'll never guess how I got away though!'

Fatty thought he could make a very good guess indeed, but he pretended to be quite bewildered.

'My word – this is a tale and a half!' he said. 'Do you really mean to say you did all that? Well then – how *did* you get away?'

'My aunt took the bottom boards out of the twins' double pram, and I curled myself up in the space there,' said Rollo, grinning. 'And she sat the twins down on top of me. They didn't half yell!'

'And then she wheeled you back here,' said

Fatty, as if overcome with admiration. 'Well, you are a one, Rollo! I didn't believe a word at first, but I do now. You're a marvel!'

Rollo beamed at once at this unexpected praise. He leaned over to Fatty and whispered, 'I could tell you something else if I wanted to!' he said. 'I could tell you where the *real* prince is! The coppers would give a lot to know what *I* know, I can tell you! Not half they wouldn't!'

20. FATTY RIDES HOME

Fatty was so astonished that he couldn't say a word! He gazed speechlessly at Rollo and Rollo grinned delightedly.

'You're a friend of my uncle's, Old Man Tallery, so it won't matter telling *you* all this,' he said, suddenly struck by the fact that he had been telling a lot of secrets! 'But don't you let on to him that I told you.'

'No, I won't,' said Fatty. 'He's not here, anyway. Where is he?'

'Well, he thinks I don't know, but I do,' said Rollo. 'He's down in Raylingham Marshes. I heard him and Joe talking when they didn't know I was near.'

'Is that where the prince is – the real prince?' asked Fatty.

Rollo grew suddenly cautious. 'Here, I'm telling you too much. What's come over me! You just forget what I said about the prince, see? I don't know where he is.'

'You said you did just now,' said Fatty.

'Well, maybe I do and maybe I don't,' said Rollo. 'Anyway I'm not telling *you*.'

'Right,' said Fatty. 'Why should I want to know anyway? But what beats me is why you had to dress up as the prince and then run away and make people think you were kidnapped. It doesn't make sense to me.'

'Well, it ought to,' said Rollo rudely. 'But maybe your brains want a bit of polishing up.'

'Go on!' said Fatty. 'You and your cheek! I don't say I'm as bright as you are, by a long chalk. I could think a hundred years and not see why all this was done!'

'Well, you look here,' said Rollo, really enjoying himself. 'There's a prince that someone wants to get rid of, see – so that he won't have the throne. Got that?'

'Yes,' said Fatty, humbly.

'But it would be jolly difficult to kidnap him and get him out of the country before his disappearance was discovered, wouldn't it?' said

Rollo. 'So all that happened was that when he was sent down to the school camps by car, the chauffeur stopped at an arranged place, the prince was whisked away in another car – and I popped into the first car, all dressed up posh like the prince!'

Fatty suddenly saw light. So *that* was the how and the why and the where! Someone wanted the prince out of the way, but didn't want the kidnapping to be discovered till he had had time to get the boy away somewhere – and with the chauffeur in the plot, it was easy! Exchange boys on the journey down, let the second boy stay a few days in the camp and behave as if he were the real prince – and then creep away to his convenient aunt, and disappear with the twins in the double pram! No one would ever think the woman had anything to do with the second 'kidnapping', which, to all intents and purposes, was the first and only kidnapping. Nobody guessed about the genuine kidnapping!

'What a plan!' said Fatty, in a tone of deepest admiration. 'Old Man Tallery is a whole lot cleverer than I thought he was. My word, next time I meet him, I'll ask him to let me come in on his next job.

There must be a lot of money in these things.'

'There is,' said Rollo, boasting hard now. 'I reckon he'll clear hundreds of pounds. I'm going to have some myself, for my part in playing the prince.'

'My word – you'll be rich!' said Fatty. 'How did you like being a prince? Didn't you ever forget your part?'

'No. It was easy,' said Rollo. 'My colouring is as dark as the prince's, and we was both little fellows, and I didn't have to speak any English – only nonsense. But when one of the big fellows – the ones who arranged all this, you know – came down to see how I was getting on and insisted on having the state umbrella up, I didn't like that. I felt a fool. All the boys yelled at me.'

'Did you enjoy being a prince?' Fatty asked him.

'Not so bad,' said Rollo. 'I slept in pyjamas for the first time in my life – lovely silk they were, all blue and gold, with buttons to match. My aunt was told to burn the pyjamas as soon as I got here, and she did, in case anyone saw them. But she kept the buttons and sewed them on a blouse. She didn't like throwing those away, they were too good.'

Fatty couldn't help thinking what a good thing

it was that Rollo's aunt had been thrifty over the buttons! If she hadn't sewn them on her blouse, if she hadn't washed it and hung it on the line, Pip would never have spotted the buttons and he, Fatty, would never have got on to the well-hidden trail!

'I suppose Old Man Tallery helped to arrange everything,' said Fatty. 'He's great, isn't he, your uncle?'

'No flies on *him*,' said Rollo proudly. 'He's a card, he is. I quite enjoyed being a prince, but when they wanted me to go swimming, I didn't half kick up a fuss. The way they talked about me not wanting to wash, too. Wash, wash, wash, clean your teeth! Many a time I wanted to talk back at those kids up at camp. I did say a few things in English – but I was a bit afraid of giving myself away if I lost my temper.'

'Of course,' said Fatty. 'Well, you seem to have done very well. I don't believe anyone suspected you weren't the real prince. Are you like him to look at?'

'Near enough,' said Rollo. 'He wasn't anything special to look at and neither am I. I was a bit scared of someone who knew the prince coming down to see me, but nobody did.'

'And you say you know where they took the prince?' said Fatty. 'Haven't they got him away from there yet?'

Rollo became secretive again. 'I'm not telling that,' he said. 'I don't want to be skinned alive by my uncle, see? He doesn't even know I heard where he's gone to.'

Fatty decided that he couldn't find out anything else from Rollo. He knew the whole plot now – very simple, very slickly carried out – the real kidnapping cleverly masked by the false one so that the police were completely bamboozled, not looking for the prince until some days after he had *really* been kidnapped!

Had the real prince been spirited away yet? Would he ever be heard of again? There really was no time to be lost if he was still being kept in hiding. Anything might happen to him at any time!

Raylingham Marshes. If Rollo's uncle, Old Man Tallery, was there, possibly the whole gang were there, and the Prince too. Where were Raylingham

Marshes? Fatty decided to look them up immediately he got home.

He got up to go. It was getting dark and only the Fair people were now left on the field. He had missed dinner – thank goodness his parents were out, and wouldn't know he wasn't there. 'Well, so long!' he said to Rollo. 'I must be going.'

'Aren't you going to wait and see my aunt?' said Rollo, who had taken quite a fancy to Fatty. 'What did you say your name was?'

'Jack Smith,' said Fatty. 'No, I can't wait. Give her all the best from me, and say I'll look in another time. She may not remember me, of course.'

She jolly well won't! thought Fatty to himself, as he went to find his bicycle and ride home. Blow! I haven't got a lamp. I forgot I might be home after dark. Hope I don't get caught by old Mr Goon!

Fatty rode off quickly. His mind was working at top speed. What a plot! No wonder it had seemed such a peculiar mystery – there had been two kidnappings, but only one – the false one – was made known!

Raylingham Marshes. Was there a house in the

marshes? Was the prince hidden there? Had Rollo got the name right, or was he doing a little make-up on his own? He was talkative and boastful and conceited – some of what he said might quite well not be true. Fatty rode along so lost in thought that he was in Peterswood before he realised it.

He rode cautiously down the road. As he had no lights he was extra careful – but suddenly a dark figure stepped out from behind a tree, and said sharply, 'Here you! Stop! What you doing, riding without a light? Don't you know it's against the law?'

Mr Goon! thought Fatty. Just my luck! He got off his bicycle, debating what to say and do.

Goon flashed his lantern at him, and saw what appeared to be a dirty tramp with a pack. Mr Goon was suspicious at once.

'This your bike?' he asked sharply.

'Might be!' said the pedlar, insolently.

'Now you come-alonga me,' began Mr Goon, 'and give a proper account of yourself. Riding without a . . .'

'Here hold my bike for a minute while I do up my shoe,' said the pedlar, and shoved the bicycle at Goon. He had to catch it to save it from falling on top of him – and while he stood there holding it, Fatty was off like a streak of lightning!

'Oho! So that's the way of things, is it?' said Goon. 'He's stolen this bike, that's what he's done.'

Goon mounted the bicycle and rode after the running figure. But it darted off down a path where cyclists were not allowed to ride, and Goon was beaten! He had no wish to ride a bicycle without lights down a path where cycling was forbidden! Ten to one, if he did, that big boy would appear from somewhere and see him! Goon got off and wheeled it carefully back to his house. The bicycle seemed somehow vaguely familiar to him. He took it into his hall and had a good look at it. Then he got out his notebook and wrote down a full description.

'Full-size. Make – Atlas. Colour – black with red line. Basket in front. No front lamp. In good condition.'

Then he wrote a full description of the man he had seen with it.

'Tramp. Cloth cap pulled down over face. Red scarf. Dirty jersey. Dirty flannel trousers. Earrings. Rude and insolent. I had to force him to give up bicycle, which I guessed was stolen. After a terrific struggle I got it, and the man ran off, scared.'

Just as he finished writing all this, the telephone rang and made him jump. He picked up the receiver.

'Police here,' he said.

'Oh, Mr Goon, is that you?' came Fatty's voice at the other end. 'So sorry to bother you – but I have to report to you that my bike's been stolen. It's gone. Not in the shed. Vanished. I'm afraid you'll never find it or the thief, but I thought I'd better report it.'

'Details of your bike please,' said Goon, in a most official voice.

'Right,' said Fatty. 'Full-size, of course. It's an Atlas, a rather nice one in good condition. It's black with a red line, and there's a basket in front. And . . .'

Goon cleared his throat and spoke pompously. 'I have it here, Frederick. I stopped a tramp with it fifteen minutes ago. Very nasty fellow he was too. Most insolent. Didn't want to give up the bike at all when I challenged him.'

'How did you get it then?' asked Fatty in an awed voice.

'Well, I struggled with him,' said Goon letting his imagination go. 'It was a bit of a struggle, you know – but I got it from him. He was so scared that he ran for his life. I brought the bike here. You can come round for it, if you like.'

'My word, you've done some pretty quick work, Mr Goon!' said Fatty admiringly. Mr Goon stood up very straight. Aha – it wasn't often that boy said things like that to him.

'I don't let the grass grow under my feet,' said Mr Goon, with dignity. 'Well, you'll be along in a minute or two, Frederick, I suppose?'

'Give me ten minutes, and I'll be there!' said Fatty cheerfully, and rang off with a click.

21. MR. GOON HAS A BAD TIME

Fatty arrived in ten minutes, looking spruce and clean. He had just had time to get out of his disguise and clean himself up. He had given himself one minute to laugh very loudly indeed at Goon's story of the tramp and the fight he had had.

Goon opened the door. He was still pompous. 'There's your bike,' he said, waving to where it stood in the hall. 'Can't beat the police, you know, Frederick.'

'Well, I must say it was pretty smart work, Mr Goon,' said Fatty so admiringly that Mr Goon told the story of the tramp all over again, adding a few more trimmings.

'Mr Goon, I'm much obliged to you,' said Fatty earnestly. 'And, in return, I must pass on a bit of news. We've discovered a bit more about the kidnapping – I know Ern told you about the prince hiding in a pram under the babies, didn't he? Well, we've found out now that that wasn't the real prince. It was a gypsy boy. The real prince is, we *think*, somewhere in Raylingham Marshes.'

Mr Goon's face slowly grew thunderous as Fatty reeled all this off. 'Now look here,' he said, 'why don't you think up some better tale? How many more princes are you going to tell me about?'

'I'm not fooling you, Mr Goon,' said Fatty. 'I said I'd help you this time, and I'm trying to. But you make it very difficult.'

'So do you,' said Mr Goon. 'What with your dressing up as foreigners, and talking foreign, and then telling Ern to tell me about princes in prams with babies, and now you say he was a gypsy, and you want me to go gallivanting off to Raylingham Marshes after another prince. Not me!'

'I don't want you to do any gallivanting at all,' said Fatty. 'All you've got to do is to ring up the Chief Inspector and tell him everything. He'll tell you what to do.'

'Look here,' said Mr Goon, beginning to turn his usual purple, 'didn't I ring up and tell the Chief all about Princess Bongawee, the Prince's sister – and it was all made up on your part to make me look small? Oh, you needn't shake your head, I know it was! Then you wanted me to tell him another idiotic story – and now this. Well, I shan't!'

'You'd better,' said Fatty. 'Or shall I? If I do, I'll get all the credit again, you know.'

'Don't you do any telephoning either,' snapped Mr Goon. 'Can't you keep out of this? I'm in charge of this case, I tell you. Interfering with the law! That's what you do all the time. You're a toad of a boy, a . . .'

'Shush shush, Mr Goon,' said Fatty, beginning to wheel his bicycle out of the hall. 'Naughty naughty! Mustn't lose temper.'

He wheeled his bicycle to the front gate and mounted it. Then he called back, 'Oh, I say, I forgot to ask you something, Mr Goon. Did that tramp you fought with do up his shoe after all?'

And, without waiting for an answer, Fatty rode chuckling down the road. Mr Goon stared after him in the darkness. He was puzzled. How did that boy know that the tramp had said he wanted to do up his shoe? Certainly Mr Goon had mentioned no such thing. Then *how* did Fatty know it?

Light suddenly dawned on Mr Goon. He

staggered into his sitting-room and sat down heavily in his chair. He put his head in his hands and groaned. The tramp had been Fatty! He had taken his bike away – and patted himself on the back when Fatty had reported it gone – and given it back to him without so much as mentioning the missing front lamp!

Why, oh why, had he made up such a wonderful story? How Fatty must have laughed up his sleeve! Mr Goon spent half an hour thinking of all the horrid things he would like to do to Fatty but, alas, he knew he would never, ever get the chance to do them. Fatty could look after himself too well!

The telephone rang and Mr Goon jumped. He picked up the receiver fiercely. If it was that boy again, he'd tell him what he thought of him!

But it wasn't. It was a message from the Chief Inspector, delivered shortly by another constable.

'That PC Goon? Message from the Chief. A report has come through from one of our men to say it is now thought that the boy at the camp was not the real prince – but someone masquerading as him. Photographs shown to boys on the field have not been recognised as the boy who was with them as the prince. The Chief says, have you had any inkling of this – if so, please send in your report.'

Mr Goon gaped. He didn't know *what* to say. Why, it seemed as if the message Ern had delivered to him from Fatty might have been correct after all then – not a fairy tale. That story about the prince getting away in the pram – and now Fatty's tale about it being a gypsy boy after all! Was it all true?

'PC Goon? Are you still there?' said the voice at the other end impatiently. 'Did you hear me?'

'Yes – oh yes,' panted Goon, feeling suddenly as if he had been running a long way. 'Thanks. Interesting report. I'll – er – think about it – and send in mine shortly.'

'Right. Goodnight,' said the voice, and the telephone clicked off.

For the second time that night, Goon sank down into his chair and put his head in his hands, groaning. Why hadn't he told the Chief all that Ern had told him? Now someone else had got the information, and got in before him. Goon began seriously to wonder if he owned as good brains as he thought himself to have.

First I ring up and tell the Chief about that

dressing-up and Princess Bongawee, which was nonsense, he thought. And then I *don't* tell him about the prince going off in the pram with those babies. That's why those kids were over at the Fair, no doubt about that – trying to trace the babies and their mother.

He sat and brooded for some time. Then he thought of the last thing Fatty had said to him – that he thought the *real* prince was in Raylingham Marshes.

Was that true? Did he really think so? Dare he ring up and tell the Chief that – or would it turn out that there wasn't such a place or something?

Mr Goon began to get into a state. He paced up and down. He clutched his head. He groaned. He'd lose his job over this if he didn't do something special now!

He got down a police map of the district. He looked up Raylingham Marshes. Yes, there was such a place. But was it just marshes and nothing else? Suppose there wasn't even a house there?

'There's only one thing to do,' said Mr Goon, making up his mind. 'I must go and see this place. Let's see, what's the time? There seems to be a station within a mile or two of the place. Is there a train I can catch?'

He looked up the timetable. There was a train, the very last train, in three-quarters of an hour. Mr Goon began to do things in a great hurry.

He took off his uniform and put on ordinary clothes. It wouldn't do to go snooping round a hide out in police uniform. He dragged on a pair of enormous, grey flannel trousers, added a grey jersey with a bright yellow border at the neck and bottom, and a cap. He put on a tweed coat, rather baggy, and then looked at himself in the glass.

Nobody would guess I was a police officer! he thought. Talk about disguises! Well, I can do a bit of that too. I'm just a hiker now, that's all. I'll put a few things in a kit-bag to make meself seem real.

He caught the train by the skin of his teeth. It arrived on time at the station near to Raylingham Marshes – Raylingham Station – a sleepy little place with one man who was porter, ticket clerk and everything.

He seemed surprised to see Mr Goon on the last train. 'Did you want to get out here, mate?' he asked.

'I did,' said Mr Goon. 'Er, I'm a hiker, you see.

I'm – er – seeing the countryside.'

'Well, don't you go hiking over them marshes in the dark,' said the porter, puzzled.

'Are there any houses in the marshes?' asked Goon.

'Not many,' said the porter. 'Two, that's all. One's a farm, on high ground, and the other's a big house. Belongs to foreigners, so people says.'

Aha! thought Goon. That's the house I want. I'll get there somehow, and snoop round. I might find the prince. I might even rescue him.

Wonderful pictures of himself carrying the prince on his back across dangerous marshes came into Mr Goon's mind. Even more wonderful pictures came after that – photographs of himself and the prince in the papers. Headlines – 'Brave Constable Rescues Kidnapped Prince'.

Mr Goon left the dimly-lit station and stepped out into the darkness. There was a lane outside the exit. He would follow that – very, very cautiously. It must lead somewhere!

The porter watched him go. 'Funny chap,' he said to himself. 'Mad as a hatter! Hiking over the marshes in the middle of the night. The police ought to be told about *him* – ought to keep an eye on him, they ought!'

But nobody kept an eye on the brave and valiant Mr Goon. He was quite, quite alone.

22. DISAPPEARANCE OF
MR GOON

Fatty had done nothing that night except to look up the map to find Raylingham Marshes, if there *was* such a place. There was, as Goon had already found. Fatty examined the map closely.

I believe I could get into the marshes from this bit of high ground here, he thought. There's a path or something marked there. Two buildings marked as well – one at one end of the marsh, one in the middle. There's a station too. Well, I certainly won't go by train – much too conspicuous.

He decided to go to bed and sleep on the whole idea. He would tell the others about it in the morning. He was much too tired to do any more 'gallivanting' about that night and, anyway, he wasn't going to lose himself in unknown marshes in pitch darkness!

The telephone rang while he was eating his breakfast next morning. The maid answered it and came into the room.

'Frederick, it's for you,' she said. 'Chief Inspector Jenks on the telephone.'

Fatty jumped. His father looked at him at once. 'You haven't been getting into any trouble, Frederick, I hope,' he said.

'I don't think so,' said Fatty and disappeared hurriedly into the hall, wondering what in the world the Chief wanted at this time of the morning.

'Frederick? Is that you?' came the Chief's crisp voice. 'Listen – Goon's disappeared. Do you know anything about it?'

'Gosh!' said Fatty, startled. 'No, I don't, sir. I saw him late last night. He – er – found my bicycle for me after I had – er – reported it gone. He certainly didn't make me think he was going to disappear.'

'Well, he has,' said the Chief Inspector, sounding annoyed. 'He didn't answer his telephone this morning and when I sent a man over, he reported that Goon was gone – not in his uniform either.'

'Don't say *he's* disappeared in his pyjamas too – like the prince!' said Fatty, still more startled.

'I don't know,' said the Chief. 'Nobody would kidnap Goon, I should imagine – not out of his own house! It's most extraordinary. You are sure you don't know anything about it, Frederick? You usually seem to know a good deal more than most people.'

'No, sir. Honestly, I didn't know he had gone – or was meaning to go anywhere,' said Fatty, very puzzled. 'I can't make it out.'

'Well, I can't stop for more now,' said the Chief. 'Ring me if you have any ideas. Good-bye.'

And before Fatty could ask him or tell him anything more, the telephone went dead. Fatty stared down at it. He was most surprised at this news.

Goon disappeared! He must have gone after I left him. It was dark then, and he was in his uniform. He must have undressed. Gosh, don't say he's gone in his pyjamas too – this is all very peculiar! Fatty quite forgot that he hadn't finished his breakfast, and went out to get his bicycle to ride round to Larry's.

Larry was surprised to see him so early. 'No time to talk much now,' said Fatty. 'Come round to Pip's, you and Daisy. There's a lot of news.'

There certainly was! The others drank in all Fatty had to say about the boy in the caravan the night before, and what he had told Fatty.

'So you see, Sid was quite right when he told us about the boy who was hiding in the pram,' said Fatty. 'And now we know why he hid – and why he pretended to be the prince, and everything.'

'But we don't know where he's been hidden – the real prince, I mean,' said Pip.

'Well, I may even know that,' said Fatty, and he told them what the boy had said. 'He said his uncle, Old Man Tallery, was in Raylingham Marshes,' he went on, 'and as he was mixed up in the kidnapping, and produced his nephew, Rollo, to impersonate the real prince, it's very likely that the prince is there too. There's probably a good hide out there, in those marshes.'

'You did awfully well last night,' said Pip. 'What time did you get back?'

'Late-ish, in the dark,' said Fatty. 'And I hadn't a lamp on my bike – and what do you think! I was caught by Mr Goon!'

'Gracious!' said Bets, alarmed. 'Did he go round and complain to your parents?'

'Of course not. He didn't know it was me. You forget, I was disguised as a tramp,' grinned Fatty, and then told them how Mr Goon had taken his bicycle and how he, Fatty, had got it back again. The others roared with laughter.

'No one will *ever* get the better of you, Fatty,' said Daisy, with the utmost conviction. 'Any more news? What a lot you've got.'

'Yes. I've kept the spiciest bit till last,' said Fatty. 'Mr Goon has disappeared! Nowhere to be found this morning, so the Chief Inspector says – and, he's left his uniform behind. Where, oh where, can he be?'

Nobody knew. They were all astounded at this last bit of news. 'Another spot of kidnapping, do you think?' asked Larry.

'I don't know *what* to think,' said Fatty. 'He certainly didn't appear to have any plans for going anywhere last night when I went to fetch my bike.'

'Of course, if you'd mentioned Raylingham Marshes to him, I would have thought he might be there,' said Bets. 'Just to get in before *you*, Fatty. But he wouldn't know, of course.'

Fatty sat up straight. 'Bets, you're a marvel!' he

said. 'Hit the nail on the head, as usual. I *did* tell him the place, of course – but what with one thing and another, I'd forgotten I'd mentioned it to him. That's where he is!'

'Do you think so *really*?' asked Bets, her face glowing at Fatty's praise.

'Of course,' said Fatty. 'But goodness knows what has happened to him. Got a timetable, Pip? He wouldn't bike all that way, and the buses wouldn't be going at that time of night. But there might be a train.'

There was, of course. 'That's what he did!' said Fatty, jubilantly. 'As soon as I'd gone, he must have got out of his uniform and put on his ordinary clothes and rushed out and caught that train – and gone hunting for the prince in Raylingham Marshes!'

'Without saying a word to anyone!' said Pip. 'What a man!'

'What are *we* going to do about it?' asked Daisy. 'Anything?'

Fatty considered. 'I don't think I'll tell this idea to the Chief. He wouldn't want to send a posse of men searching marshes for Mr Goon unless he was dead certain he was there. We'll go ourselves!'

'What! All of us?' cried Bets, joyfully.

'All of us,' said Fatty.

'And Ern too?' asked Bets, pointing down the drive. Everyone looked and groaned. Ern was coming up the drive – by himself, fortunately.

'Well, I suppose Ern may as well come too,' said Fatty. 'The more the merrier. We'll be a company of kids out walking – looking for unusual marsh flowers and marsh birds.'

'I'll look for the Marsh Goonflower,' said Bets with a giggle. 'And you can look for the Clear-Orf Bird, Pip.'

'Hello, hello, hello!' said Ern, appearing round the hedge. 'How's things? Any news?'

'Yes, a lot,' said Bets. 'But we can't stop to tell you now, Ern.'

'Spitty,' said Ern, looking disappointed. 'What's the hurry?'

'You can come with us if you like and we'll tell you on the way,' said Fatty. 'I hope you haven't got Sid and Perce parked outside the front gate, Ern, because we are *not* going to take them too.'

'I'm alone,' said Ern. 'Perce has gone to buy

some more rope for the tent – it flopped down on us last night. And Sid's gone to buy nougat.'

'*Nougat*!' said everyone astonished. 'But why not toffee?'

'Sid seems to have gone off toffee all of a sudden, like,' said Ern. 'Funny. He's never done that before.'

'Well, nougat is almost worse – so gooey,' said Bets. 'Spitty!'

'Now don't you catch Ern's disease,' said Pip. Ern looked startled.

'What disease?' he asked. 'I haven't got no spots nor anything.'

'We haven't any time to waste,' said Fatty. 'We'll go and buy sandwiches and buns and drinks down in the village. There won't be time to prepare food ourselves. We'll take the bus to the east side of the marshes and then walk.'

They left their bicycles at Pip's and went to buy their food. Soon they were on the bus to Raylingham. Fatty forbade them to talk about anything to do with the mystery. 'Someone might be on the bus that knows something about it,' he said. 'We don't want to give any information away.'

They got out of the bus at the edge of the marshes. They had talked so loudly about flowers and birds all the way that the conductor felt sure they wanted to search the marshes for them.

'You'll be all right so long as you keep to the paths,' he told them. 'See that one there? That leads right to the centre of the marsh. You'll notice other paths going off here and there, but be careful not to choose too narrow a one.'

Off they all went. Was Mr Goon somewhere there? Surely he hadn't fallen into the marsh in the middle of the night, and sunk down and down?

'Till his head's just above the surface of the marsh!' said Bets, with a shiver. 'Only his helmet showing.'

'He's not wearing his helmet,' said Fatty. 'Cheer up. It would take a long, long time for an enormous weight like Mr Goon to sink down and down and down! This is not a terribly *marshy* marsh – not in the middle of summer at any rate!'

But when Pip slipped off the path once, he soon found himself up to the knees in muddy water! He didn't like it at all, and got hastily back on to the path.

'I shan't go looking for Goonflowers just here!' he said. 'I don't feel they'd grow very well!'

23. THINGS BEGIN TO HAPPEN

The marsh was a strange place. It was intensely green and it was also full of the most irritating flies. Ern nearly went mad with them, and the others nearly went mad with Ern's continual slapping and grumbling!

'Look – there's a house or something over there,' said Fatty, suddenly. 'On that high ground, see – where there are trees.'

'How nice to see trees again,' said Daisy. 'I was almost beginning to forget what they looked like. Ern, stop slapping about. You keep making me jump, and it's too hot for that.'

'Let's take this little path,' said Fatty, stopping where a narrow path curved off the main one they were following. 'It seems to go round the back of that copse of trees – it looks almost a wood really – and we could reconnoitre without being seen.'

'What's "reconnoitre",' said Bets at once.

'Spy round – have a snoop,' said Fatty. 'If Raylingham Marshes *is* a hide out for Old Man Tallery and the prince and his kidnappers, we don't want to be caught.'

But they *were* caught! They stole down the narrow little path that skirted the copse, looking carefully down at their feet to make sure they were going to tread safely, when two men rose up from beside a turn in the path. They had been lying behind great tufts of rushes, and couldn't possibly be seen.

The children stopped, alarmed and shocked at such a sudden, silent appearance. The men looked quite ordinary country men, though both had very dark eyes, and a rather odd accent when they spoke.

'Hello,' said Fatty, recovering. 'You startled us!'

'Why do you come through this dangerous marsh?' asked one man. 'It is not fit for children.'

'Oh, we're on a walk,' said Fatty. 'A nature walk. We're not trespassing, you know – this marsh is common ground.'

'But you *are* trespassing,' said the other man, and his dark eyes snapped at Fatty. 'This land belongs to that farm over there. See it?'

'Yes,' said Fatty. 'Well, we're doing no harm.

Now we've come so far, we'll go right on to the other side.'

'Not this way,' said the first man, and he planted himself in Fatty's way. 'You can go back to the main path. I've told you, you are trespassing.'

'What's up that we can't go this way?' said Fatty, impatiently. 'Anyone would think you had something to hide!'

'I say – look!' said Larry suddenly, and he pointed up into the sky. 'What's that? A helicopter, surely! Gosh, it's not coming down into the marsh, is it? It will sink!'

One man said something savage to the other in a foreign language. Both glanced up at the hovering helicopter. Then the first one pushed Fatty firmly back.

'I'm having no nonsense,' he said. 'You'll do as you're told, all you kids. Go back to the main path and, if you're wise, keep away from this marsh, see?'

Fatty stumbled and almost fell into the water on one side of the path. Ern, angry that anyone should have dared to touch his beloved Fatty, gave the man a violent push too. He lost his balance and went headlong into the marsh!

'Shut up, Ern,' said Fatty angrily. 'What's the sense of doing that? We shall only get into trouble! Turn back, all of you, and go to the main path!'

The man who had fallen into the marsh was extremely angry. He clambered out, calling orders to the other man, still in a foreign language.

'You can come along with us,' said the second man to Fatty, grimly. 'You hear? Walk in front of us on this narrow path. We'll show you that we mean what we say when we tell you you are trespassing!'

The helicopter was still hovering over their heads. The men suddenly seemed in a great hurry. They made the children squeeze by them on the narrow path till all of them were in front. Then they made them march ahead quickly.

Nobody said anything. Fatty was thinking hard. That helicopter was about to land. Where? There must be some small landing-place cleared for it somewhere near. Who was it going to take away? The prince? Then he hadn't yet been spirited away. Those men had been on the watch for anyone coming through the marsh that day – something was going on, that was clear.

In silence, the two men hurried the children

along. Bets was frightened and kept close to Fatty. Ern was scared too, and forgot all about slapping at the flies. And all the time, the helicopter hovered about overhead, evidently waiting for some signal to land.

Round a corner, they came into a big farmyard. Pigs were in a sty, and hens wandered about. It looked very homely and countrified all of a sudden. Ducks quacked in a pond, and a horse lifted its head from a trough where it had been drinking, and stared at the little company.

A very big farmhouse lay back from the yard. Its tall chimneys showed that it was old – probably built in Elizabethan times. There was a small door in the wall of the farmhouse not far from them. The men hurried the children over to it, opened it, and shoved them all in, giving them a push if they thought anyone was not quick enough.

Down a long passage – up some narrow, curving stairs, along another passage, with wooden boards that were very old and uneven. The passage was dark, and Bets didn't like it at all. She slipped her hand into Fatty's and he squeezed it hard.

They came to a door. The man in front opened

it. 'In here,' he said, and in they all went. Fatty put his foot in the doorway just as the man was about to shut them in.

'What are you doing this for?' he asked. 'You know you'll get into trouble, don't you? We're only kids out on a walk. What's the mystery?'

'You'll be kept here for a day or two,' said the man. 'There are reasons. You came at an unfortunate time for yourselves. Be sensible and nothing will happen to you.'

He kicked Fatty's foot away suddenly and slammed the door. The six children heard the key turning in the lock. Then they heard the footsteps of the two men as they hurried away down the passage.

Fatty looked desperately round the room. It was small and dark, lined with oak panels. There was one small window, with leaded panes. He ran to it and peered out. A sheer drop to the ground! Nobody could climb out there with safety.

'Fatty! What's all this about?' said Ern, in a frightened voice. 'Sawful!'

'Shall I tell you what I think?' said Fatty, in a low voice. 'I think Prince Bongawah was taken here and hidden, when he was kidnapped from his car. And I think he's been kept prisoner here till arrangements could be made to spirit him away somehow – and that's what that helicopter is arriving for! It will land somewhere here, the prince will be hurried aboard – and nobody will ever hear of him again!'

Bets shivered. 'I don't like you saying that,' she said. 'Fatty, what are we going to do? Do you think they'll hurt us?'

'No,' said Fatty. 'I think we're a nuisance, but I think they really do believe we're only six kids out hiking. They've no idea we're hunting for old Mr Goon, or that we know anything is going on here.'

'But what are we going to *do*?' said Bets again. 'I don't like this place. I want to get out.'

'I can hear the helicopter again,' said Pip. 'It sounds nearer. It must be coming down.'

'Do you suppose Mr Goon is a prisoner too?' said Larry. 'We haven't seen or heard a sign of him. Perhaps he didn't come to Raylingham Marshes after all.'

'Perhaps he didn't,' said Fatty. He went over to the door and tried it. It was locked. He looked at the door. It was old but very stout and strong.

Nobody could possibly break it down!

'Do your trick of getting out through a locked door, Fatty,' said Daisy suddenly. 'There's a good space under the door – I believe you could manage it beautifully.'

'That's just what I was thinking,' said Fatty. 'The only thing is, I need a newspaper – or some big sheet of paper – and I haven't brought a newspaper with me today. Very careless of me!'

'I've got a comic,' said Ern unexpectedly. 'Would that do? What you going to do, Fatty?'

'Get through this locked door,' said Fatty, much to Ern's amazement. Ern fished in his pocket and brought out a crumpled and messy comic, which he handed to Fatty.

'Good work,' said Fatty, pleased. He took the comic and opened out the middle double sheet. He slid it carefully under the door, leaving only a small corner his side. Ern watched, puzzled. How was that going to open a locked door?

Fatty took a small leather case from his pocket and opened it. In it were a number of curious small tools, and a little roll of wire. Fatty took out the wire and straightened it.

He inserted it into the keyhole and began delicately to work at the key. He prodded and pushed and jiggled it – until, suddenly, he gave a sharp push and the key slid out of the keyhole on the other side of the door, and fell with a thud down to the floor.

Ern stared open-mouthed. He couldn't for the life of him make out what Fatty was doing. But the others knew. They had seen Fatty doing his locked door trick before!

'Hope it's fallen onto the paper,' said Fatty, and bent down to draw the sheet of paper back under the bottom of the door. Carefully he pulled it, very carefully. More and more of the comic appeared and, oh joy, at last the key appeared too under the door, on the second half of the double-sheet! There it was, on their side of the door. Fatty had managed to get it!

Ern gasped. His eyes almost fell out of his head. 'Coo – you are a one!' he said to Fatty. 'You're a genius, that's what you are.'

'Be quiet, Ern,' said Fatty. He slid the key into the lock on his side of the door and turned it. The door unlocked. Now they could all go free!

24. FATTY DOES SOME GOOD WORK

'Listen,' said Fatty, in a low voice. 'I don't think we'd all better go out. There's such a crowd of us, we'd be sure to be spotted. What I propose to do is this – get out by myself and have a really good look round. If there's a telephone, I shall immediately use that to get on to the Chief Inspector, and warn him to send men here at once.'

'Ooooh, *yes*!' said Bets, delighted at the idea of rescue.

'Then I shall snoop round to see if I can find the prince – though I'm afraid I won't be in time to stop the helicopter from going off with him, if they mean to take off again at once,' said Fatty.

'What about Mr Goon?' asked Larry. 'Will you look for him?'

'Well, I'll certainly keep a look out for him,' said Fatty. 'But, at the moment, the most important thing is to get in touch with the Chief, and also see if I can hold up the prince's flight. Now all you have to do is to keep quiet and wait. I'll have to lock you in again, I'm afraid, in case someone comes along and finds the door unlocked. But you know how to get out if you want to, Larry, don't you? – so you'll be all right.'

'Suppose someone comes and sees you're not with us?' said Bets, in sudden alarm.

'I don't expect they'll notice,' said Fatty. 'They haven't counted us, I'm sure! Well – slong!'

'So long!' whispered the others. 'Good luck!'

Fatty disappeared down the passage, after carefully locking the door behind him and leaving the key in the lock. He was very cautious. By good chance they had come at a most important moment, and Fatty did not mean to throw his chance away!

The telephone! That was the most essential thing for him to find. Where would it be? Downstairs, of course. In the hall, probably, which would make it very awkward indeed to talk into. He would certainly be heard.

A thought struck Fatty. Sometimes people had a telephone in their bedroom. His mother had, for instance, so that if she happened to have a cold, she could still telephone her orders to the shops, or talk to her friends.

There *might* be one in a bedroom. Fatty decided to look. It would make things so much easier if there were.

He peeped into first one room and then another. Two of them were most luxuriously furnished, considering this was a farmhouse. Fatty stood at the door of one, his sharp eyes looking all round.

Then his face brightened. A telephone in pale green stood beside the big green-covered bed at one side of the room! Gosh! Could he possibly get to it and telephone unheard? He tiptoed across the room, first shutting the door quietly behind him. He took up the whole telephone, and crept under the bed with it, hoping that his voice would be muffled there.

He lifted the receiver and put it to his ear, his heart beating fast. Would the operator answer?

With great relief he heard a voice speaking. 'Number please.'

Fatty gave the number in a low voice. 'It's the Chief Inspector's number,' he said urgently.

'Put me through quickly, will you?'

In under half a minute, another voice spoke. 'Police station here.'

'This is Frederick Trotteville speaking,' said Fatty, keeping his voice low. 'I want the Chief Inspector at once.'

There was a pause. Then came the Chief Inspector's voice and Fatty's heart lifted in joy.

'Frederick? What is it?'

'Listen,' said Fatty. 'I'm at the farmhouse in the middle of Raylingham Marshes. I'm pretty certain the kidnapped prince is here too. There's a helicopter hovering about, and I think maybe we've come at an important moment – when the prince is about to be spirited away. We're prisoners, sir, but I managed to get to a telephone. We're all here, Ern too. Can you send men along?'

There was an astounded silence. Fatty could picture the Chief's astonished face. Then his crisp voice came over the wires. 'Yes. I'll send some. Hang on till we come – and see if you can stop the prince from being taken away! If anyone can, *you* can, Frederick! Good work!'

The telephone went dead. Fatty replaced his

receiver with a sigh of thankfulness. Help would come sooner or later. Now he was free to do a bit of prowling round and see what he could find. If only he could find out where the prince was!

Fatty crawled out cautiously from beneath the bed and replaced the telephone on its little table. He tiptoed to the door. All was quiet. He opened it silently and peered out into the passage. No one was in sight.

Better look for a locked door, thought Fatty. That's the only bright idea I've got at the moment. Let's think now – the farmhouse had two wings to it and I'm in the middle. We must have been locked up in one wing. Maybe the prince is in the other.

He leaned carefully out of a window to have a look at where the other wing of the house stood out. He at once noticed a barred window. Ah, surely that would be the room!

He drew in his head, and made his way down the passage. Was there any way of reaching the other wing except by the stairs and the hall? There might be.

Fatty came to the head of the stairs. Down below he could hear the murmur of voices coming from some room – and then his eye caught sight of something through the landing window.

It was the helicopter! With its vanes whirring, it was slowly descending! Fatty watched it disappear behind a big barn-like building. There must be a landing-place there. He frowned. There was no time to lose now. The prince might be hurried off immediately!

He went to the back of the landing and found a tiny, narrow passage there. Perhaps it ran to the other wing! He followed it carefully and quietly and, as he had thought, it did run to the other wing of the house.

Now to find the locked room with barred windows! thought Fatty jubilantly, and then shrank back in fright as he heard the sound of a door being shut and locked, and a man's voice saying something loudly.

Fatty crouched behind a curtain covering a window, hardly daring to breathe. Footsteps passed by him, and went on to the big landing where the stairs were. When all the sounds had gone, Fatty came out again. He tiptoed quickly along the passage, passed two open doors – and then came to a shut one!

It was locked! But, fortunately, the key had been left in the lock. Fatty turned it, opened the door, and looked in.

A dark-faced boy with a sulky, scowling expression looked up. He was about Pip's size, and in build and colouring was very like Rollo, the gypsy boy.

'Are you Prince Bongawah?' whispered Fatty. The boy nodded, staring in astonishment at this big boy in the doorway.

'Come on then – I've come to save you,' whispered Fatty. 'Hurry up.'

The boy ran to the door and began to jabber in a foreign language.

'Shut up!' said Fatty urgently. 'Do you want to bring everyone up here! Come with me and don't make a sound!'

The boy followed him, suddenly silent. Fatty locked the door behind him. Then, very cautiously indeed, his heart thumping hard against his ribs, he led the boy down the narrow passage, across the landing where the stairs were, and along the passage that led to the other wing.

He unlocked the door where the others were

and pushed the boy inside. Everyone stared in astonishment at Fatty's grinning face and this newcomer, so dark and foreign-looking.

'I've found the prince,' said Fatty jubilantly. 'And I thought the safest place to hide him would be here. He can get into that cupboard. Nobody would dream of looking for him in a room where *we* are supposed to be prisoners!'

'Oh, Fatty – you're full of good ideas!' said Bets. 'Poor prince! He must wonder what's happening.'

The prince spoke beautiful English, and gave them all a little bow.

'I have been a prisoner for many days,' he said. 'I have been unhappy and afraid. You are my friends?'

'Oh yes,' said Bets, warmly. 'Of course we are. You'll be safe now Fatty has got you!'

'I found a telephone and got a message through to the Chief,' said Fatty, unable to stop grinning. 'Golly, what a surprise for this lot when they find the police coming through the marsh and surrounding the farmhouse!'

'Honestly, you're a genius Fatty,' said the admiring Ern. 'I think you ought to be made a Chief Inspector at once, I do!'

'Did you find Mr Goon?' asked Daisy.

Fatty shook his head. 'No – didn't see or hear a sign of him. I'm beginning to wonder if he came here after all.'

'Well, it's a good thing we *thought* he did!' said Bets, 'or we shouldn't have come ourselves! And then we'd have missed all this!'

'Did you see the helicopter come down?' asked Daisy. 'We suddenly saw it landing behind that big barn.'

'Yes, so did . . .' began Fatty, and then stopped speaking and listened. The others listened too.

They could hear shouts – and banging doors and running feet! What was up?

'They've discovered that the prince isn't in his room!' said Fatty, beaming. 'What a shock for them! *Now* there'll be a rumpus! Helicopter all ready to take him off – and no prince to be found! Get into that cupboard, Prince, and keep quiet. Don't make a sound.'

The prince disappeared into the cupboard in double-quick time. Bets shut the door on him. In silence, they listened to the excitement going on elsewhere.

Then footsteps came hurrying down their passage, sounding loudly on the wooden boards. Their door was suddenly flung open.

A swarthy-faced man looked in, his eyes blazing. 'He might be here!' he shouted. 'These kids may have got him with them somehow. Search the room!'

25. A VERY EXCITING FINISH

That was a real shock to everyone! Bets went pale. Only Fatty didn't turn a hair.

'What's up?' he said. 'Who do you think we've got here? You shut six of us up, goodness knows why, and there are six still here!'

The man shouted something at Fatty in such a savage voice that Fatty decided not to say anything more. Three other men crowded into the room and began to look everywhere. In less than a minute the cupboard was opened – and the prince was discovered!

The swarthy-faced man pounced on him and shook him! He screamed something at him in a foreign language and the boy cowered in fright. He was dragged out into the passage. Fatty followed, protesting.

'I say, look here! I say, you know . . .'

The dark-faced man turned on him, his hand

lifted – but before he could strike Fatty, a loud voice shouted down the passage.

'The police! The POLICE are coming! Tom's just seen them coming over the marsh. Someone's split on us!'

Then there was such a babel of noise and excitement that it was impossible for anyone to be heard. Fatty took the opportunity of pulling the prince back into the room, pushing all the other children in too, slipping the key from the outside of the door to the inside – and locking them all in!

As he turned the key, he grinned round at the six frightened faces. 'Cheer up! No one can get at us! We're locked in again but the key's our side all right!'

Bets was crying. 'Oh Fatty, I didn't like that man. Are we safe now? Can they break the door down?'

'They won't bother to try,' said Fatty. 'They'll be too anxious to save their own skins! We can just sit here and listen to the fun – and come out when everything is quiet!'

'There goes the helicopter again!' said Pip suddenly, and sure enough it was rising quickly over the barn. Evidently it had been warned to go.

'But it didn't take *me* with it,' said the prince exultantly, and went off into a stream of what sounded like gibberish to the children.

Not much of the excitement could be seen from the window. Two policemen suddenly appeared and made a rush for the house. One man suddenly ran helter-skelter across the farmyard and disappeared, followed immediately by a burly policeman. Yells and shouts and thumps and crashes could be heard every now and again.

'I'm rather sorry to be out of the fun,' said Fatty regretfully.

'Well, I'm not,' said Ern, who was looking extremely scared. 'Fun! Not my idea of fun. Sterrible!'

After about half an hour, silence reigned. Had all the men been rounded up? Fatty and the others listened. Then they heard a most stentorian voice.

'FREDERICK! WHERE ARE YOU? FREDERICK!'

'The Chief Inspector!' said Fatty thankfully, and ran to unlock the door and open it. He too yelled at the top of his voice.

'HERE, SIR! WE'RE ALL SAFE AND SOUND!'

He turned back to the others. 'Come on,' he

said, 'it must be safe now. Come on, Ern. Your legs too wobbly to walk?'

'Bit,' said poor Ern, staggering after the others.

The Chief Inspector met them all at the top of the stairs. He ran a swift eye over the lot. 'All of you here?' he said. 'Who's this?' He pointed to the prince.

'Prince Bongawah, sir,' said Fatty. 'I got him all right. Did you catch everyone, sir?'

'I think so,' said the Chief Inspector. He pulled the prince to him. 'You all right?' he said. 'They didn't do anything to you, did they?'

'No, sir,' said the prince. 'It was my uncle who kidnapped me. I was . . .'

'We'll hear your story later, son,' said the Chief Inspector. 'Well, Frederick, that was a spot of good work on your part. Though how in the world you managed to smell out this place – and get here on your own – and find the prince – and telephone me in the middle of everything, I don't know! And taking the whole of the Find-Outers with you too – except Buster. Where is he?'

'Had to leave him behind, sir,' said Fatty regretfully. 'I was afraid he'd fall into the marsh and drown. Pity he's out of the fun though. He does love a scrap.'

'We've got some police cars on the edge of the marsh,' said the Chief Inspector. 'At present, two of them are taking some of the men to the police station but they'll be back soon, and then I'll take you home.'

'Let's have a wander round the place then, sir,' said Fatty. 'It seems odd to have a farm in the middle of a marsh.'

They all went thankfully into the open air. A frightened woman peeped from a doorway at them.

'Who's she?' asked Fatty, surprised.

'The housekeeper', said the Chief Inspector. 'We left her for the present, as someone's got to feed the hens and the pigs and ducks.'

They wandered round the farmyard and then round to the back of the big barn, behind which the helicopter had landed. A big flat space had been cleared there for the landing.

They looked at the cleared space and then walked round it to a group of sheds nearby. They talked cheerfully as they went, all of them feeling very happy to think that everything was over.

A sudden noise made them stop. 'What was that?' said Larry. 'It sounded as if it came from that shed. Is there some animal locked in there? A bull perhaps?'

The noise came again – a loud banging noise, then a series of thuds. The door of the shed shook.

'Better look out,' said the Chief Inspector. 'Sounds rather like a bull in a temper.'

Snorts and groans and yells came next. 'It isn't a bull,' said Fatty. 'Sounds like a mixture of a man and a bull! I'll look and see – through a window, not through a door!'

The window of the shed was very high up. Fatty ran a ladder up against the wall of the shed, went up it and peered through the window. He came down again, grinning.

'Friend of yours, sir,' he said cheerfully, and unbolted the door from the outside. It burst open and out came a big, dirty, perspiring, maddened creature, his fists up, and hair standing on end.

'*Goon!*' said the Chief Inspector, almost falling backwards in his amazement. 'GOON! What on earth – is it *really* you? GOON!'

Yes, it was Mr Goon, and a sorry sight he looked.

e was filthy dirty, very angry, and looked as if he ad been sitting down in all the messes he could. traw was caught in his up-standing hair, and he anted like a dog. He stared in astonishment at the ttle company before him, and quietened down at nce when he saw the Chief Inspector.

'Morning, sir,' said poor Goon, trying to flatten own his hair.

'Where did you disappear to without leaving any essage as to your whereabouts?' asked the Chief nspector. 'We've been hunting for you everywhere.'

'I – er – got a hunch that something might be ing on here,' said Mr Goon, still sounding out of reath. 'Caught the last train, sir, and somehow I t lost in these here marshes. I found myself nking down, and I yelled for all I was worth.'

'Oh, Mr Goon! How dreadful for you!' said nd-hearted Bets. 'Did someone rescue you?'

'Rescue me!' snorted Goon, sounding rather like bull again. 'Yes, they pulled me out all right – and shed me into that cowshed and bolted me in! hat for? They should all be arrested, sir! ishandling the police! Punching me in the back!'

'Don't worry, we *have* arrested them all,' said

the Chief Inspector. 'You missed that bit of fun.'

'Coo, Uncle – you don't half look funny,' sai Ern suddenly, and went off into a loud guffaw. H uncle appeared to see him for the first time.

'ERN! You here too! What you doing her mixed up in all this?' shouted Goon. 'I'll teach yo to laugh at me!'

'Behave yourself, Ern,' said Fatty, severely. H felt sorry for poor Mr Goon. What a hash he ha made of everything – and yet he, Fatty, had give him all the information he could!

'It was jolly brainy of Mr Goon to come here, si wasn't it?' he said innocently to the Chi Inspector. 'I mean, he got here even before we di It was just bad luck he fell in the marsh. He mig have cleared the whole job up himself if he hadr done that.'

Mr Goon looked gratified. He also felt sudden very kindly towards Fatty. He wasn't such a toad a boy, after all!

The Chief Inspector looked at Fatty. 'Brains a good, courage is excellent, resourcefulness is rar he said, 'but generosity crowns everythin Frederick. One of these days, I'll be proud of you

Fatty actually blushed. Mr Goon had heard all this, but hadn't understood what the Chief Inspector meant at all. He came towards them, brushing down his clothes.

'So, it's all over, is it?' he said. 'What happened, sir?'

'You'd better go and wash,' said the Chief Inspector, looking at him. 'You've no idea what you look like, Goon. And if you've been shut up all night, you'll be hungry and thirsty. Ask the woman at the farmhouse for something to eat and drink.'

'I could certainly do with something,' said Mr Goon. 'You'll call me when you want me, sir?'

'I will,' said the Chief Inspector. 'We're just waiting for the police cars to come back.'

'Slong, Uncle,' called Ern, but his uncle did not deign to reply. He disappeared in the direction of the farmhouse – an ungainly, peculiar-looking figure, but not at all downcast. Hadn't he got there before that boy, anyhow? And hadn't that boy admitted it? Things weren't so bad after all!

'It was a peculiar sort of mystery this time,' said Bets, hanging on to the Chief Inspector's arm. At first, there didn't seem to be any clues or anything – nothing we could get hold of – and then it suddenly boiled up, and exploded all over us!'

Everyone laughed. 'Bets quite enjoyed this mystery,' said Fatty. 'Didn't you, Bets? I did too.'

'So did I,' said Ern, thoroughly agreeing. 'Not half! Spitty young Sid and Perce weren't in at the finish.'

'Yes. SPITTY!' agreed everyone, chuckling, and the Chief Inspector smiled.

'Well, let me see – when do you have your next holidays?' he said. 'At Christmas time? Right. Here's to the next mystery then – and may it all end as well as this!'

the
MYSTERY
of the
STRANGE
BUNDLE

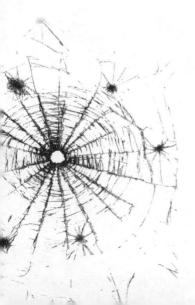

Enid Blyton

The
MYSTERY
of the
STRANGE
BUNDLE

EGMONT

First published in Great Britain 1952
by Methuen & Co Ltd.

Enid Blyton ® Blyton's Mystery & Adventure ®
Text Copyright © 1952 Chorion Rights Limited
All rights reserved
Cover photography © 2010 Martin Usborne
Images: Shutterstock

A CIP catalogue record for this title
is available from the British Library

CONTENTS

CONTENTS

1. BETS GOES SHOPPING

'Of all the miserable holidays, these just about beat the lot!' said Pip to Bets. 'Why you had to start us off on this awful flu, I can't imagine!'

Bets looked hurt. 'Well, I couldn't help it,' she said. 'Someone gave it to me before I gave it to you others. It was really bad luck that it happened at Christmas.'

Pip blew his nose violently. He was sitting up in bed, feeling decidedly better but very bad-tempered.

'*You* get it as soon as the Christmas hols begin – and you get it lighter than anyone! Then you give it to Daisy, and she gives it to Larry, and they have it all through Christmas, poor things. And then *I* get it, and poor old Fatty. What a mess-up of the Christmas hols! Hardly any left of them now!'

Pip sounded very cross indeed. Bets got up. 'All right. If you're going to be such a crosspatch,

I won't sit with you this morning. I'll go and see Fatty. I think you're very unkind, Pip, after all the games I've played with you and the books I've read you.'

She was just stalking out with her head in the air, looking very high and mighty, when Pip called to her.

'Hey, Bets – tell Fatty I'm feeling better, and ask him to get on the track of some mystery AT ONCE because I feel it's just the kind of tonic I need. And we've only got about ten days of the hols left.'

Bets grinned round at him. 'All right. I'll tell him. But Fatty can't just spin a mystery out of thin air, Pip. I think we'll have to go without one this hols.'

'Fatty can do *anything*,' said Pip, with the utmost conviction. 'I've been lying here for days, and most of the time I've been remembering all the mysteries we've ever solved with old Fatty. I've never had time to do so much thinking before. Old Fatty's a wonder.'

'I knew that without having to do a lot of thinking,' said Bets. 'All his disguises – and the way he works out the clues – and the tricks he's played on Mr Goon.'

'Oh yes!' said Pip, a broad smile on his pale face. 'It makes me feel better even to think of all those fat-headed tricks of Fatty's. For goodness sake, tell Fatty to work on some mystery or other for us – it'll do us all good. Give us some interest in life!'

'I'm going,' said Bets. 'I'll bring a mystery back for you if I can!'

'Bring some peppermints too,' said Pip. 'I've suddenly got a craving for them. No, bring a bagful of bull's-eyes, the hottest you can buy. I could do with about fifty, Bets, to go with this detective book Fatty lent me.'

'You *must* be feeling better!' said Bets. She went out of the room and put on her outdoor things. She took some money out of her moneybox. She meant to buy Fatty something too. Bets had been a very faithful visitor and friend to the rest of the Find-Outers while they had had the flu, and had spent nearly all her Christmas money on them.

She hadn't been able to help feeling guilty about giving everyone the flu and she had tried to make up for it by playing games with the invalids, reading to them, and taking them anything she thought they would like. Fatty had been very touched by the little girl's kindness. He thought the world of Bets.

Bets looked out of the garden door. Should she take her bicycle or not? It was so much quicker on a bike. She decided against it. The roads were slippery that frosty January day.

She walked down to the village and spent a good deal of money on enormous bull's-eye peppermints. Half for Pip and half for Fatty. If Pip had got to the convalescent stage of craving for sweets then presumably Fatty would soon reach it too!

She came out of the shop in time to see Mr Goon, the village policeman, sail slowly down the road on his bicycle, his nose purple with the cold air of the morning.

He saw Bets and put on his brakes too quickly. His bicycle immediately skidded on the slippery surface and Mr Goon found himself sitting down very suddenly in the middle of the road.

'Gah!' he said, glaring at Bets as if it was her fault.

'Oh, Mr Goon – are you hurt?' cried Bets. 'You sat down with such a bump!'

Mr Goon had plenty to sit down on, so he wasn't hurt, only considerably shaken. He got up and brushed down his trousers.

'These here slippery mornings'll be the death of me,' he said, looking at Bets as if she were responsible for the slipperiness. 'I just put my brakes on, see – and down I came! That's all I get for wanting to be polite and to ask after your friends. I did hear they were all down with this here flu.'

'Yes – but they're getting better,' said Bets.

Mr Goon muttered something that sounded like 'What a pity!' He straddled his bicycle again. 'Well, I must say it's been a real change for me not having that nosey-parker of a boy sticking his nose into *my* business all the time he's home for the holidays,' said Mr Goon. 'It's a funny thing how that boy sniffs out anything that's going, and gets you all into it. A good thing he's had to lie up in bed where he's out of mischief. You'll be back at school again in no time – and, for once, you won't have made nuisances of yourselves.'

'You'll get the flu yourself if you talk like that,' said Bets, stung into boldness. She was usually very scared of the policeman, especially if she met him when she was alone. 'Anyway, there's still time for something to crop up – and, if it does, we'll be on the job long before *you* are, Mr Goon!'

And, feeling rather victorious after this unexpected meeting and exchange of talk, Bets marched off with her head in the air.

'If you're seeing that big boy, tell him it's nice to know he's been kept out of mischief for once in a way!' Mr Goon shouted after her. 'I've been having a nice peaceful time, I have, without you five round my feet all the time – to say nothing of that little pest of a dog!'

Bets pretended not to hear. Mr Goon pedalled off, well satisfied. He guessed Bets would repeat everything and he knew Fatty would be mad with him – but before he could make himself a nuisance, he'd be back at school again. Toad of a boy!

Bets went to Fatty's house, let herself in at the garden door, and found Mrs Trotteville, Fatty's mother. Mrs Trotteville was fond of the little girl and smiled at her.

'Well Bets, come to see Frederick again? You really are a faithful friend. I think he must be feeling distinctly better today. I've heard the most peculiar noises coming from his room whenever I go up on the landing!'

'Oh, you don't think he's been sick again, do you?' said Bets, in alarm. 'What sort of noises?'

'Oh, voices and sounds,' said Mrs Trotteville. 'As if he's rehearsing for a play or something. You know what Frederick is like, always up to something.'

Bets nodded. She thought probably Fatty was practising various voices for his different disguises. An old man's voice – a quavering old woman's – a deep, manly voice. Fatty could imitate them all to perfection!

'I'll take you up to his room,' said Mrs Trotteville. 'He's expecting you.'

They went upstairs. Mrs Trotteville gave a sharp knock at Fatty's door.

'Who is it?' said Fatty's voice. 'I've got a visitor, Mummy!'

Mrs Trotteville looked astonished. As far as she knew, no other visitor had arrived that morning. It must have been someone the cook had ushered upstairs. She turned the handle and she and Bets went into the room.

Fatty appeared to be sunk deeply into his pillows, half-asleep. Bets could see his dark, rumpled hair but that was about all. Her heart sank. Yesterday Fatty had been sitting up, looking quite sprightly. He couldn't be feeling so well if he felt more like lying down!

She looked at his visitor. It was a plump, bespectacled woman, with an ugly, pudding-shaped black hat pulled over her forehead. A bright green scarf was wound round her neck, hiding part of her chin. Who on earth was she?

Mrs Trotteville was at a loss too. Who was this strange visitor? She advanced towards her uncertainly.

'Oh – Mrs Trotteville!' said the visitor, in a mincing kind of voice. 'You don't remember me, do you? We met at Bollingham two years ago. *Such* a nice place, isn't it?'

'Er no, I don't think I *do* remember you,' said

Mrs Trotteville, astonished. 'How did you know Frederick was ill, and who brought you up to his room? Really, er – it's kind of you – but . . .'

'Oh, your nice cook brought me up,' chattered the visitor, mopping her face with a large white handkerchief, drenched with some strong scent. 'She said you were busy so she just brought me up herself. Frederick was *so* pleased to see me. And who is this nice little girl?'

Bets was puzzled. She didn't understand this curious visitor. And why didn't Fatty sit up? Why hadn't he spoken to Bets? She looked at the mound his body made under the clothes. He must be asleep!

She poked him hard. 'Fatty! Wake up! You were awake a minute ago, because you spoke to us when we knocked at the door. Sit up and speak to me!'

Fatty took no notice. He just lay there like a log. Mrs Trotteville began to feel alarmed. She, too, went to the bed and touched Fatty.

'Frederick, are you all right? Sit up!'

Bets glanced at the visitor, who had now got up and was looking out of the window, her back to them. Her shoulders were shaking slightly. What WAS the matter? It was very peculiar and mysterious and Bets didn't like it at all.

Mrs Trotteville turned back the covers of the bed. There was no Fatty there! A dark wig had been put over a pudding basin, and bolsters had been laid in the bed. Mrs Trotteville gave a little scream.

'Fatty! Where's Fatty!'

But Bets knew where he was, of course!

2. FATTY'S TWO VISITORS

Bets swung round to the plump woman standing at the window. She ran to her and grabbed her arm. She shook it hard.

'Fatty! Fatty, you terror! You're your own visitor. Oh, *Fatty*!'

The 'visitor' collapsed into a chair. Loud explosions came from her. Yes, it was certainly Fatty all right. There was no mistaking that explosive laughter!

'*Frederick*!' said his mother, amazed and annoyed. 'Are you out of your mind? You're supposed to be in bed. What in the world are you thinking of, getting up and dressing in this ridiculous way? No, it's not funny. I'm vexed. I shall tell the doctor when he comes. Get those clothes off and get back into bed at once.'

'Oh, Mummy, give me a minute to laugh,' gasped Fatty, still collapsed in the chair. 'It was too comic to see you and Bets poking at me to make me speak, and wondering who the visitor was, and trying to be polite to her.' And Fatty went off into great laughs again.

'Well, all I can say is that you must be feeling a lot better if you can get up to such silly antics,' said Mrs Trotteville, still annoyed. 'I suppose such abnormal behaviour must mean that your temperature is normal again. Frederick, get back into bed again at once. No – not with those awful clothes on – where *did* you get them from?'

'Cookie brought them for me from an old aunt of hers,' said Fatty, pulling off the bright green scarf and the awful old hat. 'They're part of my wardrobe of disguises, Mummy. Don't pretend you don't know!'

Mrs Trotteville often had to turn a blind eye on many of Fatty's doings. There was simply no knowing what he would get up to next. She stared at the clothes in disgust.

'That *awful* scent, Frederick. I really can't even *call* it perfume! I shall have to open the window and let out the smell.'

'Yes, do,' said Fatty. 'I can't bear much more of

it myself. Gosh, I did enjoy that. Here, Bets, hang up this long black coat and skirt in my big wardrobe over there.'

He stripped off the coat and skirt, and appeared in his striped pyjamas. Bets took the coat and skirt, and was about to hang them up when Mrs Trotteville took them away from her.

'I really must tell Cook not to unload her aunt's old clothes on to him,' she said.

'Mummy, don't you dare say a word,' said Fatty, in alarm. 'Cook's a marvel. She lets me have her uncle's old things too. I've got to get proper disguises from *somewhere*. You know perfectly well I'm going to be a first class detective as soon as I'm old enough, and you have to begin practising young. Don't you say a word to Cook!'

'Frederick, I am *not* going to have the house full of old garments belonging to Cook's uncle and aunt,' said his mother firmly.

'You needn't,' almost wailed Fatty. 'I usually keep them down in my shed at the bottom of the garden – don't I, Bets? I just wanted to play this visitor trick on Bets, Mummy, that's all – so I got Cook to fetch these things from the shed for me.

Bets can take them down to the shed this very minute if you want her to.'

Fatty was now in bed. He looked beseechingly at Bets and his mother. Mrs Trotteville thought that he had suddenly gone rather pale. All this silly excitement!

'All right, Frederick. We won't say any more,' she said. 'Bets can take the things down when she goes. Put them out on the landing for now, Bets. Frederick, lie down. I'm sure your temperature must be going up again. I certainly won't let you get up for a short while this afternoon if so.'

'Mummy, can Bets stay and have lunch with me?' said Fatty, changing the subject quickly. He fully intended to get up that afternoon! 'Say she can. None of the others are coming to see me today, they're still wobbly. I'd like Bets' company – and you know she's quiet. She'd be very good for me. Wouldn't you, Bets?'

Bets beamed. To spend the day with Fatty would be marvellous. Pip was in the bad-tempered stage and too difficult to get on with amiably at the moment. It would be fun to stay with Fatty! She gazed hopefully at Mrs Trotteville, her arms full of the old clothes.

Mrs Trotteville considered. 'Well, yes, I think if Bets would like to stay, she would probably keep you from doing any further ridiculous things,' she said. 'Would you like to stay, Bets dear? And promise me that you won't let Fatty leap out of bed, or dress up, or play the fool in any way at all?'

'I promise,' said Bets happily. 'Thank you, Mrs Trotteville.'

'I'll telephone your mother and see if it's all right,' said Mrs Trotteville, and disappeared out of the room. Bets beamed again, and Fatty beamed back.

'Good old Bets,' said Fatty, snuggling down in bed. 'Gosh, I nearly burst when you and Mummy kept poking at the bolster in the bed. It wasn't a very good disguise really, but it was the best I could do on the spur of the moment. I feel better today and I was longing for a joke of some kind. I guessed you'd be coming, so I got Cookie to fetch me those things from the shed. She's a pet, is Cookie.'

'You must have been annoyed when your mother came in too!' said Bets. 'Oh, Fatty – it's nice that you're better. Have a peppermint? They're the biggest bull's-eyes I could buy. There's half for you and half for Pip.'

'I must be a lot better,' said Fatty, taking two peppermints and putting them both in his mouth at once. 'I couldn't possibly have even *sniffed* at a bull's-eye yesterday. I shouldn't be a bit surprised if I eat a lot of dinner today.'

'You look awfully pale, Fatty,' said Bets. 'Lie down for a bit. You really shouldn't have got out of bed and dressed up like that.'

'Now don't *you* start lecturing!' said Fatty. 'My legs do feel a bit funny, actually, but it was worth it. Now, spill the news. Have you got any?'

Bets faithfully gave her news. Fatty lay quiet and listened. He was feeling rather faint, but he wasn't going to tell Bets that! He hadn't realised that the effort of getting up and dressing and playing the fool would make him feel so weak. Apparently you couldn't play about with flu too much even if you *were* feeling better!

'Larry and Daisy are much better,' said

Bets. 'They're both up and about now, though they haven't been out yet. Daisy says they'll be out tomorrow if it's sunny. They're extremely bored though, and keep wishing something would happen.'

'How's Pip?' asked Fatty.

'Oh, he's better, except in his temper,' said Bets. 'Don't you go and get bad-tempered too, Fatty, when you're almost better! Oh – and I nearly forgot to tell you – I met Mr Goon this morning!'

'Ah, the great Mr Goon,' said Fatty, half-sitting up at the mention of his old enemy's name. 'And what had *he* to say?'

'Well, he said "Gah" at me, fell off his bicycle, and sat down hard in the road,' said Bets, with a giggle.

'Couldn't be better,' said Fatty, hard-heartedly. 'And what else had he got to say beside "Gah"?'

Bets told him. 'He said he'd had a nice peaceful time without that nosey-parker of a boy interfering all the time,' she said. 'He was really rather rude. He said it was a good thing you were in bed and out of mischief – and you'd be back at school again before you'd time to *do* any!'

'Ha!' said Fatty, sitting up straight now, and looking very determined. 'That's what he thinks, does he? Well, I'll be up properly tomorrow – and out the next day – and Mr Goon had better be on his guard. Things will happen as soon as I'm up!'

'What things?' asked Bets, thrilled. 'A mystery, do you mean? Oh, Fatty!'

'Yes, a mystery – even if I have to make one up myself,' said Fatty. 'If Mr Goon thinks he's *ever* going to have a nice peaceful holiday when we're home, he's wrong. Bets, we'll have some fun when I'm up. Gosh, it makes me feel better again already to think of it.'

'What sort of fun?' asked Bets, her eyes shining. 'Oh Fatty, I wish a real mystery would turn up again – but there isn't time now – we'll all be back at school before we could solve it – if one *did* turn up!'

'Never mind, we'll have some fun with old Mr Goon first,' said Fatty. 'I'll plan it. We'll all be in it. I'll think of something, don't you worry.'

Bets knew he would. There was absolutely no

one like Fatty for thinking up things. He slithered down into bed again and shut his eyes.

'Are you feeling all right?' asked Bets anxiously.

'Gosh, yes – I just got an idea, that's all,' said Fatty. 'You know how ideas come – all in a flash from your imagination – you don't even have to think of them.'

'They don't come to *me* like that,' said Bets. 'I have to think hard before I dig up an idea, and even then it's hardly ever a good one. You're a genius, Fatty!'

'Well,' said Fatty modestly, 'I wouldn't quite say *that*, you know – but I can run rings round most people, can't I? I mean, look how we've solved all those mysteries when I've been on the job, and . . .'

Fatty spent the next ten minutes unashamedly boasting, and Bets listened, unashamedly worshipping the boaster. In fact, they both had a very nice time.

'What's the time?' said Fatty suddenly. 'Surely it *must* be dinnertime, Bets. Have you got any more bull's-eyes for me? I'm starving.'

'I think I can hear dinner coming now,' said

Bets. 'Yes, it's your mother. I'll go and help her with the trays.'

Mrs Trotteville appeared, bearing a tray with two steaming platefuls of soup. Fatty eyed them in disappointment. 'Oh, Mummy! Soup again! When am I going to have a really decent meal? I'll never get better on soup!'

'You said yesterday that you couldn't possibly take even a spoonful of soup!' said his mother putting the tray down. 'Don't worry. There's roast chicken and all the etceteras if you want some.'

'That's better,' said Fatty. 'What's the pudding? Save me two helpings, Mummy.'

Mrs Trotteville laughed. 'Oh, Frederick, you do go to extremes. All right – the doctor says you can eat well now that your temperature is down. Bets, bring the tray down when you want the next course, and don't let Frederick gobble up your soup as well as his!'

3. THAT AFTERNOON

The two ate their soup in a pleasant silence. It was hot and well-flavoured. Fatty took two pieces of toast with it and crunched them up with appetite. He seemed to be hungrier even than Bets!

A distant bark came to their ears. Fatty listened and frowned. 'I do think Mummy might have let me have Buster in today,' he said. 'He'd be good for me.'

'You didn't want him in yesterday,' said Bets, spooning up the last of her soup. 'You said his bark would drive you mad.'

'Did I really?' said Fatty in surprise. 'Fancy me thinking old Buster's bark would ever drive me mad. I think he's got a very nice bark – not too yappy and not too woofy – a proper Scottie bark. I wish you'd ask Mummy if I could have him in here this afternoon, Bets. She might do it if you asked her.'

'All right. I'll ask her,' said Bets, getting up to take the tray. 'But I bet she won't let him get on the bed, Fatty. Do you really want some chicken now? I feel a bit full up already.'

'Yes. And plenty of bread sauce,' said Fatty. 'And some more toast. That soup's made me feel warm and comfortable, but it hasn't done much else. Sure you don't want me to carry the tray for you, Bets?'

'Idiot,' said Bets happily, and walked out with the tray. Mrs Trotteville was surprised to hear that Fatty really wanted chicken. She filled a plate for him and one for Bets. 'The pudding is stewed apple and rice pudding,' she said. 'He said he wanted two helpings, but I'm sure he won't want even one. There – can you manage, Bets?'

Bets arrived in the bedroom with the tray, and put it down by Fatty's bed. He eyed it with satisfaction. 'I'd better get on to that before my appetite fades away,' he said, and began to tuck in. Yes, certainly Fatty was on the mend. Nobody could eat like that if they were feeling at all ill!

He slowed down a bit before he reached the

end of the chicken and vegetables. 'What's the pudding?' he asked Bets.

'Stewed apple and rice,' said Bets. Fatty made a face.

'What a pudding to plan for someone in bed. It's bad enough to be faced with that when you're up and about. I won't have any.'

'I suppose you're pretending you would have had two enormous helpings if it had been treacle pudding?' suggested Bets, slyly. 'You're a fibber, Fatty. You can't eat another thing! Nor can I, as a matter-of-fact. I'll take this tray down now.'

'Don't forget to ask Mummy if Buster can come up this afternoon,' Fatty called to her.

Bets delivered the tray, broke the news about the lack of appetite for apples and rice, and asked about Buster.

'Well,' said Mrs Trotteville, considering the matter, 'well, I wouldn't mind if I thought Frederick would keep quiet, and not get excited with Buster tearing all over the place. Oh, and Bets, your mother said you could stay on to tea if you liked. She says Pip has got someone coming to see him this afternoon, and it would be good for you to have a change and be with Frederick for a bit. Would you like to?'

'Oh yes,' said Bets. 'But doesn't Fatty rest a bit in the afternoon? I mean – I had to sleep after my dinner when I had flu.'

'Yes, certainly he must,' said Mrs Trotteville. 'But you needn't stay with him then. You can come down here and have a book to read and then go back again when he is awake. He can bang on the floor when he has had enough sleep. And if he still wants Buster, you can take him up then.'

'Oh, good!' said Bets. 'I'll just go out into the kitchen and have a word with old Buster, Mrs Trotteville. He must be missing us all so!'

Buster gave her a frantic welcome. He tore round her on his short legs, rolled over, bounced up again, and altogether behaved as if he was about six-months-old. He barked non-stop, and the two maids sitting with their cups of tea put their hands up to their ears.

'He's going upstairs to Fatty this afternoon,' said Bets. 'Did you hear that, Buster! Going to Fatty!'

Buster thought that Bets meant he was going that very minute. He flung himself at the closed door, and barked madly. Bets laughed. 'I'll come and fetch you later on,' she said. 'In about an hour or so, Buster.'

She managed to slide out of the door before Buster could squeeze out too. She left him barking crossly. What! She had gone to see his beloved master, and not taken him, after all her promises? Wuff, wuff, wuff! Grrrrrrrr!

Bets went back upstairs to tell Fatty the good news. 'I'll settle you down if you like,' she said to him. 'Then you can go to sleep, and when you wake up, bang on the floor with this stick and I'll come up with Buster. I'm allowed to stay to tea, so we've plenty of time to talk and play games.'

'Good,' said Fatty, pleased. He was now feeling sleepy and he snuggled down. 'But don't go, Bets. There's a nice comfy chair over there, look – and you can borrow one of my Sherlock Holmes stories if you like. There's a pile on that table.'

'Your mother said I was to go downstairs and read,' said Bets. 'I'd better go.'

'No, don't,' said Fatty. 'I don't like being left alone. Stay with me, Bets.'

'Don't be silly! You don't care at all about being

alone – and you'll be asleep in a few moments!' said Bets, with a laugh.

'Bets,' said Fatty suddenly, in a voice that made her look across at him in surprise. 'Bets, you *must* stay with me! Because of the Voices!'

Bets gaped at him. Voices! Whatever did Fatty mean?

'What Voices?' she said.

'I don't know,' said Fatty, still very mysterious. 'Sometimes it's a duck, I think. And other times, it's a hen. And once it was a dog whining.'

Bets was amazed. 'What – here in your bedroom?' she asked, disbelievingly. 'Fatty, you must have had a very high temperature to think you heard Voices.'

'I tell you, there *are* Voices in this bedroom when I'm all alone,' said Fatty, leaning up on one elbow. He looked very earnest. 'There's a silly old man too, who keeps asking for a cigarette. Bets, do stay with me. If you hear the Voices, we could try and find out what they are. Do stay here and sit in that chair. But don't you say a word to Mummy, will you? She'll think I've got a temperature or something again.'

'All right. I'll stay,' said Bets, puzzled and disbelieving. 'But I believe you're making it all up, Fatty, just to make me stay here with you. You shouldn't do that.'

'Bets, as sure as I lie here, there have been Voices in my room,' said Fatty. 'Will you believe me, if you hear them? See that duck on the mantelpiece? – the china one – well, I've heard it quacking. And see that dog in the picture? He barks and whines!'

'You lie down, Fatty,' said Bets, and she pushed him down. 'You're dreaming. Or just being silly. I'm going to sit in that chair and read Sherlock Holmes. Don't say another word, or we'll have your mother up here.'

Fatty lay down. Bets sat in the chair, wondering why Fatty spoke so much about Voices. She decided that he must have had such a high temperature that he had wandered a little in his mind and heard voices that were not really there. She opened her book and yawned.

Bets fell asleep, and so did Fatty. Except for a log falling in the grate, where a bright fire was burning, there was nothing to be heard. Buster was snoozing in the kitchen, keeping one eye open for the big cat. The cat had to keep a certain distance. One paw over the line and Buster flew at her!

The clock on the mantelpiece ticked on. Half past two. Three o'clock. It was raining outside, and the afternoon was dark. It would have been too dark for Bets to read if she had been awake. Half past three. Both Fatty and Bets were perfectly still, and the fire grew rather low.

Then Bets woke up with a jump. She sat up, wondering where she was. Of course, she was in the big chair in Fatty's bedroom! How low the fire was! Fatty must still be asleep, because he hadn't put on his light, and the room was really very dark.

'Quark, quark, quark!'

Bets almost jumped out of her skin. She gazed incredulously at the big china duck on the mantelpiece. Did the quacking come from there? Her heart began to beat fast. Was this one of Fatty's 'Voices'? She stared at the duck and thought she saw it move.

'Quark, quark, quark!' There it was again – a

rather deep quack, just like the noise made by the drakes on the pond. Bets couldn't believe her eyes.

'Cluck, cuk-cuk-cuk-cuk-cuk-cuk!'

Bets was glued to her chair. That was a hen clucking now – a hen in the bedroom! But how! Why? And now there was a dog whining softly!

She glanced at the picture of the dog but could hardly see it in the darkness. It whined again and gave a little yap.

And then a quavery old voice came from the wardrobe in the far corner.

'A cigarette, please, sir. Just a cigarette!'

'Oh, dear,' said Bets in fright. 'Fatty, Fatty, wake up. Your Voices are here!'

There was a click as Fatty suddenly switched on his bedside light. He sat up in bed, looking at Bets. 'Did you hear them too?' he said. 'Listen, the old man is beginning again.' He pointed over to the wardrobe. Bets looked across at once.

'A cigarette, please, sir. Just a cigarette!'

'I don't like it,' said Bets, and she rushed over to Fatty. 'I'm frightened. Fatty, what is it?'

'Quark, quark, quark!'

'Cluck, cuk-cuk-cuk-cuk-cuk!'

'Moo-oo-oo-oo!'

'Oh, Fatty, Fatty, what is it?' wept Bets, and covered her face and ears. 'Fatty, come out of this room. I'm frightened!'

'Oh, Bets, don't cry! I didn't mean to make you cry,' said Fatty, and put an arm round the scared little girl. 'I thought you'd guess what it was at once! You are a little silly, Bets, not to guess.'

'Guess what?' asked Bets, astonished. She looked up into Fatty's smiling face. 'Fatty! It's not just a trick you're doing, is it? What is it?'

'It's a bit of a secret, Bets,' said Fatty, putting his mouth to her ear. 'I'm practising to be a ventriloquist, that's all. Didn't you really guess?'

4. A LESSON ON VENTRILOQUISM

Bets could hardly believe her ears. She stared at Fatty's grinning face in amazement.

'But – but – was it you then, making that duck on the mantelpiece quack?' she said. 'And that hen cluck, and the dog bark – and that old man ask for a cigarette? It can't be you, Fatty!'

'It is though,' said Fatty. 'I've been working at it all last term. Gosh, the noises that have come from the corners of our dorm each night! And the noises in class too. Once I even got the master to open a cupboard to see if a cat was mewing there.'

'But Fatty – how do you do it?' asked Bets, staring at him. 'I've seen ventriloquists on the stage, of course – making their dolls speak – but how do you do it? Fatty, I didn't like it!'

'Now, don't you be silly,' said Fatty. 'I wouldn't have played the trick on you if I'd thought you were going to be scared. It just shows I must be really good. There's no talking duck or hen or dog or old man in this room, Bets, you *must* know that. I wanted to try and see if I could puzzle you – I didn't mean to frighten you. Gosh, I must be a better ventriloquist than I thought!'

A voice came from the wardrobe again – or at least Bets *thought* it did!

'A cigarette, please sir – just a cigarette!'

Bets looked swiftly round at Fatty and this time she laughed. 'Oh, Fatty, you're clever, but I just saw your throat moving when you said that. How do you manage to throw your voice somewhere else though? Fatty, it's marvellous! Whatever will the others say!'

Fatty sat comfortably up in bed. 'Well,' he began, 'I'll tell you a bit about it, Bets. A man came down to our school last term to entertain us. He was a ventriloquist and he had a couple of idiotic-looking dolls, whose heads could turn from side-to-side. Their eyes could open and shut, and their mouths worked up and down. You've seen a ventriloquist, haven't you? Well, he was absolutely super, this man. I honestly couldn't see either his mouth or his throat working in even the smallest movement – and yet it was his own voice that made those dolls seem to talk – and sing too!'

'Yes. I think ventriloquists are marvellous too,' said Bets. 'I haven't the faintest idea how they do it. But *you* must know, Fatty, because you can ventil – ventrilo . . .'

'Ventriloquise,' said Fatty. 'Well, I do know a *bit* now. But I've had to get it out of books, because you can't learn interesting and really useful things like ventriloquism – or conjuring – or disguising yourself – at school. Such a pity they don't have things like that in the timetable. Wouldn't I work at them!'

'Yes, so would I,' said Bets. 'Did you have to practise ventriloquism yourself then, Fatty, with nobody to help you?'

'Yes,' said Fatty. 'But it's difficult to be anywhere by yourself at school, you know, so I had to let a few of the boys into the secret. We've got about six ventriloquists at my school now.'

'But you're the best, I bet you are, Fatty,' said Bets at once.

Fatty wished he could say he was. But honesty

compelled him to admit that another boy was better than he was.

'We've got an African boy at our school,' he said. 'A Zulu prince or something. He's the best. But that's not to be wondered at, because apparently all his uncles and great-uncles and grandfathers were able to throw their voices wherever they wanted to. Anyway, when he knew I was trying to learn to throw my voice, he showed me a few tricks.'

'Tell me, Fatty,' begged Bets. 'What tricks?'

'Well,' said Fatty, banging his pillows and settling himself comfortably, 'first of all, I'll explain the name "ventriloquism". It comes from two words – "venter", which means tummy, and "loqui", which means to speak. In other words, a ventriloquist was supposed to be a man who could speak by using his tummy in some way.'

'Do you use *your* tummy then?' asked Bets.

'As a matter-of-fact, the people who thought that made a mistake. The tummy is *not* used,' said Fatty.

'Oh. What is then?' asked Bets, intensely interested.

'Well,' said Fatty, 'as far as I can see, a

ventriloquist forms his words in the ordinary way but he lets his breath escape very slowly indeed, and he closes up his glottis – his throat – as much as he can, and opens his mouth as little as possible. Oh, and he only uses the tip of his tongue.'

Bets couldn't follow this, but she didn't much mind as she had no intention of becoming a ventriloquist herself. She was quite sure she would be no good at it at all. The whole thing sounded quite impossible to do. But Fatty, as usual, had tackled the impossible and done it!

'You *are* clever, Fatty,' she said. 'Now do some more ventriloquism and let me see how you do it.'

But she couldn't see, of course, except that Fatty's throat moved a little, and once his lips moved too. 'Just a cigarette, please, just a cigarette,' came a quavering voice which didn't appear to be anywhere near Fatty at all. She instinctively looked over to the wardrobe again. Fatty was looking there too, as if somebody was really there.

'It's strange,' said Bets. 'Really strange. How do you throw your voice like that, Fatty?'

'I don't really. You just think I do, and you look at the place where you imagine the voice is coming from, and hear it there,' said Fatty. 'That's just a trick, of course. Though this Zulu boy I was telling you about can *really* throw his voice, it seems to me. Anyway, one day it sounded to us as if there was somebody calling us from outside the classroom door but when we went to see, there wasn't anyone in sight – and old Benjamin was sitting in his chair inside the room, grinning away like anything. "I fool the English boys, I fooled you," he kept saying.'

'I wish I went to your school,' said Bets. 'You always make it sound so exciting, Fatty. Fancy you being a ventriloquist now – whatever will you be next?'

'Well, you just never know when things like that will help you,' said Fatty. 'It might come in very useful with my detective work when I'm grown-up. It's a really amusing trick, anyhow.'

There came the sound of excited barking, and the thump of leaping feet on the stairs.

'Buster,' said Fatty. 'Gosh, in all this excitement about my ventriloquist act, we'd forgotten about poor old Buster. Bets, don't say a word to mother about my ventriloquist stunt.'

Before Bets could assure Fatty that she certainly wouldn't, the door opened and in came Mrs Trotteville with a tremendously excited Buster rushing in front. He leapt straight on to the bed, of course, and flung himself on Fatty. He put his paws up on the boy's shoulders and proceeded to lick him all over the face, barking loudly.

'Mercy, Buster, mercy!' begged Fatty, and disappeared completely under the bedclothes to escape the excited dog. Buster followed at once, and a curious heaving earthquake formed itself in the bed, accompanied by yells and barks.

'Frederick! Buster must come out!' cried Mrs Trotteville. 'Oh, dear, neither of them can hear me. FATTY! BUSTER! FATTY!'

Fatty appeared eventually, his hair towsled, his eyes bright, holding Buster in such a tight grip that the dog couldn't move even a leg.

'What do you do with mad dogs, Mummy?' he asked. 'Honestly, he's quite dippy.'

'Oh, Frederick – put him down outside the bed,' said Mrs Trotteville. 'That's right, Buster. If you dare to get on the bed again, I'll set the cat on you.'

'Wuff,' barked Buster rudely. 'Wuff to that!'

'Frederick, listen,' said his mother. 'It's almost teatime. You can get up, put on your dressing-gown, and stay up for two hours. You can have tea while you're up. Bets can go and get it in ten minutes' time.'

She went out of the room, and Buster immediately leapt up on to the bed again. But this time he was not so uproarious. He had given Fatty the welcome he had been saving up for him, now he was content to lie by him, licking his hand whenever it came near his black nose.

Bets got Fatty's dressing-gown and slippers, and put the armchair in front of the fire. Fatty got out of bed. At first he meant to leap out, but somehow his legs failed to obey his orders. He found that his knees were still very shaky.

'Are you going to tell the others about your ventriloquism?' asked Bets. 'Will you teach them too?'

'No, I won't teach them,' said Fatty. 'The difficulty is not so much the *learning*, Bets, it's the practising. You make all kinds of strange noises then, and people don't like it.'

'No. I can't see Mummy being very pleased if Pip tried to learn,' said Bets. 'She says he's noisy enough already. Anyway, his school report wasn't very good. She and Daddy would be sure to think it was messing about with ventriloquism that made him not work hard at his class subjects.'

'Pity,' said Fatty, beginning on the buttered toast. 'Is there any honey to go with the toast? I always think hot, buttery toast and honey make a good pair – but usually you get one without the other. No, there's no honey. Be a pet and go and ask for some, Bets. Don't be too long, or else the honey won't be needed.'

'Why not?' said Bets, surprised.

'Because there won't be any toast left to go with it,' said Fatty. 'Go on, hurry!'

'Don't dare to eat it all! I never in my life saw such lovely drippy toast – it's just so buttery!' said Bets.

She went out to get the honey. Fatty looked down at Buster, who was sitting beside him looking up adoringly, his mouth open and his

301

tongue hanging out because of the heat of the fire. Fatty tipped up a piece of buttery toast and let two or three drops of the melted butter drip down to Buster's pink tongue. Buster was agreeably surprised. He swallowed twice and then held out his tongue again.

'Quark, quark, quark,' said Fatty, down in his throat. Buster looked at him inquiringly and wagged his tail.

'Cluck, cuk–cuk–cuk–cuk,' clucked Fatty. 'Where's that hen, Buster, where is it?'

Buster thumped his tail on the ground. But he didn't go and look for either duck or hen.

'Too sensible, aren't you?' said Fatty, with his mouth full. 'No matter where I pretend the sounds come from, you know they're made by *me*, don't you? Quark, quark, quark!'

5. MR. GOON HEARS
STRANGE VOICES

In three days' time, all the Find-Outers were apparently completely themselves again. Perhaps a spurt of brilliantly-fine weather had something to do with it. All of them felt that they must be out in the sunshine, however cold it was otherwise.

They went for their first walk together that holiday, enjoying the stroll, though only Bets really felt like running. 'I vote we pop into the café and have a hot cup of chocolate,' said Fatty, as they turned into the High Street. 'Come on, Buster, it's no use staring at cats that are safely sitting on walls. They won't come down for you to chase them! Funny that a clever dog like you shouldn't have learnt that elementary fact yet!'

They went into the little café and sat down at one of the tables there. In the summer, they had ice-cold milk there, and ice creams, or lemonade.

In the winter, the little shop did a roaring trade in hot milk, cocoa, and hot chocolate.

A short, plump woman came to serve them. 'Well, well,' she said, beaming at them, 'I thought you must have gone back to school. I've not seen you for so long. What would you like?'

'Hot chocolate, ginger biscuits, and currant buns please,' said Fatty. He drew a handful of change out of his pocket to pay. Fatty always had plenty of money!

'I'll pay,' said Larry. 'I've not spent half my Christmas money yet. You're always paying for us!'

Fatty let him pay. He knew that it often made Larry feel embarrassed when he so often had to allow him, Fatty, to pay for their treats. Anyway, Fatty could always pay for the second round of chocolate and biscuits! 'Flu seems to have enlarged my appetite,' he said. 'I've not stopped feeling hungry for two days.'

'How nice!' said Daisy. 'I like feeling hungry.'

'Only because you know you're going to get plenty to eat,' said Pip. 'It wouldn't be any fun being hungry if you thought there wasn't going to be even a bit of bread to chew for days!'

Nobody could think of an answer to that remark. Buster suddenly got up and went to the door. He barked loudly.

'Be quiet!' said Fatty. 'Behave yourself, Buster. Don't bark at that dear old lady.'

'He's not,' said Bets suddenly, peering through the shop window from where she sat. 'It's Mr Goon.'

'Well, I hope he keeps out of here,' said Pip, beginning on a currant bun. 'These are great – new as anything.'

Bets let her eyes wander round the shop. Up on the mantelpiece was a model of a cow, standing about two feet high. It had a head that would nod up and down if anyone set it going. She got up and went over to it.

'I like this cow,' she said. 'I'll set its head nid-nodding. Let's see if it manages to nod it the whole time we're here.'

She set the head nodding and went back to her chair, watching the cow. Buster began to bark again, and the five swung their heads round to the door.

Mr Goon was standing there, looking so plump

that the buttons on his tunic were stretched to bursting-point. 'Call this dog to you,' he commanded Fatty. 'Put him on a lead. I won't have him dancing round my ankles.'

'Why? Are you coming to have a drink of hot milk or something?' asked Fatty. He deftly put Buster on the lead, and made him sit down. Fatty was hoping against hope that Mr Goon was indeed coming to sit in the shop and have a drink. Fatty had a bright idea, and wanted to carry it out!

Mr Goon stalked in and sat down at the table next but one to the five children's. He called for a cup of cocoa and a bun.

'Cold outside for you again, isn't it, Mr Goon?' said the short plump woman, setting down a cup of cocoa and a bun in front of the red-faced policeman.

Mr Goon took no notice of her. He glanced across at the children. 'Ho, seems like I've had a nice quiet time these holidays,' he began. 'No nosey-parkering, no interfering with the law. That says something for the flu, that does. You must have felt funny not being able to stick your noses in a mystery.'

Nobody answered. Fatty spoke a few words to Larry, and Larry said a few back. Nobody looked at Mr Goon. He didn't like being ignored. He raised his voice.

'Or have you got a mystery on hand?' he began again. 'A nice juicy mystery to make a mess of?'

Fatty looked at him. 'Now how did you hear *that*, Mr Goon?' he said, in a surprised voice. 'Larry, have you been saying anything about our latest mystery?'

Larry rose immediately to Fatty's invitation to be absurd.

'Which case do you mean?' he said. 'The mystery of the red-nosed reindeer, or the one about the flying saucers? We've solved them both, haven't we?'

'Oh, yes. I didn't mean *those*,' said Fatty. 'Mr Goon probably knows all about those by now. They're stale news, aren't they, Mr Goon? No, Larry – I meant the mystery of the strange voices.'

'Gah!' said Mr Goon, biting violently into his bun. 'Strange voices – you don't know what you're talking about. Lot of silly make believe!'

The other four had pricked up their ears when they heard Fatty refer to strange voices. They all knew about his ventriloquial powers now, and he had practised a few of his tricks in front of them. Why had he mentioned strange voices to Mr Goon?

'Lot of silly make believe,' said Mr Goon again, and took a sip of hot cocoa. 'Strange voices! Gah!'

'Oh yes, that mystery's not solved yet, is it?' said Larry, speaking to Fatty in a voice loud enough for Mr Goon to hear. 'Curious case that – people hearing strange voices which aren't really there. Somebody casting a spell on them, I suppose.'

'Baby talk,' said Mr Goon, drinking his cocoa rather loudly.

'You may be right,' said Fatty seriously. 'But believe it or not, some people lately have been hearing ducks quack where there are no ducks, hens clucking, and people speaking – and yet there don't seem to be any there.'

'You'll tell me that cow on the mantelpiece will start to moo next,' said Mr Goon, swallowing the last of his currant bun. Fatty scribbled something quickly on a piece of paper and pushed it across the table to the others.

'Cow will moo,' he had written. 'But none of you is to hear it.'

Mr Goon wiped his mouth. 'Quacking ducks, clucking hens, mooing cows,' he observed sarcastically. 'Silly make believe. Bosh and rubbish!'

'It's a nice cow, isn't it?' said Bets, looking across at it. 'Its head is still going up and down.'

Mr Goon looked across at it too.

'Moo-oo, moo-oo, moo-oo,' said the cow, mooing in exact time to the nodding of its head. The mooing was so realistic, and so exactly in time with the nodding, that even the children, with the exception of Fatty, thought for one moment that the mooing noise did actually come from it.

Mr Goon stared at the cow, astounded. He glanced round at the children. Not one of them, of course, took any notice of the mooing, remembering Fatty's hastily scribbled instructions. They lifted up their cups and drank, Bets hoping to goodness that she wouldn't start to giggle.

Mr Goon looked at the nodding cow again. It

had stopped mooing – principally because Fatty had been overcome with an urge to laugh. But, as Goon looked at it, it gave such a large and unexpected moo that the policeman jumped violently. Then the mooing quietened and went on in time with the nodding of the animal's head.

Mr Goon swallowed hard. 'Moo-oo, moo-oo, moo-oo,' went the cow, nodding its head. Nobody would ever have believed that it was merely Fatty throwing the noise across to the mantelpiece!

Mr Goon felt rather sick. He didn't know what to make of it at all. He looked at the children again. They were taking absolutely no notice at all of the mooing cow. Neither was Buster, of course. Was it possible that they were not hearing what Mr Goon was hearing?

The little plump woman came bustling into the shop with some more buns for the children. The cow stopped mooing. Mr Goon cleared his throat and spoke to the shop-woman.

'Er – nice cow that of yours, my good woman – the one on the mantelpiece, I mean. Very life-like! You'd almost expect it to moo!'

'You will have your joke, sir,' said the little

woman. 'My, if I heard it moo, I'd think there was something wrong with me. I'd think I was going crazy!'

'That's just what we were saying,' said Fatty gravely. 'Strange voices are about – people are hearing them. What are they? A warning? Brrrrrr! I'm glad *I* don't hear them!'

'Well, we live in funny times, no doubt about it,' said the little shop-woman puzzled, and hurried off again. The cow began to moo once more, but so softly that Mr Goon was not absolutely sure if he was hearing it or not. Could he be imagining it? He gazed so earnestly at the nodding cow that Bets felt an irresistible giggle rising up from the very middle of her tummy. She knew from experience that they were the worst kind of giggles – the ones that heaved up and broke out helplessly.

'Talk, do talk,' she besought the others in a low voice. 'I'm going to laugh.'

All but Fatty talked in low voices, saying any nonsense that came into their heads. Fatty stopped making the cow moo. Mr Goon sat back cautiously. Thank goodness the cow was behaving normally now. Maybe his ears had just played him a trick.

'Quark, quark, quark!' Mr Goon jumped violently again, and looked all round. That was a duck quacking, no doubt about it.

QUARK! Mr Goon's eyes caught sight of a wild duck, beautifully stuffed, placed in a glass case at the end of the shop. He gazed at it, holding his breath.

'Quark, quark, QUARK!' The duck appeared to be looking at him out of its glass eye, and its half-open beak seemed to be quacking. Mr Goon leapt up, full of horror.

'That duck!' he said wildly. 'Did you hear it?'

'What duck?' asked Larry. 'Oh, Mr Goon – surely – surely you are not suggesting that the duck in the glass case is quacking!'

'Mr Goon, don't say you are hearing the strange voices!' said Fatty, earnestly and solemnly.

'Quark!' The noise seemed to come from somewhere behind Mr Goon. He gave a loud, hunted cry and ran from the shop, Buster almost tripping him up with his lead. And then the children collapsed over the table, crying tears

of laughter into their empty cups. 'Mr Goon,
Mr Goon, you couldn't have been funnier!'

6. SOMETHING HAPPENS AT LAST

'Oh, Fatty – HOW do you do it?' said Daisy, mopping her eyes and feeling very weak. 'The way you made that cow moo in time to its nodding was perfect. Honestly, I could have believed myself that the thing was mooing.'

'So could I,' said Bets. 'Oh, dear, don't do that sort of thing too often, Fatty – I simply won't be able to keep my giggles down if you do. Mr Goon's face! His eyes almost fell out of his head!

'He must be feeling pretty puzzled,' said Larry. 'I bet he'll wake up at night and hear noises that aren't there!'

They paid their second bill and went out. What a pity there wasn't any first class mystery to probe into! These were the first holidays in which nothing of any sort or kind had turned up. And there were only a few days left.

'Can't we spoof old Mr Goon a bit, just to have

some kind of excitement in our last few days?' said Larry. 'That laugh did me more good than a dozen days in bed!'

'Me too,' said Pip. 'I was feeling rather low this morning, but now I'm feeling fine. That's obviously what we all need – a really good laugh every now and again.'

'And Fatty's the one to give it to us,' said Bets, squeezing his arm. 'Fatty, do let's see if we can't spoof Mr Goon a bit?'

'But how?' said Fatty. 'I mean – we can't follow him around with all kinds of noises. He'd soon begin to associate them with us. If every time he hears a cow moo or a duck quack, or hears mysterious voices going on, and sees us somewhere near, well, even *he's* wide-awake enough to put two and two together – us and the noises.'

'I suppose you're right,' said Bets with a sigh, putting away her visions of pursuing Mr Goon with strange and wonderful sounds. 'Well – perhaps something will happen to give us a bit of excitement.'

It was strange that she said that – because that

very night something did happen, though nothing very startling. They didn't know about it till the next morning.

The milkman told Larry. 'Heard about the break-in at the Cedars last night?' he said. 'It's next door but one from you. It's a small house, and a man called Mr Fellows has rented it since a week or two ago. Lived there all alone.'

'What happened?' said Larry.

'Well, apparently somebody broke in, and rifled the house from top to bottom,' said the milkman. 'We don't know if Mr Fellows was there or not – anyway, he's gone this morning. Hasn't come back yet either.'

'Who discovered this?' asked Larry, quite excited to think that all this had taken place so near to his own home. Why, he might have heard something in the night – a shout, the breaking of a window, or something. However, he had been too sound asleep.

'I found the house door open, and a window broken at the back, when I took the milk early this morning,' said the milkman. 'I peeped in at the hall door and, my, what a mess the place was in! I stepped in and telephoned the police at once.'

'Oh, did Mr Goon come?' asked Larry, disappointed. He had hoped for one moment that the Find-Outers might get in first! It was still early, only just after breakfast.

'Yes. He's there now – taking notes and looking for fingerprints and the rest of it,' said the milkman. 'He's feeling important this morning. Told me to keep my big mouth shut and not tell anyone what I found – after I'd told every single one of my customers! What does he think I am – a clam?'

'Did you notice anything at all out of the ordinary?' asked Larry.

'Nothing,' said the milkman. 'I didn't stop to look round, anyway, I telephoned the police at once. Mustn't disturb anything, you know, in cases like this.'

Larry got on his bicycle and went to tell Fatty. It might be nothing, or it might be something interesting, you never knew. Fatty would soon get the old brains to work and decide if the Find-Outers were to do anything or not!

Fatty was most interested. 'This cheers me up immensely,' he said. 'It may be a potty little robbery, but we'd better go and find out. If the house really *was* rifled from top to bottom, it looks as though someone was trying very hard to find something of great importance to him. What was it – and who was it?'

They collected Pip and Bets, fetched Daisy, and all five of them, with Buster, went up to the house that stood two doors from Larry's. It didn't look as if anyone was there. Mr Goon must have come and gone. Good.

'Now then,' said Fatty. 'Examine all the paths and beds round the house. Look for usual things – footmarks, cigarette-ends, handprints on window ledges, etc. Make notes of what you find, and we'll compare later.'

'Aren't you coming with us?' asked Bets, seeing Fatty turn away.

'No. I'm going to look in the windows and see if there's anything interesting inside,' said Fatty.

But the curtains were drawn across and he couldn't see anything. He went steadily round the little house, but not one window could he see into. The front door was closed and fastened now, and the back door was locked too.

Fatty came to the broken window at the back. It was the kitchen window. Obviously the robber, or whatever he was, had got in here. Fatty stuck his hand inside and moved the curtain. The kitchen was upside down! Drawers had been pulled from the dresser and from the table. Cupboards were open and their contents dragged out on to the floor! What could the intruder have been looking for?

Fatty suddenly heard a sound inside the kitchen. He listened. What was it? He heard it again, and then peeping in at the window once more, he made out two gleaming eyes looking at him from a cupboard.

'Miaow! Miaow!' said the owner of the eyes piteously.

'Gosh, it's a kitten,' said Fatty. 'Scared to death, I expect, and nobody to feed it or care for it, poor little thing!'

The others came round the corner of the house, notebooks in their hands. 'Here!' said Fatty, beckoning. 'There's a kitten left in the house! What shall we do?'

'Get it,' said Daisy promptly.

'How?' asked Pip. 'All the doors and windows are shut tight. We've checked that.'

'This one's broken,' said Fatty. 'If I wrap my hand in a handkerchief, I think I could put it through the broken pane and do what the thief did – undo the clasp and open the window. Then I could get in and rescue the kitten.'

'Well, go on then,' said Larry, looking all round. 'There's no one about. Mr Goon won't come back yet.'

Fatty took out a big white handkerchief. He twisted it firmly round his fingers. Then he gingerly put his hand through the hole in the broken pane and tried to reach the fastening of the window. It was a casement, opening sideways once the clasp was moved.

'Got it,' said Fatty, and jerked the clasp. It slid down stiffly and he took back his hand again. He could now easily open the window.

'Done it,' he said pleased, and hopped up to the ledge. Buster began to bark, wanting to go with Fatty.

'Keep him quiet, for goodness sake,' said Fatty.

'We don't want anyone to see me climbing in!'

They hushed Buster while Fatty climbed nimbly into the kitchen. He found the tiny kitten, which crouched back in the cupboard, spitting and scared. But it soon began purring when Fatty picked it up and petted it.

'I'll find some milk,' he called quietly to the others. 'I expect it's hungry.'

He came to the pantry and looked inside. Even that was untidy, and a broken dish lay on the tiled floor. Fancy hunting in the pantry too! Whatever had the intruder been after?

'Here you are, kitty,' said Fatty, and put down a saucer of milk for the little creature. It lapped hungrily. When it had finished, it rubbed itself against Fatty's legs, purring. He bent to pick it up, but it scurried away, and ran through the doorway into the hall.

'Puss, puss!' called Fatty. 'Come back here.'

'What's up?' said Pip's voice, looking in at the window. 'Daisy says if you hand the kitten out to her she'll take it home, as she lives so near. They've got a kitten too, and it can be with hers till somebody comes back here.'

'Right. But I'll have to find it first,' said Fatty. 'It's dashed through the kitchen door into the hall. Half a minute. I'll get it. I can hear it there somewhere.'

He went out of the kitchen door into the hall. He paused there, amazed at the untidiness. Coats, shoes, and umbrellas were all in wild confusion on the floor, flung there from the hall cupboard and from a chest of drawers.

The kitten was nowhere to be seen. Fatty went into one room after another, but the little thing was hiding, whether from fright or from play he didn't know.

Fatty took the opportunity of having a good look round. There were three rooms downstairs and three above and a bathroom. Each of them was in confusion. By the soot that lay in the fireplaces, Fatty guessed that the hunter had even felt up the chimney for whatever it was that he had been looking for.

And then, as he came out from a bedroom on to the little landing, Fatty saw something in a corner, near the top of the stairs. It was bright red. He picked it up.

A child's glove, he said to himself. A very *small* glove, for a very small child. But surely there was no child here? And there's only one glove. Could Mr Fellows have been hiding a child here – kidnapped it, perhaps? – and the other fellow came to find it?

He shook his head. No, people don't look for even very small children up chimneys and in drawers. I wonder whether there are any more clothes for a child here. It doesn't look like a house where children came at all – not a single toy, not a book or a doll – and no cot.

There were no children's clothes to be seen, thrown in the muddle on the floor. All kinds of other clothes were there – men's coats, trousers, vests, shoes, hats – as well as a trouser press flung down and opened, books, cushions, papers, blankets, sheets, pillowcases . . .

'Well,' said Fatty, slipping the child's red glove into his pocket, 'I'll keep it, just in case – though in case of what I don't know! Only *one* of the pair – that's the mysterious part! Was a child here last night? – and was it dressed in a hurry, so that it dropped one glove? No, it couldn't be.'

A loud whisper penetrated to him.

'Fatty! Quick! Mr Goon's coming back. He's coming up the road. QUICK, Fatty!'

7. MR. GOON iS ASTOUNDED

Almost before Fatty had time to get downstairs, there came the sound of Goon's angry voice.

'Now then, you kids! What are you doing here? Clear orf!'

Then came the sound of Buster's barking. Fatty grinned. How many, many times had this same scene been acted? – the Find-Outers snooping round – Goon finding them – ordering them off – and Buster objecting loudly! Well, Buster could certainly look after, not only himself, but all the children too.

Fatty wondered whether he could slip out of the front door. He could hear that Mr Goon was round at the back.

'Interfering with the law!' he heard, in the policeman's angry voice. 'Poking your noses in! What's it to do with you?, I'd like to know. Clear orf!'

'Well, we live just close by,' said Larry. 'It's naturally interesting to us – to Daisy and me, I mean. If burglars are in the district, I want to get some information in case they come to rob our house too, next door but one.'

'Gah!' said Goon disbelievingly. 'Tommy-rot! Just an excuse for interfering. This here job's a potty little job – no mystery in it at all. Not worth your notice, see? And take that dog away before I lose my temper with him. Nasty yappy little mongrel!'

Fatty longed to be out there with the others. Calling Buster a *mongrel*! Why, the little Scottie had a pedigree a yard long, and all his grandparents had been champions. Fatty boiled with rage. He tiptoed to the front door. He didn't want Mr Goon to catch him in the house, even though he had the perfectly good excuse to offer about rescuing the kitten.

'Where's that big boy?' demanded Mr Goon, suddenly realising that Fatty was absent. 'Still in bed with the flu, I hope. Best place for him too. Hope he gets a relapse! WILL you call this dog off?'

Larry called Buster. 'Buster, come here. I can

find some better ankles for you if you want some.'

Mr Goon snorted. That was one of the things he did remarkably well. 'Get out of this garden, all of you,' he said. 'Any more messing about here and I'll report you. Yes, and I'll go round to your parents again too – especially yours, Philip Hilton!'

Pip hastily removed himself from the garden of the little house, taking Bets with him. He didn't want Goon to make any more complaints to his parents. They had a habit of taking Mr Goon seriously! Larry and Daisy followed, Larry holding Buster by the collar. They stood outside the front gate, wondering what Fatty was going to do.

Fatty was most unfortunate. He opened the front door from inside at exactly the same moment that Mr Goon unlocked it from the outside. Mr Goon stared at Fatty as if a thunderbolt had hit him. His mouth fell open and he went a familiar purple colour. He swallowed hard.

'Good morning, Mr Goon,' said Fatty, smoothly. 'Do come in. I'll shut the door for you.'

Mr Goon stepped in, still wordless. Then he exploded into speech.

'What you doing here? HERE, in this house that's under police supervision. You want to get locked up, I suppose – being found on enclosed premises, and up to no good, I'll be bound! HO!'

Fatty stepped back out of range of Mr Goon's explosions. 'I heard a kitten mewing here,' he said still politely. 'And being a subscriber to the RSPCA – if you know what that means, Mr Goon – I naturally had to come into the house to find it.'

'Pah!' said Mr Goon, disbelievingly. 'This here house is absolutely empty! I've been through it meself with a toothcomb already!'

'This 'ere 'ouse hisn't habsolutely hempty,' said Fatty. 'Dear me, I seem to be getting muddled. Hark, Mr Goon – can't you hear the kitten mewing now?'

'Miaow!' said the kitten, and obligingly crept out from under the hall-stand. It went to Fatty and rubbed affectionately against his legs. Then it looked at Mr Goon, hissed at him and spat.

'Most intelligent behaviour,' observed Fatty. 'I hope you believe in the kitten now, Mr Goon.'

Mr Goon did. He had to. 'Take it away and take yourself off too,' he said to Fatty. 'I've work to do here. And keep out of this, see?'

'You'll be careful of the dog here, won't you, Mr Goon?' said Fatty. 'I'm not quite sure where it is – you may possibly hear it growling somewhere, and trace it by that.'

'There's no dog here,' said Mr Goon, stalking past Fatty. 'A kitten I might have missed, being so small like, but not a dog. What do you take me for?'

'It would be better not to tell you,' murmured Fatty. 'Not here, anyway.'

He was just behind the policeman, and it was as well for Mr Goon that he couldn't see the innocent expression on Fatty's face – a look that all his school teachers knew only too well.

A blood-curdling growl suddenly came from somewhere in the house. Mr Goon stopped as if he had been shot. 'What's that?' he said.

'Sounded like the dog,' said Fatty. 'What a horrible animal it must be. I think I'll go, Mr Goon, and leave you to tackle him.'

Another growl came from somewhere, and the policeman took two hurried steps backwards, treading heavily on Fatty's foot.

'Ouch!' said Fatty. 'Look out where you're going if you want to walk backwards, Mr Goon! Well – good-bye – I'll leave you now.'

'You come and help me find that dog,' said Mr Goon, changing his mind completely about wanting Fatty to clear off. 'It might want two of us to get him. Funny I didn't see him or hear him when I was here before this morning.'

Fatty grinned behind Mr Goon's broad back. He debated whether to produce another animal noise. This ventriloquism was most useful!

'All right, Mr Goon,' he said. 'If you think it's my duty to stay and help you, I will. I'm always around when duty calls, you know.'

Mr Goon was very thankful. He began to tiptoe forward into the little dining-room. Fatty followed a few paces behind. He suddenly gave a shout that made Goon nearly fall over backwards.

'Look, look – what's that? – over there! LOOK OUT!'

Mr Goon was so anxious to get out as well as to look out, that he almost fell over Fatty, trying to rush out of the room. Fatty clutched him as he went.

'It's all right! It's all right! I just caught sight of

you in that mirror over there, Mr Goon, and it was such a dreadful sight I thought it must be someone lying in wait for us. Gosh, thank goodness it was only your reflection!'

Mr Goon was very angry and very relieved. He glared at Fatty. 'Any more of this funny business,' he began, and then stopped suddenly.

From somewhere behind came the sound of heavy grunting. Mr Goon swung round at once. 'Did you hear that?' he asked Fatty, breathlessly. 'That grunting noise. What was it? It sounded out there in the hall.'

'Yes, it did,' said Fatty, clutching at Mr Goon's arm and making him jump again. 'You go first, Mr Goon. I'm scared.'

So was Mr Goon. He tiptoed into the hall and promptly fell over the kitten which made a dart at him as soon as he appeared. He retreated into the dining-room again, bumping into Fatty. The grunting noise was heard once more, this time sounding further off.

'It's a pig!' said Mr Goon, hardly able to believe his ears. 'Sounded upstairs that time. Did you think it was a pig, Frederick?'

The more frightened and puzzled Mr Goon became, the more polite he got. At this rate, thought Fatty, he'll soon be bowing to me every time he speaks! He badly wanted to laugh, but he firmly thrust down the ever-mounting guffaw that wanted to rise up and explode.

'What sort of a fellow was it who lived here, Mr Goon?' asked Fatty, innocently. 'Was he fond of animals? He seems to have kept kittens, and dogs, and pigs, anyway.'

'How was it I didn't see the pig when I was here this morning?' marvelled Goon. 'I turned everything over and looked everywhere for clues. And yet, I didn't see the dog or the pig. Shall we go upstairs to find the pig?'

'Yes. But be careful the dog doesn't rush out at you,' said Fatty. 'You go first, Mr Goon.'

Mr Goon didn't want to go first. He pushed Fatty in front of him, and then immediately wished he hadn't because a deep and ferocious growl came from somewhere behind him. Fatty was certainly practising his new talent well!

And then a new sound came to worry poor Mr Goon. A voice came from somewhere, a groaning voice that said, 'I never did it, I never! Ooooooh! I never did it! Where's my auntie?'

Goon listened, petrified. He began to feel as if he was in a nightmare. He whispered to Fatty, 'There's a man here somewhere! This beats all! We'd better get help. I'm not going to snoop round here with dogs, and pigs, and a man groaning. What's been happening since I was here this morning?'

'Look, you stay here, Mr Goon, and I'll go and get help,' said Fatty, and moved firmly into the hall. But Mr Goon clutched at him.

'No, don't leave me here alone. Can't *you* stay while I get help?'

'Remember your duty, Mr Goon,' said Fatty, solemnly. 'There is something strange here, and it's your duty to examine it. But it's not *my* duty. I'll go and get help. Good-bye!'

Goon held on to him tightly, and then the voice began again. 'I never did it, I never! Ooooooh! I never did it! Where's my auntie?'

Goon began to shake. 'What's he mean, talking about his auntie?' he whispered. 'Come on, let's go! This is a madhouse, this is.'

'Mr Goon – why not telephone for help!' said Fatty, suddenly catching sight of the telephone in the hall. 'You'd get someone here in a trice then.'

Mr Goon was so relieved at this bright idea of Fatty's that he almost embraced him. He stumbled to the telephone and dialled a number.

Fatty heard him telephoning to another constable. He tiptoed silently out of the front door, grinning as he heard Goon's agonised voice.

'Send someone up here at once. There's a fierce dog in the house – and a pig – yes, I said a pig – P-I-G. Yes, PIG, you idiot. And a groaning man who wants his auntie. AUNTIE! Yes, I did say auntie. Are you deaf, or something? Well, how do *I* know why he wants his auntie? No, I'm not daft, but I soon shall be if you don't send someone to this address at once. Yes – I do want help – YES, there IS a dog here – and a pig – and an auntie – no, not an auntie, but a man who wants one. Oh, and there's a kitten too, I forgot to mention that.'

There was a pause as Goon listened to a few remarks from the other end of the telephone. He spluttered into it again.

'Any more sauce from you, Kenton, and I'll

report you. I'm NOT having a joke with you. You come up here at once. AT ONCE, do you hear?'

Fatty heard all this and felt that he really must go somewhere and laugh. He tiptoed round to the back of the house where there was a shed he could go into and laugh in peace. He saw the broken casement window, hanging open, as he passed. He thrust his head inside, and sent a terrible growl into the house.

Mr Goon heard it. He looked round, and found that Fatty had gone. He was alone – alone in the house with a host of terrifying things! It was too much for Goon. He fled at top speed out of the front door, and didn't stop running till he came to the bottom of the road.

Fatty heard him go. And then he laughed. How he laughed! It really was the best laugh Fatty had ever had in all his life!

B. LAUGHTER, IS GOOD FOR THE FLU

Fatty's laughter echoed across the next garden and came to the ears of the others. They had retreated to Larry's house, and had made their way into the back garden to wait for Fatty. Buster heard the laughter too, and pricked up his ears. He began to bark delightedly. Like everyone else, he loved Fatty's enormous laughter!

Larry climbed up onto the wall. He gave the piercing whistle that the Find-Outers sometimes used. Fatty heard it and saw Larry.

'Wait for me! I'm coming!' he called. He was soon in the garden with the others. They retired to a little out-house at the bottom of the garden.

'What happened? And why did Mr Goon rush out of the house so suddenly at top speed?' asked Daisy. 'We saw him flashing by the gate like dark blue lightning!'

Fatty began to laugh helplessly again. The

others had to laugh as they watched him. Pip gave him a punch and Buster leapt on him in excitement. Why was his master so pleased?

'Come on – tell us the joke,' said Pip.

So Fatty told them, and soon they were all helplessly sitting on the floor of the out-house, holding their sides, picturing Mr Goon's amazement at the thought of the grunting pig, the growling dog, and the groaning man.

'That auntie bit! Oh, what made you think of that?' groaned Larry, holding his aching sides. 'That's a touch of genius. Oh dear – only an idiot like Mr Goon would have taken all that in! What *will* Inspector Jenks think when Mr Goon makes out a report full of pigs, and dogs, and men that want their aunties?'

That made them all laugh again, but Fatty began to look a little more sober. He rubbed his nose thoughtfully. 'I hadn't thought of Mr Goon making out a report,' he said. 'Yes, I suppose he'll have to. The Chief Inspector will smell a rat, I should think. Especially if he knows I was with Mr Goon at the time all this happened.'

'He may not put you into the report,' said

Daisy, comfortingly. 'He'd leave you out if he possibly could. He hates admitting you are ever on the same job as he is.'

'He telephoned for help,' said Fatty. 'Let's go and see if he's met his help and if they're coming back.'

Just as they got to the front gate and hung over it, with Buster doing his best to squeeze underneath, Mr Goon came up the road with PC Kenton. PC Kenton had been most astonished to have Goon bump violently into him at the corner of the road.

'I just came to meet you,' explained Goon in haste. 'Thought you mightn't know where the house was. Come on.'

He scowled when he saw the five leaning over the gate. He especially scowled at Fatty for deserting him. Gah! Toad of a boy! However, he thought it best to say nothing whatever to any of them, in case Fatty was funny at his expense. Fatty could be rude more politely than anyone Goon had ever met.

'I bet Mr Goon's friend will be puzzled to find the house completely empty of kitten, dog, pig, and man,' said Fatty. He had brought the kitten with him to Daisy's. It had most conveniently jumped out of the window and landed at his feet while he had been standing laughing at the back of the burgled house. It was now playing with Daisy's kitten in a very friendly manner.

PC Kenton was indeed astonished to find nothing and no one in the house of the kind that Goon had described.

'Not even auntie!' he complained. 'I was looking forward to seeing auntie. You sure you weren't seeing things, Mr Goon?'

'I didn't *see* anything – except the kitten. I heard them, I keep telling you,' said poor Mr Goon, amazed to hear no sound of growl or grunt or groan, and to find nothing that could conceivably have made them.

'I can't think where auntie's gone,' said PC Kenton, maliciously.

'Don't keep on and on about auntie,' said Mr Goon, exasperated. 'Auntie, whoever she was, wasn't here. The man just kept on wanting her, that's all. I keep telling you.'

PC Kenton was inclined to make a joke of the

whole thing and this infuriated Goon to such an extent that he began to exaggerate.

'If you'd been here and heard a dog growling, just about to leap at you, and heard a pig grunting and stamping about on the floor above, and then heard a man groaning and groaning at the top of his voice, and dragging himself about the floor, well, you wouldn't have made a joke of it, I can tell you,' said Mr Goon.

'Well, all I can say is that the kitten, the pig, the dog, and the man, must have all rushed off together as soon as you left the house,' said PC Kenton, rather severely. 'You should have stayed and waited for me. Now we've lost all the animals and the man too. You'll have to make inquiries in the neighbourhood about them. See if anyone saw them rushing off together.'

Mr Goon lost some of his high colour. He didn't think people would take him very seriously if he went round asking a question like that. He changed the subject and, after a while, the two policemen fastened the open window, and went out of the front door, banging it behind them. The children saw them go.

Mr Goon crossed to the other side of the road with PC Kenton. He didn't want any awkward questions just then, and especially not from Fatty. They passed out of sight.

'A wonderful morning,' said Pip, with a sigh. 'I've forgotten all about the flu. I wonder doctors don't recommend this sort of thing for flu. I don't see how anyone can feel ill if they have mornings like this. I've never laughed so much in my life. What do we do now, Fatty?'

'I want to know if *you've* anything to report to me,' said Fatty. 'You had the job of going carefully round the house and spotting anything there was to see. Tell me what notes you made?'

'We didn't get much,' said Larry. 'We've pooled our notes together and here's a short report. I wrote it out while I was waiting for you.'

'Good work,' said Fatty, approvingly. 'Fire ahead.'

Larry read out his notes.

'We went carefully all round the house. We found out where the burglar came in. He didn't come in at the front door but over the wall at the bottom of the garden.'

'How do you know that?' said Fatty, at once.

'Well, there's a bed there, and there are very deep imprints of feet,' said Larry. 'Only a person jumping down from the wall could have made such deep prints.'

'Right,' said Fatty. 'Go on.'

'We traced the same footprints to a bush,' went on Larry. 'Here the man must have hidden, as there are many footmarks, all messed up together, as if he stood there for some time, occasionally peeping out.'

'Got a drawing of the prints?' asked Fatty.

'Of course,' said Pip, producing a sheet of paper from his pocket and unfolding it. 'But it's not much help – we think the man wore Wellingtons, about size eleven. Anyway, the marks are exactly the same as our own Wellington boots make, except that ours are smaller.'

'Right,' said Fatty again. 'Go on.'

'We found this cigarette-end,' said Larry, and passed a damp cigarette butt to Fatty. 'Can't tell much from that though. We could only find this one, and that was under some leaves. I expect Mr Goon found any others there were. We saw what must have been *his* enormous footprints everywhere too. But we know those all right. So we could tell them easily from the others.'

'Good thing Mr Goon has such colossal feet,' said Fatty. 'We always know *his* footmarks! Anything else?'

'Oh yes. We traced the footprints from the bush to the back of the house,' said Larry, reading his notes again. 'We couldn't see them on the lawn, of course, but we could trace them on another bed and also on a very soggy gravel path by the back of the house. There are quite a lot of marks, all mixed up, on the path under the broken window. He must have got over the wall, hidden under the bush and waited till he judged the time right for entering, then crept up the garden and broken the window. There's a half-brick just below the window. We think he broke it with that.'

'Yes. Probably,' said Fatty. 'That means that someone might have heard him just then. We'll find out. Any more?'

'Yes. There are other footprints, different ones, going from the front door, across the beds there in front of the house, then on a bit of the gravel path that leads to the back gate – then no more,' said Larry. 'They don't go straight from the front door to the front gate. If they had, we wouldn't have seen them probably, because there are so many other footprints there now.'

'I see – so you think someone else – probably Mr Fellows – ran out of the front door and, instead of making straight for the front gate, ran across the front beds to the back gate and disappeared out that way. That probably means he went down the road, not up,' said Fatty thoughtfully.

'Yes. That's all our notes,' said Larry, shutting his book.

'And they're really good too,' said Fatty. 'You've done better than old Mr Goon, I bet. Now, just let me think a bit and try to piece together exactly what happened last night.'

9. IS IT A MYSTERY?

'Silence while the great mind works,' said Larry. 'Quiet, Buster! Sh!'

Fatty worked out his ideas rapidly. He was soon ready with them.

'This is how I see it,' he said. 'Somebody wants something out of Mr Fellows. What, we don't know. Anyway, whatever it is, the man must, for some reason, break into the house – probably because he feels sure that Mr Fellows won't admit him if he comes to the front door. That means that he wants something that Mr Fellows won't want to give him.'

'Yes. That sounds right,' said Pip. 'But why did Mr Fellows tear out of the house like that?'

'Now wait a bit. Don't rush your fences,' said Fatty. 'The man hides till he thinks it's safe to break in – probably hoping that Mr Fellows is asleep, then he can face him suddenly – possibly with a gun – and get what he wants. So in he goes at what he thinks is the right moment.'

'I'd never have thought of all this,' said Bets. 'It's like an adventure story, the way you tell it!'

'In he goes,' went on Fatty, 'but for some reason he doesn't take Mr Fellows by surprise. Perhaps Mr Fellows has heard the breaking of the glass and has smelt a rat – anyway, hearing the man getting in at the back window, what does he do? He shoots out of the front door, leaving it wide open, and rushes out into the dark, dark night . . .'

'It wouldn't be so very dark,' said Daisy. 'There was moonlight last night. My bedroom was flooded with it.'

'You're right. So was mine. Good for you, Daisy,' said Fatty. 'Well, to go on – he fled out into the moonlit night – possibly taking with him whatever it was that the other fellow had come for. The other fellow found the bird flown but, not being certain if he had taken with him whatever it was he wanted, he proceeded to turn the house upside down to look for it. And he didn't leave any corner or drawer or cupboard – or even the chimneys – unsearched!'

'You *are* clever to work all this out,' said Bets. 'I never knew anyone who could put two and two together and make four so quickly.'

'Ah, but where Fatty scores is that he makes them come to *five*,' said Larry. 'He's always one up on Mr Goon or anyone else! Mr Goon makes two and two come to four – but old Fatty goes one better!'

'Thanks, Larry,' said Fatty, amused but also pleased. 'That's what all good detectives do. Now, the thing is, what was it that Mr Fellows rushed off with? It can't have been anything terribly bulky or heavy or he wouldn't have been able to run far with it – and someone might have spotted him and stopped him if he was carrying a suspicious parcel or big sack.'

'So they might,' said Daisy. 'Gosh, Fatty, if you work all this out much further you'll be telling us what it was the man was carrying.'

'I wish I could,' said Fatty. 'But I think I've found something that might be a help – though how, I can't possibly imagine!'

He produced the little red glove from his pocket.

They all stared at it, and Buster sniffed hard.

'It's a doll's glove,' said Daisy. 'Or a baby's. *Could* it have been a baby's?'

'I did play with the idea that Mr Fellows had kidnapped a baby or some very small child,' said Fatty. 'But I came to the conclusion he hadn't. There wasn't anything in the house to suggest that a small child had been there. Only this glove!'

Larry took the glove and turned it over. 'It's very clean,' he said. 'It couldn't have fitted a child of more than two, I should think. Where's your big doll, Daisy? – the one you had when you were three – it was nearly as big as you then!'

'She's packed away somewhere,' said Daisy. 'I'll go and get her. Wait a minute.'

While she was gone, Fatty turned to Pip. 'You showed me the drawing of the burglar's footprints,' he said. 'But what about Mr Fellows' footprints – you saw them go from the front door, across the front beds and on the path by the back gate. Did you take a drawing of them?'

'Gosh, yes – I forgot to show it to you,' said Pip, feeling in his pocket. He brought out a second folded sheet of paper and undid it carefully.

'Rather funny prints these, Fatty – smaller than the others and rather flat and indistinct.'

Fatty looked at them in silence. 'I think Mr Fellows ran out in his bedroom slippers,' he said. 'This print isn't of proper shoes or boots, with heels – it's a print of flat slippers. He may even have had on his night-things and a dressing-gown, with bedroom slippers – he went out in such a hurry. If he was in bed or just going, he wouldn't be fully dressed.'

'Yes, you're right. It *is* the print of flat bedroom slippers,' said Pip. 'Larry, go and get yours – they're flat, aren't they? We could see what kind of footmarks you make in them. There's a nice muddy bit over by the wall.'

Larry fetched his slippers and came back with Daisy, who had found the doll. It certainly was a nice big one. Fatty tried the glove on its hand.

'Yes, whatever child this glove belonged to couldn't have been much bigger than your doll, Daisy,' he said. 'But it beats me why the man dropped it, unless he *was* carrying a small child.'

He put the glove back into his pocket and looked at Larry, who was busy changing his

Wellingtons for red bedroom slippers.

They all followed him as he went to the muddy patch by the wall. 'Run over it at top speed,' said Fatty. Larry ran, first up, then down.

His mother, looking out of the window just then, was amazed to see Larry rushing up and down in the muddiest part of the garden in his bedroom slippers. She couldn't help noticing them because they were bright red!

She knocked at the window and opened it. 'Larry! What are you doing? Stop that silly game at once!'

'There! We might have known that Mummy would look out of the window at this very moment!' said Daisy. 'It's all right, Mummy – we're just trying to prove something, that's all.'

'Well, don't,' said her mother. 'And please tell the others it's almost one o'clock. I'm sure Pip and Bets ought to be going home.'

She shut the window and disappeared. Fatty looked hurriedly but carefully at the flat, smooth prints that Larry's bedroom slippers had made.

'Yes, they're very like Mr Fellows' footprints,' he said, comparing them with Pip's drawing. 'Do they *look* the same to you, Pip? You got a really good view of Mr Fellows' prints because you had to draw them.'

'Yes, exactly the same,' said Pip. 'Come on, Bets, we'll simply have to rush home! When's the next meeting, Fatty? Come to our house, will you?'

'Right,' said Fatty, folding up the paper and putting it into his pocket. 'We'll meet this afternoon at half past three – unless anyone's got to have a rest, because of what the doctor calls "the aftermath of the flu" – whatever that means. We've done some good work this morning – to say nothing of having had some great fun!'

Larry and Daisy went indoors with the doll and the red bedroom slippers. Pip and Bets shot off home. Fatty went more leisurely, his brain at work. There was more in this little happening than met the eye. Much more he thought. It wasn't just an ordinary burglary – and Fatty very much doubted if the 'burglar' had taken anything at all.

I bet Mr Fellows rushed off with whatever it was the man had come after, he thought. Where is he? Where did he put what he wanted to hide? Will he come back?

Mrs Trotteville was out for lunch, so Fatty was able to have a long and satisfying meal all by himself in front of the fire. He thought about the new problem all the time. It wasn't really a 'mystery' – not yet anyway – but it was certainly very interesting. When Jane the maid came in, she was surprised to find how much he had eaten.

'Dear me – yes, I do seem to have cleaned up the dishes rather,' said Fatty, gazing in surprise at the empty tureens and plates. 'I've been thinking and when I'm thinking I like plenty of food for thought, Jane. What's for pudding? French pancakes? Oh, good. How many? Ah, plenty of food for thought here!'

Jane laughed. Frederick was very funny and no mistake! She went out to tell the cook to make another French pancake for Fatty.

Fatty meant to work out a proper scheme for tackling this new problem immediately after lunch – but, unfortunately, he fell fast asleep in front of the fire with Buster curled up on the hearth rug beside him. He didn't wake up till the clock struck half past three.

He leapt up in horror. Goodness, he ought to be at Pip's by now. He pulled on his coat, remembering his mother's orders to put on a scarf. He decided to bicycle, with Buster in the front basket. He wouldn't be so late then.

He arrived at Pip's, ringing his bell furiously down the drive, much to Mrs Hilton's annoyance. Why must Fatty always announce his coming? Really, that boy wanted taking in hand! He was getting too big for his boots.

'Sorry we're late,' said Fatty, arriving in the playroom upstairs, with Buster dancing at his heels. 'I fell asleep. Can't think why.'

'We all did!' said Larry, with a grin. 'Another bit of the doctor's "aftermath", I suppose! Pip and Bets were still asleep when we came!'

'Well, we're wide awake now,' said Pip. 'And Mummy says you can all stay to tea if you like, Fatty. Our cook has made a big chocolate sponge, so you're lucky. Mother says we can finish it between us, if we like.'

'That's one good thing about having had flu,'

said Bets. 'Grown-ups think we want feeding up, and instead of Mummy saying, "Now don't be greedy," she keeps saying, "You *must* have more than that, dear. Take a second helping." Long may it last!'

Everyone agreed heartily. Pip produced the rest of the bull's-eyes that Bets had bought him, and they all took one. They sat round the fire, their cheeks bulging, feeling happy and comfortable.

'Now, let's talk,' said Larry. 'We had to break up the meeting in such a hurry this morning. Fatty, have you any plans? Is this a mystery, do you think, by any chance? I mean, it seems rather ordinary really, after the mysteries we've tackled before – but even a *little* one would be nice before we go back to school in four or five days' time.'

There were groans at the last few words. Nobody felt like school, but they were all fit enough to go back now.

'I think,' said Fatty slowly, 'I really do think this *may* be a mystery and, if so, we'll make the best of it. After all, a mystery, little or big, is always a mystery, and has to be solved. I vote we get down to it at once!'

10. A FEW PLANS – AND A GOOD TEA

Everyone was delighted to hear this, of course. Buster thumped his tail on the floor as if he thoroughly agreed. A mystery! He'd be in it too, all right!

'You all remember what we worked out this morning, don't you?' said Fatty. 'And you all know the few clues we have – two sets of footprints – and a small red glove – and a cigarette-end that really isn't worth anything as a clue because, except that it proves the intruder smoked, we can't tell much more from it – not even the kind it was.'

'Yes. That seems about all the clues,' said Larry.

'By the way,' said Fatty, remembering something suddenly. 'We know how the man got into the garden, hid, and then walked to the back window and got in – but does anyone know how he got away? I mean, he wasn't in the house the

355

next day – that is, today – so he must have got away somehow. Any ideas?'

'Yes,' said Pip at once. 'We think he went out of the front door. We thought we could make out a few of his footprints in the general muddle of footmarks going up and down the front path. Anyway, there were none going back down the garden.'

'I see,' said Fatty. 'Yes, he probably did go out of the front door – and didn't bang it in case it attracted attention to him. It's a pity we can't find anyone who saw either of the men wandering about in the middle of the night – particularly Mr Fellows, who was in bedroom slippers and, presumably, dressing-gown. That's really what we ought to do next – find someone who saw one or other of them that night.'

'I don't see how we can,' objected Daisy. 'We can't possibly find anyone who was out late that night and ask them if they saw a man in slippers and dressing-gown. They'd think we were mad.'

'Another thing we ought to find out is the time the man entered the house,' said Fatty. 'That might give us some guide.'

'Guide to what?' asked Daisy.

'I don't know,' said Fatty. 'We've just got to follow up every tiny little thing. Larry, do you know the people next door to you – at the house in between yours and Mr Fellows?'

'Yes,' said Larry. 'The mother's help there has a boy. I talk to him sometimes. He's a great bird-fellow – watches them, and knows all their names and calls.'

'Is his bedroom on the side next to Mr Fellows' house?' asked Fatty.

'I don't know,' said Larry. 'Do you want me to ask him if he heard anything funny in the night – like the breaking of glass, for instance?'

'You might as well,' said Fatty. 'You see, if we can get the time the burglar went in, say at three o'clock in the morning – we could perhaps find someone who saw Mr Fellows somewhere at that time.'

'Who?' said Larry scornfully. 'I mean, how many people are wandering about at three o'clock in the morning?'

'Nobody, usually,' said Fatty mildly, 'except Mr Goon at times. But there are such things as

357

night-watchmen – I don't know if you've ever *heard* of them, Larry – they're the men who . . .'

'All right, all right, you win!' said Larry, making a face. 'I should have thought of night-watchmen, of course. Especially as our roads are being done up now, all over the place, and there are night-watchmen to guard the tools and things left beside the road. Yes, you are right, a night-watchman might have spotted Mr Fellows in his dressing-gown. Though don't forget he might have pulled an overcoat on.'

'If it was three o'clock in the morning, he would have his pyjamas on, and they would show under an overcoat,' said Bets. 'It doesn't seem to me to matter whether he wore a dressing-gown or a coat. He'd still look a bit peculiar with pyjama trousers and bedroom slippers!'

'Well, do you propose that we go round to all the night-watchmen of the district and ask them questions about dressing-gowns and slippers?' said Larry, not at all pleased with the idea. 'Bags I don't. Night-watchmen are not awfully helpful in the daytime – if you can find them. They're sleepy and cross.'

'Well, we'll go when it's dark then,' said Fatty. 'They will presumably be wide awake then, if they have a job of watching to do. I think *I'll* go but I don't think the girls should do this, and I doubt if your mothers would let you wander round in the cold night air, Larry and Pip. The aftermath of flu would prevent such goings-on!'

'What about you then?' demanded Pip. 'Would you be allowed to?'

'I shall probably feel the need for taking Buster out for a run tonight,' said Fatty solemnly. 'My father has had to do it while I've been ill, and apparently Buster has played him up properly – run off into the bushes for ages and made Dad hunt for hours – and then he would find Buster waiting patiently for him on the front doorstep.'

Everyone laughed. 'All right, you take old Buster out for a nice long run tonight,' said Pip. 'And enter into conversation with a few night-watchmen. I can just see you sitting down on an upturned pail and warming your hands at one of those lovely holey buckets of hot cinders, and talking nineteen to the dozen!'

'And I'll have a word with the boy next door

– his name's Erb,' said Larry. 'Short for Herbert. Or for Erbert, I've never found out which. He's a nice lad, anyway. I'll give you a phone call, Fatty, if I can find out anything. I'll slip in and see him tonight – lend him a bird book, or something – and ply him with questions.'

'Right, and if as a result of your plying you find out the time of the breaking of the window, it will be a help,' said Fatty. 'I can ask the night-watchmen if they saw Mr Fellows at some definite time then. It'll make it easier for me.'

'How?' asked Bets, puzzled.

'Well, I may have an uncle who sleepwalks and who was missing at a certain time last night, and wants to know where he wandered to, for instance,' said Fatty, grinning. 'Aha! I'm going to interest quite a few watchmen in my Uncle Horatious.'

'I never knew you had an Uncle Horatious,' said Bets.

'Didn't you? He's the one that sleepwalks. I've just told you,' grinned Fatty. 'And I've got an Uncle Tobias who goes round at night looking for glow-worms – funny old fellow he is. The night-watchmen might have seen him too.'

They all laughed, and Bets gave him a punch. 'You're an idiot. You've got an imagination that's too good to be true!'

Buster got up suddenly and ran to the door, standing there with his nose glued to it.

'Buster hears tea coming,' said Pip. 'I wish I had ears like a dog. By the way, Daisy, how's the little kitten?'

'Fine,' said Daisy. 'It's a real darling. If it belonged to Mr Fellows – and I suppose it did – he must be feeling worried about it! I'd hate to desert a tiny thing like that and leave it to starve in an empty house.'

'He may come back,' said Fatty, 'and if he does, that'll make a wonderful excuse for going to see him, Daisy! I can take back the kitten, and ask him all sorts of innocent questions!'

'Good idea – if he comes back,' said Pip. 'Hurrah, Buster was right – it is the tea!'

He and Bets ran to the door and took in two large and well-loaded trays. 'Thanks,' said Pip, eyeing the trays with approval. 'Gosh, what a great chocolate sponge.'

It was a very fine tea – hot, new-made scones, sweet and buttery, strawberry jam, bread and butter, and potted salmon and shrimp paste, small ginger buns, shortbread biscuits and, of course, the large chocolate sponge, which had a thick cream filling.

'I vote we march down in a body to the kitchen after tea and give three cheers,' said Larry. 'Well, flu certainly has its good points . . . afterwards! I hope we shall all be fed just as much at school when we get there.'

'We shall be – but not in quite the same way as we are being fed up now!' grinned Pip, offering the scones round. 'I soon get fed-up at school.'

'Ha ha! Joke over,' said Larry, biting into his scone. 'Gosh, this is the most buttery scone I ever had. Buster would just love to lick my face clean after it!'

It was a lovely tea – cosy, companionable, and full of silly jokes. Buster accepted tit-bits from everyone, and was not above abstracting a biscuit from the plate when no one was looking.

They ate everything, and Pip asked everyone politely if he should go down and ask for any more. But nobody could manage another thing. Buster thumped his tail on the carpet to say that he wouldn't mind a few more biscuits but, unfortunately, nobody took any notice of him.

They played a game of *Monopoly* after tea, but had to stop before it was finished. Both Larry and Daisy had been told to get home by quarter past six, as an aunt was coming to stay.

'Will you have time to go in and see that boy next door – Erb, didn't you say his name was?' asked Fatty.

'Oh yes, I'll leave Daisy chatting brightly to Aunt Pamela,' said Larry. 'She's good at that sort of thing. Well, come on, Daisy. We must go. I'll ring you later on this evening, Fatty.'

They all went down to the kitchen and gave three cheers for their wonderful tea. The two maids were tickled and pleased. 'Go on with you,' said the cook. 'You're only doing this to get as good a tea next time you come. Oh, there's Buster. Did they give you any tea, Buster?'

Buster drooped his tail as if to say no. 'Oh, you fibber!' said Pip. 'Who stole a biscuit off the plate? You thought I wasn't looking, but I was. Good thing I was your host or I'd have had something to say to you!'

Larry, Daisy, and Fatty went to say good-bye and thank you to Mrs Hilton, who was always very strict about good manners. Then they went off together down the drive to the front gate. Fatty wheeled his bicycle.

'I hope I don't meet Mr Goon,' he said. 'I've got no light at the front. Well, so long, Larry and Daisy. Here's to the new mystery, even if it's just a tiddler – and don't forget to phone me, Larry.'

'Right,' said Larry. 'And good luck with your Uncle Horatious and your Uncle Tobias and the night-watchmen, Fatty. You'd better keep a sharp eye on those two uncles of yours in future!'

11. LARRY DOES A LITTLE WORK – AND SO DOES FATTY

Larry and Daisy arrived home just at quarter past six. Their aunt was already there. Larry chatted politely for ten minutes and then escaped, leaving Daisy to carry on the good work. He slipped up to his room and found his new book on garden birds. Erb would love to borrow that!

He went in the gate of the next door house and made his way to the back door. He rapped four times. That was the signal to Erb that he had come to see him about something.

Erb opened the door. 'Hello!' he said. 'What's up?'

'Nothing,' said Larry. 'I just wondered if you'd like to borrow my new book. It's got every single garden bird in it – all the ones we get here, of course!'

'Come in,' said Erb, eagerly. 'Mum's out. Let's have a look at the book. Coo, it's a beauty! Will you really lend it to me?'

Erb sat down at the table and opened the book. He would have been pleased if Larry had gone back home straight away and left him to it. Herbert was certainly mad on birds, Larry reflected.

He wondered how to begin his questions about the night before, when suddenly Erb gave him just the opening he needed.

'Oooh, here's a fine chapter on owls,' he said. 'And what smashing pictures. I love owls. I'm always listening out for them. There – listen – one's hooting now. Can you hear it?'

A long and beautiful quavering hoot came to Larry's ears. He sat up at once.

'Erb, did you hear any owls last night?'

Erb looked across at Larry and nodded. 'Yes, I did. They like moonlight nights, you know. One owl came so near my window that I thought he must be calling for me to come and catch mice with him. I even saw him fly past the window, though I couldn't catch the sound of his quiet wings.'

'What time did you hear him?' asked Larry. 'Did you notice?'

'Why, did you hear him too?' said Erb, surprised. 'Let's see now, I heard owls before I went to sleep – about ten that was. Then they woke me again about half past twelve – that was the time one came to my window. I got out of bed and watched for a while then.'

'Where does your bedroom face – towards our house?' asked Larry.

'No, it faces on to the next door house,' said Erb. 'The one that was burgled last night. When I looked out about half past twelve, there was still a light on downstairs in the sitting-room. Mr Fellows must have been sitting working there like he often does. Sometimes he doesn't draw his curtains, and I see him sitting at a table. But last night, the curtains were drawn. He'd got his radio on, I think. I'm sure I heard sounds coming from it.'

'I suppose you didn't hear any owls after that, did you?' asked Larry hopefully. 'There must have been a lot about, enjoying looking for mice in the moonlight.'

'Oh, there were,' said Erb. 'Something woke me later on, but I don't think it was owls. I don't really know what it was. I switched on my light and saw it was quarter past three. I went to the

367

window and listened for owls again, and I could hear some brown owls somewhere, and some little owls too, twitting like anything.'

'Had the light gone out in the sitting-room next door?' asked Larry.

'Oh yes,' said Erb. 'But the funny thing was that I thought I saw some kind of a light down in the kitchen – the room that faces our kitchen. Not the usual electric light – torch perhaps, or a candle.'

This was all very interesting. Larry wondered if the light in the kitchen had been the torch of the man who had got in through the broken casement.

'Can't you really remember what the sound was that woke you?' he asked. 'Would it be breaking glass, for instance?'

'Well, it might have been,' said Erb, wrinkling his forehead. 'Are you thinking about the burglary next door? Well, I dare say that might have been glass breaking I heard, and it might have been the light of a torch I saw in the kitchen, I couldn't swear to it – I didn't take that much notice.'

He bent his head down to the book again and became completely absorbed in it. Larry got up. He didn't think he could get anything more out of

Erb. Erb obviously took much more interest in birds than he did in burglaries. He didn't seem at all interested in the happenings next door!

'Good-bye, Erb,' said Larry, and went back home. Erb and his owls! Larry hoped he would enjoy the bird book – he deserved the loan of it in return for all the information Larry had got out of him!

He telephoned Fatty and told him the whole conversation clearly and concisely. Fatty approved.

'You are all getting really good at reporting things,' he said. 'Thanks for such interesting details. I think there's no doubt that the burglar fellow broke the window at about quarter past three – and very soon after that Mr Fellows rushed out of the house, probably with the precious goods – whatever they were – that the other chap had come for.'

'Well, I suppose you'll now decide that your respected Uncle Horatious wandered abroad sleepwalking at round about quarter past three,' said Larry, 'and half the night-watchmen in Peterswood will hear all about him – bedroom slippers and all!'

'Quite right,' said Fatty. 'How bright you are, Larry! Anyway, thanks for all you've done. Good work. See you tomorrow and tell you anything that happens tonight!'

That night, Fatty apparently went up to bed at eight o'clock, immediately after the evening meal. His mother approved. 'You've had a long day and I'm glad you are sensible enough to go up early,' she said. 'Your father and I are going out to play bridge. Don't read too late in bed, Frederick.'

Fatty duly promised, congratulating himself on his luck. He had been afraid that he would have to undress completely and get into bed, in case his mother came up to say goodnight. Now he needn't do that.

He heard his father get into the car. He heard it go purring down the drive and into the road. Good. Now he could act.

He debated on a disguise. Should he put one on, or shouldn't he? It wasn't really necessary. On the other hand, it would be fun, and he was rather out of practice disguising himself these hols. Fatty decided he *would* do a spot of disguising. He took a torch, and he and Buster disappeared cautiously down the garden to the lock-up shed where he kept his dressing-up things.

He thought he wouldn't put on anything too noticeable. He didn't want to scare the night-watchmen, dreaming over their fires! He decided on a small toothbrush moustache, his false, prominent teeth, and no wig – just his own hair. A cap of some sort? Yes, that checked one would do well. He'd wear it back to front – it would look very fetching that way.

He chose a tweed overcoat, rather too big for him, and a blue-spotted scarf. He looked at himself in the glass. Did he look like a young man asking for information about a sleepwalking uncle? He thought he did.

He set off. He guessed he must go in the direction of the river because Mr Fellows had gone out of the back gate, which meant he was presumably going in that direction and not up the road towards the hills. Now, where was the road being mended on the way to the river?

Fatty decided regretfully to leave Buster behind. Too many people knew Buster. If they met him in company with a strange young man at night, they might think somebody was stealing him. So Buster was left behind, curled up on the rug in the shed.

Fatty went to Mr Fellows' house, and looked at it. It was in complete darkness. He stood at the back gate and looked along the road. Yes, he would go down there – and when he came to the bottom, he would see if there was any sign of a night-watchman's brazier of glowing coals.

He walked down smartly. At the end, he looked this way and that. No sign of any watchman or of the road being up. He turned to the right and made his way to the next crossroad. There he had some luck.

Red lamps burned in a row, and in the midst of them was the dark shadowy shape of a watchman's hut, with the brazier of burning coals in front of it. Fatty walked along.

The watchman heard his steps and peered out. 'Good evening,' said Fatty cheerily. 'Nice fire you've got there! Do you charge anything if I warm my hands, mate?'

'Warm 'em and welcome,' said the old fellow.

'Everybody who comes by likes a warm at my fire, so he do.'

'Do you get many people late at night?' asked Fatty, spreading his fingers over the warm glow. 'I mean, after midnight?'

'I gets the policeman, Mr Goon,' said the watchman. 'Chatty fellow he is. Handles a lot of important cases, so he tells me. And I gets a fisherman or two that likes a bit of midnight fishing. Nobody about then to disturb the fish you know.'

'I wonder if you've ever seen my Uncle Horatius,' began Fatty. 'He's a funny old fellow – walks in his sleep.'

'Do he now?' said the watchman, with interest.

'Yes, he do – er, does,' said Fatty. 'I suppose you didn't see him last night, did you, wandering about in a dressing-gown – or perhaps a coat over his pyjamas – with bedroom slippers on his feet?'

The watchman went off into a cackle of laughter just like a goose. Fatty listened to it intently, he could copy that at some time – wonderful! Cackle, cackle, cackle.

'Naw, I didn't see him,' said the old man. 'Good

thing too, or mebbe I'd have thought I were asleep, and dreaming – and that's not a good thing for a night-watchman to do. But old Willie, him that's watching further along, nearer the river, he did say something about a chap in pyjamas last night. Mebbe that was your Uncle Horatius. You should ought to lock him up, Mister – he'll get himself drownded one night, sleepwalking near the river!'

'Yes. I think I *will* lock him up in the future,' said Fatty, delighted at this unexpected bit of news. 'I'll go and have a word with Willie. Hello, who's this?'

There was a ringing of a bicycle bell, and a familiar figure loomed up in the light of the nearest lamp-post. Mr Goon! Blow! What was *he* doing here?

12. A LITTLE NIGHT-PROWLING

Fatty moved off hastily, glad that he hadn't brought Buster with him. What a welcome Buster would have given the astonished Goon!

The burly policeman got off his bicycle and went over to the night-watchman. Fatty escaped into the shadows and hurried off to find Willie.

A row of red lamps again guided him. He went down a long road towards them, seeing the flash of the river at the end. The watchman's little hut was set close beside the bright brazier of burning coals.

Fatty introduced himself as before, and brought his Uncle Horatius into the conversation as soon as he could. He was afraid that Goon might turn up again! Why must he ride round the streets just when Fatty wanted them to himself!

Willie the watchman proved rather a surly fellow. He answered very shortly indeed.

'You sometimes have people asking you if they can warm themselves by your fine fire, I'm sure,' said Fatty, persevering in spite of the watchman's surliness. 'I bet my Uncle Horatius always comes to warm himself when he goes sleepwalking at nights.'

The watchman grunted. He took no interest in Fatty's uncle or in sleepwalking either.

'You might have seen him last night,' went on Fatty. 'Came out in his pyjamas and bedroom slippers. Ha, ha, ha!'

The watchman looked at Fatty. 'I seed him,' he remarked, suddenly developing quite a chatty manner. 'Leastways, I seed someone running by – pyjama legs and bedroom slippers 'e wore. Scatty fellow, I thought to myself. But he weren't old, the way he run along.'

Fatty was delighted. Ah, so Mr Fellows had run down this road. That was something! It only led to the river. Why had he gone down to the *river*?

'Was he carrying anything?' asked Fatty.

'Yes, he were. Something in his arms like, but I dunno what it was,' said the watchman. 'So he were your uncle, were he? Do he often sleepwalk?'

'On moonlight nights mostly,' said Fatty, ready to invent anything now that he had got a little information. 'You didn't see him come back, did you?'

'Naw,' said Willie, and relapsed into surliness again. Fatty was about to say goodnight when he heard the ringing of a bicycle bell again. Surely, surely that couldn't be Mr Goon once more?

But it was! Fatty escaped from the light of the burning brazier just in time. Goon sailed up to the light of the red lamps and hailed Willie.

'Are you there, my man? I want to ask you a few questions!'

Fatty hid behind a convenient bush, a really worrying suspicion forming in his mind. Was Goon cross-examining the night-watchman too – and for the same reason as Fatty was? Had he worked out the problem in the same way as the Find-Outers had? If so, Goon was growing a few brains!

'Well, Willie,' said Goon, warming himself at the brazier, first his vast front, then his rather vaster back. 'You seen anyone suspicious last night? I'm on a case again, and I'm looking out for someone.'

'You wouldn't be wanting an old uncle what sleepwalks and wears pyjamas and red slippers, would you?' said Willie.

Goon stared at him, astonished. 'Why, the old watchman away up the other road asked me that,' he said. 'I thought it was just his joke. Who's been kidding you along too?'

'A young fellow,' said Willie. 'Proper worried about his old Uncle Horatius, he was – old gent what sleepwalks at night.'

'Oh. And I suppose Uncle Horatius went for a sleepwalk last night, did he?' said Mr Goon, in such a ferocious voice that Willie was astonished.

' 'Ere! What you talking to me like that for?' he complained.

'What was this fellow like who told you this fairytale?' demanded Mr Goon.

'I didn't rightly notice him much,' said Willie. 'My eyes ain't too good now. Young, he was. Tallish. A moustache of some sort. And he was fattish too.'

Mr Goon gave an exclamation. *Fattish!* Could the owner of the sleepwalking uncle be – that boy! Was it that pest again, on the track of something as usual? Mr Goon could have shouted in rage.

The moustache was put on, of course – the sleepwalking uncle was made up. It must be – it *was* that big boy following the same clues that he, Mr Goon, had so painfully worked out himself. Where was he? Where had he gone? If Mr Goon could have got his hands on Fatty at that moment, Fatty would have had to yell for mercy!

'Now, you listen here, Willie,' said Mr Goon, suddenly making a plan. 'You listening?'

'Ay,' said Willie. 'Speak louder though. My ears ain't so good.'

Mr Goon spoke up, much to Fatty's joy. What was he going to say?

'That fellow will come back this way,' said Mr Goon. 'I want to get my hands on him, see? So when you see him coming, you holler out to him. Get him over here and keep him talking.'

'What for?' asked Willie, doubtfully. 'If he's a bad lot, I don't want to give 'im the chance of knocking me on the 'ead.'

'I'm going to hide at the other end of the road,' said Goon. 'In case he spots me. He's scared of me, dead scared. If he so much as sees the lamp on my bike, he'll run for miles. And I want to get my hands on him, see? Now, when you see him coming, you take up one of your red lamps and swing it slowly to and fro in your hands. I'll be along at once, while you're talking to him.'

'All right,' said Willie, resignedly. What with people talking about sleepwalking uncles and red slippers and bad lots and swinging lamps, Willie was fed up. He'd never get down to a nice little snooze tonight, that was certain!

Mr Goon disappeared on his bicycle. He went to the far end of the river road, got off, and hid under a tree, his bicycle beside him. Ah, he'd catch that big boy on his way back! He'd have to come back that way, because the river barred his way at the other end of the road!

Fatty debated what to do. Should he cut down to the river, make his way across somebody's back garden, and cut into the road that ran parallel with this? Or should he play a little trick on Goon?

He decided on the trick. Goon deserved one after saying that Fatty was dead scared of him! Fatty began to get to work quickly. He blackened his face with dirt. He twisted his cap the other way round, with the peak now shading his eyes. He put a white handkerchief round his neck instead of the scarf. He took off his moustache, but left in his awful teeth.

He felt about on the waste piece of ground nearby. Was there anything he could use in his trick. His hand fell upon an old sack. Good – just the thing! Fatty groped about among the rubbish left by the road-menders and came across pieces of brick and stone. He quickly slid them into the sack until it was half–full. It was very heavy.

He made his way back to the road and skirted round to the back of the watchman. Then he walked slowly by him, half-bent under the sack.

The watchman saw him, but his bleary old eyes couldn't make out who it was. He stared hard, in doubt, wishing the moon would come out from behind a cloud. He decided that whoever it was looked decidedly suspicious. It wouldn't do any harm to swing the red lamp to and fro!

He picked it up, turned himself towards Mr Goon, and swung the lamp slowly. Fatty grinned as he saw it out of the corner of his eye. He plodded on slowly, bent under the sack. If ever anyone looked a suspicious person at that moment, Fatty did!

Mr Goon saw the swinging lamp, and came quickly down the road, keeping to the shadows, his rubber-soled boots making no noise. He tried to see if Fatty was there, talking to the watchman. But to his great annoyance, when he got to the little hut there was no one there but Willie!

'Where is he? Why did you swing your lamp? He's not here!' said Goon, exasperated.

'I see a very suspicious chap shuffling down the river road,' said Willie. 'Not the chap as you wanted, but someone you'd like to get your hands on, I don't doubt. A real suspicious chap. And carrying a heavy sack too. You'd like to know what's in that sack, I reckon!'

'Ho! It certainly sounds bad,' said Goon, thinking that if he couldn't get his hands on Fatty, it would be satisfactory to get them on to someone else. 'What direction did he go in?'

'Yonder,' said Willie, nodding. And yonder went Goon, keeping to the shadows, tracking down Fatty and the suspicious sack. Fatty took a quick look back. Good! Goon was on his trail! He would lead him a nice little dance!

Down to the river plodded Fatty, and came to where the waves were silvery with moonlight. He turned down the towing-path that led to the small jetty nearby, and Goon followed stealthily, breathing so hard that Fatty could hear him.

Fatty walked slowly shuffling one foot after the other, like an old, old man. He coughed mournfully as he went, a horrible hollow cough. He suddenly stopped and put down his sack as if it was too heavy. Goon stopped too.

Fatty heaved the sack on to his shoulder again, and set off once more on his way to the jetty. He stopped suddenly again when he was almost there, and put the sack down once more, with a groan. Goon also stopped suddenly. He was very curious now. What was the old man doing with such a heavy sack? Where was he going? What was in the sack? Had he some accomplice he was meeting? Goon began to feel quite excited.

Fatty hoisted the sack on his back once again and went on his way. He came to the little wooden jetty. Moonlit water splashed against it.

Fatty went on to the jetty and sat down with his sack as if to rest.

Now was Goon's chance! He emerged from the shadows and strode heavily up to the jetty, a big figure in the moonlight.

'Now then,' he began. 'What's your name? And what have you got in that sack?'

'Bricks and stones,' said Fatty truthfully, in a sad, weary, old-man voice.

'Gah!' said Goon, in scorn. 'Nobody carries sacks of bricks and stones about, unless they're mad!'

'Mebbe I'm mad,' said Fatty, drooping his head down so that the moonlight didn't fall on his face.

'You open that sack and let me see what you've got,' said Goon, threateningly.

'No,' said Fatty, clutching the sack as if it contained rubies and diamonds.

'Come on now!' said Goon, advancing on him. 'You open that sack – and be quick about it!'

13. NEWS FROM ERB

'It don't belong to me,' said Fatty obstinately, still clutching the sack.

'Who does it belong to then?' demanded Mr Goon.

'Sh! It belongs to Mr Fellows!' whispered Fatty, on the spur of the moment, and then was horrified to realise what he had said! Mr Goon was amazed.

'Belongs to Mr Fellows!' he repeated. 'But – how did you get it? Look here, you give it to me. You are acting in a suspicious manner, and you'll be arrested in a moment!'

He grabbed at the sack, and Fatty stood up, shouting dramatically, 'No, no, don't touch it!' And then, more dramatically, he picked up the sack and flung it down into the river beside the jetty. He was very glad to get rid of it indeed. It made a most tremendous splash.

Mr Goon was bitterly disappointed. He had made up his mind that there was something very important in the sack – and now it was gone! He knelt down to look over the side of the jetty, and Fatty took to his heels at once.

Mr Goon stood up and gaped at the running figure. How could the old, shuffling fellow run like that? Mr Goon wondered if he was dreaming. He decided that he couldn't possibly catch the fellow – why, he was almost at the turning into the river-road now! What a strange thing to run like that after so much shuffling! A sentence floated into Mr Goon's mind – 'Fear lent him wings'. Well, Mr Goon hadn't got any wings. He would have to walk back at his own pace.

He knelt down again to look into the river but, of course, he could see no sign of the sack. He made up his mind to come with a boat-hook the next day and haul it up. He would find out what was in that sack if he had to go into the water himself to get it!

Willie was astonished to see yet another figure, this time racing past, instead of shuffling past. The goings-on there were in these times! It was quite certain he wouldn't get a snooze before midnight at this rate. That policeman would probably be coming back in a minute too.

Fatty fell to a walk after a bit. He guessed Mr Goon wouldn't come after him. He felt relieved to think that the policeman hadn't recognised him. But whatever had made him say the sack belonged to Mr Fellows? That was really rather idiotic, and not fair to Mr Fellows! Fatty felt distinctly uncomfortable about that.

He got home without any further adventure, feeling unexpectedly tired. Buster gave him an uproarious welcome, and Fatty discarded all his clothes down in the old shed with the little Scottie dancing round him in delight.

Then Fatty crawled tiredly up the garden path from the shed to the house. Gosh! I'm shuffling just like I pretended to, he marvelled. But shuffling's not so good when it's real!

Fatty was so tired that he was almost asleep as he climbed the stairs. He fell into bed, and immediately began to dream of red lamps following him in a threatening manner. He groaned in his sleep and Buster pricked up one ear. Then Mr Goon appeared in his dream riding on his bicycle – and fortunately the red lamps all attached themselves to him, so Fatty was at peace once more.

At breakfast the next morning, the telephone rang. The maid came in and looked at Fatty. 'It's for you, Frederick,' she said. 'Larry is on the phone.'

Fatty jumped up as if dogs were after him. There must be something up if Larry telephoned so early! He hurried to the telephone.

'That you, Fatty?' came Larry's excited voice. 'Guess what! – Mr Fellows is back! I thought you'd better know at once in case old Mr Goon doesn't know yet.'

'Gosh, yes – thanks for phoning,' said Fatty. 'But how did you know?'

'Erb told me,' said Larry. 'I was out in the garden with Daisy looking for one of the kittens that wouldn't come in, and Erb called over the wall to me. He said he was awake last night, listening to his precious owls again, when he heard the click of the gate next door.'

'Go on,' said Fatty. 'What time was this?'

'He said it was about two o'clock in the morning,' said Larry. 'He went to his window at once, wondering if it was a burglar again – but he says it was Mr Fellows. He saw him clearly in the moonlight. And he saw him again when he went into the house, because he switched the light on in the sitting-room whose window Erb can see into. And it *was* Mr Fellows all right.'

'What was he dressed in?' asked Fatty, excited by this news.

'He couldn't really see – but he *thinks* he had on a dressing-gown,' said Larry. 'He wasn't carrying anything though, so if he did rush out of the house with a parcel of some sort . . .'

'He did!' said Fatty. 'I found that out from a night-watchman last night!'

'Oh, good – well, whatever it was, he apparently didn't bring it back with him,' said Larry. 'Do you suppose he was shocked to see his house turned upside down?'

'No. He probably expected it,' said Fatty. 'Well, I'll be along at your house after breakfast. Telephone Pip and Bets, will you? We'll have to think out our next move. By the way, Mr Goon's on the same track as we are. He was very chatty with the watchmen last night too – seems to me he's been setting his brains to work. Most unusual!'

'Frederick!' called his mother. 'Your breakfast is getting cold. Do come back.'

'Good-bye, see you later, Larry,' said Fatty hastily, wondering just how much of the telephone conversation his mother had heard.

He went back into the dining-room and sat down. 'That was Larry,' he said. 'We're all going to his house this morning, if that's all right, Mummy. You don't want me for anything, do you?'

'Well, I *was* going to look through all your school clothes,' said his mother. 'But it will do another time.'

Fatty groaned. 'School! I'm usually really pleased to go back – but this flu has taken it out of me. I'd like the hols to be longer this time!'

'You look the picture of health,' said his father, putting his newspaper down. 'And judging by the number of sausages you've eaten, you feel healthy enough too. You'll go back to school on the right day, so don't try to get round your mother.'

'I'm not!' said Fatty indignantly. 'And sausages have nothing to do with how I feel. Actually, I was eating them quite absent-mindedly this morning.'

'What a waste of sausages then,' said his father, putting up his newspaper again. 'Frederick, I couldn't help overhearing part of your telephone conversation just now – I hope you are not going to get mixed up in anything to do with that absurd policeman again.'

'Not if I can help it,' said Fatty, spreading butter on his toast. 'Any news in the paper this morning, Dad?'

'Plenty. And I'm quite aware that you are hurriedly changing the subject,' said Mr Trotteville, drily.

Fatty said no more, but chewed his toast, his mind dwelling on the return of Mr Fellows. He would go and see him immediately after breakfast, taking the kitten with him – what a marvellous excuse for going! He would see what he could get out of him. He hoped that Mr Goon didn't also know Mr Fellows was back, but there was really no reason why he should have heard. Erb wouldn't have told *him*!

Good old Erb! thought Fatty, drinking his coffee. Erb had come in very useful indeed. Good thing he was so interested in night birds! He wouldn't have been nearly so useful if his interest had been in house sparrows!

Fatty took his bicycle and rode off to Larry's at top speed, with Buster in the basket. On the way, he saw Mr Goon, also on a bicycle, far in the distance. The policeman saw Fatty and waved to him frantically. He had a few questions to ask him about the night before!

Fatty knew that. He certainly wasn't going to stop! He waved back cheerily, as if he thought that Goon was simply being friendly. The policeman pedalled furiously to catch up Fatty.

Blow him, thought Fatty, and pedalled as fast as he could. He turned a corner, leapt off his bicycle, and disappeared with it into the garden of an empty house. He crouched behind the fence.

Mr Goon came by, purple and panting, and sailed up the road, marvelling that Fatty could disappear so swiftly. Fatty came out quickly, mounted his bicycle and rode off in the opposite direction. Buster was surprised at all this, but hadn't even got out of the basket!

Mr Goon's on the lookout for me, thought Fatty. I'll have some awkward questions to answer. Blow him! Does he suspect it was me last night that he followed? I wonder if he's found that sack of bricks and stones yet! He said he was going to get a boat-hook and drag it up. Well, good luck to him! It'll keep him out of the way for a bit, messing about in the river!

He arrived at Larry's out of breath. Pip, Bets, Larry, and Daisy were watching for him. Daisy was holding the kitten.

'Nobody's seen a sign of Mr Fellows,' said Larry, as soon as Fatty came up. 'We think he may be lying low for a bit. Do you think you really should go and see him? I mean, he may not be at all pleased to see you!'

'Can't help that,' said Fatty. 'I can't miss this chance. I simply must question him before Mr Goon gets at him.'

He took the kitten. 'Thanks, Daisy. Well, you funny little thing? You won't like leaving your playmate, will you, and going back to that lonely house?'

He left his bicycle at Larry's, and went up the road to the next house but one – Mr Fellows'. He looked in at the gate. Should he go to the front door or to the back? There was no sign of life in the place at all. Was Mr Fellows pretending to be still away?

I'll go round to the back, thought Fatty. I don't want Mr Goon to see me standing at the front door if he comes by.

He went quietly and cautiously round to the back. He looked in at the window there, the one that was broken. Nobody was about. Fatty debated with himself again.

It was likely that Mr Fellows would not answer any ringing or knocking if he was lying low. But *somehow* Fatty must get hold of him. How? Fatty racked his brains.

And then a splendid idea came to him. It was quite likely that Mr Fellows had been looking for the kitten, now he was back – perhaps he was worried about it. Fatty would stick his face close to the broken pane, and miaow as loudly as he could! If that didn't fetch Mr Fellows into the kitchen, nothing would!

14. AN INTERESTING CONVERSATION

'Miaow! Miaow! MIAOW!'

A most pitiful, heartrending noise penetrated into the kitchen through the broken window. The little kitten that Fatty was holding jumped when it heard his lifelike mewing. It suddenly added its own high-pitched mew.

'That's right,' whispered Fatty. 'Keep up the good work, kitty. Mew as loudly as you can!'

'Miaow!' said the kitten obligingly. 'Miaow.'

Fatty listened. He thought he heard a noise in the house. It seemed to come from upstairs.

'MIAOW-ee-ow-ee-OW!' said Fatty piercingly.

He listened again. Yes, certainly someone was moving in the house now – there were footsteps on the stairs. Then they stopped.

'Miaow,' said the kitten shrilly. It certainly was doing its best for Fatty.

A man appeared at the inner door of the

kitchen, the one that led into the hall.

That must be Mr Fellows, thought Fatty, looking at him closely. He was fully dressed, though Fatty had half-expected him to be in dressing-gown and slippers! He hadn't caught sight of the boy and the kitten yet. He was looking all round the kitchen floor as if wondering where the mewing had come from. He was a youngish fellow, with a thin face, and bright, intelligent eyes. His hair was smoothly brushed, and he didn't in the least look as if he had rushed, panic-stricken, out of his house two nights before.

'Miaow,' said the kitten again, struggling to get out of Fatty's arms. The man heard the mew and looked across to the window. He saw Fatty's head and shoulders there, and made as if to draw back at once. Then he saw that Fatty was a boy, and that he was holding the kitten.

He came forward slowly. Fatty guessed that he was annoyed at having been seen. He spoke apologetically through the broken pane.

'Sorry to disturb you, sir – but this is your kitten, isn't it? We've been looking after it through the – er – upset.'

The man smoothed back his hair. He answered cautiously. 'Yes, it's my kitten. Er – wait a minute, I'll undo the kitchen door.'

He unlocked and unbolted it. Fatty was at the door, waiting. The man stretched out his hand for the kitten, and Fatty sensed that once he had taken it, he would probably say no more than a word of thanks, and shut the door.

'I say, sir – your burglary caused quite an excitement!' said Fatty, holding on to the kitten. 'The police were here – did you know?'

Mr Fellows looked startled. 'The police!' he said. 'What for? How did they know anything about the house being empty – or, er – burgled?'

Fatty thought rapidly. Mr Fellows hadn't heard then that the milkman had reported anything – he didn't know that Mr Goon had inspected the house and found it upside down. Probably he hoped that nobody knew anything at all, either about the intruder, or about his rushing out of the house!

'I'll tell you all about it, if you like, sir,' said Fatty, stepping firmly into the kitchen. Mr Fellows now obviously wanted to know what Fatty had to say. It was news to him that the police had been into his house. He looked worried.

He shut the kitchen door and locked it. He took Fatty into the little sitting-room. Everything was now tidy and in its place. Mr Fellows had obviously been very busy since he had got back, and had cleared everything up. The kitten followed, mewing.

'Does it want any milk?' asked Mr Fellows, looking down at it. 'I'm afraid there isn't any. The milkman apparently didn't come this morning.'

'No. I expect the police told him not to as you weren't here,' said Fatty. He sat down on a chair.

'What *is* all this about the police!' said Mr Fellows irritably. 'Can't a man go away for a short while without the police coming in and snooping round! I think that is most unnecessary.'

'Well, you see, apparently burglars got in and turned the place upside down while you were away,' said Fatty, watching Mr Fellows closely. 'Didn't you find everywhere in an awful mess?'

The man hesitated. He quite obviously wasn't going to say more than he needed to.

'Yes, but I'm an untidy person,' he said. 'Er

– who did you say raised the alarm to the police?'

'The milkman,' said Fatty, stroking the purring kitten. 'He found the front door wide open when he came to leave your milk yesterday morning – walked in, saw the confusion, and telephoned the police.'

'I see,' said Mr Fellows. 'This is all news to me.'

'What time did you leave your house then?' asked Fatty suddenly. He knew quite well what time it had been, because of Erb's information, but he wanted to see what Mr Fellows had to say.

The man hesitated again. 'Oh, sometime that night,' he said. 'I – er – went to visit a friend and stayed the night with him. I came back last night to find the house a little untidy, certainly. But nothing has been stolen as far as I can see. I don't see why the police had to butt in without my permission.'

'Because of the open front door,' said Fatty, patiently. 'I suppose you did shut the front door after you when you went out, Mr Fellows?'

'Of course,' said the man, but Fatty didn't believe him. He felt sure that Mr Fellows had probably only pulled it to, not wanting the intruder in the house to hear him go. It was the intruder who had left it wide open!

Fatty debated whether or not to ask Mr Fellows what he had been dressed in when he had left the house. He decided that he wouldn't. He would only be more on his guard than ever, and would anyhow lie about it. Fatty glanced at him – he looked extremely clean and tidy and well-brushed.

Not a bit like my Uncle Horatius! thought Fatty. Now, if I want to find out if he really did wander about in a dressing-gown and bedroom slippers, I'll somehow have to slip upstairs and snoop round for them. But how?

All conversation suddenly came to an abrupt end. A big red face unexpectedly appeared at the sitting-room window, and looked in. The face owned a helmet – it was Goon!

Mr Fellows gave an exclamation. 'Who's that? Of all the brazen cheek! It's the police again! What do they think they're doing, snooping and prying on private property like this? I'll put this fellow where he belongs!'

'I certainly would, if I were you,' Fatty agreed fervently. 'A man can't call his house his own

401

these days! Are you going to let that policeman in, sir? He's speaking to you.'

Goon had just been on his rounds and had, as a matter of routine, called in at Mr Fellows' house to see if anything had happened there. As there was no smoke from the chimneys, and everything seemed quiet, he hadn't done anything but peep in at the windows. He wasn't going to enter that house alone again if he could help it!

He could hardly believe his eyes when he saw Fatty sitting there with a man who must be Fellows. He gaped at them both. Then a familiar rage boiled up in him. That boy! That toad! There he was again, poking his nose in – and getting it there before he, Mr Goon, could get in his. How did he do it?

'Open the door, sir,' bellowed Mr Goon. 'I have a few words to say to you.'

Mr Fellows glared at the red-faced policeman. He strode to the window and opened it.

'What do you mean by peering in like this at my window?' Mr Fellows asked in a furious voice. 'Can't you see I'm sitting here talking to a friend? What's the matter with you?'

'A friend?' choked Mr Goon, glaring at Fatty. 'Is that boy your friend?'

'I shall report you for this extraordinary behaviour,' said Mr Fellows. 'My house is my own, and I am not aware that I have done anything to cause the police to pry into it.'

'But – but – there's been a burglary!' spluttered Mr Goon. 'The house was all upside down, and . . .'

'There has been no burglary,' said Mr Fellows. 'As far as I know, not a single thing has been stolen. As for the house being untidy, well, I'm an untidy person. I can turn my own house upside down if I want to, can't I?'

'The front door was wide open,' persisted Mr Goon, angry and bewildered.

'I'm forgetful,' said Mr Fellows. 'I do sometimes forget to close my doors. Now, clear off – do you hear me, CLEAR OFF!'

Fatty could have hugged himself in joy. Goon was always yelling at people to clear off, and now here was someone yelling the same thing at him. But the policeman had not finished yet.

'Well, let me tell you, you've no right to go

away and leave animals to starve in the house,' he said.

'The kitten is quite all right,' said Mr Fellows coldly, and was about to shut the window when Mr Goon put an enormous dark blue arm in to stop him.

'What about the dog?' he said. 'And the pig?'

Mr Fellows stared at Mr Goon as if he had suddenly taken leave of his senses. 'What dog and what pig?' he demanded. 'Are you crazy, constable?'

'Ho! And what about the fellow who kept crying out, and wanted his auntie?' said Mr Goon, trying to force the window open.

Mr Fellows was now quite convinced that Mr Goon was raving mad. He turned to speak to Fatty – but Fatty was not there!

No, Fatty had seen a chance to creep upstairs and examine bedroom slippers and dressing-gowns, and also pyjamas. Reluctant as he was to leave the battle-ground on which Mr Fellows and Mr Goon were squabbling so fiercely, he felt that he couldn't miss this chance.

He picked up the kitten and tiptoed out of the room. He wanted the kitten with him to provide him with an excuse for going upstairs – why should anyone think it odd if the kitten fled upstairs and needed looking for?

Up the stairs went Fatty, grinning to hear Mr Goon shouting the question about the dog and the pig. Gosh, Mr Fellows would think he was quite mad!

He saw that everywhere had been tidied up. He tiptoed into the biggest room, which he guessed was Mr Fellows' bedroom. Now – where were his slippers – and pyjamas – and dressing-gown?

15. FATTY IS PLEASED

Fatty looked round the room. No slippers to be seen! He looked under the bed. Ah, a pair of red slippers lay there, rather like Larry's, but bigger. Fatty turned them upside down and examined them.

They were muddy, very muddy! Mud had even got splashed on the tops of the slippers. It was quite obvious that Mr Fellows had been wandering about the streets in these.

Fatty slipped his hand under the eiderdown and pulled out pyjamas, striped red and white. He gave a low whistle. The bottom edges of the legs were filthy dirty – splashed with mud and clay. Fatty nodded his head. Yes, that muddy clay down by the river.

Now for the dressing-gown. It was hanging in a tall cupboard. It was dirty – but it was also messed up with hay and straw – strands stuck out here and there. Where had Mr Fellows been in his dressing-gown? Fatty thought rapidly, as he shut the cupboard door.

He didn't go to stay with a friend, he hid somewhere for the rest of that night, and all day yesterday – because he didn't want to be found in his night-clothes – questions would be asked! He hid in a barn or in a haystack or rick – and crept home in the middle of last night. I bet the watchmen were surprised to see him again, if they spotted him. Gosh, they'd think my Uncle Horatius had been out again!

The angry voices downstairs had stopped. There was the sound of a window being slammed shut. Fatty dropped down on his hands and knees and began calling.

'Puss, puss, where are you? Kitty, kitty!'

A voice came up the stairs. 'What are you doing up there? Come down at once!'

'Sorry,' said Fatty, appearing at the top of the stairs. 'The kitten's run away.'

'It's down here,' said Mr Fellows. He still looked very angry. 'You clear off now. Thanks for seeing to the kitten. I've ticked that interfering policeman off, and he's gone. I've a good mind to report him.'

'I should, sir,' said Fatty earnestly.

'I think he must be mad,' said Mr Fellows, pacing nervously up and down. 'Talking about dogs and pigs and aunties.'

Fatty wanted to laugh. He glanced round, and decided that there really wasn't any more to get out of Mr Fellows, or to hunt for in the house. He had done very nicely!

'Well, good-bye, sir – and I hope the kitten will be all right now,' said Fatty. 'Sorry to intrude and all that. Fancy you not having a burglar after all!'

'Well, I didn't,' snapped Mr Fellows. 'Clear out now. I want some peace!'

Fatty cleared out, whistling softly. A most interesting interview – and how nice to find that all his ideas had been right. Those muddy slippers! My word, if Mr Goon got into the house and did a bit of snooping, he would find a few things to interest him too!

Mr Goon was lying in wait for Fatty. He emerged from behind a tree as Fatty turned down the road to go to Larry's.

'Ho!' said Mr Goon, his face purple. 'Ho!' He seemed quite unable to say anything else for the moment.

'Ho to you,' said Fatty politely. 'Many Hoes!'

Mr Goon went a deeper purple. 'So you're his friend, are you?' he said, in a choking voice. '*That's* a bit of news, that is!'

'I'm so glad,' said Fatty politely, trying to edge past.

'Do you know what you are?' said Mr Goon, losing the rest of his temper with a rush. 'You're a pest! A toad! But I've sent in my report, see – and you'll be sorry!'

'I don't see why,' said Fatty. 'I do hope you've put in the kitten, the dog, and the pig – not forgetting Auntie.'

'There wasn't any auntie,' shouted Mr Goon. 'He just *wanted* his auntie! Gah! What with you and Kenton and that fellow up yonder, my life's not worth living.'

'No. It's a poor sort of life,' agreed Fatty, suddenly seeing Larry and Daisy out of the corner of his eye in Larry's front garden. He hoped and prayed they had got Buster with them, and would have the sense to let him out of the gate.

'I suppose you think I don't know it was you muddling those night-watchmen last night?' began Goon again, going off on a new tack, with a new grievance. 'Your Uncle Horace! Pah!'

'My Uncle *Horatius*,' corrected Fatty. 'Don't muddle up my uncles, please.'

Mr Goon advanced on him, ready to tear Fatty limb from limb. Never had he felt so angry in his life. Poor Mr Goon, he was muddled and bewildered and so exasperated that he didn't know which way to turn!

'Wuff! Wuff-wuff!'

With a delighted volley of barks, Buster suddenly shot out of Larry's front gate at sixty miles an hour. He was thrilled to see Fatty, and equally thrilled to see Mr Goon, though for rather a different reason. He leapt up at Fatty, gave him a hurried lick, and then leapt at Mr Goon.

The policeman was defeated. Fatty was bad enough – but Fatty plus Buster was too much. Mr Goon gave the biggest snort of his life, flung himself on his bicycle and wobbled down the hill, one of his feet slipping frantically on a pedal. Buster flew after him, leaping and pouncing in delight.

Fatty began to laugh. He staggered into Larry's gate. Larry held him up, laughing too. The other three were there and they made their way to the shed at the bottom of the garden. Fatty collapsed on the ground, quite weak with excitement and laughter.

They held a very interesting meeting. Everyone hung on Fatty's words as he described his peculiar interview with Mr Fellows, Goon's sudden appearance, and all that Fatty had discovered in his snooping upstairs.

'Wow! Then all your reasoning was correct,' said Bets, in admiration. 'Every single thing! He *did* rush out in pyjamas and dressing-gown and slippers – and he came back in them too – after sleeping in hiding somewhere.'

'Yes. But we still don't know what he took with him when he went – or where he has hidden it,' said Fatty. 'According to Erb, he had nothing with him when he returned. He wouldn't, anyway, I suppose – because it would be senseless to take back whatever it was that was so valuable. He might find the burglar waiting for him again!'

'Yes. He's hidden it,' said Larry. 'I wonder where? We can't very well hunt in all the haystacks and ricks round about Peterswood – there are dozens of them!'

'He's very careful in all he says,' said Fatty. 'There's something going on. I wonder what it is. Gosh, we *must* try and find out before we go back to school. An unfinished mystery. How disgraceful!'

Everyone agreed, but nobody could see for the life of them how they could get any further. Mr Fellows was not likely to help them! He had something he badly wanted to hide, that was certain. *Could* they possibly go hunting in stacks and ricks? The farmers wouldn't be at all pleased.

Fatty told the others about his escapade of the night before. They laughed delightedly.

'Oh, Fatty!' said Bets. 'I never knew anyone like you in my life. And I never shall. There's just nothing you're scared of doing.'

'I was a bit scared of old Mr Goon just now,' said Fatty. 'Honestly, he looked like an angry bull. I don't blame him. I must be pretty annoying to him. I was really glad when Buster came flying out!'

'Wuff,' said Buster, thumping his tail approvingly.

'Do you think Mr Goon has got that sack of yours out of the river yet?' said Daisy. 'Whatever will he say when he finds it is full of stones and bricks! He doesn't know it was you who dumped it there, does he?'

'No. But he'll guess it was when he finds what's in the sack!' grinned Fatty. 'You should have seen me heave it in! Old Mr Goon nearly went in after it.'

'Do you think he's gone to look for it now?' asked Bets. 'He wouldn't leave it too long, would he? Let's go for a walk down to the river and see if he's anywhere about. We can bike down.'

'Yes, let's,' said Daisy. 'You've been having all the fun, Fatty – we want some now too. I'd just love to see Mr Goon digging about with a boat-hook and bringing up a sack full of stones and bricks.'

'All right. We might as well,' said Fatty, getting up. 'Walkie – walk, Buster. Come on!'

They got on their bicycles. Pip and Bets had

413

theirs at Larry's, as they had bicycled there that morning. They freewheeled down the hill towards the river.

Mr Goon was not there. Fatty spotted an old boatman friend of his, painting a boat outside his shed. He put his bicycle by a tree and hailed him.

'Hello, Mr Spicer! Getting ready for spring weather? It's been pretty cold lately, hasn't it?'

'Ay, that it has,' agreed old Spicer, beaming at the five children. He knew them all. 'Why aren't you back at school yet?'

'Term hasn't begun,' said Fatty. 'Are you letting out any boats yet, Mr Spicer? I suppose we couldn't have one this morning?'

'No. I've only got the one ready that you see down there,' said Spicer, nodding his head towards a little, freshly-painted boat bobbing by the bank.

'Well, why can't we have *her*?' demanded Larry, feeling that he would like a good row more than anything else.

'That bobby rang up and asked me to have one ready for him this morning,' said Spicer. 'What's his name now – Moon?'

'Mr Goon, you mean,' said Fatty. He winked at the others. So, Mr Goon *was* going to come and jab about in the river for the sack that Fatty had thrown in. Good!

'Ay, Mr Goon. Wants a boat-hook too,' said old Spicer, painting a bright red line with a steady brown hand. 'Seems like my boat-hooks are popular this morning. He's the second one wants a boat-hook.'

Fatty pricked up his ears. 'Who's the other fellow who wants a boat-hook?' he asked, wondering if it was Mr Fellows. Maybe he wanted to fish out a sack himself!

'I never seen him afore,' said Spicer. 'Big fellow – got a scar down his cheek, and something wrong with one eye. Not a nice piece of work at all, he wasn't. He offered me ten pounds for the loan of my longest boat-hook – said he wanted specimens of the weeds growing up and down the river for some botanist fellow.'

'I see,' said Fatty. The man wasn't Fellows, that was certain. Could he be the would-be burglar, the intruder who had caused Fellows to fly out of his house with a bundle of some kind?

16. DOWN BY THE RIVER

The others were all very interested in this piece of news too. They nodded to Mr Spicer and walked off till he was out of hearing.

'Strange,' said Fatty, in a low voice. 'I don't believe that yarn about jabbing for weeds at the bottom of the river. Let's see if we can find the fellow.'

'Don't let's go too far away,' begged Bets. 'I don't want to miss Mr Goon hunting for your sack, Fatty.'

'Well, you four go and watch Mr Goon when he comes, and I'll saunter up the tow-path as soon as I've asked Mr Spicer where the other fellow went,' said Fatty. 'Perhaps it would be as well if I wasn't here when Mr Goon finds that sack and opens it – he might throw the stones and the bricks at me!'

He went back to ask Spicer in which direction

the man with the boat-hook had gone. 'I'm interested in water weeds myself,' said Fatty, quite truthfully. There were very few things that Fatty was *not* interested in!

'He went up yonder,' said the old boatman, pointing up the tow-path. 'He can't have got very far.'

Fatty went up the path, leaving the others sitting on a seat just inside Spicer's shed. From there, they could easily see when Mr Goon came down to the boat. They waited expectantly, hoping for some fun.

Fatty wandered up the tow-path, keeping his eyes open for the man that Spicer had described. He soon saw him, coming back down the path. He had a pail with him, out of which water weed was hanging. Fatty wondered for a moment if the man really was getting weed for a botanist.

Fatty stopped as the man came up to him. 'Got any snails in your weed?' he asked politely. 'I want some for my garden pond.'

'Get some yourself then,' said the man, in a surly tone. He turned his back on Fatty, and looked down into the water.

'Can I help you?' asked Fatty. 'I know a bit about water weed.'

The man turned round, scowling. 'I don't like boys who hang round,' he said. 'You're not wanted, see? Buzz off!'

Fatty didn't buzz off. He merely sauntered on till he came to a clump of thick bushes. He disappeared round them, forced his way into the centre, and parted a few branches to look through. The bushes were of evergreen box, and Fatty was very well hidden.

He saw the man look back as if to see if Fatty was still anywhere near. But there was no boy to be seen, of course. The man went slowly on his way, looking into the water as he went. He came to a stop at last, and into the water went his boat-hook. He jabbed and poked at something and finally lifted it out. Fatty grinned. An old boot! Well, if he was collecting those, there were plenty in the river!

But the old boot went back with a splash and the man went on again, taking a look round every now and again as if to see if Fatty was still about.

He jabbed again, and brought up something

that disgusted him. He threw it back quickly. Another jab and up came a mass of weeds. He put some into his pail.

'That's just for show, Mr Scarred Cheek,' murmured Fatty, peering through the bush. 'In case anyone is watching you. Are you thinking that Mr Fellows has thrown the treasure, whatever it is, into the river? Or are you just a junk-hunter, wanting to make a few pounds on anything you find? No, I think not. Junk-hunters don't pay money for the loan of a boat-hook!'

The man went slowly on down the tow-path. Fatty grew bored. What were the others doing? Had Mr Goon arrived yet?

Mr Goon had! To the delight of the four watching children, and of Buster, who had not been allowed to go with Fatty, Mr Goon had arrived at full speed on his bicycle! He had jammed on his brakes, thrown his bicycle against a tree, and yelled to Spicer.

'Got that boat ready? And I want the boat-hook too please. I'm pressed for time.'

'The boat's ready yonder, and the hook's alongside,' shouted back Spicer. Goon grunted and went to the little boat. He got in and took the oars. The boat-hook lay beside him. Off he went, and soon began to pant with the effort of his rowing.

'Come on,' said Larry, jumping up. 'Let's go and watch. I'd better carry Buster though, or he might try and leap into his enemy's boat!'

'Let's not go too near till Mr Goon gets Fatty's sack of stones and bricks,' said Bets. 'Let's just saunter up and down, and wait till we see him pull up the sack.'

'Right,' said Larry. So the four of them, with a struggling Buster in Larry's arms, sauntered up and down in the January sunshine. Mr Goon soon spotted them and exclaimed angrily under his breath, 'Those kids again! Good thing for that big boy he's not with them. I don't know what I might do to him with a boat-hook ready to hand!'

He rowed to the jetty. He had decided that it would be much easier to drag up the sack from a boat rather than from the jetty. Mr Goon feared that he might overbalance if he had to bend down and jab about from the high little jetty!

He stopped rowing when he came to the

wooden jetty and drew in his oars. He took up the boat-hook and peered down solemnly into the water. His own red face peered back at him. Mr Goon looked deeper down and tried to see the bulk of a sack somewhere. But the water was very deep just there and, try as he could, he could not see the bottom.

He looked up at the jetty. Now where had that old fellow been standing when he dropped the sack into the water? Yes, just about there! Mr Goon began to prod and jab where he thought the sack might be.

He got hold of nothing but water weeds. He pulled up hundreds of green, slimy strands and exclaimed in annoyance. Weeds, weeds, weeds – where was that sack? He'd find out what that old man had got in his sack if it took him all morning to do it!

Mr Goon got very hot jabbing here and there. He suddenly sensed somebody looking at him, and glanced up. He frowned. Those kids! Now they had come to watch him! Like mosquitoes they were, always buzzing round him. Pity he couldn't slap them all away!

Ah! What was this? His boat-hook really had got hold of something this time – something fairly solid too – and fairly heavy! This must be the old man's sack! Mr Goon puffed and panted, heaved and hauled, trying to raise the sack.

It came up with a rush and Mr Goon nearly fell overboard. The four watching children gasped, and winked at one another. Mr Goon had got the sack, hurrah! Now what would happen?

They walked right on the jetty to see. Some way off, the man with the boat-hook stood, also watching, his attention suddenly caught by Mr Goon's antics. A little way behind him stood Fatty, ready to dart into Spicer's shed if Goon's anger was too great!

Mr Goon was so excited that he didn't even notice all these spectators. He heaved the bundle into the boat. Larry looked at it intently. It didn't look to him like a sack. It looked more like a laundry bag or something like that. Was it Fatty's sack that Goon had got – or was it something else?

Goon looked at the dripping bundle. He saw that it was a bag, not a sack, but he didn't worry about that. He had only seen the bundle on Fatty's back by moonlight. Bag or sack, he was absolutely certain that this was what the old man had thrown into the river last night!

He undid the string that tied the neck. He opened it wide. He put in his hand, wondering what he was going to find – the result of several burglaries, he had no doubt.

Ah, a big stone. That would be to weight it down – and another stone – and another. Goon fished them out rapidly and tossed them into the water. Splash!

The watching children now felt sure that this was Fatty's sack – look at all the stones! But now Mr Goon was rummaging deep in the bundle. His face took on a puzzled look. He couldn't feel anything except soft, dripping clothes – or what felt like clothes.

He drew one out. He shook it – and amazement spread over his face. It was a small red coat! He put it into the bottom of the boat and delved into the bundle again.

A pair of blue trousers – long ones, but far too small for a normal boy! Goon began to snort. He pulled out various things one by one – a red belt

– a blue tie – a blue cap with a red button on top – a pair of socks – and, finally, a pair of small red shoes with laces.

Goon couldn't make them out. Why would an old man in the night carry these things about in a sack? It didn't make sense. Why had the old fellow been so determined that he, Goon, shouldn't see into the sack, or take it?

Goon looked at the array of small garments, and his face grew purple once more. That boy! That toad of a boy! *He* must have been the old man! He had spoofed Mr Goon with a sack of dolls' clothes! Yes, that's what they were, dolls' clothes! That girl, Daisy, must have been in the trick too – she must have lent them to him – stuffed them into the sack ready to trick Goon into thinking the old man had stolen something, and to make Goon follow him!

'Gah,' said Goon, in angry disgust. 'Didn't he run like a hare when he'd dumped these into the water? I thought that was funny at the time. That boy was the fellow who talked to the watchmen, and he was the old man too. He's too bad to be true, that boy. I'll not keep my hands off him this time – I'll get him, and I'll stuff these things down his horrible neck, so I will. If I lose me job, I'll do it!'

Goon shoved the things back into the bag again. He was boiling with rage, and his hands shook. He'd report that toad to the Chief. He'd make the Chief do something about him. He'd go round and complain to Mr and Mrs Trotteville. The things he'd tell them about that boy of theirs!

He took up the oars and rowed away from the jetty, muttering to himself. The four children, seeing him look so fierce, decided to go back and warn Fatty. They set off on the tow-path at top speed.

They came up to Fatty, who was grinning. He had been too far away to see what had been taken out of the bundle. All he had seen were the three stones being tossed into the water. He had thought, of course, that they were some of the stones he had put into his own sack.

'Fatty! Goon's got some other sack, not yours!' said Daisy, in an urgent voice. 'It was full of clothes – dolls' clothes, they looked like. I'm sure he thinks you put them there to spoof him. You'd better go quick before he comes! He's SIMPLY FURIOUS!'

17. A WONDERFUL SCRIMMAGE – AND A DISCOVERY

Fatty listened. He was suddenly very interested. *Clothes*! That was a funny thing for anyone to dump into the river in a sack. Goon had got the wrong sack – he would of course.

'I'll pop into old Mr Spicer's shed, I think,' said Fatty. 'I'd like to see what Mr Goon does when he lands. He won't spot me in the shed.'

He disappeared into the big, dark shed and sat down on an upturned boat. The four children turned to watch Goon rowing nearer and nearer. The scarred-faced man also watched, looking very interested in the rowing policeman. He had given back his boat-hook and now had only his pail of water weed.

Goon, still purple in the face, drew in to the bank. He threw the mooring-rope over a post and clambered out, the boat rocking dangerously under his weight. He picked up the bag into which he had stuffed the wet clothes.

He looked at the four children nearby, scowling. 'Where's that friend of yours? I want him. I've got a few things to say to him!'

'What friend?' asked Larry innocently. Goon's scowl became even more ferocious.

'*You* know who I mean – that toad of a boy!' spluttered the angry policeman.

The old boatman heard him. He was still painting his boat, and looked amused at Mr Goon.

'He's in there,' he said, pointing to the shed. 'What you going to do to him, Mr Goon?'

'In there?' said Mr Goon, delighted. Aha! Now he'd show that boy something!

He strode into the dark shed, determined to do or die this time. He'd stuff these things down that boy's neck till he yelled. He'd smother him with them! That would teach him to play tricks on him again!

Fatty was taken by surprise when Goon walked in. Larry shouted a warning just too late. Goon was on Fatty before he knew it.

And then Mr Goon had the time of his life! He caught hold of the seated Fatty, held him in an iron grip, and began to stuff the wet, dripping garments down his neck, wrenching open his collar, tearing his shirt, but not caring in the least.

Fatty could do nothing. He was half-choked, to begin with, by having things forced down the front of his neck, and Mr Goon was extremely solid and strong. He struggled and heaved, and finally fell off the boat he was sitting on, landing on the earth floor of the shed. Still Mr Goon went on relentlessly pushing everything down Fatty's neck! Trousers, coat, socks, cap, shoes, one by one, down they went. Goon was absolutely determined to punish Fatty this time!

Larry ran at Goon and so did Pip. They tried to pull the furious policeman away. Old Spicer heard the noise and came in, astonished. He stopped, gaping, when he saw the scrimmage.

The man with the water weed came too. He watched with great interest, very great interest indeed.

At last, everything was down poor Fatty's neck. He felt wet and uncomfortable. Mr Goon stood up, panting, feeling uncommonly satisfied with himself.

'You got what's been coming to you for a very long time,' he panted. 'Now just you stop poking your nose into things, Mr Nosey-Parker! Stuffing that sack with rubbishy dolls' clothes, and stuffing me up too, making me think you were a bad old man with stolen goods. Ho! Now *you've* been stuffed up good and proper!'

'Mr Goon!' said old Spicer in a shocked voice. 'You're a policeman! You can't do things like this – to a boy too!'

'Gah!' said Mr Goon, rudely. 'You go and boil your head, Spicer. That boy won't complain of what I've done, I know that! And why? Because he's been plaguing me night and day, and interfering with the law. If he complains about me, I'll complain about him – but he won't! He's got a guilty conscience, he has. He's a bad lot, and one of these days he'll come to no good.'

'Mr Goon,' said Fatty, sitting up and trying to look as dignified as he could, with dripping garments down his neck and hanging out of his collar. 'Mr Goon. I give you my word of honour I didn't spoof you with these things. I've never seen them before in my life. You owe me an apology.'

'I owe you a lot of things,' said Mr Goon, 'yes, a whole lot. But not an apology. You put those things into that sack to spoof me, made me waste half a morning for nothing, and you got what you deserved – you got them in the neck! And what's more, you can keep them! Or give them back to that girl to dress up her dolls!'

And, with a perfectly marvellous snort, Mr Goon marched out of the shed. He bumped into the man with the water weed.

'Excuse me,' began the man, 'I'd just like to know where . . .'

Mr Goon snorted at him rudely and walked past, shoving him out of the way. He was feeling fine. Oh, Mr Goon was on top of the world at that moment. He could have put the Chief Inspector in his place, too, with a few well-chosen words – if only he had been there. But he wasn't, which was perhaps just as well for the triumphant Goon.

'Oh, Fatty, Fatty, are you hurt?' said Bets, in tears. She was very scared. 'Oh, Fatty, are you all right?' She began to sob.

'I'm fine, Bets,' Fatty assured her getting up and feeling himself all over. 'Don't cry, Bets, please don't. It was a wonderful fight.'

'It wasn't, it wasn't,' sobbed Bets. 'I hated it. I hate Mr Goon. I shall tell the Chief Inspector.'

'No. Mr Goon only got back at me for all the maddening things I've done to him,' said Fatty. 'He'll feel better now. You were wonderful to come to my rescue, Bets. Now please don't cry any more. That upsets me much more than Mr Goon's attack!' He put his arm round Bets.

'Cry baby,' interposed Pip, in his nice, brotherly way. 'Shut up, Bets. Don't make a fool of yourself.'

'Let her alone, Pip,' said Fatty. 'She's really scared – and I don't wonder. Goon looked a pretty nasty bit of work when he flung himself at me. But what a peculiar thing to do – to stuff these things down my neck! Ugh! They're really wet and smelly.'

'Let's get back home and fish them out,' said Larry, seeing two or three interested children coming up on their way home from school. 'Come on, Fatty. We'll get our bikes.'

Mr Spicer grinned good-bye and patted the red-eyed Bets as she passed. The water weed man stood silently watching. The school children nudged one another and grinned. Fatty really looked very strange just then.

They got on their bicycles. Fatty had recovered now. He felt a new respect for Mr Goon. Fancy him thinking of such a thing – and doing it too! Fatty shivered as he felt some cold, wet drops running down his chest.

They rode to Fatty's house and went to his shed. They locked the door. Fatty looked round. 'Hey, where's old Buster? He never came to my rescue!'

'He went off with old Spicer's terrier,' said Larry, suddenly remembering. 'Spicer said his dog would show Buster how to catch rabbits in the fields behind the boathouse, and off they went. I never thought another thing about him! Things got so exciting that I forgot about old Buster.'

'Well, I do think he might have come to my help,' said Fatty, half-vexed. 'He'd have enjoyed it too – free nips at any portion of Mr Goon that he fancied!'

'He'll come home when he's found out that, as usual, rabbits aren't really catchable,' said Daisy. 'Oh, Fatty, you *are* wet. You'd better strip off your coat and shirt and vest and put on dry ones.'

'Larry, you go indoors and get me some,' said Fatty. 'Mummy's out, so she won't want to know what you're doing, carrying my underwear about!'

Larry disappeared. Fatty took off his coat, pulled off his shirt, and stripped off his vest. It was then easy to get rid of the damp, smelly things that Goon had put down his neck. Fatty looked at them in distaste.

'Nasty wet things! Who could have been such an idiot as to dump dolls' clothes into a sack, weight them with stones, and sink them in the river. It doesn't make sense.'

'I'll take them to the dustbin,' said Daisy, gathering them up. 'That's the best place for them.'

She lumped them together – trousers, coat, tie, shoes, socks, belt, shirt, everything – and went out to the dustbin. They heard her put on the lid and then back she came again.

Larry came in too with some clean, dry clothes. Fatty was about to put them on when he wriggled.

'I've still got something down me somewhere,' he said. 'I can feel a nasty, cold, wet patch on my tummy. Perhaps it's a wet sock. Wait a minute – I really must get it.'

He wriggled his hand down and caught hold of something. 'Got it,' he said. 'I thought I felt one last thing. It's a red sock.'

He flung it down on the floor of the shed and then began to dress himself rapidly in dry clothes. Bets bent down to pick up the little red woollen thing. It was limp and shapeless.

'It's not a sock,' she said. 'It's a glove – a little red glove.'

Fatty swung his head round quickly and incredulously. Bets had got the little glove and was pulling the fingers straight. Fatty snatched it from her.

'A little red glove. *Another* one!' he said, jubilantly. 'The pair to the one I've got in my pocket! Where is it? Look! Exactly the same!'

He pulled the first little red glove out of his trousers pocket, and put it beside the one that Mr Goon had stuffed down his back. They were an exact match!

Everyone stared at the two gloves. How very, very extraordinary!

'But, what does it mean?' asked Daisy, at last. 'You found that first glove in Mr Fellows' house.'

'And Mr Goon stuffed the second one down my neck! He's given us the biggest clue yet!' said Fatty. 'Oh, dear, dear, old Mr Goon – you've nearly solved the mystery for us by stuffing things down my neck!'

18. THAT NIGHT

There was a silence after this rather peculiar statement. Nobody could quite follow it. What did Fatty mean?

'Don't stand round me looking daft like that!' said Fatty. 'Don't you *see* what this means? It means that the bag of clothes that Mr Goon hooked up is the bundle that Mr Fellows rushed off with and threw into the river – to hide! The bundle that the other fellow was after, for some reason or other!'

'But how do you know?' asked Daisy.

'Well, because I picked up one of the red gloves in a corner of the landing in Fellows' house!' said Fatty, impatiently. 'He must have pushed everything quickly into a bag to rush off to hide it somewhere, but one of the little gloves dropped out!'

'Oh, I *see*,' said Larry. 'Yes, your red glove does

prove that this bundle was the one that Fellows rushed off with in such a hurry. But, Fatty – why are these dolls' clothes so important?'

'We'll get them and see,' said Fatty. 'Daisy, go and haul them out of the dustbin again. We'll go through them carefully. There must be *some*thing to tell us why they are apparently of such importance.'

Daisy and Larry went off to get them but just as they were going back to the shed with them, they heard the voice of Mrs Trotteville's cook.

'You children! Do you know it's nearly half past one! Your mother's been telephoning here for you, Daisy, and so has Mrs Hilton for Pip! And Frederick's lunch has been waiting for him for a long time.'

'Oh, blow, blow, blow!' groaned Larry. 'Just when we were going to do something REALLY exciting!' He hurried to the shed and told the others.

Fatty looked longingly at the bundle of wet clothes. 'Well, we must wait till this afternoon. Anyway, the clothes will be drier by then. I'll take them up to my room and dry them by the fire.'

'Promise you won't examine them till we come back?' said Bets urgently.

'I promise,' said Fatty. 'Go on, now, all of you – and I hope you don't get into a row.'

They all left at top speed, fearing that they certainly *would* get into a row.

They did. Two really angry mothers met them at their doors. 'A quarter to two! What *are* you thinking of?'

The dreadful result was that not one of the four was allowed to go down to Fatty's that afternoon, nor even to leave the house! Larry and Daisy sat disconsolately in their playroom and Pip and Bets sat in theirs. Fatty waited till three o'clock and then phoned. He wasn't even allowed to *speak* to the others.

Larry's mother was cross. 'You should really not keep Larry and Daisy so late,' she said. Fatty apologised humbly and gloomily.

Mrs Hilton said a good deal more. Fatty felt even humbler when she had finished. He could hear Bets' voice calling to her mother at the end.

'Mummy! Mummy! Ask Fatty if Buster is back, please, please ask him.'

Mrs Hilton asked him. 'Yes – tell Bets he arrived an hour ago, covered in sand and awfully hungry,' said Fatty. 'I won't let him go off with old Spicer's dog again.'

He heard Mrs Hilton's receiver click down. He turned and glared at Buster who was sitting nearby, looking very guilty.

'To think you deserted me when Mr Goon attacked me!' said Fatty. 'Shameful dog! To go rabbiting when your master is in danger! Brrrrrrrr!'

Fatty went up to his room and looked longingly at all the things he had put in front of the fire. They were perfectly dry now. How he longed to examine them! But no, he had promised, and it simply didn't occur to Fatty to break such a promise. He bundled all the clothes into a drawer.

The rest of the day was extremely dull. The mystery was at a standstill till the others could come and look at the curious clothes. Buster was still feeling guilty and was not at all lively. It began to pour with rain.

The other Find-Outers were not allowed out at

all that day. They sat and moped and sulked. How maddening to be kept in just when they really had got somewhere! Bets and Pip talked about the dolls' clothes.

'Funny that they should be important enough for someone to break into Mr Fellows' house and turn the place upside down for them,' said Pip.

'I bet Mr Fellows will be going out with a boat-hook too, to try and get them back,' said Bets.

'Strange that those dolls' clothes should be for a boy, not for a girl,' said Daisy to Larry.

'How mad Mr Goon would be to know that he had made a present of such an enormous clue to Fatty,' said Larry. 'I guess nobody has ever had a clue stuffed down their neck before. Just like Mr Goon!'

They all went to bed early. Both Larry's mother and Pip's were still annoyed, and only Fatty's mother was good-tempered that day – but that was because she had been out to lunch, and hadn't been kept waiting like the others!

Fatty was tired. 'More "aftermath",' he supposed. He switched off his light early and fell into a sound sleep. His parents were up in town that evening, having driven up to a theatre and a dance afterwards. They would not be back until about one o'clock in the morning, perhaps later.

At half past ten, the whole house was in darkness except for a small light left on in the hall. The two maids were in bed and asleep. Buster slept soundly too. So did Fatty.

He was suddenly awakened by Buster barking loudly. WUFF, WUFF, WUFF! He sat up with a jerk and turned on the light. A quarter to one.

'Shut up, Buster. It's only Mummy and Dad you can hear!' said Fatty, sleepily. 'Do shut up. Surely you know the sound of their car by now!'

But Buster wouldn't stop. He leapt from the bed to the floor and barked frantically. Fatty threw a book at him.

'Shut up, I tell you! It's only Mummy coming home. You know she and Dad are out. Come here, Buster.'

Buster took not the slightest notice. Fatty thought there really might be something the matter. He jumped out of bed, pulled on his dressing-gown and opened the door. A frightened voice called to him.

'Frederick? Is that you? Why is Buster barking? Is there someone in the house?'

'I expect it's just my parents coming back,' said Fatty. 'You go to bed again. Buster's gone downstairs at top speed, so you may be sure if there's anyone down there, he'll be after them!'

Buster was still barking frantically somewhere downstairs. Fatty decided to explore. He was about to go downstairs when he caught sight of his mother's bedroom. The door was open and the landing light streamed into it. It was in utter confusion!

'Gosh!' said Fatty, switching on the light. 'Look at that. Burglars! While we were all asleep!'

He looked in his father's dressing-room and into the guestroom. Both had had their drawers and cupboards rifled and turned out. Fatty ran downstairs. Buster was standing by an open window in the sitting-room, barking madly.

'It's no good barking *now*, Buster,' said Fatty, glancing round the sitting-room, which was in as much muddle and confusion as the other rooms. 'The thief is gone – he must have been about to come into my room when you heard him and awoke. He's gone out of the same window he came in by. I wonder what he's taken. Not Mummy's jewellery, I hope.'

There came the sound of a car up the drive. It was his parents returning home. Fatty heaved a sigh of relief. Now they could take matters in hand.

Mr and Mrs Trotteville were horrified when they came indoors and saw all the confusion in so many rooms. Mrs Trotteville rapidly looked through her jewellery and valuables. They were all intact.

'It's peculiar,' she said, after about twenty minutes' search. 'I can't see that *any*thing has been taken. Even the pearl necklace I left on my dressing-table hasn't been taken. What did the thief come for?'

Fatty suddenly knew! The intruder must have been the same one who had searched Mr Fellows' house. And he had been looking for the same thing – the dolls' clothes! But why – why – why?

Fatty raced up to his room to see if they were still safe. Yes, they were there in the drawer into which he had thrown them. What a blessing he hadn't left them down in the kitchen to dry, as he had first thought of doing. He had only taken them up to his room so that awkward questions would not be asked by anyone who saw such strange things drying on the kitchen airer!

But how did the burglar know that the clothes were now in Fatty's house? Fatty soon thought that one out. The man with the water weed! He had been looking on while Mr Goon had stuffed the wet clothes down Fatty's neck. *He* had been looking for them that morning too – but it was Mr Goon who had found them – and thrown them away on Fatty!

How wild the water weed man must have been when he saw something he badly wanted being stuffed down a boy's neck! He must have asked old Spicer who Fatty was and where he lived – and then he had come to try and get the clothes back that night.

Fatty looked at the clothes in the drawer. 'There's something extraordinarily valuable about you,' he said solemnly. 'Maybe we'll find out tomorrow.'

He heard his mother talking to his father. 'Are you going to phone the police?'

'No, I'm not,' said his father's voice. 'I don't want that flat-footed policeman stamping all over my house late at night! There's nothing gone, as far as I can see. We'll let Mr Goon sleep in peace!'

'Thank goodness,' said Fatty, sliding into bed. 'I just don't feel like seeing Mr Goon again tonight.'

19. EXAMINING THE CLOTHES

To Fatty's relief, his father decided next day not to inform Mr Goon of the attempted robbery at all. Mr Trotteville had no great opinion of Mr Goon, and was not disposed to waste a morning with him.

'He'd ask asinine questions, and waste everybody's time,' said Mr Trotteville. 'Just have new fastenings put on all the windows, my dear, and another bolt on the front and back door. And perhaps Buster had better sleep downstairs.'

Buster had other views, however. He had heard suggestions like this before, but however firmly he was put into a basket in the hall and told to be on-guard, he was invariably to be found lying on Fatty's bed in the morning. As Mr Trotteville said, it was most extraordinary the way that Buster could find his way through a closed bedroom door!

447

Fatty telephoned the others. 'Come on down as soon as you can,' he said. 'I've news. We've had robbers in the night. No – nothing taken, as far as I can see. Old Buster drove them off. Hurry up and come down.'

They met down in the shed at the bottom of Fatty's garden. Fatty kept a good lookout for the water weed man, as he called him, when he took the clothes down to the shed. He wouldn't have been surprised to have him pounce on him from behind a tree! However, Buster trotted happily in front, and nothing untoward happened at all. Fatty was safely ensconced in the shed when the others came tapping at the door.

He shut the door and locked it. He pulled the curtains over the windows, and lit the little oil-lamp so that they were not in complete darkness.

'Why all the mystery?' asked Daisy, surprised. 'Going to do conjuring tricks, or something?'

'No. But that water weed man is somewhere around, I bet,' said Fatty. 'And I don't want him peeping in at the window while we're examining those clothes. He's dead keen on getting them. He's made two break-ins already in different houses to get them. I don't want to have to give them up at gun-point.'

'Gracious, Fatty!' said Bets, in alarm.

'It's all right, Bets. And now for the clothes,' said Fatty, taking them out of the box he had put them in. 'Use your eyes well – there's obviously something we mustn't miss! Now, the trousers first!'

He shook out the blue trousers. They were long ones, with little buttons at the top. 'No pockets,' said Fatty. 'Don't dolls' clothes ever have pockets, Bets?'

'Oh yes, sometimes,' said Bets. 'Aren't they dear little trousers? – a boy doll would look nice in those. Let me have them, Fatty.'

Bets took them. She turned them inside out. There was nothing that would tell them anything – they were just trousers with buttons. Bets passed them round to the others, and then Fatty put them down.

'Red belt for the trousers,' he said, and passed it round. 'Quite ordinary. A little brass buckle, a bit rusty – due to the river water, I suppose.'

It was duly examined. Then came the socks.

Those were turned inside out too. Bets hunted for any name marked on them, but there wasn't one.

'Dolls never have their names marked on their clothes, silly,' said Pip, when Bets remarked why she was looking so carefully.

'Mine do,' said Bets. 'I borrowed Mummy's marking tape and ink, and I've marked all my biggest doll's clothes with her name – Pamela Mary. Pass the shoes, Fatty. Gosh, aren't they small!'

'Well, they're small for a child, but big for a doll,' said Fatty. 'Very nice shoes, though – strong and well made – not like the usual dolls' shoes. These have real laces in too.'

'I suppose these clothes *couldn't* belong to some child – some tiny little child?' said Larry.

'Well, I suppose they might,' said Fatty. 'But for the life of me, I can't see why they're so important, whether they belong to a doll or a child! Not worth breaking into two houses for anyway!'

Bets undid the laces and did them up again. They really were nice little shoes! She showed one to Buster. He sniffed at it.

'Buster, who does it belong to?' said Bets. 'Go

on, tell us! Surely you can tell by the smell! Whose smell is it?'

'Wuff!' said Buster, and pawed at the shoe. Bets dodged it away, and Buster sprang at it. He got it in his mouth and ran off with it triumphantly. He stuffed it into a corner and sat down on it, as if to say, 'It's mine now.'

'Bring it here, Buster,' said Bets. 'It's ours!' Buster took it into his mouth and ran round the shed to hide it somewhere. He was in a silly mood that morning and had already run off with Daisy's handkerchief and Fatty's pencil.

'Don't take any notice of him,' said Fatty. 'He's got one of his show-off fits on. Probably feels very grand because he scared off a burglar last night. All right, Buster, be an idiot if you want to. Look, here's the coat, complete with buttons and collar!'

That was examined too. Fatty ran his hands down the lining. Could there be anything hidden there that might be of value? No, he could feel nothing.

Everyone examined it solemnly. It was a well made little coat, of good material, strong and very little worn.

'The longer we look at these things, the more puzzled I feel,' said Fatty. 'Who wore them – and why should they have been stolen? At least, I suppose they *were* stolen . . .'

'By Mr Fellows, do you mean?' asked Larry. 'But how do we know he stole them?'

'Well, why should he have them and hide them as he did?' said Fatty. 'What beats me is why they are apparently of such importance. Here's the tie, look – and the cap. Nice cap. Very nice indeed. Quite a cheeky cap, in fact!'

He set it on his large head at a comical angle. Bets laughed. 'You look terrible, Fatty. Take it off.'

'Even battier than usual,' said Pip, and got a punch from Fatty. Buster, always ready for a battle, flung himself on the two boys, barking. Fatty sat up and pushed him away.

'Where's that shoe?' he said, severely. 'You bring it back here, and we'll admit you into the family circle again. And what have you done with my pencil? If you've chewed the end off, you can count it as your dinner, because you won't get any more!'

Buster retired to his corner, his tongue hanging

out. Bets thought he looked sweet. She liked him when he was 'showing off'!

'Is that all the clothes?' asked Daisy, examining the cap carefully when Fatty handed it round. 'I simply can't see anything out of the ordinary about these things at all – except that they're better made and stronger than ordinary dolls' clothes. I can't think why they are important.'

'Neither can I. But they must be,' said Fatty. He gazed at the pile of clothes rather gloomily. 'I wouldn't a bit mind Mr Goon having stuffed them down my neck if only they'd prove to be really worthwhile – help us with this rather peculiar mystery. Though I'm beginning to think we may be making a mountain out of a molehill, and that it's not a mystery at all.'

'Well, we've only got two or three days more to solve it,' said Bets. 'I don't think I could *bear* to go back to school without knowing the solution of this strange little mystery. Do you suppose we ought to take these dolls' clothes back to Mr Fellows?'

'Well, yes – I suppose we should,' said Fatty. 'I actually hadn't thought of that. We could ask

453

him what *his* explanation is – we might find out something after all! We'll take them this afternoon. He'll be astonished to see them, I bet! He probably thinks they're still safe in the river!'

'I do WISH we'd managed to find some clue hidden in the clothes,' said Bets. 'I'm sure there must be. Let me go through them just once more, Fatty, before you put them away.'

'You think you might discover something that all five of us couldn't see?' said Pip, scornfully. 'What a hope!'

'It's always a good thing to have another check on anything if you feel you must,' said Fatty, handing the bundle of clothes to Bets. 'They're all there, Bets, except the shoe that Buster took. Hey, Buster, bring back the shoe, old fellow.'

But before Buster could do as he was told, Bets gave a loud exclamation that made everyone jump. She was examining the little red coat, and she looked up, her eyes shining.

'Look – we missed this – a little white handkerchief embroidered with daisies, and it's got a name embroidered on it too – very small!'

'Where was it?' asked Fatty, almost snatching the tiny hanky.

'There's a very small pocket here inside the coat-cuff,' said Bets, showing the others. 'So well hidden that none of us saw it. Fatty, what's the name on the hanky?'

Fatty spread out the tiny hanky so that all the Find-Outers could see the little daisies on it and the name that was embroidered all round them, making a circle of the letters.

Fatty spelt it out. 'E-U-R-Y-C-L-E-S. Eurycles! What a name.'

'Never heard it in my life,' said Larry. 'It's Greek, isn't it?'

'Yes. Greek,' said Fatty. 'Wait – wait – I've heard it before. Who was Eurycles? I'm remembering – yes, I'm remembering. EURYCLES! Of course, I remember now. What a clue!'

20. MR. EURYCLES - AND A TALK WITH GOON

The others stared at Fatty in excitement. What was the clue? Who was Eurycles the Greek? And why did it matter who he was?

'Listen,' said Fatty. 'Eurycles was a Greek who lived ages ago, but he happened to be a very well-known Greek, because he had a peculiar gift – he was a ventriloquist! He was such a good one that he's never been forgotten, and he had dozens of pupils.'

'I thought ventriloquists were all modern,' said Daisy, in astonishment. 'I mean, I thought it was something that people had thought of in the last century.'

'Good gracious, no – it's a very old art,' said Fatty. 'It was well known in Greece, and all kinds of nations have practised it – the Zulus, for instance – and the Eskimos. And Eurycles the Greek was a very fine ventriloquist. I read about him when I was teaching myself to ventriloquise and to throw my voice to a distance.'

'Yes, but why should this doll's hanky have an old Greek ventriloquist's name on it?' said Daisy. 'And why is it important? I simply don't understand, Fatty. Do explain.'

'Now listen,' said Fatty, thrilled. 'When hankies are embroidered with somebody's name, that name usually belongs to the owner of the hanky, doesn't it? Right, either the one who owned that hanky and wore these clothes was called Eurycles – or his *master* was. Mr Eurycles – what could he be but a ventriloquist, and what could these clothes belong to but his talking doll?'

The others followed this with interest, and at the end Pip exclaimed, 'Of course, of course, of course – why didn't we think of it? The clothes were worn by a big doll belonging to a ventriloquist – that's why they are a bit smaller than a child's and rather big for an ordinary doll, and that's why they are very well made.'

'Yes. And I bet he is owned by someone whose stage name is Mr Eurycles, after the old Greek ventriloquist,' said Fatty, jubilantly. 'I see daylight at last!'

'Well, it's more than I do,' said Larry. 'What kind of daylight can you see? It's true that we think we know who the clothes are worn by, and probably the name of the man who owns the doll who wears the clothes . . .'

'That lived in the house that Jack built!' said Daisy, with a giggle.

'Well,' said Fatty, 'we've only got to find Mr Eurycles and ask him why the clothes are so important – why they were in Mr Fellows' custody, why they were important enough for someone to try and steal them twice, and why Mr Fellows fled out in the night to dump them in the river? Once Mr Eurycles tells us that, the mystery is solved!'

'But how do we find Mr Eurycles?' said Pip, after a pause. 'It might take ages. And we're going back to school so soon.'

There was a silence, which deepened into gloom. Only Fatty remained confident.

'I'll telephone the place that sells things for conjurers and ventriloquists,' he said. 'They'll soon tell me if there's a Mr Eurycles.'

'Or Mr Fellows might tell us,' said Daisy, suddenly.

'Yes, he might,' said Fatty. 'And he might not. If he's stolen the clothes himself from Mr Eurycles, he won't want to say very much. I'll tell you what we'll do – we'll take the clothes to him this afternoon and see his face when we show them to him – and we'll fire a few questions at him before he's got time to recover from his surprise.'

'Right,' said Larry. 'Well, let's put them away till we're ready to take them. I'm sure I heard your mother in the garden just now, Fatty, and she might want to know why we're all playing with dolls' clothes if she walks into the shed!'

The clothes were bundled anyhow into a box. Fatty shut down the lid.

'There's the hanky, look,' said Bets, holding it out to him. 'It's such a dear little hanky. I suppose I couldn't keep it in my pocket till we take the clothes to Mr Fellows, Fatty? I won't blow my nose on it.'

'Yes. You keep it,' said Fatty. 'And congratulations on finding the one thing that led us to the right solution! We're well on the way to solving the whole thing now! Very good, Bets!'

Bets blushed, and put the little hanky into her pocket. It *was* a bit of luck finding that tiny pocket in the sleeve of the little red coat!

'I vote we go and have some hot chocolate again at the café,' said Fatty. 'And some macaroons if they've made any fresh ones. I feel just like three or four macaroons.'

'Yes, all gooey and crunchy,' said Pip. 'I suddenly feel like a macaroon too. Come on. You do have some bright ideas, Fatty.'

They went out of the shed with Buster delightedly prancing round their ankles. Fatty locked the door, and they all went up the path to the garden gate.

They bicycled to the café with Buster running beside them. Fatty thought it would be good for him to have a quick run. 'Take off some of his fat,' he said. 'A fat Scottie is an offence to the eye. Do you hear that, Buster?'

'Wuff, wuff,' panted Buster. Bets giggled.

'He says that a plump master is also an

offence to the eye!' she said. Fatty stared at her in amazement.

'Bets! You've got very bright – and very cheeky all of a sudden!'

'I know. It just popped into my head,' said Bets, with another giggle. 'Sorry, Fatty. Look out, you nearly wobbled over Buster.'

'There's Mr Goon,' said Larry suddenly. 'Look – coming round the corner on his bike. Let's hope he doesn't hang round us.'

'He's probably hoping we won't hang round *him*,' said Fatty, getting off his bicycle and putting it outside the café window. 'Come on in. I smell fresh macaroons!'

They all trooped in. The little shop-woman beamed at them. They were very good customers indeed! Children always were. They ate twice as much as any grown-up who came into her shop!

'Hot chocolate for everyone, please – and macaroons,' said Fatty, sitting down at a table.

'Five macaroons?' asked the shop-woman, with a twinkle.

'Gosh, no – ten, to start with, just so we won't look too greedy,' said Fatty, with a grin.

'They're newly made,' said the little woman, warningly. 'Don't you eat too many.'

'Are you trying to put us off your magnificent macaroons?' said Fatty. 'What a hope! Ten, please – just to start with.'

Mr Goon came in. He was looking worried. 'You all right?' he said to Fatty, in an offhand voice. Fatty stared at him, amazed.

'Why this sudden concern for my health, Mr Goon?' he said. 'Why shouldn't I be all right? Are *you* in good health? Let me see your tongue. Say ninety-nine – or one hundred and sixty-two and a half, if you like.'

'Perhaps he's feeling sorry he behaved so badly yesterday,' said Bets, unexpectedly, giving Mr Goon a really fierce glare. 'Stuffing things down people's necks.'

'Shut up, young Bets,' said Fatty. 'It was a good scrum while it lasted.' He looked at Mr Goon, puzzled. It wasn't like the bad-tempered policeman to feel concerned about anything he had done to Fatty. There was something behind this. Fatty wondered what it was.

The hot chocolate and macaroons arrived.

Fatty threw another glance at Mr Goon. He was standing looking round the café, as if he had something to say and didn't know how to begin. What *could* have happened?

'Hot cocoa, sir – and a bun or macaroon?' said the little shop-woman. 'Just newly made.'

'No thanks – er – well, yes, I think I will,' said Goon, changing his mind suddenly. He sat down at the table next to the children's. He really did look worried.

He made the five children feel so uncomfortable that they fell silent. Buster was tied to the leg of the table, but even he didn't seem inclined to bait Mr Goon that morning.

Mr Goon suddenly cleared his throat with an enormous noise. 'Now he's going to talk!' whispered Pip.

'Er – you heard from Chief Inspector Jenks lately?' blurted out Goon, suddenly.

'Not a word,' said Fatty promptly. Goon at once looked vastly relieved. He edged his chair a little nearer to the children's table.

'See here,' he said to Fatty, 'I want a talk with you. Friendly-like.'

463

'You mean you won't fling yourself at me and stuff things down my neck?' said Fatty, attacking a macaroon. 'In a word – friendly-like.'

'It's like this,' said Goon, with his mouth full. 'You see – well – it's like this, Frederick. Er, well . . .'

'Get on, Mr Goon, and say what you want to say,' said Fatty, beginning to be impatient. 'Good gracious – you sound as if you can't say gah to a goose this morning.'

Bets gave a sudden giggle. Gah to a goose. That was just like Fatty.

Goon made a great effort and came to the point. 'It's like this,' he said. 'You remember that time we were in Mr Fellows' house together – the time you *said* you were looking for the kitten?'

'Yes,' said Fatty.

'Well, do you remember hearing a dog growl and a pig grunt, and a man groaning?' said Mr Goon, earnestly.

'The one who longed for his auntie?' said Fatty. 'I've often wondered if she ever went to comfort him. Yes, I remember. Why? What about it?'

'Well, I made out a report for the Chief

Inspector, see?' said Goon. 'Put it all in, pig and all. And the man who said he never did it and kept on about his auntie.'

'Yes. Do get to the point,' said Fatty. 'I can hardly wait!'

'I sent in the report,' said Goon, miserably. 'And the Chief don't believe a word of it. Not one word! He wasn't half snorty about it over the phone this morning. So I told him you were there too, Frederick, and heard the whole lot. I said you were a proper witness of all the facts, though I hadn't said so in the report.'

'I see,' said Fatty, at once understanding not only Goon's gloom but also his sudden anxiety to be on good terms with him! 'You want me to back you up, I suppose?'

'Yes. You see, you did hear all those noises too, didn't you?' said Goon anxiously.

'I bet you exaggerated everything in your report,' said Fatty. 'I'll back you up in any facts, but not in any exaggerations, Mr Goon. That's flat.'

Goon drummed his fingers on the table top. 'I may have let meself go a bit,' he admitted. 'I don't rightly remember. But the thing is – you were with me, Frederick, and you did hear things, didn't you?'

'All right, Mr Goon. But I don't see why you had to go and write a fairytale about the silly happenings in Mr Fellows' house,' said Fatty, crossly. He was beginning to feel distinctly uncomfortable himself. Suppose the Inspector demanded full explanations? Fatty would feel extremely small. He could only hope that nothing more would come of this.

'Thanks, Frederick,' said Goon, breathing more easily. 'We've had our scraps, like, and called each other bad names – but I knew I could depend on you to back up the truth. Thanks.'

He paid his bill and got up to go. A voice came weakly from the corner of the café. 'I never did it, I never, I never! I never did it, I . . .'

But Goon was gone – gone like a hare before the hounds. With one horrified glance at the corner, he tore out of the café. Was he being haunted? That voice, that awful voice!

21. A DREADFUL SHOCK

There was a startled silence. The voice had come so suddenly, and sounded so pathetic! Then Pip gave Fatty a vigorous punch.

'Gosh, you startled me! You might warn us when you're going to do that, Mr Eurycles!'

'I swallowed half my macaroon,' complained Larry. 'You made me jump.'

'Oh, Fatty, how *do* you do it?' said Bets. 'You sent poor Mr Goon out at sixty miles an hour! I bet he's puzzled – he didn't wait for "I want Auntie"!'

'Serves him right,' said Fatty. 'What does he want to go and write an idiotic report about pigs and dogs and groaning men for? They weren't important. I bet he spread himself too – put in bits about snarling, and the patter of pigs' feet, and the sound of a wounded man dragging himself over the floor! I know Mr Goon!'

'And now, I suppose, as he's told the Chief you

467

were there, you'll be asked all about it too,' said Bets. 'Whatever will you say to him? Will you tell him it was all you?'

'I don't know,' said Fatty, looking gloomy. 'Blow Mr Goon! I bet he was worried in case I said I wouldn't back up his poppy-cock story. But I'll have to.'

'Any more macaroons, Fatty?' asked Pip. 'There's one left.'

'No, thanks. This has rather spoilt my appetite,' said Fatty.

'Well, you've had four macaroons, if not five, so you can't have much appetite left to spoil,' remarked Larry. 'Finish up the macaroon, Pip?'

Surprisingly enough, no one wanted it. 'I'll go a splash and buy it for Buster,' said Pip. 'He's been so good and quiet.'

Buster was surprised and thrilled. He gulped the macaroon down at once.

'I call it a waste of a macaroon to gulp it down without a single crunch,' said Pip, looking at Buster. 'You dogs haven't learnt the art of eating yet. Wasn't he good with Mr Goon this morning, Fatty?'

'Yes. He must have known Mr Goon was in need of comfort, and wanted someone to hold his hand and say "There, there" to him,' said Fatty, still cross. 'Gone all soft-hearted, Buster? Gah!'

They got up and went off to find their bicycles. Fatty paid the bill. It was a very large one, considering it was only for hot chocolate and macaroons. Still, as Fatty said, school was looming horribly on the horizon and they might as well make hay and eat macaroons while they could!

They biked back to Fatty's, as there was still an hour before lunch. 'But we MUST leave in good time today,' said Pip. 'I really believe Mother will send us to bed on bread and water if we're late again. You're lucky not to have a fierce mother, Fatty.'

'Oh, ours isn't *fierce*, Pip,' said Bets, protesting. 'She's just keen on rules being kept. I wouldn't change our mother for anything.'

'Nor would I, idiot,' said her brother. 'But you can't deny she was pretty fierce yesterday. The thing is, we MUST leave early.'

'Let's go down to the shed again,' said Larry. 'I

left a book there. It's a detective story I thought you mightn't have read, Fatty.'

'Fatty's read every single detective story that's ever been written!' said Bets. 'He's . . . why, Fatty, what's up?'

Fatty had thrown his bicycle suddenly to the ground when they came to the shed, and had rushed up to the door with a cry. He swung round.

'Someone's been here! The lock's forced! The door's ajar – and just LOOK at the inside of the shed!'

The five stared at the shed. Fatty had swung the door open, and inside were piled all the shed's contents in an incredible muddle. All Fatty's 'disguises' had been torn from their pegs or from their chest and had been flung down. Boxes had been opened and their contents thrown out. It was a scene of utmost confusion and chaos.

'Oh, Fatty!' said Bets, trembling. 'Oh, Fatty!'

'Look at that!' said Fatty, angrily. 'That burglar fellow has been HERE while we were out – and he's messed up everything – and what's more, I'll bet he's taken those dolls' clothes!'

Fatty was right. The precious clothes were

gone. Their biggest, finest clue! The box into which Fatty had thrown them was empty. Not even a sock was left! The thief had found at last what he had looked for so persistently.

Fatty sat down on a box and groaned. This was a real shock to him. 'Why did we leave the things here?' he almost wailed. 'Why didn't we take them with us? Now we're finished – nothing to show for all our work at all!'

'It must have been the thief we heard in the garden when we thought it was just your mother,' said Larry. 'Oh, Fatty, isn't this a blow?'

'Well, we can't take the clothes and tackle Mr Fellows now,' said Pip. 'I don't see that there's anything we can do. Whatever made us leave the things here for the thief to get? And we even go out and leave the coast clear for him. We must have been mad.'

'We were worse. We were fatheads,' said Fatty, in deep dejection. 'I blame myself. How could I be such a mutt?'

It was no good talking about it. The thing was done. The thief had come and gone and had taken what he wanted away with him. Fatty heard a sound near the shed and went out to see if it was the gardener.

It was. 'Mr Hedges, have you seen any stranger about this morning?' he asked. 'Someone's been into my shed.'

'Well, I'll be blowed!' said Hedges. 'That would be that fellow with the scarred cheek, I expect. A nasty chap he looked. I turned him away once. He was trying to make me give him an order for manure. I found him in the garden! He said he was looking for me, Frederick – but I guess he was looking about for what he could steal.'

Fatty nodded and went back to the others. He was very down in the dumps. 'It was the water weed man all right,' he said. 'The gardener said he had a scarred cheek, so that proves it was the fellow we know. Blow, blow, blow! I'll never forgive myself for this.'

'Let's tidy up,' said Bets. 'We can't leave you to put everything back in its place by yourself. Come on, Daisy, I'll hand you Fatty's disguises to hang up.'

Everyone was soon busy putting the shed tidy again. It took quite a long time. As Bets was picking up a few things, she gave a sudden exclamation.

'I've just remembered – the tiny hanky with daisies on it and the name Eurycles is in my pocket,' she said. 'The thief wouldn't have found it with the other clothes.'

Everyone stared at it. 'Well,' said Fatty, fingering it, 'you'd better keep it for yourself, Bets – it's not much good to us now.'

Bets put the tiny hanky back into her pocket. She felt rather bad. It was all that was left of their wonderful collection of clues. She went on tidying up everything with the others.

'Better shove all the rest of the things into that chest,' said Fatty at last, looking at his watch. 'You ought to go. It's getting near dinnertime.'

So the last few armfuls were flung higgledy-piggledy into the chest, and the lid was shut down. Then the four got their bicycles, shouted good-bye to Fatty, and raced off.

Fatty went slowly back to the house. He was very depressed. Things had been going so well. Now all they had left of their biggest clue was the tiny hanky with 'Eurycles' embroidered on it. And a fat lot of good that was, Fatty reflected. Was there much point in trying to find out if there was a ventriloquist called Mr Eurycles? Fatty thought not. He was beginning to feel fed-up with the whole thing.

'Oh, there you are, Frederick,' said his mother, as he came slowly in. 'Dear me, you do look miserable! Cheer up! A great friend of yours telephoned this morning but you were out, so he's telephoning this afternoon.'

'Who's that?' asked Fatty, not at all interested. It was probably one of his school friends, he thought. How boring! He would see enough of them in a few days! Poor Fatty was indeed feeling depressed!

'It was Chief Inspector Jenks,' said his mother, expecting Fatty to be delighted. He thought the world of the Chief, who knew all the children very well, and had often welcomed their help in many curious mysteries.

But, far from pleasing him, the news made Fatty feel more down in the dumps than ever. Now he'd have a very difficult and awkward telephone conversation with the Chief. Chief Inspector Jenks had a high opinion of Fatty's capabilities, but a low opinion of some of his jokes. Fatty felt that things were getting worse than ever.

He ate a very poor lunch, though whether it was because he was worried, or had had too many macaroons, he didn't know. Probably both, he thought.

The telephone rang immediately after the meal ended. 'That's the Chief Inspector, Frederick,' said his mother. 'You answer it, will you?'

Fatty went. He picked up the receiver. 'Hello!' he said. 'This is . . .'

'Ah, Frederick!' interrupted a voice. 'It's you. Good. I wanted to speak to you.'

'Delighted, sir,' said Fatty, most untruthfully.

'Listen, I've had a most extraordinary report in from Goon,' said the Chief. 'He's sent in plenty of peculiar reports in his time – but this beats them all. It's so extraordinary that I didn't believe it. But when I telephoned him, he not only swore it was true but said that you would back him up. He said you were a witness to all the things in his report – though why he didn't mention you were there, when he wrote his report, I don't know.'

'Quite, sir,' said Fatty, politely.

'Apparently Goon went to inspect a house that was empty and that had been reported as burgled,' said the Chief, sounding very businesslike and brisk. 'He says that there was a kitten there, mewing – a dog which growled most ferociously, and snarled, and was ready, so he infers, to eat him up – and a pig – a *pig*, P-I-G – that grunted somewhere and stamped about overhead. Really, Frederick, I am ashamed to quote from this report!'

Fatty couldn't help grinning into the telephone. Goon had certainly let himself go!

'Go on, sir,' he said.

'And to crown everything, Goon reports that there was a wounded man in the house, who was groaning and dragging himself about somewhere, crying out "I never did it, I never. Oooooh, I never did it. Where's my auntie?" It sounds quite incredible, Frederick.'

'It does, sir,' said Fatty, trying to keep his end of the phone very business-like, and not give away anything.

There was a pause. 'Are you still there,

Frederick?' said the Chief. 'Well, I may as well tell you that as soon as Goon told me you were in the house with him, I smelt a rat! Not a dog or a pig or any other animal, Frederick, but a rat. Do you understand me?'

'Er – yes, I think I do, sir,' said Fatty.

There was another pause. Then the Chief's voice came again, a harder note in it. 'I imagine I am correct in thinking that you had something to do with the extraordinary things in this report?' he rapped out.

'Well, yes, sir,' said Fatty, wishing this one-sided conversation would end. He didn't like the sound of the Chief's stern voice at all!

'Exactly what did you have to do with it?' asked the Chief. 'Please be a little more explicit, Frederick. I'm getting tired of this yes-sir, no-sir business. You usually have plenty to say for yourself.'

'Yes, sir. Well, it's like this,' said Fatty, desperately. 'I've been practising ventriloquism, and . . .'

'Practising *what*!'

'VENTRILOQUISM,' shouted Fatty.

'Oh, ventriloquism,' repeated the Chief. 'Good

heavens! I didn't think of that. Bless us all – *ventriloquism*! What next? What an absolute menace you are, Frederick. There's no other word for it – a menace.'

'Yes, sir,' said Fatty, sensing that the Chief was not feeling *quite* so angry. 'I say, sir, there's a bit of a mystery on here – and I want to get hold of a ventriloquist myself. A man called Mr EURYCLES. How can I find out about him?'

There was a startled pause. 'Did you say Eurycles?' came the Chief's voice in amazement. 'Now why do you want to see *him*? Wait – don't say a word more over the telephone – not a word. I'm coming straight over. Keep your mouth shut till I come!'

22. AN EXCITING MEETING

There was a click as the Chief put down his receiver. Fatty put back his too, feeling rather dazed. What an abrupt ending! Why was the Chief so astonished? Did he know about their little 'mystery' then? Did he actually know anything about Mr Eurycles?

It was all very puzzling. Fatty rubbed his nose. He wasn't altogether pleased at the idea of seeing Chief Inspector Jenks that afternoon. He didn't particularly want the subject of dogs and pigs and groaning men reopened, and it might quite well be.

Mrs Trotteville was curious to know what the conversation had been about. She had heard the word 'ventriloquism', because Fatty had shouted it so loudly.

'What's this about ventriloquism, Frederick?' she asked. 'Did I hear you say you were practising it? I do wish you wouldn't. I suppose that explains all those peculiar noises that keep coming from your room when you are up there alone.'

'Yes, Mummy. But don't you get all hot and bothered about it,' said Fatty. 'I'll be back at school in a very short time. Then the house will be nice and quiet. By the way – er – the Chief Inspector is coming over here this afternoon. Do you mind if I get the other four along? They'll like to see him – especially Bets.'

'Yes, get them along if you like,' said his mother. 'But, Frederick – I hope all this doesn't mean you've been mixing yourselves up again in matters that don't concern you. I really did hope you'd not lead the others into trouble these holidays.'

Fatty was indignant. 'I *never* lead them into trouble! Mummy, how can you say such a thing! Why, even the Inspector has often told me that . . .'

'All right, Frederick,' said his mother. 'I am not going to argue with you. Telephone the others and see if they can come to tea. There is a nice new batch of cakes in today – and I brought in some macaroons from the café. You haven't had any for a long time.'

Not so very long, thought Fatty, pleased at the idea of a few more that afternoon. He went to telephone the others but, remembering the Chief's injunction to 'keep his mouth shut', he gave them no hint as to the unexpected visit, though he would dearly have liked Bets to know. She was very fond of the 'high-up policeman,' as she used to call him.

It's a pity we've got to tell the Chief that we were idiotic enough to leave the dolls' clothes unguarded, so that they were stolen, thought Fatty. That won't be a very good mark for me! I can't think how I was such a fathead. Well, the deed is done.

The Chief arrived first, in his big, black, shiny car, driven by a police-driver and, surprisingly, with him came a distinguished-looking man in plain clothes.

Fatty was at the door when the car came up the drive and stopped outside. He welcomed the Chief with pleasure. The big, burly, good-looking man grinned at Fatty.

'Well, you menace? I've a good mind to cast you off and have no more to do with you!' He turned to the tall, quiet man by his side.

'Sir, this is the boy I was telling you about. He plagues the local police, but at times he's been very useful to me. He's dependable and responsible, so you can tell him what you like. Let me introduce Frederick Trotteville.'

Fatty shook hands solemnly. He noticed that the Chief didn't tell him the tall man's name. It was obvious that he was a very big noise, Fatty thought. Probably in the Secret Service – or Scotland Yard. Anyway, a bit hush-hush. Fatty looked at him in awe.

They all went into the sitting-room, where a bright fire was burning. Mrs Trotteville had gone out to one of her bridge afternoons. Fatty was thankful. He didn't particularly want his mother to be present if his escapades with Goon were to be gone into.

They sat down. 'Now, first of all, Frederick, what do you know about Mr Eurycles?' asked the Chief, coming straight to the point as usual.

'Not much,' confessed Fatty. 'I'd better tell you

everything from the beginning, sir, then you'll see how we finally arrived at Mr Eurycles. It's a funny little story – we got mixed up in it somehow – but it's rather interesting.'

'Fire away,' said the Chief, 'we're listening. I may take a few notes as you relate your tale, but don't let that worry you. Now then?'

Fatty was just beginning his tale when he heard the loud ringing of four bicycle bells, and Buster began to bark and paw at the door.

'Oh – it's the others, sir,' said Fatty, apologetically. 'Do you mind if they come in too? I mean – they were all in it.'

'Fetch them in,' said the Chief, and Fatty went to the window, threw it up, and yelled, 'Hey, all of you! Come in here. Quick!'

The four parked their bicycles in a hurry, and rushed in at the garden door. What was up? They burst into the sitting-room, and stopped in amazement when they saw their old friend, Chief Inspector Jenks, tall and burly as ever, a wide smile on his good-humoured face.

Bets flung herself on him, and as usual he swung her high in the air and she shrieked. The others crowded round eagerly. What fun to see the Chief again – and how exciting! What did it mean?

The tall, quiet man also stood up, smiling. He seemed very much amused with all this. The Chief introduced the four newcomers to him, one by one. But again he did not say who the stranger was. The tall man was very courteous, and his shrewd, dark eyes rested in turn on each child's face. Fatty guessed that he didn't miss much!

'What have you come for? Not just to see *us*?' cried Bets.

'I came because I think you may have a tale to tell me that will help me in something else,' said the Chief. 'Frederick was just about to tell it when you arrived. Sit down, and we'll hear it.'

Everyone sat down, Bets as near the big Chief as she could possibly get. Fatty began again.

He described the breaking into Mr Fellows' house, and what the milkman had reported. He told how he and the others had gone to have a look at the house, which was so near Larry's.

'And, I suppose you managed to find an excuse

for a little breaking-in yourself, Frederick?' said the Chief.

'Well, there was a kitten left behind,' said Fatty, grinning. 'And while I was looking for it in the house, Mr Goon appeared.'

'I see – and then the dog, and the pig, and the groaning man began to haunt the house too, I suppose,' said the Chief. 'All right, we won't go into details. I've had too many already from Goon. I know all this bit, actually. It was fully reported to me at once. Tell me the bits I'm not likely to know.'

So Fatty told him of the question he had put to himself – who could have seen Mr Fellows rushing out at night? He went on to describe his talks with the night-watchmen – and regretfully he decided that he must also tell of his impersonation of the old man with the sack, and describe how he had led Mr Goon to the jetty and tipped in the sack of stones.

'Most reprehensible,' murmured the Chief.

'Yes, sir,' agreed Fatty, hurrying on. He told how the five of them had gone down to see if Mr Goon would drag out the sack next day and what he would do when he found he had been spoofed – he described the watching water weed man, which caused both the Chief and his plainclothes friend to sit up straight and look at one another.

'Give me a full description of this man, please,' said the Chief and, helped by the others, Fatty gave a very full description indeed.

'Excellent,' said the Chief. 'Most observant lot you are! I wouldn't be surprised if you told me everything the fellow had in his pockets! Wait a minute now – you say Goon arrived just then?'

'Yes, sir,' said Fatty. The Chief took a sheaf of papers from his pockets and chose one, which he read quickly to himself.

'This is Goon's report of that morning,' he said. 'But it's confused and lacks detail. I think we'd better get him along here too, now that he comes well into the tale. I may want to ask him a few questions.'

'Shall I telephone him, sir?' said Larry, at once. What a wonderful meeting! Goon would just about complete it. Poor Goon – he didn't shine on these occasions.

The Chief nodded and began to make some

notes, which he passed to the stranger. Larry telephoned, got Mr Goon at once, and gave him the Chief's message.

'What did he say?' inquired the Chief, when Larry returned.

'Well – er – not much, sir,' said Larry, embarrassed. 'Actually he just said "Lovaduck". Nothing else.'

Everyone laughed. Bets began to play with Buster, but it wasn't more than two minutes before Goon came sailing up the drive on his bicycle. He was met at the door by Fatty, who ushered him solemnly into the rather crowded sitting-room.

Goon was very nervous. He hadn't taken off his bicycle clips, nor had he stopped to brush his uniform which showed traces of his dinner. He slipped his helmet off and put it on the floor.

'Sit down, Goon,' said the Chief. 'I'm glad you came so quickly. Er – we have been hearing quite an interesting little tale from Frederick, here, and we thought you should hear it too – though no doubt you already know a good deal.'

Goon looked hurriedly and beseechingly at Fatty.

He sat down heavily, and Buster at once capered round his ankles. Fatty called him off sternly.

'Shut up, Buster. This is a serious meeting.' He turned to the Chief again. 'Shall I go on, sir? Well, that morning, Mr Goon did come down to the river, as we expected. And he took a boat and rowed to the jetty where I'd thrown in the sack of stones the night before.'

A snort came from Goon, but nobody took any notice of it. 'Mr Goon found a sack, sir – but it wasn't the sack I'd thrown in – it was another one.'

Goon stared at Fatty, his mouth open. What! That boy *hadn't* put in that sack? Then who had?

'Mr Goon opened the sack, sir, and it was full of very peculiar things. Clothes, sir – dolls' clothes – coat, trousers, belt, tie, socks – and a glove to match the one I told you I'd found in Mr Fellows' house. That made us guess the sack was the one that Mr Fellows himself had hidden in the river – so we took all the clothes home.'

'But, wait a minute, how did you get them? I thought *Goon* had them in the sack he pulled up,' said the Chief, puzzled.

'Well,' said Fatty, looking embarrassed, 'he – er – well, he *gave* them to me, sir. Gave me every single one! You look surprised – well, so was I!'

23. A STRANGE TALE

'But I don't understand,' said the Chief. 'These clothes were a most important clue. Goon, what in the world made you hand them over to Frederick?'

Mr Goon swallowed hard. His face was going a peculiar colour. That boy! That toad of a boy! Here he was in trouble again because of that boy. He couldn't think for the life of him what to answer.

But Bets answered for him. 'He didn't *give* them to him,' she said, indignantly. 'He stuffed everything down Fatty's neck – all wet and slimy too!'

'Be quiet, Bets,' said Fatty, uncomfortably. 'I'd asked for it.'

'What peculiar behaviour, Goon,' said the Chief, astounded. 'No wonder your report was hard to follow. Is it a habit of yours to stuff things down people's necks when you are annoyed?'

'No, sir,' muttered Goon, his eyes on the floor. 'How was I to know those clothes were important, sir? I wouldn't have stuffed them down his neck if I'd thought they'd got anything to do with this case. I was – well, I was downright annoyed that morning, sir.'

'I didn't mind,' said Fatty earnestly, sorry for poor Goon at that moment. 'As a matter-of-fact, I rather enjoyed it. It was very clever of Mr Goon to stuff every single thing down my neck – shoes and all!'

'Shoes? Did you say *shoes*?' said the Chief, at once. He made a quick note. 'Well, we will now leave this subject of stuffing clothes down necks, as I see it is rather painful to Goon, and get on with the next part of the tale.'

Fatty told how they had dried out the clothes – how there had been a breaking-in to his own house that night, but nothing was taken – how he had interviewed Mr Fellows, and got nothing but evasions – and, finally, how they had examined the clothes that very morning and how Bets had made her interesting discovery.

Goon was now listening intently. This was all new to him.

'We found nothing of interest at all, sir,' said Fatty. 'Until Bets here found a tiny pocket hidden in the sleeve-cuff – and in it was a handkerchief embroidered with daisies, and the name I told you – Eurycles. Bets, where's the hanky?'

Bets produced it proudly. In an intent silence, the Chief and his friend examined it. Mr Goon gaped. What was all this? What did a doll's handkerchief matter?

'What did you deduce from this handkerchief then?' asked the Chief.

'Well, first I recognised the name Eurycles,' said Fatty.

The stranger spoke directly to Fatty for the first time.

'Why did you recognise it? It is not a usual name,' he said.

'No, I know that, sir,' said Fatty. 'In fact, *I'd* never met anyone of that name in my life, though for all I know there may be plenty of Greeks called Eurycles. I recognised it because – well, because I'm a bit of a ventriloquist, as I told the Chief here.

You see, there was once a Greek called Eurycles who was a very famous ventriloquist indeed. I read about him in my book on ventriloquism.'

'Remarkable,' said the stranger, in his soft voice. 'And so you thought that the clothes must belong to a doll owned by a modern ventriloquist called Mr Eurycles?'

'Yes, that's right,' said Fatty. 'I was at a dead end as regards this mystery, and I thought perhaps if I could find out if there *really* was a ventriloquist using the old Greek name as a stage name, I could ask him a few questions. I thought *he* might be able to solve this peculiar mystery for us. That's why I asked the Chief on the telephone if he knew of anyone called Eurycles and how I could get in touch with him.'

'I see. Again I say, it's most remarkable,' said the tall man. 'Well, you'll be interested to know that there *is* a modern ventriloquist who uses Eurycles as his stage name – and that those clothes you speak of, do belong to his doll. And you'll also be interested to know that we have been searching everywhere for the clothes.'

'Why?' asked Fatty, astonished. 'Gosh, what a

lot of people are interested in those clothes!'

'I propose to tell you a little story myself now,' said the Chief's friend. 'A story which you must keep to yourselves. You are not to ask me any questions about it, you must accept my tale as it stands. It will tell you why my friend, the Chief Inspector here, was amazed when you spoke of Mr Eurycles to him.'

This was all very astonishing. Every eye was on the quiet stranger as he began his tale.

'You know the Chief Inspector and you know that I am a friend of his, in the same kind of service – we work to preserve the law and order of our country, to keep out enemies, to secure for this country the things that are right and proper.'

He paused. Everyone felt very solemn, and Bets found that she was holding her breath.

'Very well. It is our duty to discover and watch any man or woman who is working against this country and its laws. There are many of them, some in high-up places, some in lowly ones. Our duty is to watch, to sift out what we hear, and to report whenever we find anyone suspected of misdeeds against the country and its laws.'

'Spies?' whispered Bets.

'Not only spies – but any man or woman of evil intent,' said the tall man. 'Mr Eurycles was one who helped us in this. He was a clever ventriloquist who went everywhere with Bobby-Boy, his talking doll. He went to both high and low places, and gathered a great deal of information for us. Mr Fellows was his assistant.'

'Oh!' cried Daisy. 'Was he really? So that's how *he* comes in!'

'One day, one of Mr Eurycles' friends came to him with a list of names,' went on the Chief's friend. 'They were names that we wanted more than anything else! Names of people undermining every industry in our country – provoking strikes, sabotage, anything that would harm Britain – and there was also other information, very valuable indeed to us. Mr Eurycles put the information into his usual hiding-place – in the clothes that Bobby-Boy wore.'

Everyone listened intently, especially Mr Goon.

'That night, Mr Eurycles was kidnapped. The kidnappers took Bobby-Boy also, knowing that either on Mr Eurycles or on his doll, the list of names was hidden. But the ventriloquist managed to throw the doll out of the window of the car that kidnapped him.

'Following the car was one of our police cars, as it happened – not because the police suspected that Mr Eurycles was in the first car, but because they knew it to be a stolen car. When the doll was thrown out, the police in the car behind thought it was a small child and stopped their car, of course, to see.

'They lost the first car and returned to headquarters. Mr Fellows had by then reported the kidnapping of his master, the ventriloquist, so the doll, Bobby-Boy, was handed to him. Apparently he knew that Mr Eurycles had hidden something of value in the clothes, but he had no idea what. So he took the clothes into his keeping, hoping that his master would soon turn up.'

'Oh, *I* see! And then the kidnappers found out that the list wasn't on Mr Eurycles but somewhere in the doll's clothes, and have been hunting for it ever since!' cried Daisy.

'And that's why Mr Fellows ran out with the clothes in the middle of the night, when someone broke into his house – and he sank them into the river, meaning to get them again sometime,' said Pip, seeing everything now. 'And then the water weed man, who was the burglar, saw Mr Goon stuffing them down Fatty's neck, and so the next place he broke into was Fatty's. Goodness, we were in the middle of something terribly exciting, and we didn't know it!'

'Why didn't Mr Fellows look for the valuable list himself and take it?' asked Bets. 'Then he could have thrown the clothes away.'

'I imagine that he wasn't able to find it – and, anyway, he didn't know what to look for,' said the Chief. 'But *we* shall be able to find it. We have had information as to where it is. If you'll just produce the clothes, Frederick, we will show you where the invaluable list is hidden, a most dramatic ending to what you called "just a little mystery"!'

There was a dead silence. All the excitement drained out of the children as they remembered the disastrous happening of the morning.

'What's the matter?' said the Chief, surprised. 'You *have* got the clothes here, haven't you? What are you looking like that for?'

'It's awful to have to tell you, sir – but, they're gone,' said Fatty, in a low voice. 'We – we went out of the shed where we kept them, locked it behind us, and when we got back the shed was broken open – and all the clothes were gone.'

Bets burst into tears. 'What shall we do? Oh, we didn't know it was so important! Oh, Fatty, what shall we do?'

24. GOOD OLD BUSTER!

The Chief Inspector whistled through his teeth and looked at his plainclothes friend.

'This is a set-back!' he said. 'A real shock. Our scarred-faced friend again, I suppose. He's certainly determined this time!'

'That list is important to him – and to a lot of others who would like it destroyed,' said the tall man grimly. 'And, unfortunately, it is important to us too.' He turned to Fatty.

'*All* the clothes went – he took the lot?' he asked sharply.

'Yes, all except for the little hanky Bets found, which you've seen,' said Fatty. 'But if you like, we can go down to my shed and have another look in the box where we put them. But I'm pretty certain it's empty, sir.'

They trailed down to the shed, Mr Goon too, all of them feeling most depressed. To have such an exciting mystery – and then to have the right ending snatched away just as they were being so successful! It really was bad luck.

They looked into the box. It was, as Fatty said, well and truly empty. Then Bets suddenly remembered something and cried out loudly.

'The shoe that Buster took! Did we find it and hide that away too? Or did we forget it and leave it in whatever corner Buster put it?'

'We forgot it. I didn't put it in,' said Fatty. 'But would just one shoe be of any use to you, sir?'

'My word, yes – more than you'd think, if it was the right shoe!' said the Chief. 'Here, Buster boy, find that shoe!'

And, as if Buster completely understood, he ran round the shed, hunting into this corner and that – and, finally, after sniffing under an old sack, he disappeared beneath it, worried at something – and came out proudly with a doll's red shoe in his mouth!

'It's the shoe. He's found it,' said Fatty, in delight. 'Good old Buster. Clever dog, Buster.'

Buster wagged his tail proudly. The Chief

took the shoe at once and he and his friend examined it closely.

'It may be the one. Can't tell without examining it,' said the Chief. 'Anyone got a sharp penknife?'

Fatty had, of course. He always kept his pockets full of things that might conceivably come in useful some day.

The Chief took the knife and sat down on a box. He turned the shoe upside down and, with all the Find-Outers breathing heavily down his neck, he began to try and prize away the heel.

'Strongly made,' said the Chief. 'Ah – up it comes!'

The heel came away from the shoe, and the children saw a neat little hollowed-out compartment in the heel itself. In it was a thin sheet of paper tightly folded.

'It's here,' cried the Chief, as excited as the five children. His fingers delicately eased the paper from its hiding-place. He handed it, folded, to the tall man, whose eyes were now gleaming.

He unfolded the paper very carefully, and ran his eyes down a list of names and notes. They were all written in most minute writing, impossible to make out at a distance. Mr Goon, craning his neck to see if he could read anything, could only make out a blur.

'This is it,' said the tall man, a ring of triumph in his voice. 'There's a whole year's work here – invaluable, Jenks! And to think how nearly we lost it – if it hadn't been for that dog running off with the shoe as he did, and hiding it, we'd have lost it for good!'

'The thief must just have seen the bundle of clothes in the box, thought everything was there, and picked the whole lot up,' said Fatty. 'And gone off with it in delight. What a shock when he finds only one shoe!'

'Perhaps he'll come back and try and find it,' suggested Larry. 'You could catch him then.'

'Oh, we know where to pick him up now,' said the Chief. 'My word, look at this name on the list – and that – whew! This is going to make a stir!'

'It is. It's going to make several dozen people extremely uncomfortable,' said the tall man, grimly. 'What a haul! I can't believe it – and all because of these kids. Marvellous, aren't they?'

'Well, they've certainly done some good work in their time,' said the Chief, smiling. 'Very good work. They call themselves the Five Find-Outers and Dog, you know. And the things they've found out – they could really have books and books written about them!'

'But Buster's really the hero of *this* mystery!' said Bets, picking up the little Scottie and hugging him. 'Aren't you, Buster? Did you know that shoe was important, Buster? Is that why you hid it? Fatty, I'd be quite ready to believe that Buster *did* guess, you know!'

'What are you going to do now?' asked Larry, turning to the Chief.

'Well, just a few bits of work,' said the Chief. 'We must go and drop in on Fellows, to begin with, and set his mind at rest. And we must send somebody to gather in Mr Scarred-Face – or the water weed man, as you call him. He won't be wanting water weed for some time after this!'

'I do hope you'll get Mr Eurycles back some day,' said Bets. 'I hope nothing horrid's happened to him.'

'I'll let you know when he does appear again,'

said the Chief. 'I have a feeling that once we get after the people whose names are on this sheet of paper, our Mr Eurycles will find himself unexpectedly free. Quite a lot of these people will flee the country soon!'

'Er, can't we give these children a little reward for their enormous help?' said the tall man, getting up from his box and almost bumping his head against the roof.

'Oh, no, thank you,' said Fatty at once. 'That would spoil everything – we wouldn't want to solve mysteries for a reward. We do it because it's fun – and we like helping the Chief.'

'My dear fellow, there are so few people left in the world who will do things without expecting payment or reward, that I think we'll let the Find-Outers go their own good way,' said the Chief to his friend, quite seriously. That made the five feel extremely proud.

'Right,' said the tall man. 'Well, we must be going. Still, there are two things I'm going to do for these, er – what do they call themselves? – these Find-Outers and Dog. I am going to get my butcher to send his biggest and juiciest bone to this remarkably clever dog . . .'

'Wuff,' said Buster, wagging his tail most appreciatively.

'And when Mr Eurycles turns up again, I shall ask him if he would be good enough to give Frederick here a few first class lessons in ventriloquism,' said the tall man. 'He'll be delighted to do that.'

Fatty blushed with pleasure. 'Oh, sir – thank you. I don't want any reward, as you know – and I'll pay for the lessons. Gosh, wouldn't I like them! Thanks very much.'

The Chief and his friend departed. The police car revved up and disappeared down the drive. Only Mr Goon was left with the five children. They looked at one another.

Poor old Goon. He hadn't had much of a look-in this time. The Chief hadn't even said a word of farewell to him. Even Buster had done better than Goon!

'Well,' said Fatty, in a jovial tone, 'what about tea? It must surely be ready by now. Anyway, *I'm* ready for it. Mr Goon – will you join us?'

Mr Goon was so astounded at this invitation

that he could only gape. He was not a generous enemy, like Fatty, and never would be. He hardly understood this invitation, and his mouth opened and shut like a goldfish.

'Well, do answer, Mr Goon,' said Fatty. 'We'll celebrate the occasion, and I'll open the big tin of chocolate biscuits I got for Christmas. Will you, won't you, will you, won't you, Mr Goon?'

'I will,' gasped Goon, almost as if he was getting married. 'Thanks. I take it very kind of you after – er – after some of the things that have happened.'

'Well, don't you go stuffing things down my neck again!' said Fatty, leading the way in.

Goon gave a sudden grin. 'And don't you go making up dogs, and pigs, and what-not,' he said.

Bets didn't want Goon to stay to tea, but she said nothing. She liked Fatty's generous gesture, and she knew that poor Mr Goon hadn't had a very good time in this mystery – but nothing was going to persuade her to sit next to him, or even to address a word to him. She would never, ever forgive him for stuffing those things down Fatty's neck!

It was a most hilarious tea. Everyone was pleased that the little mystery had turned out to be a genuine, large-size one, and had ended so triumphantly for Buster.

Buster, of course, was amazed to find his old enemy suddenly belonging to the family circle. He gave a few fierce growls and then, as everyone made so much fuss of him, and Daisy actually addressed him as Hero Dog, he joined in the general enjoyment.

Mr Goon enjoyed himself too. Well, well – to think that toad of a boy could behave like this! After his fourth macaroon, and third piece of chocolate cake, Mr Goon was ready to be Fatty's best friend!

And then a loud grunting noise was heard under the table! 'What's that?' cried Bets, in alarm. Mr Goon looked under the table, amazed. Only Buster was there.

The others looked at Fatty's grinning face and laughed. And then, from just behind the astounded Mr Goon, came an all-too-familiar voice. 'I never did it, I never! Ooooh, I never did! Where's my auntie?'

Oh, Fatty! What are we to do with you? Tell us about your next mystery, do!

the MYSTERY
of the
MISSING
NECKLACE

Enid Blyton

the
MYSTERY
of the
MISSING
NECKLACE

EGMONT

First published in Great Britain 1947
by Methuen & Co Ltd.

Enid Blyton ® Blyton's Mystery & Adventure ®
Text Copyright © 1947 Chorion Rights Limited
All rights reserved
Cover photography © 2010 Martin Usborne
Images: Shutterstock

A CIP catalogue record for this title
is available from the British Library

CONTENTS

CONTENTS

1. OH, FOR A MYSTERY!

Pip and Bets sat in their garden, in the very coolest place they could find as the August sun was blazing hot.

'A whole month of the summer hols gone already!' said Pip. 'And except that we've been away to the seaside for two weeks, absolutely nothing else has happened. Most boring.'

'The boringest hols we've ever had,' said Bets. 'Not even the smell of a mystery to solve! And not even Larry, Daisy, Fatty, or Buster to play with – they've been away at the sea for ages!'

Larry and Daisy were friends of Pip and Bets, and so was Frederick – or Fatty as everyone called him. Buster was his Scottie dog, loved by all the children.

The five children called themselves the Five Find-Outers and Dog, because for the last four holidays they had tackled curious mysteries and solved them all – much to the annoyance of the village policeman, Mr Goon.

'But now it seems as if you and I, Pip, are the only Find-Outers left,' said Bets. 'I don't feel as if the others will ever come back! Soon the hols will be over, you'll all be back at boarding-school again, except me, and we shan't solve any mystery at all these hols.'

'There are still four weeks left, so cheer up!' said Pip. 'And the others come back this week – and I bet old Fatty will have heaps of new disguises to try out on us! We'll be on the look out for him this time, though – and we jolly well won't be taken in!'

Bets laughed. She remembered how Fatty had disguised himself as a French boy, and deceived them all beautifully. And in the last holidays he had produced all kinds of disguises, which he wore with a red wig and eyebrows. There was no knowing what old Fatty would be up to next!

'But *this* time he won't deceive us,' said Pip again. 'I shall be very suspicious of any peculiar-looking stranger who tries to talk to me, or comes to call on us. I shall say to myself, "It's you all right, Fatty," and I shan't listen to a word!'

'Do you think there will be a mystery for us to solve these hols?' asked Bets. 'I do so like looking for clues, and making out lists of suspects, and crossing people off the list when we've made enquiries – and finding the real suspect at the end!'

'We've been jolly lucky so far,' said Pip, sitting up and looking round for the bottle of lemonade he had brought out. 'We've been able to solve every single mystery. We can't always be successful, though. I don't expect even real detectives are always successful. Bets, you pig, you've finished the lemonade. Go and ask Gladys for some iced water.'

Bets was too lazy to move. She rolled over out of Pip's reach, and yawned loudly. 'I'm bored! I want the others to come back so that we can have games with them. I want a mystery – a really good one. And I want to solve it before Old Clear-Orf does!'

Old Clear-Orf was Mr Goon the policeman. He told children and dogs to 'clear orf' whenever he saw them. He disliked all the Find-Outers intensely, and never had a good word to say for them. Pip and Bets hadn't seen much of him in the summer holidays, and were very glad, for he had often been to their parents to complain of the

521

behaviour of the Five Find-Outers. Bets was afraid of him, because when he lost his temper he shouted, and was very unpleasant indeed.

'Bets, didn't you hear me tell you to go in and fetch some iced water?' said Pip crossly. 'Go on!'

'I'm not going to be ordered about by you,' said Bets, rolling a bit further away. 'I suppose you order all the little boys about in your school, and then when you come home you think you can order me about too. Well, I shall soon be ten, and you're not to!'

'Don't you cheek me, young Bets!' said Pip, sitting up.

'I think you're a horrid brother to have,' said Bets. 'I'd much rather have Fatty. He's always kind to me!'

'He wouldn't be, if you were his sister,' said Pip. 'He hasn't got any sisters – if he had, he'd know what a nuisance they are. Now – are you going to go and . . .'

'Yes, I'll get it!' said Bets, getting up, 'but only because *I'm* thirsty, and *I* want some to drink, see? I don't mind bringing you out a little too, as I'm going to get some for myself, but I'm really going for myself, and . . .'

Pip pretended to be getting up, and Bets fled. If only the others would come back! She and Pip were getting tired of one another.

Bets hadn't long to wait before the others came back. In two days' time Larry, Daisy, Fatty, and Buster all turned up together, looking so brown that Pip and Bets had to gaze earnestly at them to make sure they really were their friends. Buster wasn't brown, of course – he was still jet black, and he flung himself on Pip and Bets in joy and delight, barking and licking and whining as if he had gone mad.

'Buster, darling! You're fatter! Oh, Larry, I'm glad you're back! Daisy, you're terribly brown. And oh, Fatty – you've *grown*!'

Fatty certainly had grown in the last four months. He was taller, taller even than Larry now, and much taller than Pip, who didn't seem to have grown at all in the last year.

'Hello, everyone!' he said, and Bets gave a cry of surprise.

'Fatty! You've got a different voice! It's a

grown-up voice! Are you putting it on – disguising it, I mean?'

'No,' said Fatty, pulling Bets' hair teasingly. 'It's just broken, that's all.'

'Who broke it?' said Bets, in alarm, and the others roared at her till their sides ached.

'Bets, don't be silly. You know that when they grow up, boys get deep voices like men's, don't you? Well, when boys' voices change like that we say that their voices *break* – that's all. We don't mean broken in half, or smashed to pieces!'

'Oh, Fatty – I don't know you with such a deep voice,' said Bets, half-alarmed. 'You don't sound the same. You *look* like Fatty – but you don't sound like him! I wish you had your old voice.'

'Bets, you've no idea what a difference it makes to me, now I've got a proper grown-up voice,' said Fatty earnestly. 'It means that I can disguise myself as a grown-up instead of always like some kind of boy! It gives me much more scope – and I've got some fine grown-up disguises!'

Bets immediately changed her mind about not liking Fatty's new voice. More disguises! Now life would be exciting and thrilling and unexpected things would happen. Fatty would disguise himself as all kinds of grown-up people – the Find-Outers would have a simply gorgeous time. She stared at Fatty happily.

'Oh, Fatty! You've only been able to dress up as telegraph boys or butcher boys or messenger boys before! Now you can be all kinds of things – old men with beards – a postman – a dustman – a window-cleaner with a ladder! Oh, Fatty, do be all those things and let's see you!'

Everyone laughed. 'Give me a chance!' said Fatty. 'I'm going to practise a bit these hols. I didn't have much chance whilst I was away, because Mother wouldn't let me take much luggage – but I don't mind telling you I'm going to collect a few things now! I've got taller too, so I can almost wear grown-ups' things. By the time our next mystery comes along I shall be able to tackle it in whatever disguise is necessary.'

'You do sound grown-up,' said Bets. 'Doesn't he, everybody?'

'Well, as a matter of fact,' said Fatty, swelling up a little with pride, 'I'm the tallest boy in my form now, and you should just see the muscles in my arms. I'll show you!'

'Same old Fatty!' said Larry. Best in everything, aren't you? Nobody to beat you!'

Fatty grinned and bent his arm and showed them how his muscles came up in a big lump. Bets looked on in awe, but Larry and Pip did not seem to be much impressed.

'Fair!' said Larry. 'I've seen better ones on a boy of twelve!'

'Huh! You're jealous!' said Fatty, good-humouredly. 'Now then – let's hear any Peterswood news, Pip and Bets. The village seemed pretty crowded when I came through it just now.'

'Too jolly crowded for anything!' said Pip. 'This hot weather is drawing the people to the river in their hundreds! We get coaches all day long – and down by the river there are all sorts of shows to amuse the people when they get tired of the river, or it's raining.'

'What sort of shows?' asked Fatty, lying down on the grass, and tickling Buster on his tummy. 'Any good?'

'Not much,' said Pip. 'There's a waxwork show – pretty dull really – you know, figures made of wax, all dressed up – and there are those bumper cars – they're quite fun for the first two or three times you go in them. . . .'

'And a hoopla game,' said Bets. 'You buy three wooden rings, and you try to throw them over any of the things arranged on a big round table – and if the ring goes right over anything, you can have whatever you've ringed. I like that game.'

'You would!' said Pip. 'She spends her pocket money on hiring the wooden rings – and then wins a mouldy little brooch worth hardly anything, that Mother can't bear and won't let her wear!'

'Well, Pip, you spent your money once, and you didn't win a thing!' began Bets hotly. But Fatty interrupted.

'Sounds as if Peterswood is going quite lively!' he said. 'We'll have to make up a party and go down to all these shows one wet afternoon. If it ever *is* wet again!'

'Fatty, will you go in one of your new grown-up disguises?' asked Bets excitedly. 'Oh, do! It would be lovely to see you acting like a grown-up, and taking everybody in!'

'I'll see,' said Fatty. 'I'd like to take in Old

Clear-Orf, I must say! He's up to all my boy-disguises now – he'd see through them at once – but I bet he wouldn't see through a grown-up disguise!'

'What will you go as?' asked Daisy.

'Don't know,' said Fatty. 'And listen, all of you – if you can get any old things of your fathers' – you know, old hats they don't want, or boots, or even old coats – they'd come in mighty useful for me. I'm afraid if I take too many of my father's things, he'll be annoyed. Mother doesn't let him keep any of his old things, she gives them away – so he's only got rather newish clothes.'

'We'll do what we can,' promised Larry, and Pip nodded too. Anything to help old Fatty to disguise himself! Bets sighed with joy to think that Fatty was back again. Now life would really be exciting once more. And oh, if *only* a mystery turned up, how heavenly the rest of the hols would be!

2. MR. GOON IS VERY ANNOYING

It was lovely to be all together again, day after day. The Five swam in the river, went for long bicycle rides, lazed in the garden, squabbled, drank pints of iced drinks, and ate hundreds of ices. Buster liked both lemonade and ices and had his full share. He got rather fat and Pip teased him.

'You're too fat to go after rabbits, Buster!' he said. 'Why, even a mouse would escape you now. You don't walk any more, you waddle. You don't breathe, you wheeze! You . . .'

'Oh, don't tease him so,' said Bets, who was always quite certain that Buster could understand every single word said to him. 'He *doesn't* waddle. I bet if he saw Old Clear-Orf this very minute he'd be after him like a shot!'

'By the way, what's happened to Mr Goon?' asked Fatty. 'I saw him yesterday, in a great hurry and looking extremely important.'

'Probably solving some mystery we don't know anything about,' said Larry gloomily. 'There have been a lot of burglaries lately, and perhaps Mr Goon is getting at the bottom of them.'

'Yes – but the burglaries haven't been in his district,' said Fatty. 'They've mostly been miles away. I've read about them in the paper. Lady Rexham's jewels were stolen only last week – and somebody else's famous diamonds the week before. It's a clever gang of thieves – but they're not working this district, as far as I know.'

'I wish they were!' said Bets. 'Then we could catch them. You could put on one of your new disguises, Fatty, and track them down.'

'It's not as easy as all that, Bets, and you know it!' said Fatty, with a laugh. 'You just think of all the difficulties we had in our other mysteries.'

'We haven't seen you in any grown-up disguise yet, Fatty,' said Daisy. 'Do put one on, so that we can spot you in it, if we can.'

'I've been practising in my bedroom,' said Fatty. 'I don't want to try anything out on you till I'm perfect. I'll try it on you when I'm ready, I promise. And I'll give my second-best pen to anyone of you that spots me first, see?'

'Oooh, Fatty!' said Bets. 'Can you really spare it?'

'I'll certainly give it to any of the Find-Outers if they're bright enough to spot me in my first grown-up disguise,' said Fatty. 'It's a bargain!'

'I bet I'll spot you first,' said Larry. 'The girls won't, I'm sure. Pip might – but I'll be first!'

'We'll have to leave Buster behind when we try to do the spotting,' said Pip. 'Or he'll simply rush up to you and bark madly to tell everyone it's you!'

'Yes. Buster's out of this,' said Fatty, and Buster cocked up his ears at his name. 'Sorry, Buster, old boy – but tomorrow you must stay at home with the cat.'

'Oh, Fatty – are you going to dress up *tomorrow*?' asked Bets, in delight. 'Really tomorrow? Well, you won't deceive *me*! I shall look at everyone with an eagle eye!'

'Right,' said Fatty. 'But all the same – I have a feeling that my pen will still be safely in my pocket tomorrow night! You may be quite good Find-Outers – but I'm a bit cleverer than any of you!'

'You're certainly best at boasting!' said Larry 'That trumpet of yours must be quite worn out by now.'

'What trumpet?' said Bets, in curiosity. 'I've never seen Fatty with a trumpet.'

'No, but surely you've heard him blowing his own trumpet?' said Larry. 'It's deafening at times! It's . . .'

And then Fatty sat up and flung himself on Larry and there was a great deal of shouting and yelling and squealing, with Buster plunging into the middle of the brawl and getting wildly excited too.

Mrs Hilton, Pip's mother, appeared. 'Children! You do know I've visitors in the garden, surely? If you want to yell and squeal and fight, will you go somewhere else? What about a nice walk?'

'Oh, *Mummy* – it's too hot for a walk!' groaned Pip.

'Well, I should have thought it was much too hot to fight,' said Mrs Hilton disapprovingly. 'Really, Larry and Frederick, you look very dirty and untidy!'

'Sorry, Mrs Hilton,' said Fatty meekly, and Larry tried to smooth his hair down. 'We'll go for a walk. I forgot you had people to tea in the garden. I really do apologise.'

Fatty had marvellous manners with grown-up people, and Mrs Hilton began to smile again. 'Go down to the dairy and get yourselves an ice cream each,' she said. 'Here's the money, Pip.'

'Oh thanks, Mummy,' said Pip, and they all got up, pleased. It was the fourth ice cream that day, but it didn't seem worth while mentioning that to Mrs Hilton. Fatty's mother had already provided ice creams and so had Larry's, and Fatty had generously given them one each as well. Now this was the fourth lot. Goody!

They walked sedately down the garden and round the drive to the gates. They went to the dairy, which made real cream ices that were most delicious, and sat down at the little table in the window to eat them.

Mr Goon passed by on his bicycle as they sat there. He pedalled furiously, his face hot and red.

'Spot of hard work for Mr Goon,' said Fatty, letting a cold spoonful of ice cream slide as slowly down his throat as possible. 'Looks busy, doesn't he?'

Before they had finished their ices, Mr Goon came pedalling back again, as furiously as before. The police station was just opposite the dairy, and the children watched the policeman go smartly up the steps. Then they saw his head behind the frosted window pane of one of the rooms in the police station, talking to somebody else. Mr Goon was talking the most and was nodding vigorously.

'Never seen Mr Goon so busy before!' said Fatty, in astonishment. 'Do you think he's really got a case to work on – a mystery to solve that we don't know anything about?'

'Golly, here he comes again!' said Pip, as Mr Goon scuttled out of the police station, buttoning a big sheaf of papers into his breast-pocket. 'He's simply bursting with importance.'

'He's feeling jolly pleased about something,' said Fatty. 'I *should* be mad if something had cropped up in Peterswood whilst I've been away, and we don't know anything about it!'

Mr Goon jumped on to his bicycle and pedalled away again. It was maddening to sit there and watch him so busy and important and not know why. Fatty felt as if he was bursting with curiosity.

'He's on to something!' he said. 'He really is. I know that look on his face. We *must* find out what it is!'

'Well, you find out then,' said Larry. 'And if he tells

you, you'll be lucky! It's what Mr Goon has dreamed of for months – a mystery all to himself, that the Five Find-Outers don't know anything about!'

'I can't bear it!' said Fatty, and let the last spoonful of ice cream go down his throat. Then he looked dismayed. 'Oh I say – do you know, I was so puzzled about Old Clear-Orf and his mystery that I ate that ice cream without tasting it. What a fearful waste. I'll have to have another.'

The others looked at him. 'There's no more money,' said Pip. 'We spent it all.'

'I've got some,' said Fatty, and dug his hand into his pocket. He always had plenty of money, much to the envy of the others, who had pocket money each Saturday and had to make that do for the week, like most children. But Fatty had plenty of rich relations, who seemed to pour money into his pockets in a most lavish way.

'Mummy says it's bad for you to have so much money,' said Pip. 'She's always saying that.'

'It probably is bad for me,' said Fatty, 'but I'm not going round telling my relations to stop giving me tips. Now, who wants another ice cream? Bets?'

'Oh, Fatty, I couldn't,' sighed Bets sadly. 'I'd love

to, but I know I can't. I feel a bit sick already.'

'Well, go outside,' said Pip unfeelingly. 'No thanks, Fatty. I don't feel sick, but I shan't eat any supper if I have another, and then Mummy will stop all ice creams for a week, or something awful.'

Larry and Daisy said they couldn't possibly eat another either, so Fatty had a second one all by himself, and this time he said he tasted every spoonful, so it wasn't wasted as the first one had been.

Mr Goon came back on his bicycle, just as the children left the shop. 'There he is again!' said Fatty admiringly. 'I've never seen him move so quickly. Good evening, Mr Goon!'

Mr Goon was just getting off his bicycle to go into the police station again. He glanced at Fatty, and took no notice of him. Fatty was annoyed.

'You seem extremely busy, Mr Goon,' he said. 'Solving another mystery, I suppose? Nice to get the old brains to work, isn't it? I could do with a bit of that myself, after lazing away most of these holidays.'

'Oh? You got some brains then?' said Mr Goon sarcastically. 'That's good hearing, that is. But

I'm busy now, and can't stop to talk about your brains, Frederick. There's big things going on, see, and I've got plenty to do without wasting my time talking to you.'

'Big things?' said Fatty, suddenly interested. 'What, another mystery, Mr Goon? I say – that's . . .'

'Yes, another mystery,' said Mr Goon, almost bursting with importance. 'And I'm IN CHARGE of it, see? I'm the one that's tackling it, not you interfering kids. And not a word do I tell you about it, not one word. It's secret and important, and it's a matter for the police!'

'But Mr Goon – you know how we . . .' began Fatty anxiously; but the policeman, feeling for once that he had got the better of Fatty, interrupted loftily.

'All I know about you is that you're a conceited, interfering kid what ought to be put in his place and kept there – you and your nasty barking dog! This here case is mine, and I'm already getting on with it, and what's more I'll get promotion over this as sure as my name is Theophilus Goon,' said the policeman, marching up the steps to the police station. 'You clear orf now!'

'What a blow!' muttered poor, disappointed Fatty, as Mr Goon disappeared through the door. He and the others walked home slowly, discussing all that Clear-Orf had said.

'To think of that fat policeman at work on a perfectly gorgeous new mystery that we don't know a thing about!' said Fatty, looking so miserable that Bets put her arm through his. 'It's maddening. And the worst of it is that I simply don't see how we are going to find out a thing, if Mr Goon won't tell us.'

'Even Buster's upset about it,' said Bets. He's got his tail right down. So have you, poor Fatty. Never mind – you're going to try out your grown-up disguise tomorrow – that will be a bit of excitement for you, Fatty. And for us too!'

'Yes, it will,' said Fatty, cheering up a little. 'Well – I'll be getting back home now. Got to practise my disguise a bit before I try it out on you all tomorrow. So long!'

3. FATTY DISGUISES HIMSELF

Next morning Larry had a note from Fatty.

> *Go down to the sideshows by the river this*
> *afternoon. I'll meet you somewhere in disguise.*
> *But you won't know me!*
> *Fatty*

Larry showed the note to Pip and Bets when he went to see them that morning. Bets was thrilled. 'What *will* Fatty be dressed in? I bet I'll know him! Oh, I can't wait for this afternoon to come!'

Larry's mother gave him some money to spend at the sideshows when she heard they were all going there that afternoon. They set off at two o'clock, ready to spot Fatty, no matter how well he was disguised.

As they walked down the village street an old bent man came shuffling up towards them. He stooped badly and dragged his feet, which were in old boots, the toes cracked and the heels worn down. He wore a straggly sandy-grey beard, and had shaggy grey eyebrows, and he looked extremely dirty. His coat sagged away from his bent shoulders, and his corduroy trousers were tied up with string at the knees.

His hat was too large for him and was crammed down over his head. He had a stick in his hand and used it to help himself along. He shuffled to a bench and sat down in the sun, sniffing loudly.

'That's Fatty! I know it is!' said Bets.

'It's just the sort of disguise he'd put on. Isn't he clever?'

The old fellow sniffed loudly and then wiped his hand across his nose. Bets giggled. 'Oh dear! Fatty is really simply marvellous. I do think he is. He must have been practising that awful sniffle for ages.'

Larry went over to the old man and sat down beside him. 'Hello, Fatty!' he said. 'Jolly good, old boy! But we all recognised you at once!'

The old man took absolutely no notice at all. The others joined Larry and sat there, giggling. Pip gave the old man a punch in the ribs.

'Hey, Fatty! You can stop pretending now. We know it's you!'

The old man felt the punch and looked round indignantly, his eyes almost hidden under his shaggy eyebrows. He moved a little way away from Larry and Pip.

'Fatty!' said Pip. The old man put his hand behind his ear, and said 'Wassat?'

'He's pretending to be deaf now!' said Bets, and giggled again.

'Ah?' said the old man, looking puzzled. 'Wassat?'

'What does "Wassat" mean?' asked Bets.

'It means "What's that" of course,' said Larry. 'Hey, Fatty, stop it now. Give up, and tell us we're right. We all spotted you at once.'

'Wassat?' said the old man again, and put his hand behind his ear once more. It was a very peculiar ear, large and flat and purple red. Bets gazed at it and then nudged Daisy.

'Daisy! We've made a frightful mistake! It's not Fatty. Look at his ears!'

Everyone gazed at the old fellow's ears. No – not even Fatty could make his ears go like that. And they were not false ears either. They were quite real, not very clean, and remarkably hairy. In fact, they were most unpleasant ears.

'Golly! It *isn't* Fatty!' said Pip, gazing at the ears. 'What *must* the old man think of us?'

'Wassat?' said the old man again, evidently extremely puzzled at the children's familiar behaviour towards him.

'Well, thank goodness the poor old thing is deaf,' said Daisy, feeling ashamed of their mistake. 'Come on, Larry, come on, Pip. We've made an idiotic mistake! How Fatty would laugh if he knew!'

'He's probably hiding somewhere around and grinning to himself like anything,' said Pip. They left the puzzled old man sitting on his bench and went off down the street again. They met the baker, and Bets gave him a long and piercing stare, wondering if he could by any chance be Fatty. But he wasn't. He was much too tall.

Then they met the window-cleaner, and as he was just about Fatty's height, they all went and pretended to examine his barrow of ladders and pails, taking cautious glances at him to find out whether or not *he* could be Fatty in disguise.

'Here! What's the matter with you kids?' said the window-cleaner. 'Haven't you ever seen ladders and pails before? And what are you giving me them looks for? Anythink wrong with me today?'

'No,' said Larry hurriedly, for the window-cleaner sounded rather annoyed. 'It's just that – er – these sliding ladders – er – are rather interesting!'

'Ho, *are* they?' said the window-cleaner disbelievingly. 'Well, let me tell you this . . .'

But the children didn't listen to what he had to tell them. They hurried off, rather red in the face.

'Wait! We shall get into trouble if we go squinting at everyone to find out if they really are Fatty,' said Larry. 'We'll have to look at people a bit more carefully – I mean, without them knowing it.'

'There he is – I'm sure of it!' said Bets suddenly, as they went over the level-crossing to the riverside, where the sideshows were. 'Look – that porter with the moustache. That's Fatty, all right!'

The porter was wheeling a barrow up the platform, and the others stood and admired him. 'He wheels it exactly like a *real* porter,' said Bets. 'Why do porters always wear waistcoats and no coats at railway stations? I'm sure that's Fatty. It's just the way he walks.'

She raised her voice and hailed the porter. 'Hey, Fatty! Fatty!'

The porter turned round. He set his barrow down on the ground and walked towards them looking angry.

'Who are you calling Fatty?' he demanded, his face red under his porter's cap. 'You hold your tongue, you cheeky kids!'

The children stared at him. 'It *is* Fatty,' said Bets. 'Look, that's just how his hair sticks out when he wears a hat. Fatty! We know it's you!'

'Now you look here!' said the porter, coming nearer. 'Calling me names! You ought to be ashamed of yourself, you should!'

'It *isn't* Fatty, you idiot,' said Pip angrily to Bets. 'Fatty isn't as short in the arms. *Now* you've got us into trouble!'

But very luckily for them, a train came thundering in at that moment and the porter had to run to open and shut doors and see to luggage. The children hastily left the level-crossing and ran down to the river.

'You *stupid*, Bets! You'll get us all into trouble if you keep on imagining everyone is Fatty,' said Pip. 'Calling out "Fatty" like that – especially as the porter *was* fat. He must have thought you were disgustingly rude.'

'Oh dear – yes, I suppose it did sound awfully rude,' said Bets, almost in tears. 'But I did think it was Fatty. I'll be more careful next time, Pip.'

They came to the sideshows, which made a kind of fair alongside the river road. There was a roundabout, the hoopla game, the bumper cars, and the waxwork show. The children looked at the people crowding in and out of the Fair, and tried to see anyone that might be Fatty.

Bets was scared now to recognise anyone as Fatty. She kept seeing people she thought might be Fatty and followed them around till she knew they weren't. The others did the same. Some people saw that they were being followed and didn't like it. They turned and glared.

'What you doing, keeping on my heels like this?' one man snapped at Larry. 'Think I'm going to give you money for the roundabout?'

Larry went red and slipped away. He imagined

Fatty somewhere near, tickled to death to see the Find-Outers trying in vain to spot him. Where *could* he be?

'I think I've found him!' whispered Bets to Pip, catching hold of his arm. 'He's the man selling the roundabout tickets! He's just like Fatty, only he's got a black beard and thick black hair, and gold earrings in his ears.'

'Well, he doesn't sound "just like Fatty" to *me*!' said Pip scornfully. 'I'm tired of your spotting the wrong people, Bets. Where's this fellow?'

'I told you. Selling roundabout tickets,' said Bets, and though Pip felt quite certain that not even Fatty would be allowed to sell roundabout tickets, he went to see. The man flashed a grin at him and held up a bunch of tickets.

'A lovely ride!' he chanted. 'A lovely ride on the roundabout.'

Pip went and bought a ticket. He looked hard at the man, who gave him another cheeky grin. Pip grinned back.

'So it *is* you!' he said. 'Jolly good, Fatty!'

'What you talking about?' said the roundabout man in surprise. 'And who are you calling Fatty?'

Pip didn't like to say any more somehow, though he really was quite certain it was Fatty. He got on the roundabout, chose a lion that went miraculously up and down as well as round and round, and enjoyed his ride.

He winked at the ticket man as he got off and the man winked back. 'Funny kid, aren't you?' said the man. Pip went to the others. 'I've found Fatty,' he said. 'At least, I suppose it was Bets who did, really. It's the man who sells the tickets for the roundabout.'

'Oh no it isn't,' said Larry. 'Daisy and I have found Fatty too. It's the man who stands and shouts to people to come and have a go at the hoopla. See – over there!'

'But it *can't* be!' said Pip. 'He'd never be allowed to have a job like that. No, you're wrong. I don't think *that* can be Fatty.'

'Well, and *I* don't think the roundabout ticket man is right, after all,' said Bets unexpectedly. 'I know I *did* think so. But I don't any more. His feet are much too small. He's got silly little feet. Fatty's got enormous feet. However much you disguise yourself you can't make big feet into small ones!'

'I bet Fatty could!' said Daisy. 'He's a marvel. But I still think Fatty's the hoopla man – the one who shouts to people to come and try.'

'And *I* think he's the ticket man at the roundabout,' said Pip obstinately. 'Well – we'll see. We'll have some fun, get tea over there, and wait for Fatty to show himself in his own good time!'

4. FUN AT THE FAIR

Having more or less decided the question of Fatty's disguise, though Bets was very doubtful indeed, the four children had some fun.

Bets bought some of the wooden hoopla rings from the man that Larry and Daisy were certain was Fatty in disguise, and managed to ring a dear little clock. She was really delighted. She held out her hand for the clock, her eyes shining with joy. 'It will do nicely for my bedroom mantelpiece,' she said happily.

'Sorry,' said the hoopla man. 'The ring didn't go quite over the clock.'

'But it *did*,' said poor Bets. 'It did. It didn't even touch the clock. It was the best throw I've ever done!'

'You didn't ring it properly,' said the man. The other hoopla man, that Larry and Daisy thought was Fatty, looked on, and said nothing. Daisy, certain that it *was* Fatty, appealed to him, sorry to see little Bets being cheated out of the cheap little clock.

'She *did* win it, didn't she? Make this man let her have it!'

'Sorry. She didn't ring it properly,' said that man too.

And then Bets walked off, dragging the others with her. '*Now* do you think that man is Fatty?' she said fiercely. '*He* would have let me have the clock at once! Fatty is never unkind. He can't be Fatty!'

'Well – he might *have* to say a thing like that, argued Larry. 'The other man might have got angry with him. I still think it's Fatty.'

They went on the roundabout, and in the bumper cars. Pip took Bets, and Larry went with Daisy, and with many squeals and yells they crashed into one another, and shook themselves and the little cars almost to pieces. It really was fun.

'Now let's go into the waxwork show,' said Larry.

'Oh, it's too hot,' said Daisy. 'Really it is. Besides, I don't much like waxwork figures – they scare me a bit – they look so real, and yet they never even blink!'

'*I* want to see them,' said Bets, who had never been inside a waxwork show in her life, and was longing to. 'They've got Queen Elizabeth in there, all dressed up beautifully, and Napoleon, with his hand tucked into his waistcoat, and Nelson with one arm and one eye, and . . .'

'Oh well, let's go in and see all these wonderful persons,' said Daisy. 'But it's a marvel to me they don't all melt in this weather. I feel as if I'm melting myself. We'd better have ice creams after this.'

They paid their money and went in. The show was in a small hall. A red-headed boy took their money, scratching his head violently with one hand as he handed them tickets with the other. Bets stared at him. Could *he* be Fatty? Fatty had a red-headed wig and eyebrows, and he could put freckles all over his face, just like the ones this boy had. But Fatty had said he would be in a *grown-up* disguise – so he couldn't be this boy. Still – Bets couldn't help staring hard at him.

'Stare away!' he said. 'Never seen red hair before, I suppose!'

Bets went red and joined the others. All round the little hall, arranged on steps that raised each row of figures up behind the others, were the wax people. They stood there, still and silent, fixed looks on their pink faces, staring without blinking.

Pip and Larry liked them, but the two girls felt uncomfortable to have so many strange figures looking at them.

'There's Queen Elizabeth!' said Pip, pointing to a very grand-looking wax figure at the end of the little hall. 'And there's Sir Walter Raleigh putting down his cloak for her to walk on. They're jolly good.'

'What grand clothes she wears,' said Bets, 'and I like her big ruff. And look at all her beautiful jewellery. I'm surprised people don't steal it!'

'Pooh! All bought at Woolworth's!' said Pip. 'I say – here's Nelson. I didn't know he was such a little chap.'

'Oh – and here's Winston Churchill,' said Bets in delight. 'With his cigar and all. He looks the best of the lot!'

'Look – there's a girl selling sweets,' said Larry suddenly, winking at Pip. 'Here, Bets, go and buy some chocolate for us.' He gave the little girl some money and she went to the sweet girl, who stood nearby with a tray of bags and boxes.

'I'll have some chocolate, please,' said Bets, and held out her money. The girl didn't take it. She looked steadily over Bets' head and said nothing.

'SOME CHOCOLATE, PLEASE,' said Bets loudly, thinking that perhaps the girl was deaf. The girl took absolutely no notice at all, and Bets was puzzled.

Then she heard the others exploding behind her, and guessed in a flash the trick they had played. 'Oh! This girl is a waxwork too! You beasts! I've been trying to buy chocolate from a waxwork figure.'

'Oh, Bets! Anyone can take you in, simply anyone!' said Pip, almost crying with laughter. 'To think you're one of the Find-Outers, too! Why, you can't even spot when somebody is a waxwork!'

Bets hardly knew whether to cry or to laugh, but fortunately she decided to laugh. 'Oh dear! I really did think she was a proper person. Look at that horrid red-headed boy over there laughing at me!'

They examined all the wax figures closely. There were a good many of them. Among them was a policeman rather like Mr Goon, but taller and not so fat.

'I'd like to stand Old Clear-Orf in here!' said Pip, with a giggle. 'He looks just about as stolid and stupid sometimes. And I say – look at this postman. He's quite good, except for his idiotic grin.'

It was really very hot in the waxwork show and the children were glad to go out. The red-headed boy at the entrance made faces at Bets, and she tried not to look.

'What a horrid boy!' she said. 'I can't think how I thought he could be Fatty. Fatty wouldn't behave like that, even in disguise.'

'Let's go and have some tea,' said Daisy. 'Look, this place has got ices and home-made cakes.'

'Cakes and an iced lemonade for me,' said Pip. 'I'll have an ice later if I can manage it. I wish old Fatty could join us. Wonder if he's looking on at us, in his disguise. I'm sure he's the ticket man at the roundabout. That man's mop of curly black hair is too good to be true.'

They had a very nice tea, and ate twenty-four cakes between them. They finished up with ices, washed down by a rather sweet lemonade, and then felt able to go out into the sun once more.

'Let's go and sit down by the river,' said Bets.

'It will be cooler there. There's always a breeze by the water!'

They made their way out of the Fair. Bets suddenly caught sight of a lovely patch of bright colour, and she stopped. 'Pip! Look at those balloons! I do love a balloon. Have you got enough money to buy me one?'

They all went over to where the old woman sat, holding her bunch of bright balloons. She was a shapeless old dame, with a red shawl over her shoulders and head, though the day was hot. Untidy hair hung in wisps over her brown, wrinkled face, but she had surprisingly bright eyes.

'Balloon, young man?' said she to Pip, in a cracked old voice.

'No thanks,' said Pip. But Bets pulled his arm.

'Oh, do buy me one, Pip. Oh, I wish Fatty was here. *He'd* buy me one. They're so pretty!'

'Well, but they're expensive!' said Pip, looking at the price label hanging from the string of balloons. 'It's robbery. No, I can't lend you money for that. Mummy would think I was mad.'

'She can have one for half price,' croaked the old woman kindly. Bets looked at Pip.

'Oh, all right,' he said, and pulled out the money. 'But mind you give me the money back when you get home, Bets.'

'Oh thank you, Pip,' said Bets, and took the money. She looked at all the balloons, swaying gently in the breeze, and couldn't make up her mind which one to buy. The reds were so nice and bright, the greens were so pretty, the blues were like the sky, the yellows were like sunshine – oh, which should she have?

'Well, come on after us when you've made up your mind,' said Pip impatiently. 'We're not going to stand here all evening waiting for you, Bets.'

The others went off to the river-bank. Bets stared at the lovely balloons.

'Pretty, aren't they?' said the old woman. 'You take your time in choosing. I don't mind!'

Bets thought what a kind old woman she was. 'It was so nice of you to let me have one at half price,' she said. 'Really it was. Do you make a lot of money, selling balloons?'

'Not much,' said the old dame. 'But enough for an old lady like me.'

Bets chose a blue balloon and the old woman

held out her hand for the money. It was a very dirty hand, and it closed over the money quickly. Bets wondered why so many of the Fair people had such dirty hands and faces.

Then she noticed something that made her stare. The old woman's hand was certainly extremely dirty – but the nails on it were remarkably clean! Much cleaner than Bets' own nails!

How odd! thought Bets, still staring at the clean, well-kept nails. Why should this old woman keep her nails so clean, and her hands so dirty?

Bets then looked hard at the old woman's dirty brown face, all wrinkled up. She looked into the surprisingly bright, twinkling eyes – and she saw that they were Fatty's eyes! Yes, there wasn't an atom of doubt about it – they were Fatty's own bright, intelligent eyes!

'Oh, Fatty!' whispered Bets. 'Oh, it really is you, isn't it? Oh, do say it is?'

The old woman looked round quickly to make sure no one was listening.

'Yes. It's me all right,' said Fatty, unwrinkling his face as if by magic, and straightening his bent back. 'Jolly good disguise, isn't it? But HOW did you know it was me, Bets? You're too cute for anything!'

'Sh! There's somebody coming,' whispered Bets. 'I'll go. Where will you meet us?'

'Go home at six and I'll meet you somewhere,' said Fatty hurriedly, and screwed his face up into all kinds of wrinkles again. Bets saw that he had cleverly painted the places where the wrinkles came, so that no one could possibly see that they were not always there. Fatty was simply marvellous!

'Don't tell the others!' said Fatty. 'Keep it dark for a bit.' Then he raised his voice and, in a feeble croak, called 'Balloons! Fine strong balloons!'

Bets went off, her eyes shining. She had found Fatty – and oh, *wasn't* he clever! He really, really was.

5. THE OLD BALLOON WOMAN

Bets went to join the others, very pleased with herself. Her blue balloon floated behind her, tugging at its string.

'Here she is at last!' said Pip. 'We thought you were never coming, Bets. What's up with you? You look bursting with something.'

'Do I?' said Bets. 'Fancy that! By the way, I've a message from Fatty. We're to go home at six and he will meet us somewhere.'

'Who gave you that message?' said Pip, at once.

'That's *my* secret,' said Bets annoyingly.

'Did you speak to Fatty himself?' demanded Larry. 'Is he the hoopla man?'

'I shan't tell you,' said Bets. 'I'm going to keep my secret for a bit!'

And she wouldn't say another word, which annoyed the others very much. Fancy young Bets knowing something *they* didn't know!

At six o'clock they made their way back through the Fair, across the level-crossing, and up the lane from the river. Sitting on a bench, with her balloons, was the old balloon woman, waiting for them. She got up as they came.

'Balloons!' said she. 'Strong balloons!'

'No thanks,' said Pip, and walked on.

The old woman walked with him. 'Buy a balloon!' she said. 'Just to help me, young man!'

'No thanks,' said Pip again, and walked a little faster. But the old dame could walk surprisingly fast too. She kept up quite easily with Pip!

'*Do* buy a balloon!' she said, her voice cracking.

How long she would have pestered Pip nobody knew – but Bets suddenly exploded into a series of helpless giggles that took the others by surprise. They stared at her.

'What *is* the matter?' said Pip, exasperated.

'Oh, dear!' gasped Bets. 'Oh dear – I'm sorry. But I can't help it. It's all so f-f-f-funny!'

'*What's* funny?' shouted Pip. And then he stared – for the old balloon woman, pulling her skirts above her knees, and showing shoes and bare legs, was doing a lively jig in front of him and round him, making peculiar noises all the time.

'Don't, Fatty, don't! I shall die of laughter!' said Bets, holding her aching sides.

The others stared as if their eyes were about to fall out. 'What – it's *Fatty*?' said Pip. '*Fatty*! It isn't. I can't believe it!'

But it was, of course. As soon as Fatty unscrewed his face, as Bets called it, and got rid of his lines and wrinkles, everyone could see quite well it was Fatty.

Larry and Daisy were speechless. So Fatty hadn't been the hoopla man, or the roundabout man either. He was the old balloon woman instead. Trust Fatty to think out a disguise that nobody would guess!

Or had little Bets guessed it? The others looked at her smiling face. Larry dragged the balloon woman to a wayside seat, and they all sat down.

'Is it really you, Fatty?' said Larry.

The old woman nodded.

'Of course! Golly, this disguise must be super if I could take you all in as well as that!'

'Did Bets guess?' demanded Pip.

'She did,' said Fatty. 'She suddenly guessed when

she was buying her balloon, and you had all gone off without her.'

'But how did she guess?' said Pip, annoyed.

'Goodness knows!' said Fatty. 'How *did* you guess, young Bets?'

'Oh, Fatty – it was such a silly thing – I don't really like to tell you,' said Bets. 'I'm sure you'll think it was a silly way to guess.'

'Go on – tell me,' said Fatty, with much interest.

'Well, Fatty – you see, you had very dirty hands, like so many of the Fair people,' said Bets. 'But I couldn't help seeing that you had nice, clean nails – and it did seem to me a bit funny that somebody with dirty hands should bother to keep their nails so clean.'

'Well, I'm blessed!' said Fatty, looking down at his dirty hands, and examining the well-kept nails. 'Who would have thought of anyone noticing that? Very very careless of me not to get some dirt into my nails when I made my hands filthy. I never thought of it. Bets, you are very clever. Most intelligent.'

'Oh, Fatty – not really,' said Bets, glowing all over her face at such generous praise.

'Well, I must say I think it was jolly cute of young Bets to notice a thing like that, said Larry. 'I really do. We all had a chance of noticing, because we all stood in front of you. But it was Bets who spotted it. Jolly good, Bets!'

'She wins my second-best pen,' said Fatty. 'I'll give it to you when I get home, Bets. In fact I wonder if I should give you my best one. That was a really smart bit of work. Bright enough for a first class detective!'

Daisy praised Bets too, but Pip was rather sulky. He was afraid his little sister would get swollen-headed. 'If you say much more, Bets will want to be head of the Find-Outers,' he said.

'Oh no, I shan't,' said Bets happily. 'I know it was only a bit of luck, really, Pip. You see, I actually put the money into Fatty's hands, and that's how I noticed the clean nails. Pip, I'll lend you the pen *whenever* you want it. See?'

That was so like Bets. Not even a cross elder brother like Pip could sulk for long with Bets. He grinned at her.

'Thanks, Bets. You're a good Find-Outer, and a good little sport too!'

'I say – look out – here's Mr Goon!' suddenly said Larry, in a low voice. 'Better pretend we're not with Fatty, or Mr Goon will wonder why we are hobnobbing with an old fair woman!'

So they all got up, and left Fatty behind on the seat, with his string of balloons bobbing over his head. Mr Goon was on his bicycle as usual. He pretended not to notice the children at all. He always seemed busy and important these days!

But he got off his bicycle when he saw the old woman. Fatty was drooping over, pretending to be asleep.

'Here, you!' said Mr Goon. 'Move on! And where's your licence to sell balloons?'

The others heard this, and looked alarmed. Did you have to have a licence to peddle balloons? They were sure Fatty hadn't got one.

Fatty took no notice, but gave a gentle snore. Mr Goon shook the shoulder of the balloon woman, and Fatty pretended to awake with a jerk.

'Where's your licence?' said Mr Goon.

'What did you say, sir?' said Fatty, in a whining voice. 'Want to buy a balloon, sir? What colour do you fancy?'

'I don't want a balloon,' said Mr Goon angrily. 'I want to see your licence.'

'Oh, ah, my licence?' said Fatty, and began to pat all over his extremely voluminous skirts, as if to find where a licence could possibly be hidden. 'Somewhere about, sir, somewhere about. If you can just wait a few minutes, kind sir, I'll find it in the pocket of one of my petticoats. An old woman like me, sir, she wants plenty of petticoats.'

'Gah!' said Mr Goon rudely, mounted his bicycle and rode off, ringing his bell furiously at a small dog that dared to run across the road in front of him. Was he, the Great Goon, in charge of a first class case, going to wait whilst an old pedlar woman fished for ages in her petticoats for a licence he didn't really want to see? Gah!

When Mr Goon was safely out of sight the others went back to Fatty, amused and half-alarmed. 'Oh, Fatty! How *can* you act like that with Mr Goon? If only he'd known it was really you!'

'I enjoyed that,' said Fatty. 'Good thing Mr Goon didn't wait to see my licence though, because I haven't got one, of course. Come on – let's get back home. I'm dying to take off these hot clothes. I've got layers of petticoats on to make me fat and shapeless!'

On the way up the village street they passed the bench where they had spoken to the old man on their way to the Fair that afternoon. Bets pointed him out to Fatty.

'Fatty. Do you see that old fellow, sleeping on that bench over there? Well, we thought he was *you*! And we went and called him Fatty, and Pip gave him a poke in the ribs!'

Fatty stood and looked at the old chap. 'You know, it would be quite easy to disguise myself like him,' he said. 'I've a good mind to try it. Honestly, I believe I could.'

'But you couldn't make your ears like his,' said Bets. 'He's got awful ears.'

'No, I couldn't. But I could pull my cap down lower than he does, and hide my ears a bit,' said Fatty. 'Yes, that would be a very good and easy disguise indeed. I'll try it one day. Did Pip really poke him in the ribs?'

'Yes. And the old fellow kept on saying, "Wassat? Wassat?" ' said Pip, with a giggle. 'He's deaf, poor old thing.'

The old man suddenly opened his eyes and saw the children looking at him. He thought they must have spoken to him. He cupped one of his ears in his hand and croaked out his favourite word, 'Wassat?'

The old balloon woman winked at the children and sat down beside the old fellow. 'Fine evening,' she said, in the cracked voice the children were beginning to know well.

'Wassat?' said the old man. Then he sniffed, and wiped his nose deftly with the back of his hand. Fatty did exactly the same, which made Bets giggle in delight.

'FINE EVENING,' said Fatty. 'AND A FINE MORNING TOO!'

'Don't know nothing about mornings,' said the old man surprisingly. 'Always sleep till midday, I do. Then I gets up, has my bit of dinner, and comes out into the sun. Mornings don't mean nothing to me.'

He sniffed again. Fatty watched all he did. Yes, it would be a marvellous thing to do, to disguise himself as this old fellow. Sniffs, deafness, and all – Fatty could do it!

'Come on, Fatty!' said Pip, in a low voice. 'We really will have to get back. It's getting late.'

Fatty got up and joined them. They soon parted and went their different ways – Pip and Bets down their lane, and Larry and Daisy up theirs. Fatty went in at his back gate, and his mother caught sight of the old balloon woman, as she stood in the garden, cutting sweetpeas for the table.

She thought, is she trying to sell balloons here?

She waited for the balloon woman to come back again, but she didn't. So, rather curious, Mrs Trotteville went to the kitchen door and looked in. There was no balloon woman to be seen – only Cook, red in the face, cooking the dinner.

'Where did that old balloon woman go?' said Mrs Trotteville, in wonder. But Cook didn't know. She hadn't seen any old woman at all. And no wonder – for at that moment the old balloon woman was stripping off layers of petticoats down in the shed at the bottom of the garden – to come forth as a very hot and rather untidy Fatty.

What a peculiar thing for a balloon woman to vanish into thin air! thought Mrs Trotteville. And so it was.

6. A VISIT TO INSPECTOR JENKS

Fatty had much enjoyed his fun as the old balloon woman, and so had the others. He gave Bets the silver pen and she was really delighted.

'I've never had such a lovely pen,' she said. 'Thank you so much, Fatty.'

'The holidays are going too fast,' said Pip, rather gloomily. 'And we still haven't got a mystery to solve, though we know that Mr Goon has.'

'Yes, I know,' said Fatty, looking worried. 'I can't bear to think of Mr Goon getting busy on his mystery, and we haven't the least idea what it is. Though it *may* be all those burglaries that are cropping up all over the place, you know – I expect most of the police are keeping their eyes skinned for the gang that is operating such big thefts.'

'Can't we keep our eyes skinned too?' said Bets eagerly. 'We might see the gang somewhere.'

'Idiot! Do you think they go about in a crowd

569

together, all looking like burglars?' said Pip scornfully. 'They're too jolly clever. They have their own meeting places, their own way of passing on messages, their own ways of disposing of the jewels they steal – haven't they, Fatty? And they are not ways *we* would be likely to find out, even if we did keep our eyes skinned!'

'Oh,' said Bets, disappointed. 'Well – can't we ask Inspector Jenks if there really *is* a mystery here, and ask him to let us help?'

'Yes – why can't we?' said Daisy. 'I'm sure he'd tell us. We've helped him such a lot before.'

Inspector Jenks was their very good friend. He was what Bets called 'a very high-up policeman,' and he belonged to the next big town. In the four mysteries the children had solved before, Inspector Jenks had come in at the end, and been very pleased indeed at all the children had found out. Mr Goon, however, had not been so pleased, because it was most annoying to him to have those 'interfering children messing about with the law' – especially when they had actually found out things he hadn't.

'I think it's a very good idea of Bets,' said Fatty. 'Very good indeed. If he knows what the mystery is that Mr Goon is working on – and he's sure to – I don't see why he can't tell us. He knows we'll keep our mouths shut and do all we can to help.'

So the next day the Five Find-Outers, with Buster in Fatty's basket, rode on their bicycles to the next big town, where Inspector Jenks had his headquarters. They went to the police station there, and asked if they could see him.

'What! See the Inspector himself!' said the policeman in charge. 'Kids like you! I should think not. He's a Big Man, he is, too busy to bother with kids.'

'Wait a bit,' said another policeman, with a nice face, and very bright blue eyes. 'Wait a bit – aren't you the kids that helped with one or two difficult cases over in Peterswood?'

'Yes, we are,' said Fatty. 'We wouldn't want to bother the Inspector if he's busy, of course – but we would like to ask him something rather important. Important to us, I mean.'

'Shall I go in and tell the Inspector then?' said the first policeman to the other one. 'Don't want my head bitten off, you know, for interrupting without due cause.'

'*I'll* tell him!' said the blue-eyed policeman. 'I've heard him talk about these kids.' He got up and went out of the room. The children waited as patiently as they could. Surely their old friend would see them!

The policeman came back. 'He'll see you,' he said. 'Come on in.'

The children followed him down a long stone-floored passage, and then down another. Bets looked about her half-fearfully. Was she anywhere near prisoners in their cells? She hoped not.

The policeman opened a door with a glass top to it, and announced them. 'The children from Peterswood, sir.'

The Inspector was sitting at an enormous desk, piled with papers. He was in uniform and looked very big and grand. His eyes twinkled, and he smiled his nice smile.

'Well, well, well!' he said. 'The whole lot of you at once – and Buster too, I see! Well, how are you? Come to tell me you've solved the mystery that's been worrying us for months, I suppose!'

He shook hands with them all, and Bets beamed at him. She was very fond of this big high-up policeman.

'No, sir, we haven't come to tell you we've solved any mystery, unfortunately,' said Fatty. 'These are the first hols for ages that we haven't had a mystery to solve. But sir, we know that Mr Goon has got one he's working on, and we thought perhaps we could work on it too. But we don't know what it is.'

'Yes, Goon's on it,' said the Inspector. 'In fact, most of the police force of the country seem to be on it too! But it's not one that you can be mixed up in. I don't think you could help at all, first-rate detectives though you are!'

'Oh!' said Fatty, disappointed. 'Is it – is it all these big burglaries, sir?'

'Yes, that's right,' said the Inspector. 'Very clever, they are. The thieves know just what jewels to steal, when to get at them, and lay their plans very carefully. And we don't know one single one of the men! Not one. Though we have our suspicions, you know! We always have!'

He twinkled at the listening children. Fatty felt desperate. Surely the Inspector could tell them more than that. Surely Mr Goon knew more? Else why was he so busy and important these days?

'Mr Goon looks as if he knew quite a lot, sir,' said Fatty. 'Is there anything going on in Peterswood at all?'

The Inspector hesitated. 'Well,' he said at last, 'as I said, this is not a thing for children to be mixed up in. Definitely not, and I am sure you would agree with me if you knew what I know. Peterswood is not exactly mixed up in it – but we suspect that some of the gang go there – to meet perhaps – or to pass on messages – we don't know.'

The children's eyes brightened immediately. 'Sir!' said Fatty, at once, 'can't we just keep our eyes open, then? Not snoop round too much, if you don't want us to – but watch and see if we hear or spot anything unusual. Children can often see and hear things that grown-ups can't, because people suspect other grown-ups, but they don't notice children much.'

The Inspector tapped with his pencil on his desk. Fatty knew that he was weighing up whether or not to let them keep a watch on things in Peterswood, and his heart beat anxiously. How he hoped they would be allowed just to have a little hand in this Mystery! It seemed a pretty hopeless one, and Mr Goon was sure to do better than they could, because he knew so much more – but Fatty simply couldn't *bear* to be left out of it altogether!

'All right,' said the Inspector at last, and put his pencil down. 'You can keep your eyes open for me – but don't plunge headlong into anything foolish or dangerous. Just keep your eyes open. It's barely possible you children might spot something, simply *because* you're children. Report to me if you find anything suspicious.'

'Oh, *thank* you!' said everyone at once, delighted.

'It's jolly good of you, sir,' said Fatty. 'We will find out something! And we'll be as careful as Mr Goon!'

'Well, I'm afraid he will come out on top this time,' said the Inspector, his eyes twinkling. 'He knows so much more than you do. But I can tell you no more than I have done. Good-bye – and it's been so nice to see you!'

The children went. They got on their bicycles and rode back home, thrilled and pleased. They all went to Pip's garden, and sat down importantly in his summerhouse, right at the top of the garden.

'Well – we've got a mystery after all!' said Fatty. 'Who are the gang that steals all these jewels? Mr Goon's on the job, and he's got a flying start – and now we'll be on it too. Has anybody noticed anything suspicious in Peterswood lately?'

They all thought hard. But nobody could think of anything in the least suspicious. Things seemed to be pretty much as usual, except that the hot weather had brought crowds of people into the little riverside village.

'I can't think of a thing,' said Larry.

'It's not a very *easy* mystery,' said Daisy, frowning. 'There doesn't seem anywhere to begin.'

'Can't we do it the usual way – find clues, and make a list of suspects?' said Bets.

'Right!' said Pip scornfully. 'You tell us what clues to look for, and who to put down on a list of suspects!'

'There are no clues to look for, and we don't even know where to look for suspects,' said Larry mournfully. 'I wonder what Mr Goon knows.'

'He's probably got a list of men he's suspicious of,' said Fatty thoughtfully. 'And he's also probably got all details of all the burglaries committed lately.

I'd better get some back numbers of the news-papers and read them up. Not that it will help us very much, really.'

There was a long pause. 'Well,' said Pip, at last. 'What's the plan? What are we going to do?'

There simply didn't seem *any*thing to do! All they knew was that it was possible that the thieves sometimes met in Peterswood.

'I think it wouldn't be a bad idea for me to disguise myself as that old deaf fellow, who sits on that sunny bench in the middle of the village,' said Fatty. 'We know he isn't there in the mornings, so that would be the time for me to go and sit there. I might be able to spot something suspicious. Men passing notes to one another as they meet – or making remarks in low voices – or even sitting on that bench and talking.

Everyone looked doubtful. It didn't seem at all likely, really. Bets guessed that Fatty wanted the fun of disguising himself again. 'You had certainly better not be there in the afternoon!' she said. 'People would begin to wonder, if they saw *two* old fellows, exactly alike, sitting on the same bench!'

'Yes. Mr Goon would have a fit!' said Larry, and everyone laughed.

'Don't you think it would be better if you chose some other disguise, not disguise yourself like that old fellow?' said Pip. 'Just in case you did both wander along at the same time? There doesn't really seem any point in dressing up like that dirty old man.'

'There isn't, really. I just feel I'd like to, that's all,' said Fatty. 'You know, if you're as good an actor as I am, there are certain parts or characters that appeal to you much more than others. I loved being that old balloon woman – and I shall love to be that old man. I can act him exactly right.'

He gave a realistic sniff and wiped his nose with the back of his hand. The others laughed, and did not tease him over his boasting of being such a good actor.

'You're disgusting!' said Daisy. 'Don't for goodness sake start doing that sort of thing in front of your parents! They'll have a fit!'

Fatty got up and hobbled out into the garden, shuffling like the old man. He bent his back and dropped his head. He really was an extremely good actor.

Then he gave another frightful sniff and wiped his nose on his sleeve.

A horrified voice spoke to him. 'Frederick! Haven't you a handkerchief? What disgusting behaviour!'

And there was Pip's mother, come to fetch them in to a meal. Poor Fatty! He went red to the ears, and produced an enormous handkerchief at once. How the others laughed!

7. SOMETHING RATHER PECULIAR

With the help of the others, Fatty managed to get together some old clothes very like the old man on the bench had worn. Pip produced a very old gardening hat belonging to his father. Larry found an old coat hanging in the garage.

'It's been there for years, as far as I remember,' he said. 'Nobody ever wears it. You might as well have it. It's got mildew inside the pockets, so be careful how you put your hands in them!'

It was easy to get an old shirt and scarf. Fatty produced a torn shirt of his own, and found a scarf down in the garden shed, which he must have left there months before.

He dragged the shirt in the dirt, and it was soon as filthy as the old man's. He dirtied the scarf a little more too.

'What about the shoes?' he said. 'We want really old ones. That old man's were all cracked open at the toe.'

The shoes were a real problem. Nobody's father had shoes as old as that.

Then Daisy had a brain-wave. 'Let's look in all the ditches we pass!' she said. 'There are always old boots and shoes in ditches, I don't know why. We might find some there.'

Sure enough they did! Larry came across a dirty, damp old pair, open at the toes and well worn at the heels. He tossed them to Fatty.

'Well, if you think you really do want to wear such horrible things, there you are! But you'll have to dry them or you'll get damp feet, and have a streaming cold.'

'He'll be able to sniffle properly then,' said Bets. She too had been practising the old man's sniff, much to her mother's annoyance.

'I'll put them under the tank in the hot cupboard,' said Fatty. 'They'll soon dry there. They should just about fit me. I don't at all like wearing them, but, after all, if it's important to solve the mystery, it's important to put up with little things like this!'

The trousers seemed quite impossible to get.

Nobody's father wore the kind of coarse corduroy that the old man wore. Could they possibly buy a pair in the village shop and make them torn and dirty for Fatty to wear?

'Better not buy them in Peterswood, in case the news gets round,' said Fatty. 'I wouldn't want old Mr Goon to know I'd bought men's trousers – he'd be sure to snoop round and find out why. He's got more brains lately, somehow.'

'We'll walk across the fields to Sheepridge,' said Daisy. 'We might buy a pair there.'

Halfway across the fields Pip gave a shout that made everyone jump. He pointed to an old scarecrow standing forgotten in a field. It wore a hat without a brim, a ragged coat – and a pair of dreadful old corduroy trousers!

'Just what we want!' said Fatty joyfully, and ran to the scarecrow. 'We'll give them back to him when we've finished with them. Golly, aren't they holey? I hope they'll hang together on me.'

'I'd better give them a wash for you,' said Daisy. 'They really are awful. If you wear your pair of brown shorts under them, Fatty, the holes won't show up so much. There are really too many to mend.'

Happily the Find-Outers went back to Larry's. Daisy washed the trousers, but not much dirt came out of them because the rain had washed them many a time. Bets couldn't imagine how Fatty could bear to put on such horrid old clothes.

'Duty calls!' said Fatty, with a grin. 'Got to do all kinds of unpleasant things, Bets, when duty calls. And a really good detective doesn't stop at anything.'

The next day they held a dress rehearsal and dressed Fatty up in the old clothes. He had already got a ragged, sandy-grey beard, which he had cut more or less to the shape of the old man's. He had shaggy grey eyebrows to put on too, and wisps of straggly grey hair to peep out from under his hat.

He made himself up carefully. He put in some wrinkles with his grease paints, and then screwed up his mouth so that it looked as if he hadn't many teeth.

'Oh, Fatty – you're marvellous!' cried Bets. 'I simply can't bear to look at you, you look so awful. Don't stare at me like that! You give me the creeps! You're an old, old man, not Fatty at all!'

'Wassat?' said Fatty, putting his hand behind his ear. He had very dirty hands indeed – and this time he had remembered to blacken his nails too. He really looked appalling.

'What's the time?' he asked, for he had taken off his wrist-watch, in case it showed. 'Oh, twelve o'clock. Well, what about shuffling off for a snooze in the sun, on that bench? My double won't be there, because he said he never goes out till the afternoon. Come on. I'll see if I can play my part all right!'

'We'll all come,' said Pip. 'But we'll not sit near you. We'll go and have lemonade in that little sweetshop opposite the bench. We can keep an eye on you then, and see what happens.'

Fatty, after sending Larry down his garden path to the back gate, to see if the coast was clear, shuffled down, hoping that nobody in his house would spot him. He didn't want his mother to get curious about the odd old men and women that seemed to haunt her back gate.

Once out in the road, the other four children kept near to Fatty, but not near enough to make anyone suspect they were with him. He shuffled along, dragging his feet, bent and stooping, his hat well down over his ears.

'He's just *exactly* like that old fellow we saw!' whispered Bets to Daisy. 'I'd never know the difference, would you?'

Fatty did a loud sniff and the others grinned. He came to the sunny bench and cautiously sat himself down, giving a little sigh as he did so. 'Aaaah!'

He was certainly a marvellous actor. He sat there in the sun, bending over his stick, the very picture of a poor old man having a rest. The others made their way to the little lemonade shop, and sat down at the table in the window to watch him.

Just as they were finishing their lemonade a man came by on a bicycle, whistling. He was a perfectly ordinary man, in perfectly ordinary clothes, with a very ordinary face. But, when he caught sight of the old man, he braked very suddenly indeed, and looked at him in some astonishment.

He got off his bicycle and wheeled it over to the bench. He leaned it against the seat and sat down by Fatty. The children, watching from the shop opposite, were surprised and rather alarmed. Had this man seen something suspicious about Fatty's disguise? Had he guessed it was somebody pretending? Would he give Fatty away?

Fatty, too, felt a little alarmed. He had been enjoying himself thoroughly, getting right 'under the skin' of the old man, as he put it to himself. He had seen the look of surprise on the man's face. Now here he was sitting beside him. Why?

'What you out here for, in the morning?' said the man suddenly, in a very low voice. 'Thought you never came till the afternoon. Anything up? Expecting anyone?'

Fatty was taken aback to hear this low and confidential whisper. Obviously the man thought him to be the old fellow, and was amazed to see him out in the morning. But what did all the questions mean?

Just in time, Fatty remembered that the old man was deaf. He put his hand to his ear and put his ear towards the man, so that he should not look directly into his face. He was afraid that he might be recognised as a fraud if the man looked into his eyes.

'Wassat?' said Fatty, in a croaking old voice. 'Wassat?'

The man gave an impatient exclamation. 'Of course – he's deaf!' He gave a quick look round as

586

if to see if anyone was near. Then somebody else cycled slowly by and the man sidled a little way away from Fatty, and took out a cigarette to light.

The cyclist was Mr Goon, perspiring freely in the hot sun. He saw the two men at once, and got off his bicycle. He pretended to adjust the chain. The four children in the shop watched him with interest, hoping that he wouldn't go and say anything to Fatty.

Buster saw Mr Goon, and with a delighted yelp he tore out of the sweetshop, and danced round the policeman's feet. Larry rushed after him, afraid that Buster would go and lick Fatty's face, and give the show away to Mr Goon. But Buster was fully engaged with the angry policeman, and was having a perfectly lovely time.

Fatty got up hurriedly and shuffled away round the nearest corner without being noticed by Mr Goon, who was rapidly losing his temper. All the others, seeing that Fatty wanted to get away before Mr Goon noticed he was gone, began to join in the fun, pretending to call Buster off, but only succeeding in exciting the little Scottie more than ever!

When at last Buster was safely in Larry's arms, and Mr Goon could look round at the bench, it was empty! Both the men had gone. Mr Goon looked extremely angry.

'That there dog!' he said, dusting his trousers down violently. 'I'll report him, I will. Interfering with me doing my duty, that's what he did. And now where are them two fellows gone? I wanted to put a few questions to them!'

'They've disappeared,' said Daisy. Mr Goon did one of his snorts.

'No need to tell me that. I've got eyes in my head, haven't I? I may have lost a most important clue! See? Where's that boy that's always with you? I bet he's at the bottom of this!'

'He isn't here,' said Larry truthfully. 'You'll probably find him at home if you badly want to see him, Mr Goon.'

'I wouldn't care if I never set eyes on him again, the cheeky toad!' said Mr Goon, mounting his bicycle rather ponderously and wobbling a little. 'No, nor any of you neither. As for that dog!'

He was about to ride off, when he stopped, wobbled again, and spoke to Larry.

'Where were you just now?'

'In the sweetshop, having lemonade,' said Larry.

'Ho,' said Mr Goon. 'And did you see that old fellow sitting on that bench?'

'Yes, we did,' said Larry. 'He seemed half asleep and quite harmless.'

'And did you see that other fellow talking to him?' demanded Mr Goon.

'Well – he may have spoken to him. I don't know,' said Larry, wondering why the policeman was asking all these questions.

'You'd better come alonga-me,' said Mr Goon, at last. 'I'm going to call on that old fellow, see, and I want you to back me up when I tell him I want to know about the other fellow.'

The children felt distinctly alarmed. What! Mr Goon was going to visit the *real* old man – who would probably be in bed – and ask him questions about the other man, whom he hadn't been there to see! Whatever would the poor old fellow say? He wouldn't in the least know what Mr Goon was talking about!

8. THE FIRST CLUE – AND A PLAN

'I don't think we've got time to . . .' began Larry. But Mr Goon pooh-poohed him.

'It's my orders,' he said pompously. 'You may be witnesses. You come alonga me.'

So the children went with Mr Goon, Buster struggling wildly against the lead to get at the policeman's ankles. They turned one or two corners and came to a little pair of cottages at one end of a lane. Mr Goon went to the first one and knocked.

There was no answer at all. He knocked again. The children felt uncomfortable and wished they were at home. No answer. Then Mr Goon pushed hard at the door and it opened into a room that was plainly half sitting-room and half bedroom. It was very dirty and smelt horrid.

In the far corner was a small bed, piled high with dirty bedclothes. In it, apparently asleep, his grey hairs showing above the blanket, was the old man. His clothes were on a chair beside him – old coat, corduroy trousers, shirt, scarf, hat, and shoes.

'Hey, you!' said Mr Goon, marching in. 'No good pretending to be asleep, see? I saw you a few minutes ago in the village street, on the bench.'

The old man awoke with a jump. He seemed to be extremely surprised to see Mr Goon in his room. He sat up and stared at him. 'Wassat?' he said. It really did seem to be about the only thing he could say.

'It's no good pretending to be in bed and asleep,' roared Mr Goon. 'You were on the bench in the middle of the street just now. I saw you!'

'I ain't been out of this room today!' said the old man, in a cracked voice. 'I always sleeps till dinner, I do.'

'You don't,' shouted Mr Goon. 'You didn't today. And I want to know what that fellow said to you when he came and sat beside you on the bench.'

Bets felt sorry for the old man. She hated it when Mr Goon shouted so. The old fellow looked more and more puzzled.

'Wassat?' he said, going back to the word he loved.

'See these children here?' said Mr Goon, beside himself with annoyance at the old man's stupidity. 'Well, they saw you there too. Speak up now you, kids. You saw him, didn't you?'

'Well,' said Larry, hesitating. 'Well . . .' He really didn't know what to say. He knew quite well it hadn't been the old man on the bench – and yet how could he say so without giving Fatty away?

Pip saw his difficulty and rushed in with a few clever words. 'You see, Mr Goon, it's difficult to say, isn't it, because an old man in bed and an old man dressed don't look a bit the same.'

'Well, look at his clothes then,' said Mr Goon, pointing to the clothes. 'Aren't those the very clothes he was dressed in?'

'They might not be,' said Pip. 'Sorry, Mr Goon, but we can't help you in the matter.'

Larry thought it was about time to go, for Mr Goon's face was turning a familiar purple. So he and the others hurriedly went back up the lane and made their way to Fatty's, longing to tell him all that had happened.

They found Fatty in the woodshed at the bottom of his garden, trying to make himself a bit respectable. All his old man clothes were in a sack, ready for use again. He was just smoothing down his hair when the others poured in.

'I say!' began Fatty, his eyes bright. 'That was a bit peculiar, wasn't it? I mean – that man being so surprised to see me – and sitting down and saying things to me. I almost forgot I was deaf and shouldn't hear them!'

'What did he say?' asked Pip, and Fatty told him. The others listened breathlessly.

'And then up comes Mr Goon, spots this fellow, and makes an awful to-do about adjusting his bike-chain, in order to have a good squint at the chap,' said Larry. 'Looks suspicious to me. I mean – it looks as if Mr Goon knew the fellow and wanted to know what he was up to.'

'Is it a clue?' asked Bets eagerly.

'You and your clues!' said Pip scornfully. 'Don't be silly, Bets.'

'I don't think she *is* silly,' said Fatty thoughtfully. 'I think it *is* a clue – a clue to something that's going on – maybe even something to do with the mystery. You know what the Inspector said – that it is thought that Peterswood may be the meeting place of the thief-gang – the place where messages are passed on, perhaps, from one member to another.'

'And perhaps the old man is the fellow who takes the messages and passes them on!' cried Daisy. 'Oh, Fatty! Is he the chief burglar, do you think?'

'Course not,' said Fatty. 'Can you imagine a poor feeble old thing like that doing anything violent? No, he's just a convenient message bearer, I should think. Nobody would ever suspect him, sitting out there in the sun, half asleep. It would be easy enough for anyone to go and whisper anything to him.'

'But he's deaf,' objected Daisy.

'So he is. Well then, maybe they slip him messages,' said Fatty. 'Golly – I feel we're on to something!'

'Let's think,' said Larry. 'We shall get somewhere, I feel, if we think!'

They all thought. Bets was so excited that not a single sensible thought came into her head. It was Fatty as usual who came out with everything clear and simple.

'I've got it!' he said. 'Probably Peterswood *is*

the headquarters of the gang, for some reason or other, and when one member wants to get in touch with another, they don't communicate with each other directly, which would be dangerous, but send messages by that old fellow. And, Find-Outers, if I go and sit on that bench day in and day out, I've no doubt some of the members of the gang will come along, sit by me, and deliver messages in some way, and . . .'

'And you'll learn who they are, and we can tell the Inspector, and he'll have them arrested!' cried Bets, in great excitement.

'Well, something like that,' said Fatty. 'The thing is – the old man always sits there in the afternoon, and that's really when I ought to sit there, because it's then that any messages will come, But how can I sit there, if *he's* there?'

'That's why that man was so surprised this morning,' said Daisy. 'He knew the old man never *was* there in the mornings – and yet it seemed as if he was, this morning! He never guessed it was you. Your disguise must have been perfect.'

'It must have been,' said Fatty modestly. 'The thing is – can we possibly stop the old fellow from going there in the afternoons? If we could, I could sit on that bench, and you could all sit in the sweetshop and watch.'

'We can't drink lemonade for hours,' said Bets.

'You could take it in turn,' said Fatty. 'The thing is, we *must* take notice of what the messengers are like, so that we should recognise them again. I shan't dare to look at them too closely, in case they suspect something. So you would have to notice very carefully indeed. I shall take whatever messages they pass on to me, and leave it to you to see exactly what the men are like that come to see me on that bench.'

'What about that one this morning?' said Larry suddenly. 'That must have been one of them. Now – what exactly was he like?'

Everyone frowned and tried to remember. 'He was simply too ordinary for anything,' said Larry at last. 'Ordinary face, ordinary clothes, ordinary bicycle. Wait though – I'm remembering something about that bicycle. It had a – it had a hooter on it, instead of a bell!'

'So it had!' said Pip, remembering too. Daisy and Bets hadn't noticed that. In fact, they couldn't remember a thing about the man at all.

'A hooter,' said Fatty thoughtfully. 'Well, that might be a bit of a help in tracing the man. We'll keep a look out for bikes with hooters. But the thing that's really worrying me *is* – how can we stop that old man from sitting on the bench in the afternoons, so that *I* can go instead?'

Nobody knew. 'The only thing is,' said Fatty at last, 'the absolutely only thing is – for me to slide down on the bench beside him, and pretend to be one of the messengers myself – and tell him not to sit out there for two or three days!'

'Ooooh yes!' said Pip. 'Because Mr Goon may be watching. You could say that.'

'I could. And it will probably be quite true,' said Fatty, with a groan. 'Old Mr Goon has got his suspicions too, and is on the right track. We've tumbled on it by accident. There I shall sit, under Mr Goon's eye all the afternoon! I bet no messenger will come if they know that he's watching.'

'If we see a likely-looking stranger hanging about, we could get Mr Goon away for a bit,' said Larry. 'And I know how we could do it too! We could go round a corner and toot a hooter! Then

Mr Goon would think to himself, Ha, hooter on a bike! Maybe the man I want! and go scooting round the corner.'

'Yes, that's quite well worked out,' said Fatty. 'The thing is – Mr Goon probably hasn't noticed the hooter on the man's bike.'

'Well, tell him then,' said Larry. 'He'll be awfully bucked at that. Let's go and tell him now.'

'Come on then. We'll go and look for him,' said Fatty. But just then Larry looked at his watch and gave an exclamation. 'Golly! We'll be terribly late for lunch! We'll have to tell Mr Goon this afternoon.'

'I will,' said Fatty. 'See you later!'

That afternoon Mr Goon, enjoying a brief after-dinner nap, was surprised to see Fatty coming in at the door, and even more surprised when the boy presented his bit of information about the hooter on the bicycle.

'I don't know if it will be of any use to you, Mr Goon,' he said earnestly. 'But we thought you ought to know. After all, it's a clue, isn't it?'

'Ho! A clue to what?' demanded Mr Goon. 'You aren't interfering again, are you? And anyway, I noticed that there hooter myself. And if I hear it tooting, I'll soon be after the cyclist.'

'What do you want him for?' asked Fatty innocently.

Mr Goon stared at him suspiciously. 'Never you mind. And look here, how is it you know all about this here hooter, when you wasn't with the others? You tell me that.'

'Oh, *they* told me,' said Fatty. 'I'm afraid you're angry with me for trying to give you a clue, Mr Goon. I'm sorry. I didn't know you had already noticed the hooter. I won't trouble you with any of our information again.'

'Now look here, there's no harm in . . .' began Mr Goon, afraid that perhaps Fatty might withhold further information that might really be of use. But Fatty was gone. He visited a shop on the way home and bought a very nice little rubber hooter. Mr Goon was going to hear it quite a lot! In fact, he heard it a few minutes later, just outside his window, as he was finishing his nap. He shot upright at once, and raced to the door.

But there was no cyclist to be seen. He went back slowly – and the hooter sounded again. Drat it! Where was it? He looked up and down the road once more but there really was no sign of a bicycle. There was only a boy a good way down, sauntering along. But he hadn't a bicycle.

He had a hooter, though, under his coat, and his name was Fatty!

9. FATTY DELIVERS HIS MESSAGE

The next afternoon Fatty did not dress up as the old man, but instead, put on his balloon woman's petticoats and shawl again. The others watched him, down in the shed at the bottom of Fatty's garden. Bets thought she could watch him for days on end, making himself up as different people. There was no doubt at all that Fatty had a perfect gift for dressing up and acting.

'I'll go and sit on the seat beside the old man,' said Fatty. 'He's sure to be there this afternoon, waiting for any possible messages – and you can snoop round and see if Mr Goon is anywhere about. If he isn't, I'll take the chance of telling the old man not to appear for a few afternoons as the police are watching. That should make him scuttle away all right if he's in with the gang!'

'I'll come and buy another balloon from you,' said Bets eagerly. 'That will make it all seem real.'

'Oh, it'll be real enough,' said Fatty. 'All I hope is that Mr Goon won't come and ask me for my licence again.'

'He won't, if you are sitting in the middle of the village street, and he thinks you've got to hunt all through your petticoats for it, and make him look silly,' said Larry. 'He can't bear to be made to look silly. And anyway, he won't want to draw attention to himself if he's watching for any possible gang members. He won't think *you're* one.'

'Quite right,' said Fatty. 'Well reasoned out, Larry. Now – am I ready?'

'You look simply marvellous,' said Bets admiringly. 'You really do. I can't think how you manage to make your face go so different, Fatty. It doesn't look a bit like you.'

'Oh, I practise in front of a mirror,' said Fatty. 'And I've got some marvellous books about it. And, of course, I've got the *gift* – you see . . .'

'Oh, shut up, Fatty,' said Larry good humouredly. 'We all know you're marvellous, without *you* telling us!'

The balloon woman suddenly screwed up her face, and her mouth went down at the corners in a most pathetic manner. She fished out a big red handkerchief, decidedly dirty, and began to weep most realistically.

'Don't be so unkind to me,' she wept, and the others roared with laughter. Fatty peeped out at them from the corner of his hanky. 'A poor old woman like me!' he wept.

Larry looked quickly out of the window of the shed.

'Quick! There's your mother, Fatty. What shall we do?'

There wasn't time to do anything. Mrs Trotteville was even then looking in at the door. She had come to speak to the children, but when she saw the old balloon woman, she was very much astonished.

'What are you doing here?' she asked sharply. 'I saw you going down the garden path the other day.'

Bets spoke up before Fatty could answer.

'She sells lovely balloons,' she said. 'I want to buy one, Mrs Trotteville.'

'There's absolutely no need to buy one in the garden shed,' said Mrs Trotteville. 'You can buy one in the street. I don't want pedlars or tramps in the garden. I am surprised that Buster did not bark.'

Buster was there, of course, sitting at the balloon woman's feet. He looked as if she was his best friend – as indeed she was, if only Mrs Trotteville had known it.

'Where's Frederick?' asked Mrs Trotteville, looking all round for Fatty.

'Er – not far away,' said Larry truthfully. 'Er – shall I go and look for him, Mrs Trotteville?'

'Oh no. I suppose you are all waiting for him,' said Mrs Trotteville. 'Well, I'm afraid this woman and her balloons must go – and please do not come into the garden again!'

'No, mum,' said the balloon woman. They all went out of the shed and up the path to the front gate.

'That was a narrow squeak,' said Larry, when they were safely out in the road.

'Narrow squeaks are exciting!' said Pip.

They made their way to the main street of the village. There, on the sunny bench, was the old man as usual, bent over his stick, looking half asleep.

'I'll go and sit down by him,' said Fatty,

swinging his voluminous skirts out round him as he walked. 'You walk behind me now, and keep a watch out for Mr Goon. Bets can tell me if he's anywhere about when she comes to buy a balloon. You can all go and have lemonade in that shop, to begin with.'

The balloon woman sat down on the bench with her bunch of balloons. The old man at the end of the seat took no notice of her at all. The balloons bobbed in the wind, and passers-by looked at them with pleasure. A mother stopped to buy one for her baby, and the four watching children giggled as they saw Fatty bend over the baby in the pram and tickle its cheek.

'How does he know how to do things like that?' chuckled Larry. 'I'd never think of those things.'

'But it's those little touches that make his disguises so real,' said Daisy, in admiration. They went into the lemonade shop and sat down to have a drink. A man was sitting at a table nearby, lost in a big newspaper. Larry glanced at him, and then gave Pip a kick under the table. Pip looked up and Larry winked at him, and nodded his head slightly towards the man.

The others looked – and there was old Clear-Orf, in plainclothes, pretending to read a newspaper, and keeping an eye on the bench across the road, just as they too intended to do!

'Good afternoon, Mr Goon,' said Larry politely. 'Having a day off?'

Mr Goon grunted bad-temperedly. Those children again! They seemed to turn up everywhere.

'You having a lemonade too?' said Pip. 'Have one with us, Mr Goon. Do.'

Mr Goon grunted again, and returned to his newspaper. He was in plainclothes and looked rather strange. The children couldn't remember ever having seen him in anything but his rather tight-fitting uniform before. He wore flannel trousers, a cream shirt open at the neck, and a belt that he had pulled too tight. Bets thought he didn't look like Mr Goon at all.

She finished her lemonade. 'I'm going to buy a balloon,' she said. 'The one I bought at the Fair has gone pop. Order me an ice, Pip, and I'll be back to have it soon. We *are* all going to have ices, aren't we?'

'Where's that boy?' asked Mr Goon, as Bets got up.

'Boy? What boy?' said Larry at once, pretending to be puzzled.

Mr Goon gave a snort. 'That boy Frederick. Fatty, you call him. You know quite well who I mean. Don't act so daft.'

'Oh, *Fatty*! He's not far off,' said Larry. 'Do you want to see him? I'll tell him, if you like.'

'*I* don't want to see him,' said Mr Goon. 'But I know he's always up to something. What's he up to now?'

'*Is* he up to something now?' said Larry, a surprised look on his face. 'How mean of him not to tell us!'

Bets giggled and went out. She crossed the road to where the old balloon woman sat, her skirts almost filling half of the bench.

'May I have a blue balloon, please?' she said. She bent over the bunch of balloons and whispered to Fatty. 'Mr Goon is in the lemonade shop – in plainclothes. He looks so funny. I think he's watching the old man. You'll have to watch till you see Mr Goon go off, and then give your message.'

'Have *this* balloon, little Miss!' said the balloon woman, winking at Bets to show that her message

607

had been heard. 'This is a fine strong one. Last you for weeks!'

Bets paid for it, and went back to the shop. Larry had just ordered ices. He raised his eyebrows at Bets to ask her if she had delivered the message all right. She nodded. They began to eat their ices slowly, wondering if the policeman meant to stay in the shop all the afternoon.

They had almost finished their ices when the telephone went at the back of the shop. The shop woman answered it. 'For you, please, Mr Goon,' she said.

Mr Goon got up, went to the dark corner at the back of the shop, and listened to what the telephone had to say. Larry took a look at him. Mr Goon could not possibly see across the street to the bench from where he stood. Now would be Fatty's chance to give his message to the old man!

'It's hot in here,' said Larry, suddenly standing up. 'I'm going out for a breath of air. You come when you've finished your ices.'

He went out of the shop and shot across to the bench. He sat down beside the balloon woman. 'Mr Goon's telephoning,' he said. 'Now's your chance.

He can't see across the street from where the telephone is.'

'Right,' said Fatty. He moved nearer to the old man and nudged him. The old fellow looked round at once. Fatty slipped a note to him and then moved back to his end of the bench.

The old man deftly pocketed the note and sat for a few minutes more. Then, with a grunt, he got up and shuffled off round the corner. Larry followed him, at a sign from Fatty. As soon as he was safely round the corner the old fellow opened the slip of paper and looked at it. Then he took a match, lit the paper, and let it drop to the ground, where it burnt away.

He did not go back to his bench. Instead, he shuffled off in the direction of his home. Larry went back to the bench and stood beside the old balloon woman, pretending to choose a balloon.

'Did he read the note?' said Fatty, in a low voice.

'Yes. And he's gone off home now, I think,' said Larry. 'What did you put in the note?'

'I just put that he'd better not come to this seat for three afternoons as the police were watching it.' said Fatty. 'He'll think it was from a member of the gang, I expect. He will think they'd asked me to pass the message to him, as they wouldn't want to be seen doing it themselves, if the seat was watched. Well, let's hope we've got him out of the way for a few days!'

'I'll have this balloon,' said Larry, as some people passed. 'How much?'

Taking the balloon with him, he went back to the door of the shop. Mr Goon was still telephoning. Good! The others got up and went out. They all sauntered down the road, thinking how cross Mr Goon would be when he stopped telephoning and found that the old man was gone.

The balloon woman went too. It had been decided that she should go to Pip's garden, in case Mrs Trotteville, Fatty's mother, should spot her again, going down her garden-path, and make trouble. Pip's mother was out for the day, so it would be safe for Fatty to go there and change back to himself.

Soon all the Find-Outers, and Buster, were in Pip's summerhouse. Fatty changed as quickly as he could.

'I shan't use this disguise more than I can help,'

he said, pushing all the petticoats and skirts into
the sack he kept them in. 'It's far too hot!'

he said, pushing all the petticoats and skirts into the sack he kept them in. 'It's a too heavy.'

10. EVERYBODY DOES SOMETHING

Plans were laid for the next few days. 'These may be very important days,' said Fatty. 'We may be able to learn a lot – right under Mr Goon's nose, too, if he's going to do this watchdog act of his!'

'What exactly are we going to do?' said Daisy, thrilled. 'You're going to disguise yourself as that old man, we know, and take his place, hoping for a message from one of the gang. But what are *we* to do? We must have something interesting so that we can do our share as Find-Outers.'

'Woof,' said Buster.

'He wants a job too,' said Bets, with a laugh. 'Poor Buster! He can't understand why you have to dress up as somebody different, Fatty. You don't look or sound the same to him – you only *smell* the same. And when you go out as the balloon woman or the old man, we have to lock Buster up and leave him behind, and he hates that.'

'Poor old Buster-dog,' said Fatty, and at once Buster rolled himself over on his back to be tickled. His tongue came out, and his tail wagged so violently that it wagged his whole body and made it shake from end to end.

'Now,' said Fatty, taking out his notebook and opening it. 'Let's just have a look at what we know. Then we'll make our plans – and you shall each have something to do.'

'Good,' said Larry. 'I know you've got to do all the important work, Fatty, because you really are a born detective – but we do want something as well.'

'We don't know very much yet,' said Fatty, looking at his notes. 'We know that Mr Goon is watching the old man because he suspects what we do – that he receives messages to pass on – and we feel certain that for some reason or other the headquarters are here in Peterswood. We have also seen one of the members of the gang – the fellow with a hooter on his bike – but that's about all we *do* know.'

'It's not very much,' said Larry. 'Not a scrap more than we knew the other day.'

'We also know that the old fellow is likely to

keep away from that seat for a while,' said Fatty. 'Mr Goon doesn't know that. We're ahead of him there. *We* know that the old man who will be sitting on the bench this afternoon, and tomorrow and probably the next day too, will be *me* – and not that old fellow.'

'Yes, that's one up to us,' said Pip.

'Now,' said Fatty, shutting his notebook and looking round, 'tomorrow afternoon – in fact, each afternoon that I sit out on that bench, one or more of you must be in that sweetshop, watching carefully to see if anyone gives me a message – and it's your job to notice every single detail about him very carefully indeed. See? That's most important.'

'Right,' said Larry.

'And the other thing for you Find-Outers to do is to try and discover which cyclists have hooters on their bikes, instead of bells,' said Fatty. 'It would be a help if we could discover who that man was that came and spoke to me on the bench the other morning. We could watch him, and find out who his friends were, for instance.'

'I don't see how we can possibly find out who has a hooter on his bicycle,' said Pip. 'We can't go and look into everyone's bicycle sheds!'

'You could go to the shop that sells hooters and talk to the shopkeeper, and ask him if he sells many hooters, and maybe even get him to tell you the names of the buyers,' said Fatty.

'Oh yes,' said Pip. 'I hadn't thought of that.'

'I thought of it the other day when I went to buy that hooter,' said Fatty. 'But I hadn't time to talk to the man then – well, actually it's a boy in the shop I went to. I should think he'd love to have a good old jaw with you.'

'I'd like to go and talk to him,' said Bets. 'With Daisy.'

'You and Daisy and Pip can go, if you like,' said Larry. 'And I'll watch the seat from the sweetshop. Then, when you come back with all the information you can get you can take your turn at sitting in the shop and having lemonade, and I'll go and try and find out something else.'

'Buster can go with the ones who are going to the hooter shop,' said Fatty. 'But he mustn't go to the sweetshop. He would smell me all across the road, and come bounding out, barking. Mr Goon would soon think there was something funny about Buster making up to a dirty old man!'

The next afternoon Larry went to the sweetshop opposite the bench, and ordered a lemonade. Mr Goon was there again, reading his newspaper. He was once more in plainclothes, and he scowled at Larry when he came in.

'Why, Mr Goon! Here again!' said Larry, pretending to be most surprised. 'You *are* having a nice holiday! Do you spend all your time in here?'

Mr Goon took absolutely no notice. He felt very angry. Here was he, forced to spend his afternoons in a hot, smelly, little shop, watching a bench out there in the sun – and he couldn't even have peace! Those children had got to come and poke fun at him. Mr Goon eyed Larry's back grimly, and thought of all the things he would like to do to him and the other Find-Outers.

Then Mr Goon straightened up a little, for the old man was coming shuffling along to his bench. Larry watched him. He knew it was Fatty, of course, but Mr Goon didn't. Larry marvelled at the way Fatty lowered himself slowly down on to the bench. That was just exactly the way bent old people did sit down! Fatty never made a mistake in his acting.

Fatty took out a pipe and began slowly to fill it. Then he coughed. It was a horrible, hollow cough, and bent him double. Larry grinned. The cough was new. He supposed Fatty must have heard the old man, and had practised the cough till it was quite perfect.

Larry turned to Mr Goon.

'There's that old man you made us go and see the other day, Mr Goon. Funny about him, wasn't it? Did you ever find out what you wanted to know?'

Mr Goon again took no notice, but rustled the paper noisily.

But just then two men came along, stopped by the bench and sat down. At once Mr Goon began to watch the men with much concentration. So did Larry. Were they going to pass a message to Fatty?

The men had papers. They opened them and began to discuss something. They stayed there for quite a time, but neither Mr Goon nor Larry could spot any message being given or received. The old fellow at the end of the bench still leaned over his stick, his head nodding occasionally.

Then he sat upright, gave a loud sniff and wiped the back of his hand across his nose. Larry was amused to see the two men give him a disgusted look. They folded their newspapers, got up, and, still talking, walked off down the street.

Mr Goon leaned back and wrote down a few notes. Larry wondered if he thought they were the members of the gang. He was certain they weren't. For one thing he was sure that one of them was a friend of his father's.

Larry began to be bored. He had finished his lemonade. He really didn't want another, and he felt that he couldn't possibly eat an ice at that moment. The shop woman came up to him.

'Anything else, sir?' she asked. Larry said no thank you.

'Well, you go, then,' said Mr Goon's voice. 'No need for you to hang about here if you've finished your everlasting lemonade, see?'

This was awkward. Larry was supposed to watch the bench and Fatty until the others came back. He couldn't very well leave his post. But just at that moment the others *did* come back! They clattered in, chattering.

Larry stood up at once. 'Hello, you others! I'm glad you've come for me. I suppose Pip wants to stay and have a lemonade as usual. Well, you girls and I will go off and leave him guzzling!'

For a wonder even Bets sensed that Larry wanted to leave only one of them behind. So the girls went off with Larry, and left Pip to seat himself at the window table, with a glowering Mr Goon nearby. Was he *never* going to get rid of these children!

Larry took the girls off, and when they were safely round the corner, he told them how Mr Goon had ordered him to go. 'So I thought we'd better only just leave Pip behind,' he said, 'and then that still leaves two more of us to go in singly and drink lemonade or eat ices. I think Mr Goon is getting suspicious of us!'

'Larry! We had a most interesting time at the shop where the hooters are sold,' said Bets. 'Listen!'

She told Larry all about it. She and Pip and Daisy had gone into the shop, which sold bicycles, tyres, pumps, bells, hooters, torches, toys, prams, and many other things. There was a young boy in charge.

'Afternoon,' he said, when they all trooped in. 'And what may I do for *you*?'

'We want a hooter, please,' said Bets.

'Well, you're lucky,' said the boy, going over to a shelf and getting down a rubber hooter. 'We only had these in last week. First we've had for months!'

The children tried it. It hooted very nicely indeed. Parp-parp! Parp-parp!

'Do you sell many?' asked Pip, whilst the two girls ambled round the shop, pretending to look at everything.

'Only sold three this week,' said the boy.

'All to cyclists?' asked Pip.

'How should I know?' said the boy. 'The customers don't wheel their bikes into the shop with them!'

Pip didn't quite know what to say next. He joined the girls, and they all examined the contents of the rather interesting shop.

'You've got an awful lot of things here,' said Daisy. 'Do you remember all the prices and everything?'

' 'Course. I've got a good memory,' said the boy. 'At the end of the day I remember every blessed thing I've sold!'

'Gracious!' said Daisy admiringly. 'I bet you don't remember every customer too!'

'Oh yes, I do,' said the boy proudly. 'Never forget a thing, I don't!'

'Well – I bet you don't remember the customers who bought the three hooters!' said Daisy, quick as a flash. Pip and Bets thought how clever she was!

' 'Course I do,' said the boy. 'One was the fellow that lives down the road at Kosy Kot. The second one was a fellow with rather odd eyes – one blue and one brown – I don't know his name and never saw him before. But I'd know him again all right. And the third one was a boy who seemed in a bit of a hurry.'

That was Fatty, thought the three children. Daisy smiled at the shop boy. 'What a memory you've got!' she said. 'You really are a marvel. Well, we must be going. Got your hooter, Bets? Well, come on, then!'

They hurried out of the shop, rejoicing. The man at Kosy Kot – and a man with odd eyes. They might be clues, they really might!

11. LOOKING FOR MORE CLUES

Pip was having a boring time in the sweetshop. There was nothing to see outside, except the old man on the bench. Nobody went near him at all. Mr Goon breathed heavily behind Pip, evidently finding the shop a very hot place to be in on this blazing day. Pip made his lemonade last out a long time and then, to Mr Goon's annoyance, asked for an ice.

'You children seem to live here,' said Mr Goon, at last.

'You seem to, as well,' said Pip. 'Nice shop, isn't it?'

Mr Goon didn't think so at all. He was sick and tired of the shop – but it was the best place to watch that old man from, no doubt about that!

'You look hot,' said Pip sympathetically. 'Why don't you go for a row on the river, Mr Goon? It would be cool there. Seems a pity to spend all your holiday cooped up here.'

Mr Goon gave one of his snorts. He wasn't on holiday. He was on a case, a most important case. And for reasons of his own he had to wear plainclothes. But he couldn't explain all that to this irritating boy.

Bets came in next, and Pip was very glad to see her. 'Going to have an ice?' he said. 'Well, sorry I can't wait with you, Bets. So long!'

He went out and, to Mr Goon's annoyance, yet another of those children, Bets this time, settled down at the window table, obviously intending to be there for some time. Bets was afraid of the policeman, so she kept her back to him and said nothing at all, but kept a sharp eye on the old man opposite on the bench. She thought how bored poor Fatty must be!

Fatty had a coughing fit, and Bets watched in alarm. The cough seemed so very real that she felt sure poor Fatty must be getting a terrible cold.

Then Fatty had a fit of the sniffles, and hunted all over himself for a handkerchief, at last producing a violent red one. Then he got up and hobbled round a bit, as if he had got stiff with sitting. Nobody in the world would have guessed he was anything but a poor, stiff old man.

Bets enjoyed the performance immensely. She knew that Fatty was putting it on for her benefit. Fatty liked little Bets' admiration.

All the Find-Outers were glad when that day was over. It really began to be very boring, taking turns at sitting in the sweetshop, and watching for something that didn't happen. As for Fatty, he was terribly bored.

'Tomorrow I'm going to supply myself with plenty of newspapers to read,' he said. 'I simply can't spend hours coughing and sniffing. And all for nothing too. Not a soul passed me a message or anything.'

'We found out something interesting at the hooter shop, though,' said Bets, and she told Fatty about the two men who had bought hooters that week.

'One who lives at Kosy Kot, and one man with odd eyes,' she said. 'The boy didn't know where he lived. And the third person who bought a hooter was you, of course.'

'Has that shop only sold three hooters all these

months, then?' said Fatty, surprised.

'Well, they've only just got them in,' said Pip. 'That's why. So, if that fellow who spoke to you the other day on the bench *is* a member of the gang, he's either living at Kosy Kot – or he's wandering about somewhere with odd eyes – one blue and one brown!'

'We'd better try Kosy Kot first,' said Fatty, pleased. 'You did well, Find-Outers. How did you get all this information?'

'Well, Daisy did, really,' said Pip, and he told Fatty how it had happened. Fatty banged Daisy on the back.

'Jolly good,' he said. 'Very quick-witted. Now – who's going to tackle Kosy Kot?'

'Isn't it a dreadful name?' said Pip. 'Why do people choose names like that? Can't we go down into the village and find it tomorrow morning? It's too late now.'

'Right,' said Fatty. 'We will. I shan't have to masquerade as that old fellow till the afternoon, so I can come with you. Meet at Pip's tomorrow morning, ten o'clock sharp.'

So, at ten o'clock, they were all there, Buster

too. They set off to find Kosy Kot. They met a postman and he told them where it was.

They soon found it. It was a little bungalow set in a trim little garden. At the back was a shed.

'I bet that's where they keep the bicycles,' said Fatty. 'Now – how can we get a peep inside?'

'I know!' said Pip. 'I've got a ball. I could chuck it into the garden, and then we could go and ask if we might get it back – and you could peep into the shed, Fatty. If a bike is there with a hooter on, we'll wait about for the man who lives here, and see if we recognise him as the one who spoke to you, and had a bike with a hooter. We might recognise the bike too, if we see it.'

This seemed a good and simple plan. So Pip proceeded to carry it out. He threw the ball wildly, and it flew into the garden of Kosy Kot, actually hitting against the bicycle-shed.

'Blow!' said Pip loudly. 'My ball's gone into that garden.'

'We'll go and ask if we may get it,' said Daisy. So into the gate they went and up to the front door.

A woman opened it. 'Please, our ball has gone into your garden,' said Pip. 'May we get it?'

'Yes, but don't tread on any of the beds,' said the woman, and shut the door. The children went round to the back of the house. To their annoyance they saw a man there, digging. He stared at them.

'What do you kids want?'

'Oh – excuse us, please, but your wife said we might come and get our ball,' said Fatty, politely. 'I hope you don't mind.'

'Well, get it, then,' said the man, and went on digging. Fatty made for the shed and pretended to hunt round about. The door was open and he looked inside. It was full of garden tools and old sacks – but there was no bike there at all. How annoying!

'Haven't you found it?' said the man, and came over to look too. Then Fatty gave an exclamation and picked up the ball. He looked at the neat little shed.

'Useful sheds those, aren't they?' he said, 'Jolly good for bikes. Wish I had one like that.'

'Oh, I don't use it for bikes,' said the man. 'We haven't any. I use it for my garden tools.'

'Oh,' said Fatty. 'Well – thank you for letting us get our ball. We'll be going now.'

They went out into the road and crossed over to talk. 'Hasn't got a bike! But that boy at the shop distinctly said that the man at Kosy Kot bought a hooter,' said Bets indignantly. 'He *must* have got a bike. Why should he pretend he hasn't got one?'

'It's a bit suspicious,' said Pip. They walked on, puzzled. Suddenly, round the corner, they heard the noise of a hooter! Parp-parp! Parp-parp! The children clutched at one another, thrilled. A hooter! Perhaps it belonged to the man with odd eyes! Perhaps it would be his bicycle coming round the corner!

But, round the corner, ridden at a tremendous pace, came a child on a tricycle. He ran right into Fatty, who gave a yell, and hopped round on one leg, holding his right foot in his hand.

'You little idiot! What did you come round the corner like that for?' yelled Fatty.

'Well, I hooted!' said the little boy indignantly. 'Didn't you hear me? I hooted like this.'

And he pressed the rubber hooter on his tricycle and it parp-parped loudly. 'It's a new hooter,' he said. 'My daddy bought it for me. You should have got out of the way when you heard me coming round the corner.'

'We weren't expecting a tricycle,' said Pip. 'We thought the hooter was on a bike, coming along the road, not on the pavement.'

'Well, I'm sorry,' said the little boy, beginning to pedal again. 'But I did hoot. I hoot at every corner. Like this.'

Parp-parp went the hooter and the five children watched the little boy pedal swiftly down the pavement, then cross the road, and disappear into the gate of Kosy Kot.

'I feel like saying "Gah!"' said poor Fatty. 'Wasting our time looking for a hooter that's on a child's tricycle – and getting my foot run over!'

'Never mind,' said Bets consolingly. 'You'll be able *really* to limp this afternoon, when you're the old man again.'

They all went back to Pip's. It didn't seem any use trying to find the owner of the other hooter. They couldn't possibly go round looking at everyone in Peterswood to see who had odd eyes. It was very disappointing about the tricycle.

'I think this is a very *slow* sort of mystery,' said

Bets. 'It will be time to go back to school again before we've even *begun* to solve it!'

'What's the date?' said Pip. 'Let me see – it must be the seventh of September – no, the eighth. Gracious, we really haven't much more time!'

'Perhaps something will happen soon,' said Larry hopefully. 'You know how sometimes things sort of boil up and get terribly exciting all of a sudden.'

'Well, it's time this one did,' said Fatty. 'It's been in the refrigerator long enough!'

Everyone laughed. 'I wouldn't mind sitting in a fridge myself,' said Daisy. 'Let's get our swimming things and go and swim in the river. I'm so hot.'

So down to the river they went, and were soon splashing about happily. Fatty, of course, was a very fine swimmer, and could swim right across the river and back. Bets splashed happily in the shallow water. The others swam about lazily just out of their depth.

Bets thought she would swim out to them. So off she went, striking out valiantly. She didn't see a punt coming smoothly through the water, and before she could save herself, she felt something brush past her shoulder, and screamed.

The punt slid on, unable to stop, but a boat following behind, swung round, and a man caught hold of her and held her.

'You're all right, aren't you?' he said, bending over her. 'Can you swim?'

'Yes,' gasped Bets, striking out again. 'Fatty! Fatty! Come here quickly!'

The others swam over to the frightened little girl. They helped her to the shore and she gazed after the distant boat, and gulped.

'Oh,' she said, 'oh, I've missed the most wonderful clue! But I couldn't help it! Oh, Fatty, the man in that boat had odd eyes – one blue and one brown. I couldn't help noticing them when he caught hold of my shoulder. And now the boat is gone – and I never even noticed its name!'

'Oh, *Bets*!' said everyone, and Bets looked ready to cry. 'Didn't you notice what colour it was, or anything?' asked Larry.

Bets shook her head. 'No – I suppose I was too frightened. Oh, I'm so sorry. It was such a wonderful clue – and a suspect, too – and I've lost them both!'

12. SOMETHING HAPPENS AT LAST!

That afternoon things really began to happen. Fatty disguised himself once more as the old man (who was keeping remarkably well out of the way), and went to the bench in the village street as usual. He limped most realistically this time, because his foot had swollen up from being run over by the tricycle.

He had provided himself with plenty of news-papers to read, and he sat down as carefully as ever, letting out a little groan as he did so.

In the sweetshop opposite sat Mr Goon, clad as usual in flannel trousers and a cream shirt open at the neck. He looked extremely hot, and was beginning to long for some bad weather – frost and snow if possible! Mr Goon had never felt so hot in his life as in this blazing summer.

Larry went into the shop and sat down to order lemonade. Mr Goon was getting used to the fact that one or other of the Find-Outers always seemed to be there. He took no notice of Larry. He just propped his paper up in front of him, and kept a watchful eye on the old fellow nodding on the bench across the street.

It looked as if Fatty had gone sound asleep. Larry yawned and wished he could go to sleep too. Then he noticed something. A man was standing in the shady doorway of a nearby shop, and he seemed to be watching the old man. Was he thinking of giving him a message?

Mr Goon also spotted the man, and sat up straight. The man looked up and down the street.

The village was empty and deserted on this hot afternoon. A car drove by and disappeared. A dog ambled round a corner, lay down, and fell asleep. Larry and Mr Goon watched the silent man breathlessly.

The man sauntered across the road and stood for a few minutes looking in the window of a shop. Then he strolled over to the bench and sat down near the old man.

Fatty was pretending to be asleep, but he spotted the man out of the corner of his eye, and something told him that the man was no chance companion.

He was there for a purpose. Fatty jerked himself upright as if he had suddenly awakened, and sniffled loudly. He wiped his nose with his sleeve and then leaned over his stick again. Then he coughed his dreadful cough.

'Awful cough you've got!' said the man. Fatty took no notice, remembering that he was deaf. He coughed again.

'AWFUL COUGH YOU'VE GOT!' repeated the man.

Fatty turned, put his hand behind his ear and croaked out a familiar word, 'Wassat?'

The stranger laughed. He took out his cigarette case and offered the old man a cigarette. There was only one left in the case. As soon as Fatty had taken it, the man filled his case from a packet.

'Thank you, sir,' croaked Fatty, and put the cigarette into his pocket. His heart beat fast. He felt sure that there must be some kind of message in the cigarette. What would it be? He did not dare to look closely at the man, but hoped that Larry was taking note of all his clothes and everything.

Larry was. And so was Mr Goon! Both were mentally repeating the same things. 'Grey flannel suit. Blue shirt. Black shoes. No tie. Grey felt hat.

Moustache. Tall. Slim. Long nose. Small eyes.'

The man got up to go. He disappeared quite quickly round a corner. Fatty thought that he, too, had better disappear quickly, before Mr Goon could get hold of him and get the cigarette-message, whatever it was, away from him. So he, too, got up, and with most surprising agility in such an old man, he shot round another corner.

And then he saw something most aggravating! Coming towards him was the *real* old man, corduroy trousers, dirty scarf and all! He was out for a walk, though he did not mean to go and sit on the bench.

Fatty could not risk being seen by the old man, for he guessed he would be amazed and alarmed at the sight of his double. So he popped into the nearest gate and hid himself under a bush.

He was only just in time! Mr Goon came round the corner with a rush – and almost bumped into the real old man! He clutched him tightly.

'Ha! Got you! Now you give me that cigarette right away!'

The old man looked most alarmed. He shrank away from the red-faced Mr Goon, not in the least knowing who he was, for he did not recognise the policeman dressed in plainclothes.

'Where's that cigarette?' panted Mr Goon.

'Wassat?' croaked the old man. Goon heard footsteps behind him and saw Larry. Larry was horrified to see what he thought was Fatty in the clutches of the policeman. He stayed nearby to see what was going to happen. The old man tried feebly to get away from Goon, but the policeman held on grimly.

'You let go,' said the old fellow. 'I'll get the police, see? Catching hold of me like this! I'll get the police!'

'It's the police that have got *you*,' said Goon, shaking him. 'I'm GOON! GOON the POLICEMAN! Now, give me that cigarette, please!'

This was too much for the poor old man. He almost fell down in fright. He hadn't the faintest idea what Goon wanted him for, nor did he know why Goon kept on shouting for a cigarette.

Mr Goon snorted, caught hold of the old fellow by the collar of his coat and marched him down the street. 'You can come to the police station with me,' he said. 'And I'll search you there and get that cigarette! See!'

Larry watched them go, feeling rather scared, for he still thought it was Fatty that Mr Goon had got.

He had the fright of his life when he suddenly saw another old man peering out from under a bush at him!

'Larry! Have they gone?' said this old man, in Fatty's voice. Larry almost jumped out of his skin.

'*Fatty*! I thought it was *you* that Mr Goon was taking away! Golly, I'm glad it wasn't.'

Fatty came out from under the bush. 'The real old man happened to come walking up here just as I was hurrying to get away from Mr Goon!' said Fatty, with a grin. 'So I hopped in at this gate and hid, and Mr Goon grabbed the old fellow and ordered him to give up the cigarette he hadn't got. Phew! That was a very close shave!'

'Fatty! Is there a message in that cigarette?' said Larry eagerly. 'Can we find out? I saw that fellow give you one. I watched him for a long time. So did Goon.'

'Let's go to Pip's,' said Fatty. 'We're safer there than anywhere, because his garden is so big. Don't walk with me. Go in front, and when you come to a corner, whistle if you want to warn me.'

Larry walked on in front. He did not whistle at any of the corners, because there seemed to be nobody about in Peterswood at all that hot

September afternoon. In ten minutes Fatty was safely in Pip's summerhouse. He did not strip off his old clothes, because he had no others to change into. He waited there whilst Larry went off to collect the others, and he hoped that no grown-ups would think of poking their noses into the summerhouse that afternoon. They would not be pleased to find a dirty old tramp there!

Fatty longed to examine the cigarette and see what was inside it. But he waited patiently till the others came tearing up the path, pouring into the little summerhouse with excited faces.

'Fatty! Larry's told us all about it! What's the message? Is there one in the cigarette? Have you looked?'

'Of course not. I waited for you all,' said Fatty. He took the cigarette from his pocket. It was rather a stout, fat one. It had tobacco at each end – but when Fatty had scraped out as much tobacco as he could, he found that the middle of the cigarette was not made of tobacco at all – but was stuffed with a tight roll of paper!

'Oh!' said Bets, almost too excited to breathe. 'A secret message! Oh, Fatty!'

Fatty unrolled the paper. He flattened it with his hand. The five of them leaned over it, their breaths hot against one another's cheeks. Buster tried in vain to see what all the excitement was about, but for once in a way nobody took the slightest notice of him!

The message proved to be very puzzling and disappointing. All it said was:

> *One tin black boot-polish.*
> *One pound rice.*
> *One pound tea.*
> *Two pounds syrup.*
> *One bag flour.*

'Why! It's only a grocery list!' said Daisy. 'Just like Mother often gives me and Larry when we go shopping for her. Whatever does it mean, Fatty?'

'I don't know,' said Fatty. 'It must mean something. I hope it's not in a secret code.'

'What's a secret code?' asked Bets.

'Oh, a way of writing messages so that only the persons receiving them know what they mean,' said Fatty. 'But somehow I don't think this is a code.

After all, that old man had got to read it and understand it, and I'm quite sure he hasn't brains enough to understand a code.'

'Then could there be another message, but written in secret ink?' said Pip suddenly. 'You know how you taught us to write secret messages, in between the lines of an ordinary letter, don't you, Fatty? Well, could there be a message written between these lines, in secret ink?'

'Yes, there could,' said Fatty. 'And that's what I think we shall find! Good for you, Pip. Can you go and get a warm iron? If we run it over the paper, the secret message will show up.'

Pip ran off. Gladys was actually ironing in the kitchen, and though she was very surprised to think that Pip should want to borrow the warm iron to take into the garden for a minute, she let him. He came tearing up to the summerhouse with it in his hand.

'I've got it!' he said. 'Here you are. Put the paper out flat on the wooden table. That's right. Now I'll run the iron over it.'

He ran the warm iron over the spread-out bit of paper. Then he lifted it off and looked at the message. 'There's another one coming up, look –

between the lines of the other!' squealed Daisy, in excitement. 'Iron it again, Pip, quick! Oh, this is too thrilling for words!'

Pip ironed the paper again – and this time another message showed up very clearly indeed. The words came up, looking a strange grey-brown colour, and began to fade almost as soon as the children had made them out.

Tell Number Three. Waxworks, Tuesday,
9 pm – Number Five

'Golly!' said Pip. 'Look at that! Tell Number Three – that must be one of the gang. And Number Five must be another.'

'Waxworks, Tuesday, 9 pm' said Fatty, and his eyes gleamed. 'So that's one of their meeting places. Down in the waxworks hall, where all those figures are. *Now* we know something!'

'We really do,' said Bets. 'What are they meeting about, Fatty?'

'I don't know – but I shall find out,' said Fatty. 'Because – I shall be there on Tuesday night!'

13. IN MR. GOON'S CLUTCHES

The children were full of excitement when they heard Fatty say this. 'What! Go down to the waxworks, and attend the gang meeting!' said Larry. 'You wouldn't dare! You'd be discovered, however well you hid yourself!'

'It's the only way of finding out who all the gang are,' said Fatty. 'I shall see them, hear them talk and plan – my word, this *is* a bit of luck!'

'No wonder Mr Goon wanted to get hold of that cigarette from the old man,' said Daisy. 'He would give anything to have this message!'

'He'll wonder what the old chap's done with it!' said Fatty, with a grin. 'He'll have searched him from top to toe – but he won't have found that cigarette!'

They talked excitedly for some time and then Fatty said he really must go home and get out of his hot, smelly old man clothes. The others walked down to the gate with him, leaving an angry Buster tied up in the summerhouse.

Meanwhile Mr Goon had had a most disappointing time. He had found no cigarette at all on the old man. He was angry and puzzled, and he shouted at the old fellow, getting redder and redder in the face.

'You can stay here till you tell me what you did with that cigarette, see?' he yelled. 'I'll lock you up till you do. Now then – are you going to tell me?'

The old chap had turned sulky. He knew nothing of any cigarette, he hadn't been sitting on the bench, he didn't know what the bad-tempered policeman was talking about. So he sulked and said nothing at all, which made Goon madder than ever.

'Right!' said Goon at last, getting up. 'I'll talk to you some more tomorrow.'

He went home and changed into his uniform. Then he decided to go and see 'that boy Larry' and ask him if he, too, had noticed the man giving the old fellow a cigarette that afternoon. Mr Goon couldn't help being puzzled by the old chap's firm denials of any knowledge of a cigarette. But Larry must have seen the gift, and would bear witness to it.

But Larry was out. 'Try at the Hilton's,' said Larry's mother. 'Oh, I do hope the children haven't been misbehaving themselves, Mr Goon.'

'Er, no – for a wonder, no, Mam,' said Mr Goon, and went off majestically.

He arrived at Pip's just as the children were escorting Fatty, still disguised as the old man, out of the front gate. Fatty stared at Mr Goon, and Mr Goon stared back disbelievingly. What! Hadn't he just locked that old man up? And here he was again, free, and walking about! Mr Goon began to feel as if he was in a peculiarly unpleasant dream.

'Er – good evening, Mr Goon,' said Larry. Mr Goon took no notice of him.

'Here, you!' he said, grabbing at Fatty's arm. 'How did you get out? Haven't I just locked you up? What are things a-coming to, I'd like to know! Here I've just locked you up and I meet you walking into me, bold as brass!'

Mr Goon looked so amazed and disbelieving that Fatty badly wanted to laugh. He was at a loss to know what to say.

'Wassat?' he said at last, putting his hand behind his ear.

That was too much for Mr Goon. He caught hold of Fatty's collar and marched him quickly up the lane.

'You've been "wassating" me long enough!' said the annoyed Mr Goon. 'I don't know how you got out – but I do know you're going in again – and this time I'll lock the door on you meself! And there you'll stay till you see sense if it takes you a month!'

Fatty didn't like this at all. He debated whether or not to let Mr Goon into the secret of his disguise. But before he had made up his mind, he was at the police station. Mr Goon was unlocking a door, and Fatty was being pushed into the dark, narrow little room behind.

And in it was the real old man! He stared at Fatty and Fatty stared at him. The old chap let out a howl. He was beginning to feel he must be mad. Why, here was himself staring at him! What was happening?

Mr Goon heard the howl and looked into the room – and then he saw the *two* old men! Exactly alike. As like as peas in a pod. Mr Goon sat down heavily on a chair and mopped his forehead with a big handkerchief. He felt dazed. What with vanishing cigarettes, men that got locked up and then got out – and now two old men exactly alike – well, Mr Goon began to feel that he must be lying asleep and dreaming in his own bed at home, and he fervently hoped that he would soon wake up.

'Lemme get out of here!' said the real old man, and tried to push past Mr Goon. But the policeman caught hold of him. He wasn't going to have any more disappearings. He was going to get to the bottom of things.

Fatty saw that things had gone far enough, and he did not like the thought of his parents knowing that he was locked up at the police station. So he spoke to Mr Goon in his ordinary voice, and gave that poor man another terrible shock.

'Mr Goon! I'm not really an old man. I'm Frederick Trotteville.'

Mr Goon's mouth fell open. He gulped once or twice, staring at Fatty as if he couldn't believe his eyes. Fatty twitched off his beard, and then Mr Goon did indeed see that it was Fatty. He dragged him out of the dark little room, slammed and locked the door, and took Fatty into an office.

'Now you just tell me the meaning of all this here!' he said.

'Well,' said Fatty, 'it's a long story, but I'll tell you everything, Mr Goon,' and he launched into the tale of all that the Find-Outers had done, and how he had disguised himself as the old man, and sat there to trap a message from the gang.

'What about that cigarette?' said Mr Goon when he had got his breath back a bit. 'What about that? That's a most important thing!'

'Is it really?' said Fatty, in pretended surprise. 'Well, we undid the cigarette, of course, Mr Goon, and inside we found nothing of importance at all, really – just a silly grocery list. We were terribly disappointed.'

Fatty did not mean to tell Mr Goon what he and the others had discovered in the message – the few lines in secret ink. No, he would keep that to himself, and go to the meeting on Tuesday night, and see what he could find out. *He* wanted to solve the mystery, he, Fatty, the chief of the Find-Outers. He did not stop to think whether it was dangerous or not.

Mr Goon grabbed hold of the message. He spread it out. He frowned. He read it through two or three times. 'Must be a code,' he said. 'I'll look up my codebook. You leave this to me.'

'Er – well – I'll be going now,' said Fatty, after watching Mr Goon frowning at the list of groceries for a few minutes.

'If you hadn't given me this here bit of paper, I'd have locked you up,' said Mr Goon. 'Interfering with the law. That's what you're always doing, you five kids. Ho, yes, I know you think you've got a fine friend in Inspector Jenks, but one of these days you'll find he's fed up with you, see? And I'll get my promotion and be a big noise, and then just you look out!'

'Oh, I *will* look out,' said Fatty earnestly. 'Thanks for warning me, Mr Goon. Er – what about that old fellow? Are you still going to keep him locked up?'

'Yes, I am,' said Mr Goon. 'And your own common sense will tell you why – that's always supposing you've got any, which I very much doubt – I don't want him warning the gang that I'm on their track. If he's here, under my nose, he can't do much warning.'

'I think you're quite right, Mr Goon,' said Fatty solemnly. 'I couldn't agree with you more. I think –'

'I'm tired of you,' said Mr Goon. 'You clear orf double quick, before I change my mind about locking you up. I'm sick and tired of you. Messing about – interfering – dressing up – gah!'

Fatty scuttled off. He went home and quickly changed out of his old man clothes, and then shot up to Pip's to tell everyone what had happened.

'I had to give him the cigarette message, worse luck,' he said. 'It was the only thing to keep him quiet. But I don't believe he'll make head or tail of it, and I bet he won't test it for a secret message as we did. You should have seen his face when he pushed me into the same room as the real old man, and saw two of us there! I thought he would go up in smoke!'

The others roared. They were most relieved to see Fatty back safe and sound. Bets had been imagining him locked up in a dreary cell, with only bread and water.

'He's keeping the old man under his eye for a few days,' said Fatty, 'in case he gets the wind up about all this, and warns the other members of the gang. I'm pleased he's doing that. I expect the meeting will wonder why Number Three doesn't turn up on Tuesday, whoever he is. Well, they'll have to wonder!'

'I think it's awfully dangerous for you to go down to the waxworks on Tuesday,' said Daisy. 'I do, really. I think you ought to go and tell the Inspector about it, Fatty.'

'Oh no,' said Fatty. 'I want us to solve this mystery before we see the Inspector again. I shall be quite safe.'

'I don't see how you can say that,' said Larry, who agreed with Daisy that it might be dangerous. 'The men will surely not be fools enough to hold their meeting without being certain there's no spy there.'

'They won't discover *me*,' said Fatty. 'I shall wear a disguise!'

'I don't see how that will help you,' said Larry. 'Even if you are in disguise, you'll be a stranger to the men, and they'll want to know who you are.'

'I shan't be a stranger to them,' said Fatty, exasperatingly. 'Nor to you, either.'

The others stared at him. 'What do you mean?' said Pip at last. 'What are you getting at?'

'I shall be somebody the gang have seen often enough before, if they have held their other meetings in the waxworks hall. They'll know me so well they won't even look at me!'

'What do you *mean*?' said Daisy, getting annoyed. 'Don't talk in these silly riddles.'

'Well,' said Fatty, and he lowered his voice to a mysterious whisper, 'well – I shall be disguised as one of the waxworks, silly! Napoleon, I think, because he suits me most!'

There was a complete silence. All the Find-Outers stared at Fatty in the greatest admiration. What an idea! No member of the gang would suspect any of the waxwork figures! Bets could just imagine Fatty standing stiff and straight as the waxwork Napoleon, staring fixedly in front of him – seeing and hearing everything.

'What a really marvellous idea!' said Larry, at last. 'Oh, Fatty – I should never have thought of that if I'd thought for a month. You'll be right in the lions' den – and they won't even *smell* you!'

'It *is* rather a good idea, isn't it?' said Fatty,

swelling up a little. 'That's one thing about me, you know – I've always got plenty of ideas. My form master said only last term that my imagination was . . .'

But the others didn't in the least want to hear what Fatty's form master had said. They wanted to talk about Tuesday night and what Fatty was going to do.

Tuesday night! Bets thrilled every time she thought of it. This mystery was really getting too exciting for words. Oooh – Tuesday night!

14. A VERY BOLD IDEA

That weekend dragged along very slowly indeed. Tuesday was such a long time in coming! The only thing that enlivened it at all was that on the two or three occasions when the children met Mr Goon, Fatty had his hooter tucked under his coat, and sounded it as soon as they had passed the policeman.

This made him jump, and he looked round in hope of seeing the cyclist who had once stopped and spoken to the old man. But he never did, of course. He hailed the children suspiciously the third time it happened.

'Did you hear that hooter?' he asked. They all nodded vigorously.

'Did you see a bike going by then?' said the policeman.

'A bike? All by itself with a hooter?' asked Pip, and the others grinned.

'Gah!' said Mr Goon, enraged as usual. 'You clear orf! I wouldn't put it past you to carry one of them hooters about, just to annoy me, like!'

'He's getting quite bright, isn't he?' said Larry, as they walked off. 'I shouldn't be surprised if he does get promotion one of these days. He's really trying to use those brains of his a bit. We'd better not hoot any more when we pass him. He's quite likely to go and complain about us if we do – and ever since he went up to my house and asked for me the other day, Mummy's been warning me not to get into trouble.'

Fatty was preparing himself very earnestly for Tuesday night. He knew how important it was, and he also knew that, unless all his details were absolutely perfect, he might be in considerable danger.

He and the others spent a long time in the waxworks, much to the surprise of the red-headed boy, for it was very hot in there, and not many people visited the little hall these blazing days.

But Fatty had to study the figure of Napoleon very carefully indeed. He meant to get into the hall somehow on Tuesday evening, and dress himself up in Napoleon's clothes. Would they fit him? He asked Daisy what she thought.

'Yes, I should think they'd fit you very well,' she said, considering first Napoleon and then Fatty. 'You had better take a few safety pins in case something doesn't quite meet. The hat will be fine – just your size, I should think. What about hair, Fatty?'

'I can manage that all right,' said Fatty. 'I rather think my own will do, if I smarm it down a bit, and pull a few pieces out in front, like old Napoleon has got. And, er – I don't know what you think – but – er – I'm not really *unlike* Napoleon in features, am I?'

The others stared at him. 'Well,' said Pip honestly, 'I can't see any likeness at *all*. Not the slightest.'

'Do you *want* to look like Napoleon?' said Bets in surprise. 'I don't think he looks very nice, really. And I don't like those men that go about thinking they want to conquer the whole world. Napoleon must have been very brainy, of course, and *you're* brainy, Fatty. But, except that you're brainy, I don't see that you're very like Napoleon.'

Fatty gave it up. He stared once more at the

figure of Napoleon, in its grand uniform, cocked hat, medals, epaulettes, and stars. It was a fine uniform and Fatty was longing to get into it. Well, he hadn't got long to wait now.

He tried to memorise exactly at what angle Napoleon wore his hat, exactly how he held his hands, exactly how he stared so blankly in front of him. Napoleon fortunately stood in the very front row of figures, so Fatty, as Napoleon, would be able to hear and see everything very well indeed. A little shiver went down his back when he thought of standing there, perfectly still, listening to the plans of the gang, and memorising their appearance.

It was a very bold idea indeed. Not one of the other Find-Outers would have dared to do it. But Fatty, of course, would dare anything. Bets thought that he wouldn't even turn a hair if he met a roaring lion, the kind she met in her bad dreams, and which scared her terribly. Fatty would probably speak to it kindly and pat it, and the lion would lie down and roll over for Fatty to tickle it on its tummy – like Buster did!

The red-headed boy, curious at their sudden

intense interest in Napoleon, came over and joined them.

'What's exciting you about *him*?' he said. 'Who is he? Oh – Napoleon. What was he? Some sort of soldier?'

'Don't you *know*?' said Bets, in astonishment. 'Didn't you learn history at school?'

'I've never been to school,' said the red-headed boy. 'I belong to the Fair, and us kids hardly ever go to school unless we have to. We move about from place to place, you see, and before we're popped into some school, we've moved on again. I can read, but I can't write.'

'Why are you in the waxwork show?' asked Fatty. 'Does this hall belong to the Fair people?'

'Oh no – they've only hired it,' said the boy. 'The waxworks belong to my uncle. He's the fellow that runs the hoopla. I used to help him with that, but now I have to do the waxworks, and it's jolly dull.'

Fatty wondered if any of the Fair people were in the gang of thieves. Well, he would know on Tuesday night.

The children went and studied other figures

carefully too, so that the red-headed boy wouldn't get suspicious about their sudden interest in Napoleon. They had a good look at the wax figure of the policeman as well. He really did look a bit like Mr Goon! There he stood, on the second step, not far from Napoleon, his helmet on perfectly straight, the strap round the chin, and the belt a little tight.

The red-headed boy disappeared out of doors for a minute. Fatty at once went back to Napoleon and studied the clothes well, to make sure that he could take them off the wax figure fairly easily.

'Hope they're not *stuck* on in any way,' he said to the others anxiously. Daisy pulled at them.

'Oh no,' she said. 'They are put on just like ours – and look, the trousers are held up by braces. You'll be all right, Fatty. But you'll have to be here long before nine, or you'll never have time to undress yourself *and* Napoleon and then dress yourself up again.'

'I wish you wouldn't, really, Fatty,' said Bets, looking up at him with scared eyes. 'I shall hate to think of you standing so near the gang – whatever would they do to you if they discovered you?'

'They won't,' said Fatty. 'I shan't give myself

away, you may be sure of that. I've already been practising standing still for ages, in my bedroom, in exactly that position. Buster simply can't understand it. He does all he can to make me move!'

The others laughed. They could quite well picture Fatty standing solemnly in his room, perfectly still, with a most astonished Buster trying in vain to get a movement or a sound out of him!

'Come on – let's go now,' said Fatty. 'It's much too hot in here. Hello – there's Mr Goon – and in uniform again! He looks better in uniform than in plainclothes, I must say. Not that he's much to look at in either!'

Mr Goon was standing just outside the waxworks hall, apparently about to go in. He scowled when he saw the children. Funny how those kids always seemed to turn up everywhere!

'What you doing here?' he asked, in a suspicious voice.

'Passing the time away, Mr Goon, just passing the time,' said Fatty airily. 'What are *you* doing here? Is your holiday over? You must miss your little trips to the sweetshop.'

Buster was on the lead, or he would certainly

have darted at his enemy. But Fatty, seeing the black look on Mr Goon's face, hastily dragged him away.

'Wonder what he's done with that grocery list!' said Daisy, with a giggle. 'Put it with his clues, I expect. Well, we know more about that than he does!'

Bets wanted to go down by the river, so the others went, too, meaning to walk home by the river path. Bets stared hard at everyone in boats, and Pip noticed her.

'Why ever are you glaring at everyone who's in a boat?' he asked.

'I'm not glaring,' said Bets. 'I'm just looking to see if I can spot anyone with odd eyes, that's all. I did see the odd-eyed man in a boat, you know, when that punt knocked against me – and I might quite well see him again.

'What would you do if you did?' demanded Pip. 'Jump in and arrest him?'

'It's quite a good idea of Bets,' said Fatty, always quick to defend the little girl. 'After all, if the man was in a boat once, he might be again. And if we saw him on the river we could get the name of the boat, and, if it was privately owned, we could find out the name of the owner.'

'The only thing is – people go by so quickly that it's difficult to see if their eyes are odd or not,' said Bets.

'I say, Fatty, how are you going to get your face all pink like Napoleon's?' asked Larry, looking at Fatty's very brown face.

'Easy,' said Fatty. 'I shall put a little layer of pink wax all over my face and let it set. I know how to do it. It's in a book I've got.'

Fatty had the most extraordinary collection of books. He seemed to be able to find out from them anything he wanted.

'You'll have to do that before you set out, won't you?' said Daisy. Fatty nodded.

'Yes. Larry will have to go with me if the night isn't dark enough to hide me, and warn me if anyone is coming who might be likely to spot me. But now that there's no moon, I ought not to be noticed much in the twilight.'

'I do want Tuesday to come!' said Bets. 'I really can hardly wait! I wish I was going to see you all dressed up as Napoleon, Fatty. You'll look simply grand. Oh, Tuesday, hurry up and come!'

15. TUESDAY NIGHT AT LAST

Tuesday night did come at last. For once in a way it was a cloudy night, and it almost looked as if the longed-for rain was coming. It was a little cooler, and everyone was thankful.

'How are you going to manage about your father and mother tonight?' asked Pip. 'I mean – you want to set off about 7.30, don't you? And that's the time you have dinner with them.'

'They're away for a couple of nights,' said Fatty. 'Bit of luck, that. Larry, you come to dinner with me, and we'll have it at seven, together. Then you can walk down with me to the hall, to make sure no one will see me.'

'Right,' said Larry. 'I will. Wish I was going to come into the hall with you, too, and see everything. Will you come back and tell us what's happened, Fatty, even if it's very late? I'll keep awake.'

'All right. But I'd better not go to Pip's,' said

Fatty. 'Mrs Hilton is sure to hear me if I call up to Pip. Her room is just nearby.'

'Oh, *Fatty*! We can't possibly wait till the morning!' cried Bets.

'You'll have to,' said Fatty. 'I can't go round to you all and tell you what's happened. Anyway, you'll be fast asleep, Bets!'

'I shan't. I shan't sleep a wink all night,' said Bets.

The day dragged by very slowly. At half past six Fatty left Pip's, with Larry, and the two of them went to Fatty's house. They were to have dinner early, at seven – then their adventure would begin. All the children felt excited, but only Fatty did not show it. He appeared to be as calm as ever.

The two boys made a very good meal indeed. Then Fatty put the pink stuff on his face and after that they set out to go down to the river. They meant to take the path over the fields, then go by the water side, and so come to the Fair without meeting a lot of people.

They arrived at the waxworks hall. 'How are you going to get in?' whispered Larry, suddenly seeing that the place was shut and in darkness.

'Didn't you spot me undoing the catch of one of

the windows when we were here this morning?' whispered Fatty. 'I'm going to get in there. I say – what about you coming in too, in case I get into difficulties over dressing? You can easily hop out of the window afterwards.'

'Yes, I will,' said Larry, pleased at the idea of watching Fatty dress himself as Napoleon. 'Where's the window?'

'It's this one,' said Fatty, and looked cautiously round. 'Anyone about? Not a soul! Here goes, then!'

He opened the window quietly, hauled himself up and dropped down into the hall. Larry followed. The boys shut the window carefully, in case anyone noticed that it was open.

The hall wasn't dark, because a lamp from the Fair nearby shone into it, and gave a faint and rather eerie light to the still waxworks.

The boys looked round them. The figures somehow seemed more alive than in the daytime, and Larry gave a little shiver. Silly fancies crept into his head. Suppose wax figures came alive at night and walked and talked! What a dreadful shock it would give him and Fatty!

'They all seem to be looking at us,' whispered

Larry. 'They make me feel quite creepy. Look at Nelson – he's watching us all the time!'

'Idiot!' said Fatty, walking over to Napoleon. 'Come on – help me to undress him, Larry.'

It was a funny business, undressing the rather plump figure of the wax Napoleon. It wasn't easy, either, because Napoleon didn't help in any way! In fact, it almost seemed as if he quite deliberately tried to make things difficult for the two boys!

'If only he'd raise his arms a bit, or give a wriggle, or something,' whispered Larry. 'We could get his things off easily then. But he just makes himself as stiff as possible!'

Fatty chuckled. 'I'd get a shock if he *did* raise his arms or wriggle!' he said. 'I'd just as soon he didn't. There – his coat's off, thank goodness – but I've torn his high collar a bit. Now for his trousers.'

Soon poor Napoleon stood stiff and straight in nothing but some kind of shapeless under-garment. The boys lifted him up and carried him to a cupboard. They put him inside and shut the door. Then Fatty proceeded to undress himself very quickly. He stuffed his own clothes into the cupboard with Napoleon.

Then, with Larry's help he put on Napoleon's clothes. They fitted him quite well, and he only had to use one of Daisy's safety pins. He pulled on the coat, and the medals made a little jingling noise.

'Fatty! You look marvellous in that uniform!' said Larry, in admiration. 'You honestly do! Now the hat – golly, it fits as if it was made for you!'

Fatty made Larry hold up a small mirror and looked at his face in it. It was all covered with pink, and looked very like the faces of the wax figures around. Fatty pulled a strand of hair on to his forehead, just like the one the wax Napoleon had had. Then he put his hand under his coat, stood absoutely still and stiff, and stared straight in front of him.

Larry couldn't find enough words of praise. 'Nobody, *nobody* could possibly guess you weren't a wax figure!' he said. 'You're marvellous, Fatty! Honestly, you're more of a wax figure than Napoleon was before! I wish you could see yourself, I really do. Golly, it's wonderful!'

Fatty was pleased. He beamed modestly at Larry, but not too broadly in case the wax on his face cracked a bit.

'It's only your eyes that are different from the other wax figures,' said Larry. 'They've got a proper light in them – the others haven't. Yours shine.'

'Well, I hope they won't shine too much!' said Fatty. 'Now, you'd better go, Larry, old boy. It's about half past eight, isn't it? The men might be here early.'

'Right,' said Larry – and then he suddenly stood stock-still in fright. It sounded as if someone was fumbling at the door of the hall!

'Go, quickly!' said Fatty, in a whisper, and Larry fled, threading his way carefully between the silent figures till he came to the window at the back of the hall. He opened it cautiously, climbed up and dropped out, shutting it again at once. He dived under a bush and sat there, hardly daring to breathe, mopping his forehead with his handkerchief.

He pictured the gang walking in silently, and he felt glad he was not Fatty, all alone there, hidden in the rows of waxwork figures. Golly, he'd only got out just in time!

Fatty was waiting in the greatest excitement for the hall door to open. Who would come in? The leader of the gang? All the men? Would he know any of them?

The fumbling at the door went on. Somebody seemed to be having difficulty with the key. But at last it turned and the door opened quietly. Somebody stepped in, and shut the door – and locked it! Why lock it? Fatty was puzzled. Weren't the others coming in too, then?

The silent-footed person moved down the hall, and the light from the Fair lamp outside shone down on him. Fatty got a most tremendous shock.

It was Mr Goon!

Mr Goon! thought Fatty, and he almost fell off his step. Old Clear-Orf! *Mr Goon*! But – is he one of the gang then? Mr Goon here, with the thieves! What's it all mean?

Mr Goon proceeded to do a few very peculiar things. He walked behind Fatty, until he came to one of the wax figures. Fatty did not know which one, for he dared not move or turn round to see what Mr Goon was doing.

Mr Goon then lifted up the figure, and, panting noisily, carried it to a big window, where a voluminous curtain hung. Then Fatty was able to see which figure Mr Goon was carrying.

It was the wax policeman! Mr Goon carefully placed him behind the curtain, and then creaked back to the place where the wax figure had stood.

And, in a flash, Fatty understood everything. He almost groaned in disappointment.

Of course – Mr Goon has read the secret message in that grocery list after all – he found out, as we did, that a meeting of the gang will be held here tonight – and he got the same brain-wave too. He thought he'd come and be one of the wax figures, and listen in to everything! Golly – he's got more brains and pluck than I'd have thought he had!

Poor Fatty! It was a great shock and disappointment to him to know that the policeman would hear everything, and be able to solve the mystery after all. He would know the gang – and their plans – and would be able to arrest the whole lot of them at once!

But surely he wouldn't dare to tackle the whole gang single-handed? No – that couldn't be his plan. Then what was it? Fatty stood and puzzled his brains, angry and miserable to think that Mr Goon should have been clever enough to think of exactly the same idea as the Find-Outers.

But it was much more difficult for *me*, thought Fatty. I had to undress the figure of Napoleon and dress myself up again – Mr Goon only had to go and stand in the place of the wax policeman. We always did think that that wax figure was like Mr Goon! Blow! Everything's spoilt.

Fatty would have given anything to turn round and see what Mr Goon looked like, standing stiffly there some way behind him. Mr Goon was breathing very heavily, as he always did when he was excited. Fatty wondered if he would remember to breathe quietly when the gang came in! Then Mr Goon did a little cough, and cleared his throat.

Of course, he thinks there's nobody here at all, thought Fatty. So it doesn't matter what noises he makes. I want to cough, myself – but I daren't, because Mr Goon would be very suspicious at once. What a shock it would give him, to hear one of the waxworks cough. I wonder if he'd get scared and go flying out of the hall at once! No, I don't think he would!

Mr Goon shuffled his feet a little and sniffed.

Then he got out his handkerchief and blew his nose.

Fatty immediately wanted to blow his too! It was most irritating wanting to sniff and cough and blow his nose when he dared not make a single movement. Fatty disliked Mr Goon intensely at that moment. Spoiling everything! Enjoying himself sniffing and coughing. Waiting for his big moment – and thinking of promotion!

There came the sound of voices outside. Then a key was put into the door, and it opened. Ho! thought Fatty, Mr Goon had a duplicate key, had he? He made his plans well. Locked the door after him, too, so that the men shouldn't get suspicious, as they would have if the door had been unlocked!

Four men came in. Fatty strained his eyes to try and see what their faces were like. But one and all wore soft hats pulled well down over their foreheads. They did not light a lamp, nor did they even use torches. The faint light from the Fair lamp outside seemed to be enough for them.

They got chairs and sat down. They waited for a while, saying nothing. Fatty wondered why. Then he knew.

'Where's Number Three?' said one of the men

impatiently. 'He ought to be here. Didn't you warn him, Number Five?'

'Yes, I sent him a message,' said another man. 'In a cigarette I gave to old Johnny. He'll turn up soon.'

They waited in silence again. One of the men pulled out a watch and looked at it.

'Can't wait any longer,' he said. 'The job's on tonight.'

'Tonight?' said another man. 'Where? All of us in it this time, or not?'

'All of us,' said the first man. 'Except Number Three, as he's not here. It's the Castleton pearls tonight.'

'Whew!' said two of the men. 'Big stuff!'

'Very big,' said the first man. 'Now see here – these are the plans. You, Number Two, have got to drive the car, and you . . .'

Fatty and Mr Goon watched and listened intently. Mr Goon remembered not to breathe loudly, and as for Fatty, he was so excited that he hardly breathed at all. They heard all the details of the new robbery to be pulled off that night. But try as he would Fatty could not see clearly the face of any of the men at all.

He began to think hard. The men would soon be gone. Once they were gone he would get to the telephone and tell the Inspector all he knew – and the robbery could be stopped. Then he remembered Mr Goon. Blow! Mr Goon would be in charge of this, not Fatty.

Poor Mr Goon was not feeling very happy just at that moment. He wanted to sneeze. He could feel it coming quite distinctly. He swallowed violently and wriggled his nose about. No – that sneeze meant to come. Whooosh-ooo!

16. MR GOON PLAYS A MEAN TRICK

It wasn't a very big sneeze, because Mr Goon had tried most valiantly to stop it, and it came out in quite a gentlemanly manner. But it was enough to startle all the men, and Fatty too, almost out of their skins!

The men sprang to their feet at once, and looked all round the hall. 'What was that? There's somebody here! Somebody spying on us!'

Fatty was suddenly frightened. The men's eyes gleamed under their hats, and he could hear a savage tone in the voice of the man who spoke. The boy kept absolutely still. Silly, idiotic old Mr Goon, to give the game away like that!

'There's somebody here! Who is it? Show yourself!' shouted one of the men. Neither Mr Goon nor Fatty made any movement, and all the wax figures stared stolidly at the group of men.

'It's creepy in here, with all those figures looking

at us,' said the first man. 'But one of them's real! No doubt about that! Come on – we'll soon find out. I've got a torch.'

Fatty's heart beat fast. He hoped and hoped that the men would find Mr Goon before they found him. But most unfortunately Fatty was in the front row, and Mr Goon wasn't.

One of the men had a powerful torch. He walked over to Nelson and flashed it in his face. Nelson stared unblinkingly in front of him. 'He's wax all right,' said the man, and passed to the next figure, a tall soldier. He flashed the torch in his face.

The soldier didn't make a movement at all. It was obvious that he was wax, for there was a little crack down one cheek, where he had once struck his face, when being carried from one place to another.

One after another the wax figures had the torch flashed into their faces, and one after another they stared unblinkingly past the man's head. Fatty began to tremble a little. Would he be able to stare without blinking too? He hoped so.

His turn came. The torch was flashed suddenly in his face, and the boy could not help a sudden blink. His eyes did it automatically, although he did his best not to. He hoped the man hadn't noticed. But there was something about Fatty's bright, shining, living eyes that caught the man's attention at once, as well as the blink. He grabbed at Fatty's arm, and felt it to be warm and soft.

'Here he is!' he said. 'Here's the spy. Standing here staring at us, listening to everything!'

Poor Fatty was dragged down off his step and pulled into the middle of the hall. He was frightened, but he meant to put a bold face on it.

'Who are you?' said the first man, and shone his torch into Fatty's face.

'Napoleon,' said Fatty, trying to brave things out. 'Just doing it for a joke!'

'He's only a boy,' said one of the men, pulling off Napoleon's hat. 'How old are you?'

'Fourteen,' said Fatty.

The men stared at him. 'What are we going to do with him?' said one. 'Can't take him off in the car with us – too risky. And we can't waste time dumping him anywhere, because if we're not on time with this job, we'll fail. What he wants is a jolly good questioning and a good thrashing, and he'll get it – but not now. It's time we went.'

'We'll be back here again tonight with the stuff,' said another man. 'We'll tie him up, gag him, put him into the cupboard over there, and lock him in. He can't give the game away then. We'll deal with him when we come back. He can't know anything about the job tonight, except what he's just heard, so he won't have warned anyone.'

'Right,' said the other men, and then began a bad time for poor Fatty. He was rolled up in a curtain, with his hands and feet tied, and a big handkerchief was bound across his mouth. Then he was popped into the cupboard with Napoleon, and the door was shut and locked on him.

His only comfort was that Mr Goon was still there, posing stolidly, quite unsuspected. As soon as the men had got away, Mr Goon would surely come to his rescue and untie him. Then he, Fatty, would be in at the last, after all.

He could hear nothing in the cupboard. He did not hear the men go out of the hall and lock the door. He did not see Mr Goon wait on his step for a few moments and then relax and give a deep sigh. Mr Goon had had a most surprising and unpleasant time himself from the moment he had sneezed to the moment the men had at last gone.

When he had sneezed, he had felt certain that the men would search the figures and find him. He had no idea at all, of course, that Fatty had been one of the figures too. When the boy had been found and hauled off his stand, Mr Goon's eyes had almost fallen out of his head. What – somebody else in the hall – somebody who must have been there when Mr Goon himself had come in and changed places with the wax policeman? Who was it!

Mr Goon recognised Fatty's voice as soon as the boy had spoken. He went purple with rage. That interfering boy again! So he, like Mr Goon himself, had read the secret message – and he hadn't told the police. The bad, wicked . . . well, words failed Mr Goon as he stood there thinking about Fatty.

The policeman shook when he thought that the men would probably find him next. When they did not think of looking any further, his heart beat a little less fast. Well, serve that boy right, if he got caught! He deserved to! Keeping information from the police! Mr Goon's face went red again.

He had been so very pleased with himself at thinking of this idea – posing as the wax policeman, and listening in to the gang and their plans. Well, he knew a lot now, he did – and if only those men would go off to the job and leave him alone, he'd soon do a spot of telephoning, and arrange to catch them all neatly – red-handed, too! Mr Goon glowed when he thought of it.

But the men hadn't gone yet. They were tying up that boy. The policeman watched with pleased eyes the efficient way in which the men rolled Fatty up in the curtain, his hands and legs well and truly bound, and a handkerchief over his mouth. Ha! That was the way to treat people like Fatty!

Mr Goon watched the men pop Fatty into the cupboard and turn the key on him. Good! Now that boy was properly out of the way. If only the men would go, Mr Goon could step down and get busy. He smiled as he thought of how busy he would get. Inspector Jenks would be surprised at his news. Yes, and pleased, too.

The door closed and the men were gone. Mr Goon heard the sound of a car starting up. He thought it would be safe to step down into the hall, and he stood there, looking round, feeling extremely pleased with himself.

Fatty was struggling hard in the cupboard. He had read books that told him the best way to wriggle free of bonds, but, except that he had managed to get his mouth away from the handkerchief, he wasn't having much luck with his hands and feet! He did all the things the books had advised him to, but it was no good. He couldn't get his hands free.

In his struggles, he fell against Napoleon, and that gentleman over-balanced, and struck his head against the back of the cupboard. He then rolled on to Fatty, who yelled.

Mr Goon, about to open the door and go out, heard the yell. He paused. He didn't mean to set Fatty free. Not he! That boy had got what he deserved, at last, and he, Mr Goon, wasn't going to rob him of it. No – let him stay in the cupboard and think about things. Maybe he'd think it was best not to interfere with the law again.

But when Napoleon fell with such a crash, Mr Goon felt a stirring of his conscience. Suppose that boy was being suffocated? Suppose that handkerchief stopped his breathing? Suppose he'd wriggled about, and fallen and hurt himself? He was a friend of the Inspector's, wasn't he, though goodness knew why the Inspector should bother himself with a boy like that. Still. . . .

Mr Goon thought he might spare half a minute to investigate. But he wasn't going to unlock that cupboard. No, not he! He wasn't going to have that there boy rushing out on him, all untied, and playing some more of his tricks. No, Fatty was safer locked up in a cupboard.

So Mr Goon went cautiously to the cupboard and knocked smartly on the door. Fatty's struggles ceased at once.

'Who's that?'

'Mr Goon,' said the policeman.

'Thank goodness!' said Fatty fervently. 'Unlock the door and untie me, Mr Goon. We've work to do! Have those men gone?'

Mr Goon snorted. Did this boy really think he was going to let him help him! After he had deliberately not told him about that secret message, too!

'You're all right in there,' said Mr Goon, 'you

don't want to come messing about with thieves and robbers, you don't!'

Fatty couldn't believe his ears. Did Mr Goon really mean he was going to leave him there, in the cupboard, when all the fun was going on? He wriggled about in agony at the thought, and spoke beseechingly.

'Mr Goon! Be a sport! Unlock the door and let me out!'

'Why should I?' demanded Mr Goon. 'Did you tell me about that secret message? No, you didn't. And I know your parents wouldn't want you mixed up in this business tonight, see? They'll thank me for leaving you here. I'll come and get you later, when we've done all the arresting and everything.'

Fatty was desperate. To think of Mr Goon doing it all, whilst he was shut up in this smelly cupboard!

'Mr Goon! Don't be mean. It was *your* sneeze gave the show away – and instead of catching *you*, they caught *me*. It's not fair.'

Mr Goon laughed. It was rather a nasty laugh. Fatty's heart sank when he heard it. He knew then that the policeman meant to leave him where he was. He could make all kinds of excuses for it – that he hadn't time to free Fatty – that he meant to come back almost at once – anything would do. Blow Mr Goon!

'Well – see you later,' said Mr Goon, and he walked over to the door. Fatty groaned. Now he would have to stay in the cupboard till the fun was over. It was too bad. After all his fine plans, too! What would Inspector Jenks say? He would be very pleased with Mr Goon, who certainly had used his brains in this mystery, and worked hard on it.

Poor Fatty! He lay in the cupboard in great discomfort, with rope biting into his wrists and ankles. It was all Mr Goon's fault. What did he want to go and sneeze like that for, and give the game away? He had come out of it very well himself – but he had messed everything up for poor old Fatty.

Suddenly Fatty heard a slight sound and he pricked his ears up. It sounded like the window opening. Was there somebody coming in? Was one of the gang coming back?

Then Fatty heard a low voice – a voice he knew very well indeed.

'Fatty! Are you here anywhere? Fatty!'

It was Larry! Fatty's heart beat for joy and he struggled to a sitting position in the cupboard. 'Larry! I'm locked up in the cupboard where we put Napoleon! Let me out! Quick, let me out!'

17. MR. GOON GETS A FEW SHOCKS

Larry rushed over to the cupboard. The key was still in the lock. He turned it and the door opened. And there was poor Fatty, still wrapped up in the curtain.

'Fatty! What's happened?' cried Larry. 'Are you hurt?'

'Not a bit – except that my wrists and ankles are aching with the rope round them,' said Fatty. 'Got a knife, Larry? Cut the rope.'

Larry cut the ropes, and soon Fatty was unwrapping himself from the curtain. He tossed it into a corner with the cut ropes. He took off Napoleon's uniform, and put on his own clothes. Then he shut and locked the cupboard door.

'Oh Larry!' he said, 'wasn't I glad to hear your voice! But don't let's talk in here. Let's get back home, quick!'

'My parents think I'm in bed,' said Larry. 'I'll come to your house, if you like. Your parents won't be there, will they? Come on.'

'Right. We'll tell about everything when we get back,' said Fatty.

They made their way back over the fields as fast as they could. They soon got to Fatty's house and let themselves in cautiously. They went up to his room and Fatty flung himself on the bed, rubbing his ankles ruefully.

'Larry! How did you manage to come back and rescue me?' he asked. 'I'd have been there for hours, if you hadn't. That beast Mr Goon wouldn't let me out. Now – you tell me your story first.'

'There isn't really anything to tell,' said Larry. 'I went back home and told Daisy all we'd done. And then, about half past nine, when I was in bed, Pip turned up, and threw stones at my window.'

'Whatever for?' said Fatty.

'Well, Bets sent him,' said Larry. 'Pip said she was awfully upset, and wouldn't go to sleep, and kept crying and saying she knew you had got into danger. You know the silly feelings Bets gets sometimes.'

'So Pip, thinking it would be fun to hear how you'd got on, dressing me up as Napoleon, told Bets he'd go round and see you,' said Fatty. 'It would make Bets feel better, and be a bit of excitement for old Pip. I see that – but what made you come along down to the waxwork hall?'

'I don't exactly know,' said Larry. 'You know, once before Bets got the idea that you were in danger, and it turned out she was right. And I just thought – well, I thought it might be a good idea if I slipped down to the waxwork hall and just had a snoop round to see what was happening.'

'Golly! I'm glad Bets had one of her feelings,' said Fatty thankfully. 'And I'm glad you came down, Larry, old boy.'

'So am I,' said Larry. 'When I got there, the hall was in darkness and there was nobody about at all. So I opened that window, got in, and called your name. That's all.'

There was a silence. Fatty suddenly looked extremely gloomy. 'What's up?' said Larry. 'You haven't told me what happened yet – or why you got locked up. Were you discovered after all?'

Fatty began his tale. Larry listened in astonishment. So Mr Goon had been there too! When Fatty came to Mr Goon's sneeze, and related how he, Fatty, had been caught because of it, and not Mr Goon, Larry was most sympathetic.

'Poor old Fatty! So Mr Goon got all the information, left you there, the beast, and has gone to do the arresting and reporting. Quite a busy evening for him!'

'He said he'd come back and let me out of that cupboard when the fun was over,' said Fatty, beginning to grin. 'He'll be surprised to find I'm gone, won't he?'

'He will,' said Larry. 'He won't know what's happened. Let's pretend to him that we don't know where you are, shall we? We'll go and ask him about you tomorrow – he'll have twenty fits if he thinks you've vanished. He won't know *what* to think!'

'And he'll feel most uncomfortable because he'll know he jolly well ought to have let me out,' said Fatty. 'Well, I'm going to bed, Larry. You'd better go and get some sleep too. Oh, I do feel so disappointed – after all our work and disguises and plans – for Mr Goon to solve the mystery and get all the credit!'

The boys parted and Larry ran swiftly home. He wondered what Mr Goon was doing. He thought about the Castleton Mansion and wondered if the thieves were at work – if the house was being quietly surrounded – if Mr Goon was doing some arresting. Well, maybe it would all be in the papers tomorrow.

Mr Goon had certainly done some good work that night. He had surrounded the mansion with men whilst the thieves were actually inside. He had arrested all four of them – although one, alas, had got away in the struggle – and Mr Goon was feeling very pleased with himself indeed. The escaped thief would soon be caught. Not a doubt of that.

It wasn't until past midnight that Mr Goon suddenly remembered that he had left Fatty locked up in the cupboard in the waxworks hall.

Drat that boy! he thought. I could go to bed now, and sleep easy, if it wasn't for getting him out of that cupboard. He's had a nice long time there to think over all his misdeeds, he has. Well, I'd better get along and let him out – and give him a few good words of advice too. He's missed all the fun this time – and *I've* solved this mystery, not him! Ha!

Mr Goon cycled down to the waxworks hall

and, leaving his bicycle outside, went into the hall. He switched on his torch and walked to the cupboard. He rapped smartly on it.

'Hey, you!' he said. 'Ready to be let out yet? We've done everything, and now that the fun's over, you can come along out!'

There was no answer. Mr Goon rapped loudly again, thinking that Fatty had gone to sleep. But still there was no answer. A little cold feeling crept round Mr Goon's heart. Surely that boy was all right?

Hurriedly Mr Goon turned the key in the lock and opened the door. He shone his light into the cupboard. Napoleon looked back at him, standing there in his under-garment – but no Fatty! Mr Goon's hands began to tremble. Where was that boy? He couldn't get out of a locked cupboard! Or could he? Mr Goon remembered how Fatty had apparently passed mysteriously through a locked door in the last mystery.

Mr Goon poked Napoleon in the ribs to make sure he was wax, and not Fatty. Napoleon did not flinch. He looked straight at Mr Goon. Yes, he was wax all right.

Mr Goon shut the door, puzzled and upset. Now where was that boy? Had somebody carried him off? He had seen him bound and gagged, so he couldn't have escaped by himself. Well then, what had happened?

Mr Goon went home slowly, pedalling with heavy feet. He ought to have let that boy free before he had gone after the gang. Suppose he didn't turn up in the morning? What explanation could he give to the Inspector? He was seeing him at ten o'clock.

Mr Goon gave a heavy sigh. He had been looking forward to that interview – now he wasn't so sure. That boy was very friendly with the Inspector. If it came out that anything had happened to him, Inspector Jenks might ask some very very awkward questions. Drat the boy!

Fatty slept soundly that night, tired out with his adventures. Mr Goon slept too, but not so soundly. He dreamt about his great success in arresting the gang – but every time he was about to receive words of praise from the Inspector, Fatty came into the dream, tied up, begging for help. It was most disturbing, because he woke Mr

Goon up each time, and then he found it hard to go to sleep again.

At nine o'clock the Five Find-Outers were all together in Pip's garden, going over and over the happenings of the night before. All of them were most indignant with Mr Goon for leaving Fatty in the cupboard.

'We're going to make him think Fatty's been spirited away,' said Larry, with a grin. 'We'll wait about the village for him, and each time he passes any of us we'll ask him if he's heard anything of Fatty.'

So, at half past nine, the children, with the exception of Fatty, of course, hung about near Mr Goon's house, waiting for him to come out. Larry was at the corner, Pip was near the house, and Daisy and Bets were not far off.

Larry gave a whistle when he saw Mr Goon coming out, wheeling his bicycle, ready to ride over to see the Inspector. He looked very smart indeed, for he had brushed his uniform, cleaned his belt and helmet and shoes, and polished his buttons till they shone. He was the very picture, he hoped, of a smart policeman awaiting promotion.

'I say, Mr Goon!' called Pip, as the policeman prepared to mount his bicycle. 'Do you know where our friend, Frederick, is?'

'Why should I?' scowled Mr Goon, but his heart sank. So that boy had vanished!

'Well, we just wondered,' said Pip. 'I suppose you haven't seen him at all?'

Mr Goon couldn't say that. He mounted his bicycle and rode off, his face red. He hoped that boy Fatty wasn't going to cause a lot of trouble, just as he, Mr Goon, had got things going so very nicely.

He passed Daisy and Bets. Daisy called out 'Oh, Mr Goon! Have you seen Fatty? Do tell us if you have!'

'I don't know where he is,' said Mr Goon desperately, and cycled on. But at the corner, there was Larry!

'Mr Goon! Mr Goon! Have you seen Fatty? Do you know where he is? Do you think he's disappeared? Mr Goon, do tell us where he is. Have you locked him up?'

'Course not!' spluttered Mr Goon. 'He'll turn up. He'll turn up like a bad penny, you may be sure!'

He rode on, feeling most uncomfortable. Where

could the boy be? Had that thief who escaped gone back to the Hall, and taken Fatty? No, that couldn't be, surely. But WHERE WAS that boy?

The Inspector was waiting for Mr Goon in his office. On his desk were various reports of the happenings of the night before, sent in, not only by Mr Goon, but by two other policemen who had helped in the arrests, and by plainclothes detectives who had also been on the case.

He also had reports on what the three prisoners had said when questioned. Some smart work had been done, there was no doubt about that – but something was worrying the Inspector.

Mr Goon saw it as soon as he got into the office. He had hoped and expected to find his superior officer full of smiles and praise. But no – the Inspector looked rather solemn, and a bit worried. Why?

'Well, Goon,' said the Inspector, 'some good work appears to have been done on this case. But it's a pity about the pearls, isn't it?'

Mr Goon gaped. 'The pearls, sir? What about them? We've got them, sir – took them off one of the gang.'

'Ah, but you see – they are not the stolen pearls,' said the Inspector gently. 'No, Goon – they are just a cheap necklace the man was going to give his girl! The *real* pearls have vanished!'

18. THE MYSTERY IS NOT YET ENDED

Mr Goon's mouth opened and shut like a goldfish. He simply couldn't believe his ears.

'But, sir – we got the thieves red-handed. And the one that escaped was only the one on guard in the garden, sir. He hadn't anything to do with the thieving. It was the three upstairs who did that – and we've got them.'

'Yes, you've got them, and that was a very good bit of work, as I said,' said the Inspector. 'But I'm afraid, Goon, that one of the upstairs thieves, when he knew the game was up, simply threw the pearls out of the window to the man below. He must have pocketed them, and then, when he was arrested, struggled so violently that he managed to escape – *with* the pearls. Pity, isn't it?'

Mr Goon was most dismayed. True, they had got three of the gang – but the pearls were gone. He had waited to catch the men red-handed – had actually let them take the pearls, because he felt so certain he could get them back, when the men were arrested – and now, after all, the robbery had been successful. One of the gang had got them, and would no doubt get rid of them in double quick time.

'It's – it's most unfortunate, sir,' said poor Mr Goon.

'Well – let's hear your tale,' said the Inspector. 'You only had time to send in a very short report – what's all this about posing as a waxwork?'

Mr Goon was proud of this bit, and he related it all in full to the interested Inspector. But when he came to the part where he had sneezed, and the men had caught Fatty, instead of himself, Inspector Jenks sat up straight.

'Do you mean to tell me that Frederick Trotteville was there?' he said. 'Posing too? What as?'

'Napoleon, sir,' said Goon. 'Interfering as usual. That boy can't keep his nose out of things, he can't. Well, sir, when the men had gone to do the robbery, I crept out after them, and I went to the telephone box and . . .'

'Wait a bit, wait a bit,' said the Inspector. 'What happened to Frederick?'

'Him? Oh well – nothing much,' said Goon, trying to gloss over this bit as quickly as possible. 'They just tied him up a bit, sir, and chucked him into a cupboard. They didn't hurt him. Of course, if they'd started any rough stuff with him, I'd have gone for them, sir.'

'Of course,' said the Inspector gravely. 'Well I suppose you went and untied him and let him out of the cupboard before you rushed off to telephone.'

Mr Goon went rather red. 'Well, sir – to tell you the truth, sir, I didn't think I had the time – and also, sir, it was a dangerous business last night, and I didn't think that boy ought to be mixed up in it. He's a terror for getting into the middle of things, sir, that boy is, and . . .'

'Goon,' said the Inspector, and the policeman stopped abruptly and looked at his superior. He was looking very grave. 'Goon. Do you mean to say you left the boy tied up in a locked cupboard? I can hardly believe it of you. What time did you let him out?'

Mr Goon swallowed nervously. 'I went back, sir, about midnight – and I unlocked the cupboard door, sir – and – and the cupboard was empty.'

'Good heavens!' said the Inspector, startled. 'Do you know what had happened to Frederick?'

'No, sir,' said Mr Goon. The Inspector reached out for one of his five telephones.

'I must ring his home to see if he is all right,' he said.

Mr Goon looked more downcast than ever. 'He's – well, he seems to have vanished, sir,' he said. The Inspector put down the telephone, and stared at Mr Goon.

'Vanished! What do you mean? This is very serious indeed.'

'Well, sir – all I know is that the other kids – the ones he's always with – they keep on asking me if I know where their friend is,' said Mr Goon desperately. 'And if they don't know – well, he might be anywhere!'

'I must look into the matter at once,' said the Inspector. 'I'll get in touch with his parents. Now finish your story quickly, so that I can get on to this matter of Frederick Trotteville at once.'

So poor Mr Goon had to cut short his wonderful story, and blurt out quickly the rest of the night's happenings. He felt very down in the mouth as he cycled back home. The pearls had gone after all! What a blow! And now this wretched boy had disappeared, and there would be no end of a fuss about him. Privately Mr Goon thought it would be a very good thing if Fatty disappeared for good. Oh, why hadn't he let him out of that cupboard last night? He had known that he ought to – but it had seemed such a very good way of paying out that interfering boy!

Where could Fatty be? Mr Goon pondered the matter deeply as he turned into the village street. Had the escaped thief gone back to the Hall, and taken Fatty prisoner, meaning to hold him up for ransom, or something? Mr Goon went cold at the thought. If such a thing happened, he would be held up to scorn by everyone for not having freed Fatty when he could.

He was so deep in thought that he did not see a small dog run at his bicycle. He wobbled, and fell off, landing with a bump on the road. The dog flew round him in delight, barking lustily.

'Clear orf!' shouted Mr Goon angrily, and suddenly recognised Buster. 'Will you clear orf!'

He looked round to see who was in charge of

Buster – and his mouth fell wide open. He was so astonished that he couldn't get up, but went on sitting down in the road, with Buster making little darts at him.

Fatty was standing there, grinning down at him. *Fatty!* Mr Goon stared at him. Here he'd been reporting to the Inspector that Fatty had vanished – and the Inspector had gone all hot and bothered about it – and now here was that same boy, grinning down at him, large as life and twice as natural.

'Where've you been?' said Mr Goon at last, feebly pushing Buster away.

'Home,' said Fatty. 'Why?'

'*Home*?' said Mr Goon. 'You've been at home? Why, the others kept asking me where you were, see? And I reported your disappearance to the Inspector. He's going to start searching for you.'

'But Mr Goon – why?' asked Fatty innocently. 'I'm here. And I got home all right last night, too. All the same, it was jolly mean of you to leave me in that cupboard. I shan't forget that in a hurry.'

Mr Goon got up. 'How did you get out of that there cupboard?' he asked. 'All tied up you were, too. Do you mean to say you untied yourself, and unlocked that cupboard and got out all by yourself?'

'You never know, do you?' said Fatty. 'Well so long, Mr Goon – and do telephone the Inspector to tell him not to start searching for me. I'll be at home if he wants me!'

He went off with Buster, and poor Mr Goon was left to cycle home, his head spinning. 'That boy! First he's locked up, then he disappears, then he comes back again – and nobody knows how or when or why.' Mr Goon couldn't make head or tail of it.

He didn't enjoy ringing up the Inspector and reporting that he had just met Fatty.

'But *where* had he been?' said the Inspector, puzzled. 'Where was he last night?'

'Er – at home, sir,' said poor Mr Goon. 'It was the other children put me off, sir – asking me if I knew where he was, and all that, sir.'

The Inspector put down his receiver with an impatient click. Really, Goon was too idiotic at times! The Inspector sat looking at his telephone, thinking deeply. He had had reports from all kinds of people about this case – but not from one person, who appeared to know quite a lot about it

– and that was Frederick Trotteville! The Inspector made another telephone call. Fatty answered it.

'I want you to cycle over here this morning and answer a few questions, Frederick,' said the Inspector. 'Come straight along now.'

So, with Buster in his basket, Fatty rode off to the next town, wondering a little fearfully what the Inspector wanted to know. Would he think he had been mixing himself up in this mystery a bit too much? He had warned the Find-Outers not to get mixed up, because it might be dangerous.

The Inspector was friendly, but businesslike, and he listened to the whole of Fatty's tale with the greatest interest, especially to the tale of Fatty's various disguises.

'Most interesting,' he said. 'You've got a gift for that kind of thing, I can see. But don't over-do it. Now – you've heard all about the arrests, I suppose?'

'I only know what's in the paper this morning, sir,' said Fatty. 'I knew it was no good asking Mr Goon anything. I'm a bit fed up that he managed the mystery after all, whilst I was locked up in the cupboard.'

'He should have let you out,' said the Inspector

shortly. 'Very remiss of him. Not the kind of thing I expect from a police officer. Well, Frederick, three arrests were made, as you know – but the man on guard in the garden below escaped. And, most unfortunately, he appears to have escaped with the Castleton pearls!'

'But the papers said they were found in one of the arrested men's pockets!' said Fatty.

'We've got later news,' said Inspector Jenks. 'Those pearls were only cheap ones, bought by one of the men as a gift for his wife – or stolen from somewhere else probably. They're only worth a few pounds. The real pearls have gone.'

'I see,' said Fatty, and he cheered up considerably. 'So – the mystery isn't quite over, sir. We've got to find out where the pearls are? Can you find the man who escaped, do you think? He might split, and tell where he put the pearls.'

'We *have* got him,' said the Inspector grimly. 'The news came in ten minutes ago. But he hadn't got the pearls, and won't say where he's put them. But we happen to know that Number Three of the gang is usually the one who disposes of the stolen jewels – and it's likely that this fellow we've just arrested has put the pearls in some agreed place, for Number Three, whoever he is, to fetch, when all the hue and cry dies down.'

'You don't know who Number Three is, do you, sir?' asked Fatty.

'Haven't any idea,' said the Inspector. 'We more or less had our suspicions of the other four – but Number Three we've never been able to guess at. Now, Frederick, I'm not altogether pleased at the way you mixed yourself up in all this, when I warned you not to, because it was dangerous – now you just see if you can't solve the rest of the mystery, and find those pearls before Number Three does. There's no danger now – so you Five Find-Outers can go ahead.'

'Yes, sir,' said Fatty, looking rather subdued. 'We'll do our best. We've got just a few things to go on. I'll work them out and see what can be done. Thanks for giving us a chance to solve the mystery of the missing pearls! Good-bye, sir!'

19. NUMBER THREE AGAIN

Fatty went straight to Pip's. He felt sure he would find the rest of the Find-Outers there, waiting for him. They were outside the summerhouse, making Larry tell them over and over again all that had happened.

'Here's Fatty!' cried Bets. 'What did the Inspector say, Fatty? Wasn't he angry with Mr Goon for leaving you in that cupboard?'

'He wasn't very pleased with him – at least he didn't *sound* very pleased,' said Fatty. 'He didn't sound very pleased with me either! Seemed to think I shouldn't have got so mixed up in this mystery. But how *could* I keep out of it?'

'I expect he thought it was dangerous,' said Bets, 'and so it was, last night. Oh, Fatty, I knew you were in danger. I really, really did.'

'Good old Bets!' said Fatty, giving her a hug. 'I'm jolly glad you had one of your funny feelings about me – if you hadn't sent Pip to Larry, and Larry hadn't come along to the waxworks hall, goodness knows how long I'd have been shut up in that cupboard. By the way – the mystery is still not *quite* ended!'

Everyone sat up at once. 'What do you mean?' said Daisy.

Fatty explained about the missing pearls and Number Three. 'The Inspector thinks that Number Five, who escaped with the pearls last night, had time to put them in some safe place, before he was caught this morning. He will probably try and get a message to Number Three – the gang member who wasn't there last night and so is still at large – and till Number Three gets that message about the pearls and finds them, *anyone* might find them! And it's up to us to do it!'

'I see,' said Larry slowly. 'But how in the world can anyone find them if they don't even know where to look? It's impossible.'

'Nothing's impossible to a really good detective,' said Fatty. 'I agree that it's a very difficult mystery to solve – but I think if only we can get hold of Number Three somehow, and shadow him, he might lead us to the necklace!'

'What do you mean – shadow him?' asked Bets.

'Follow him, silly – always keep him in sight,' said Pip. 'Spot where he goes, or where he hangs about. He's sure to hang about the place where the pearls are, waiting for a chance to get them.'

'That's right,' said Fatty. 'The thing is – *who* is Number Three and how can we get hold of him?'

There was a silence. Nobody knew the answer.

'What do we know about Number Three?' said Fatty, considering. 'We know he rides a bike that has a hooter on it. We know he has odd eyes, one blue and one brown. And we know he rows a boat. I rather think, as we've seen him in Peterswood twice that he must live here.'

There was another silence. None of the things they knew about the odd-eyed man seemed to be of any help in finding him. Then Pip suddenly gave an exclamation.

'I think I know what to do!'

'What?' said everyone eagerly.

'Well, we're sure that Number Five hid the pearls somewhere, and we're pretty certain he'll get a message to Number Three, *some*how – has probably sent one already, in case he himself got caught by the police and put into prison. Now who would he send that message to, to deliver to Number Three?'

'The old man, Johnny, of course!' said Fatty. 'He's the one they always use, apparently, when they want to send messages to one another. So – if we watch old Johnny again – sooner or later we'll see Number Three go quietly up to him . . .'

'Sit down beside him – and receive the message!' said Larry. 'And if we shadow him, after that, we shall spot where he goes. Maybe he'll lead us straight to the necklace!'

Everyone felt much more cheerful and hopeful. 'That's a brain-wave of yours, Pip,' said Fatty. 'I'm surprised I didn't think of it myself. Very good.'

All the Find-Outers loved a word of praise from their leader. Pip went quite red with pleasure.

'I suppose that means we must go and sit in that smelly little lemonade shop again,' said Daisy. Fatty considered.

'Only one of us had better shadow Number Three closely,' he said. 'If he sees five of us tailing him he's bound to get a bit suspicious. I'll do the shadowing – if you don't mind, Pip, though it *was* your idea – and you can all follow me at a safe distance.'

'I don't mind a bit,' said Pip generously. 'I'm sure you'll be much better at shadowing than I shall. Where will you wait? And shall we have bikes or not?'

'Better have bikes,' said Larry. 'He was on a bike last time he went up to the old man. If he's walking we can always leave our bikes somewhere, and walk after him.'

'Yes, that's a sound idea,' said Fatty. 'What's the time? Almost dinnertime. The old fellow doesn't come out till the afternoon, so we'll meet just before two, at the bottom of my lane, with bikes.'

'But, Fatty, do you think the old man will come out and sit on your seat, after your warning, and after what he will have read in the papers today?' asked Larry. 'Won't he be afraid?'

'Yes, probably he will,' said Fatty. 'But if he has a message to deliver, I think he'll risk it. I bet the gang pay him well for this go-between business.'

Now that there was something to do again the Find-Outers felt very cheerful. They went to their dinners pleased that there was still a mystery to solve. If only they could find those pearls before Mr Goon did!

Mr Goon, of course, was exercising his mind too, about the missing pearls. He too knew that if only he could spot Number Three, he might be led to the pearls. But he had not got as far as reckoning out that it would be a good idea to watch old Johnny again, to see if Number Three came to receive a message!

That afternoon four of the Find-Outers sat in the little sweetshop, on the opposite side of the road to the bench where the old man so often sat. Fatty was not with them. He was leaning against a tree not far off, apparently deep in a paper, his bicycle beside him. He was watching for the old man to come. How he hoped he would!

The bicycles belonging to the others were piled against the side of the sweetshop. The four children in the shop were eating ices, and watching the bench opposite as keenly as Fatty was.

Some one came shuffling round the corner. Hurrah! It was the old man, complete with sniffle and cough. He sat himself down gingerly on the bench with a little groan, just exactly as Fatty used to do.

Then he bent himself over his stick handle and seemed to go to sleep. The children waited, whilst their ices melted in the saucers. Had Johnny got a message to deliver from Number Five to Number Three?

A noise made them jump violently. It was the sound of a hooter! Fatty jumped too. He lifted his head cautiously from his paper, and saw a man riding down the High Street on a bicycle. It had a hooter instead of a bell.

The man rode to the bench, hooted, and got off his bicycle. He stood his machine against the kerb and went to sit down on the bench close to the old man.

The old fellow did not even look up. How would he know if it was Number Three or not then? He was deaf and would not hear a whisper. Fatty puzzled his brains to think.

Of course! he thought suddenly. That loud hooter always tells the old man when Number Three is coming to sit on the bench beside him. Of course! Gosh, that's clever.

The old man took absolutely no notice of the other man. Fatty watched very carefully, but he could not see any movement of the old man's mouth, nor could he see the giving of any paper message.

For a few moments the two men sat together, and then old Johnny sat up a little straighter, and began to draw patterns in the dust with the end of his stick. Fatty watched more carefully to see if the old man was talking, under cover of his movements. But he could not make out that he was – unless he could talk without moving his lips, as a ventriloquist can!

After a minute or two the other man got up and went to his bicycle. He got on it, hooted, and rode slowly over to the sweetshop. The four children in there stiffened with excitement. What was he coming over there for?

Bets gave a gasp as he came in, and Pip kicked her under the table, afraid she might give them away. Bets took one look at the man and then began to finish her ice, making rather a noise with her spoon.

'Box of matches, please,' said the man, and put a coin down on the counter. Nobody liked to look at him in case he became suspicious of them.

He went out, lighting a cigarette. *'He's got odd*

eyes!' said Bets. 'He's the one! Hooter on his bike – and odd eyes! Oooh – it's getting exciting.'

Fatty, waiting by the tree outside, saw the man go in and out of the shop. The boy folded up his paper quickly, and mounted his bike as the man went swiftly by him. He followed him at a discreet distance, wondering if he had had any message, and if he was going to lead him to the pearls!

'Come on,' said Larry, going out of the shop quickly. 'We've got to follow too.'

The man rode down to the Fair. He wandered round a bit and then went to the hall of waxworks. But he only just put his head inside, and came out.

Fatty popped his head inside too, but except that it was full of people looking at the waxworks, there was nothing different to see. Napoleon was dressed and back in his place, and the red-headed boy was relating an extraordinary tale of how, in the night, Napoleon had apparently got out of his place, undressed and put himself to bed in a cupboard.

'Storyteller!' said some listening children. 'What a fib!'

'And what's more,' said the red-headed boy, thoroughly enjoying himself, 'that wax policeman over there – do you see him? Well, *he* got up in the night and went and stood himself behind that curtain. Such goings-on!'

Fatty longed to hear more of this, but the man he was following had gone, and Fatty had to go too, or lose him. The man had put his bicycle beside the hedge and padlocked the back wheel, so Fatty knew he meant to stay around for a while.

The other Find-Outers came up, and Fatty winked at them. 'Looks as if we're going to spend an hour or two in the Fair!' he said.

The man wandered about most aimlessly. He didn't even have a ride on the roundabout, or try for a hoopla gift, or go in a bumper car – he just trailed about. Every now and then he passed the waxworks hall, and looked inside. But he didn't go in at all. Fatty wondered if he was waiting for somebody to meet him there.

I don't believe he knows where the pearls are! thought Fatty. Or surely he'd go straight to them! My word what a crowd there is at the Fair today!

The man evidently thought the same. He asked a question about it of the man at the hoopla stall. 'Quite a crowd today! What's up?'

'Oh, it's a trip from Sheepsale, a kind of outing,' said the man. 'They're going at four o'clock, then the place will empty a bit. Good trade for us, though!'

The man nodded. Then he made his way through the crowd to his bicycle, and unpadlocked it. Fatty followed him. It was clear that the man couldn't do whatever he wanted to do, because the place was too crowded. Probably he would be coming back. It was up to Fatty to follow him. He would leave the others down in the Fair, because he was sure that he and the man would be back there sooner or later, when the trippers had gone.

He had time to give a quick message to Larry. Then off he went over the level-crossing on his bicycle, following the man as closely as he dared. Round the corner they went, the man hooting with his little hooter – parp-parp.

And round the corner on *his* bicycle came Mr Goon! The two almost collided. Mr Goon, who had heard the hooter, glued his eyes on the man at once. Was he Number Three? He must be! He seemed to be the only man within miles who had a hooter on his bicycle, instead of a bell, for some peculiar reason that Mr Goon couldn't guess.

Mr Goon made up his mind to follow Number Three at once, and keep him in sight. Visions of pearl necklaces floated in front of his eyes. Number Three knew where those pearls were, Mr Goon was sure of it. Off he went after Number Three.

And behind him went Fatty, annoyed and angry. Was Mr Goon going to get in first *again*! Mr Goon heard someone behind him and turned. He scowled.

That fat boy again! Was *he* after Number Three too. 'Gah!' said Mr Goon to himself. 'The interfering Toad!'

20. A NICE LONG RIDE - AND AN IDEA

And now, of course, Mr Goon spoilt simply everything! Number Three couldn't possibly help guessing that he was being shadowed by the fat, panting policeman! For one thing, Goon didn't keep a fair distance away, but pedalled closely to Number Three's bicycle – so close to it that if Number Three had to brake suddenly, his shadow would almost certainly bump into him!

Fatty cycled on, some way behind the other two, thinking hard. It was too bad of Old Clear-Orf to butt in like this, just as the Find-Outers had really got going again. For one moment Fatty knew what Mr Goon felt like, when others interfered! He, Fatty, had often interfered with the policeman's working out of a mystery – and now here was Mr Goon doing the same thing. And he'd done it the evening before, too, in the waxworks hall. It was most exasperating.

Number Three, giving occasional scowling glances behind him, saw that Mr Goon was hot on his trail. He didn't really need to look round him to see the policeman, because he could hear him well enough too – Mr Goon's puffs and pants were terrific.

A little grin curled the corners of Number Three's lips. Mr Goon wanted a bicycle ride, did he? All right then, he could have it, with pleasure. Number Three would take him for a long, long ride through the countryside, on this hot, sultry afternoon!

Fatty soon began to have an inkling of the way in which Number Three's mind was working, for the man suddenly seemed to have a tremendous desire to cycle up all the steep hills it was possible to find.

He was a strong, muscular fellow, and he sailed up the hills easily enough – but poor Mr Goon found it terribly hard work, and Fatty wasn't very happy either. He began to puff too, and to wish that he had given Larry or Pip the job of shadowing this extremely active fellow.

The wretched man knows that Mr Goon is following him because he suspects him of knowing where the pearls are, and he's going to lead him a fine old dance, up hill and down dale! thought Fatty, his legs going round and round furiously, and the perspiration dripping into his eyes. He's either going to tire old Mr Goon out, and make him give up – or else he's going to give him the slip somehow.

Still the three went on and on, and Fatty's clothes stuck to him horribly, he was so hot. Number Three didn't seem to tire in the least, and had a most uncanny knowledge of all the nasty little hills in the district. Poor Mr Goon went from red to scarlet, and from scarlet to purple. He was in his hot uniform, and even Fatty felt a bit sorry for him.

He'll have a fit if he goes up any more hills at top speed, thought Fatty, wiping his forehead. So shall I! Golly, I'm absolutely melting. Phew!

Mr Goon was absolutely determined that he wasn't going to be shaken off by Number Three. He knew that Fatty was behind him, and that if he, Mr Goon, failed in the chase, Fatty would go triumphantly on. So Mr Goon gritted his big teeth and kept on and on and on.

A big hill loomed up in front. Mr Goon groaned from the bottom of his heart. Number Three sailed up as usual. Mr Goon followed valiantly. Fatty, feeling that this was absolutely the last straw, went up it too.

And then he felt a peculiar bumping from his back tyre. He looked down in alarm. Blow, blow, blow! He'd got a puncture!

Poor Fatty! He got off and looked at his tyre. It was absolutely flat. No good pumping it up, because it would be flat again almost at once – and, in any case, if he stopped to pump it up he would lose Number Three and Mr Goon.

He took a quick look up the hill and caught sight of a triumphant Mr Goon looking back at him with a grin on his face. Then he and Number Three disappeared over the top of the hill. Fatty waved to Mr Goon.

'I wish you a nice long ride!' he said pleasantly, and mopped his forehead.

Fatty saw a familiar vehicle coming towards him. It was the grocery van that sometimes delivered to Peterswood. Fatty recognised the driver and hailed him and the van stopped.

'Hi, could you take a message to the next garage please?' said Fatty. 'I've got a puncture and

I'm miles from home. Please ask them to send out a taxi.'

'Well, why don't you hop in, as I'm going quite near to Peterswood and can take you most of the way?' said the driver.

'Oh, thanks very much,' said Fatty, and put his bicycle in the back of the van, then climbed into the seat next to the driver. He was very hot and tired.

After about twenty minutes, the driver stopped. 'Peterswood is just over the hill there,' said the driver. 'You can walk there quite easily.'

'Very many thanks,' said Fatty, and jumped down. He took his bicycle and waved to the departing grocery man. Then he walked smartly off in the direction of Peterswood. He went home and put away his punctured bike. His father's bicycle was in the shed, so Fatty borrowed that, and off he went, quite cheerful, on his way to the Fair to see what the others were doing.

They were wondering what had happened to Fatty. They hadn't liked to leave the Fair, so they had had tea there, and were now conversing with the red-headed boy at the waxworks, hearing for the twentieth time, the extraordinary tale of Napoleon's escapade in the night.

'Oh, *Fatty*!' cried Bets, when she saw him. 'You've come back at last! Whatever happened? And how dreadfully hot you look!'

Buster welcomed Fatty uproariously. He had been left behind with Larry, in case Fatty had to do some quick shadowing. Fatty looked at him.

'I feel as if *my* tongue's hanging out like Buster's, I'm so hot and thirsty,' he said. 'I must have an iced ginger beer. Come and sit with me whilst I have it, and I'll tell you what's happened!'

'Did Number Three lead you to the missing pearls?' asked Bets excitedly, as Fatty went to the ginger beer stall. He shook his head.

'Come on over to the grass here,' he said, and led the way. He flung himself down and drank his ginger beer in long, thirsty gulps. 'Golly! This is the very best drink I've ever had in my life!'

Soon he was telling the others about the wildgoose chase that Number Three had led both him and Mr Goon. They listened eagerly. How annoying of Mr Goon to butt in like that! They laughed when they thought of the poor, hot, fat policeman pedalling valiantly up hill and down after Number Three.

'What a shame you had a puncture,' said Bets. 'Still, Fatty, I'm sure Number Three would never lead you or Mr Goon to where the pearls were, once he knew he was being followed! He might not have known that *you* were shadowing him – but he simply couldn't *help* knowing that Mr Goon was!'

Fatty finished his iced ginger beer and ordered another. He said he had never been so thirsty in his life. 'When I think of poor, hot Mr Goon, pedalling away still for dear life, and feeling as thirsty as I am – well, all I can say is that I'm jolly glad I got a puncture!' said Fatty, drinking again. 'I should think Mr Goon will end up somewhere in Scotland, by the time he's finished this bike ride!'

'All the same,' said Larry, 'it's a bit sickening that we aren't any nearer solving the mystery of where those pearls are hidden. Instead of the man leading us *to* them – he seems bent on going as far from them as he can!'

'I wonder if that old fellow *did* give him a message,' said Pip, frowning. 'You're sure you didn't see any sign of a message at all? Let's think now. All that old Johnny did was to mess about in the dust, drawing patterns with his stick. Nothing else.'

Fatty was drinking his ginger beer as Pip said this. He suddenly choked and spluttered, and Bets banged him on the back. 'Whatever's the matter?' she said.

Fatty coughed, and then turned a pair of bright eyes on the Find-Outers. 'Pip's hit it!' he said. 'What a lot of blind donkeys we are! Of course – *we saw that old chap giving the message to Number Three under our very noses* – and we weren't smart enough to spot it!'

'What do you mean?' said everyone, in surprise.

'Well – he must have been writing some kind of message with his stick, in the dust, of course, for Number Three to read!' said Fatty. 'And to think it was there for us to read, too, if only we'd gone over and used our eyes. We're bad Find-Outers. Very bad indeed.'

The others looked excited. Pip slapped Fatty on the shoulder. 'Well, come on, let's go and see if the message is still there, idiot! It might be!'

'It might. But it's not very likely now,' said Fatty,

getting up. 'Still, we'll certainly go and see. Oh – to think we never thought of this before. Where are my brains? They must have melted in this heat!'

The Find-Outers, with Buster in Fatty's basket, set off back to the village street. They came to the bench. It was empty – but obviously people had been sitting there, for there were paper bags strewn about. The children looked eagerly at the dust in front of the seat. Would there still be a message they could read?

21. HUNT-THE-NECKLACE!

There were certainly some marks in the dust, but not many, for somebody's feet had evidently scuffled about just there. Fatty sat himself down in exactly the same place in which the old man had been. He stared hard at the dust.

So did the others. 'That looks like a letter W,' said Fatty, at last, pointing. 'Then there's a letter half rubbed out. And then that looks like an X. Then all the rest of the letters have been brushed out where people have walked on them. Blow!'

'W – something – X,' said Larry, who was good at crosswords, with their missing letters. 'W – A – X – it might be that.'

And then exactly the same thought struck all the Find-Outers at the same moment.

'WAXworks! That's what the word was!'

They stared at one another in the greatest excitement. Waxworks! Were the pearls hidden somewhere in the waxworks hall? It was a very likely place, a place that all the gang knew well. And Number Three had kept looking in at the door that afternoon.

'He kept peeping in – but he couldn't go and get the pearls, because there were too many people there!' said Fatty. 'Golly, we've got the idea now! That's the hiding-place – in the waxworks hall! Now we've only got to go there and hunt, and we'll find the pearls somewhere – in the cupboard, perhaps, or under a floorboard.'

'Let's go and look for them straightaway,' said Larry, getting up. 'Come on.'

'We can't very well, under the nose of that red-haired boy,' said Fatty. 'Still, we'll go down to the hall anyway.' They set off and soon came to the Fair again.

'There's the red-headed boy over there – he's gone to his tea or something,' said Bets, pointing. 'Has he left the hall empty for once?'

They hurried to see. There was a badly written notice stuck on the locked door. 'Gone for tea. Back soon.'

'Aha!' said Fatty, his eyes gleaming. 'This

couldn't be better for us. We'll get in at that window, Larry. It's sure to be open still.'

It was still unfastened, and the children climbed in excitedly, almost tumbling on to the floor in their eagerness to go hunting for the pearls.

'Behind the curtains, in the cupboards, up the chimney, every place you can think of!' said Fatty, in a thrilled voice. 'Go to it, Find-Outers. Solve the mystery if you can!'

Then such a hunt began. Every cupboard, every shelf, every nook and cranny in that Hall were searched by the bright-eyed Find-Outers. Buster, eager to help, though without the faintest idea of what they were looking for, scrabbled about too, having a vague hope that it might be rabbits.

Fatty even examined the floorboards, but none of them was loose. At last, when it seemed as if every single place had been searched, the five children sat down to rest and discuss the matter.

'I suppose it *is* here, that necklace!' said Daisy. 'I'm beginning to think it isn't.'

'*I* feel as if I'm playing Hunt-the-Thimble,' said Bets. 'Where *is* the thimble? It must be in some jolly good place, that necklace!'

Fatty stared at Bets. 'Bets,' he said, 'supposing we went out of the room, and you had to hide a pearl necklace somewhere here, what difficult place would you think of?'

Bets looked round the hall and considered. 'Well, Fatty,' she said, 'I've always noticed that when people play Hunt-the-Thimble, the most difficult hiding-places to find are the easiest ones really.'

'What do you mean?' demanded Pip.

'Well,' said Bets, 'I remember looking *every*-where for the thimble once – and nobody found it – and yet where do you think it was? On Mother's finger!'

Fatty was listening hard to Bets. 'Go on, Bets,' he said. 'Suppose you had to hide that pearl necklace here, in this hall – where would *you* hide it? It would have to be a good place, easy to get at – and yet one where ordinary people would never dream of looking for a valuable necklace.'

Bets considered again. Then she gave a little smile. 'Well, *I* know where I'd put it!' she said. 'Of course I'd know! And it would be under the noses of everyone, and yet nobody would notice it!'

'Where?' cried everyone.

'I'll tell you,' said Bets. 'See Queen Elizabeth over there, in her grand clothes and jewels, standing looking so proud and haughty? Well, I'd put the pearl necklace round her neck with all the other necklaces, of course – and nobody would ever guess that among the false Woolworth ones there was a REAL one!'

Fatty leapt to his feet. 'Bets, you're right. I'd got that idea half in my own mind, and now you've said all that, I'm sure you're right! I bet the necklace is there! Clever old Bets!'

They all ran to the stately wax figure of Queen Elizabeth whose neck was hung with brilliant necklaces of all kinds. Among them was a double necklace of beautifully graded pearls, with a diamond clasp – at least, the children felt sure it was a diamond one. Fatty lifted the necklace carefully off the figure's neck, undoing the clasp first.

The pearls shone softly. It was clear even to the children's eyes that they were not cheap ones, bought at a store. They were lovely, really lovely.

'These must be the missing pearls!' said Fatty, exultantly. 'They really must! Golly, we've found them. *We've* solved that mystery! What will the

Inspector say? Let's go and ring him up.'

They climbed out of the window and hurried to their bicycles. Fatty had the wonderful necklace safely in his pocket. He couldn't believe that they really had found it – and in such an *easy* place too!

'But a jolly clever one,' said Fatty. 'To think it was under the eyes of scores of people today – and nobody guessed! It was safer on Queen Elizabeth's neck than anywhere else!'

'Look out – there's Mr Goon!' said Larry.

'And Inspector Jenks with him!' cried Bets in delight. 'Shall we tell him?'

'Leave it to me,' ordered Fatty. 'Good evening, Inspector. Come to hunt for the necklace too?'

'Frederick,' said the Inspector. 'I believe you were bicycling after the member of the gang called Number Three this afternoon, weren't you?'

'Yes, sir,' said Fatty. 'With Mr Goon, as well, sir.'

'Well, unfortunately he gave Mr Goon the slip,' said the Inspector. 'Mr Goon rang me up, and I came over, because it is imperative that we keep an eye on Number Three, if we can, owing to his knowledge of where the pearls are hidden. Did you by any chance see the man, after you had got your puncture?'

'No, sir,' said Fatty. 'Haven't set eyes on him.'

The Inspector gave an annoyed exclamation. 'We *must* get Number Three. We've found out that he is the ring-leader, the man we want most of all! And now if he gets those pearls, wherever they are, and clears off, sooner or later these burglaries will start all over again. He will find it quite easy to start a new gang.'

Mr Goon looked very down in the mouth. He also looked hot and tired.

'He's a clever fellow, sir,' he said to the Inspector. 'Very clever. I don't know how he managed to give me the slip, sir.'

'Never mind, Mr Goon,' said Fatty comfortingly. '*I* can tell the Inspector where the pearls are, and how you can catch Number Three if you want to.'

Mr Goon stared disbelievingly at Fatty. 'Gah!' he said. 'You make me tired. Talking a lot of tommy-rot! I don't believe a word of it!'

'What do you mean, Frederick?' said the Inspector, startled.

Fatty drew the pearl necklace out of his pocket.

Mr Goon gasped and his eyes bulged more than ever. The Inspector stared in amazement too. He took the pearls from Fatty. All the children crowded round in excitement.

'Frederick! These *are* the missing pearls! A double row of the very finest graded pearls there are,' said the Inspector. 'My dear boy – where *did* you get them!'

'Oh – we played a little game of Hunt-the-Thimble with Bets – and she told us where they were,' said Fatty, and Mr Goon gave a disbelieving snort. 'They were round Queen Elizabeth's neck, in the waxworks hall, Inspector – a very clever place – and Bets thought of it!'

'Certainly a very clever place,' said the Inspector, 'and a very clever thought of yours, little Bets, if I may say so!' he said, turning to the delighted little girl. 'They must have been shining there under the noses of hundreds of people today – and nobody so much as guessed! But now, Frederick – how do you propose that we lay hands on Number Three?'

'Well, sir – he knows that the pearls were hidden in the waxworks hall,' said Fatty, 'and maybe